**In a whirl of black like the flurry of wings
I was between them, the blade tip almost
grazing my stomach.**

"Stop!" Her voice burst out of me, pitched for festivals, to carry over musicians or screaming warriors. "Lay down your swords!"

The raider's eyes widened. The sword slipped from his hand into the dust. Behind me I heard the thunk as Aren's dropped as well. The raider sank to his knees beside it. "Great Lady," he said.

"Lay down your swords!" I shouted again. A burly raider with a cut bleeding across his cheek threw his down, fear and awe competing.

"On your knees to Death!" I shouted, and they went down like a wave, warriors of Pylos and raiders alike, all across the square before the palace, across to the Temple of the Lady of the Sea, like grain before the wind.

Praise for BLACK SHIPS

BLACK
SHIPS

By Jo Graham

Black Ships

Hand of Isis

BLACK SHIPS

JO GRAHAM

www.orbitbooks.net

New York   London

Copyright © 2008 by Jo Wyrick
Excerpt from *Hand of Isis* copyright © 2008 by Jo Wyrick
All rights reserved. Except as permitted under the U.S. Copyright Act of 1976, no part of this publication may be reproduced, distributed, or transmitted in any form or by any means, or stored in a database or retrieval system, without the prior written permission of the publisher.

Orbit
Hachette Book Group
237 Park Avenue
New York, NY 10017
Visit our website at www.orbitbooks.net

Orbit is an imprint of Hachette Book Group. The Orbit name and logo are trademarks of Little, Brown Book Group Limited.

Printed in the United States of America

Originally published in trade paperback, March 2008
First mass market edition, December 2009

10 9 8 7 6 5 4 3 2 1

For my father, Glenn Wyrick,
who gave me The Last of the Wine
when I was eleven and a half

Latium

Seven Hills (Rome)

Cumae • ▲ *Mt. Vesuvius*

İTALY

Prison of the Winds
(Mt. Etna)

GREECE

Aegean

Mycenae •

Pylos

Mediterranean

© 2007 Jeffrey L. Ward

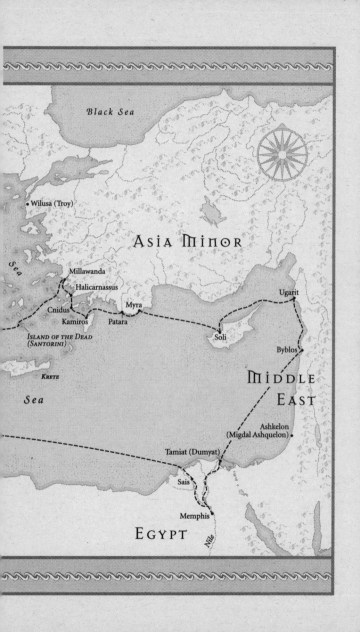

At Pylos in particular groups of women are recorded doing menial tasks such as grinding corn, preparing flax, and spinning. Their ration quotas suggest they are to be numbered in the hundreds.... At Pylos there is even an enigmatic To-ro-ja (woman of Troy), "servant of the god."

—Michael Wood, *In Search of the Trojan War*

PYTHIA

You must know that, despite all else I am, I am of the People. My grandfather was a boatbuilder in the Lower City. He built fishing boats, my mother said, and once worked on one of the great ships that plied the coast and out to the islands. My mother was his only daughter. She was fourteen and newly betrothed when the City fell.

The soldiers took her in the front room of the house while her father's body cooled in the street outside. When they were done with her she was brought out to where the ships were beached outside the ring of our harbor, and the Achaians drew lots for her with the other women of the City.

She fell to the lot of the Old King of Pylos and was brought across the seas before the winter storms made the trip impossible. She was ill on the vessel, but thought it was just the motion of the ship. By the time she got to Pylos it was clear that it was more than that.

King Nestor was old even then, and he had daughters of the great houses of Wilusa to spin and grind meal for him, slaves to his table and loom. He had no use for the daughter of a boatbuilder whose belly already swelled with the seed of an unknown man, so my mother was put to the work of the linen slaves, the women who tend the flax that grows along the river.

I was born there at the height of summer, when the land itself is sleeping and the Great Lady rules over the lands beneath the earth while our world bakes in the sun. I was born on the night of the first rising of Sothis, though I did not know for many years what that meant.

My mother was a boatbuilder's daughter who had lived all her life within the sound of the sea. Now it was a morning's walk away, and she might not go there because of her bondage. Perhaps it was homesickness, or perhaps something in the sound of my newborn mewing cries, that caused her to name me Gull, after the black-winged sea-birds that had swooped and cried around the Lower City.

By the time the autumn rains came, I was large enough to be carried in a sling on my mother's back while she worked.

I know it was not that year, but it is my first memory, the green light slanting through the trees that arched over the river, the sound of the water falling over shallow stones, the songs of the women from Wilusa and Lydia as they worked at the flax. I learned their songs as my first tongue, the tongue of the People as women speak it in exile.

There were other children among the linen slaves, though I was the oldest of the ones from Wilusa. There were Lydians older than I, whose mothers had come from far southward down the coast, and a blond Illyrian from north and west of Pylos. Her name was Kyla; she was my childhood friend, the one who paddled with me in the river while our mothers worked. At least until she was also put to work. I knew then what my life would be — the steady rhythm of beating the flax, of harvest and the life of the river. I could imagine no more. The tiny world of the river was still large enough for me.

The summer that I was four was the summer that Triotes came. He was the sister-son of the Old King, tall and blond and handsome as the summer sun. He stopped to water his horses, and talked with my mother. I thought it was odd.

A few days later he came again. I remember watching them talking, Triotes standing at his horses' heads, ankle deep in the river. I remember thinking something was wrong. My mother was not supposed to smile.

He came often after that. And sometimes I was sent to sleep with Kyla and her mother.

My fifth summer was when my brother was born. He had soft, fair baby hair, and his eyes were the clear gray-blue of the sea. I looked at my reflection in the river, at my hair as dark as my mother's, eyes like pools of night. And I understood something new. My brother was different.

Triotes threw him high in the air to make him laugh, showed him to his friends when they led their chariots along the road. He was barely a man himself, and he had no sons before, even by a slave. He brought my mother presents.

One night I heard them talking. He was promising that when my brother was older he would bring him to the palace at Pylos, where he would learn to carry the wine cups for princes, where he would learn to use a sword. He was the son of Triotes, and would be known as such.

Later, when he had gone, I crept in beside my mother. My brother, Aren, was at her breast. I watched him nurse for a few minutes. Then I lay down and put my head on my mother's flat, fair stomach.

"What's the matter, my Gull?" she said.

"I am the daughter of no man," I said.

I do not think she had expected that. I heard her breath catch. "You are the daughter of the People," she said firmly. "You are a daughter of Wilusa. I was born in the shadow of the Great Tower, where the Lower Harbor meets the road. I lived my whole life in the sound of the sea. Your grandfather was a boatbuilder in the Lower City. You are a daughter of Wilusa." My mother stroked my hair with her free hand, the one that did not support Aren. "You were meant to be born there. But the gods intervened."

"Then won't the gods intervene again and take us back?" I asked.

My mother smiled sadly. "I don't think the gods do things like that."

And so I returned to the river. I was old enough to help the women with the flax in the green cool twilight along the water. And this, I knew, was where I would spend my life.

I don't remember the accident that changed all that.

We often played along the road that paralleled the river. It was nothing more than a packed track, rutted from chariots and carts. I remember the chariot, much finer than Triotes', the blood bay horses, the gleaming bronze. I remember staring transfixed. I remember my mother's scream, high and shrill like a gull herself.

It was fortunate that the rains had begun and the road

was muddy. The wheel passed over my right leg just above the ankle, snapping the bones cleanly, but not cutting my foot off, as I have seen happen since. The road was muddy, and the surface gave.

I remember little of that winter. I don't remember how long I spent on the pallet in the corner where my mother had given birth to Aren. Perhaps it's childhood distance. Perhaps it's the essence of poppy that the oldest of the slave women gave me for the pain. I vaguely remember picking at the wrappings around my leg and being told to stop. And that is all.

I do remember the Feast of the Descent, when the Lady returns to the world beneath and greets Her beloved. The dry season was beginning, and the poppies were dying in the fields, the river running shallow and slow.

My right leg was half the thickness of my left above the ankle, and my right foot twisted, the toes turned inward and the heel out. I could stand, just. All that long spring I tried to walk again. By the height of summer I could stumble slowly, holding on to things for balance, but it was clear that I would never run or dance again.

More important, it was clear that I would never work all day in the shallows of the river.

I did not know why my mother left Aren sleeping with Kyla's mother and took me walking away from the river, up the long dusty track in a way we had never gone. I asked her over and over where we went, but she did not answer, though she carried me part of the way when the road went steeply uphill. I was light enough for six years old.

There was a turn in the road, and we stopped to rest. My mother brought out a water bottle and we shared it. I looked down and away at the size of the world. The river was a track of green, swirled like a snake across the yellows and browns of the landscape. Behind us, the mountains rose in serrated tiers to peaks as dark and as strange as clouds.

"There," my mother said. "Gull, do you see that?" She pointed to a silver smudge at the end of the river. "There's so much dust in the air, it's hard to see. That's the sea!"

I looked. The world ended, and the silver began.

"Are there gulls there?" I asked.

"Yes," she said. "That's where gulls live."

"Can we go there?" I asked.

"No," she said.

We put the water skin away and kept climbing. It was not much farther to go.

The track ended at a clearing, the great towering cypress trees green and mysterious, tangled among rocks on the mountainside. I thought at first it was a desolate place and deserted. But there was the buzzing of flies and the smell of goat dung. I looked again and saw that there was a shed off to the side of the track and downhill, a steep path leading down to it. There was another that led upward, between the great trees. That is the one we took.

My mother walked slowly now. The loam sank beneath our feet. The air was hushed and humid.

There was a cleft before us, a cave opening twice as tall as wide, a little taller than my mother. Before it stood a polished black stone, rounded and featureless.

My mother called out a greeting, and her voice seemed very loud in the wood.

A woman appeared in the entrance. I had been expecting something frightening, but she had the red, sweaty face of a woman who has been working when it's hot, the mended plain tunic of a servant. "What do you want?" she asked.

"To speak with Pythia," my mother said, squaring her shoulders.

The woman seemed to size her up. "Pythia is very busy. Have you brought an offering? I see no birds or young goat."

"I have brought my daughter," my mother said. "Her name is Gull."

I thought she would tell us to leave, but at that moment I heard a scraping sound just within the entrance. I suppose my eyes went wide. What stood in the doorway was not a woman.

Her hair was as black as night, piled and curled in elaborate pins made of copper. Her long robes were true black. Her face was as white as the moon, her lips black, and her eyes outlined in black as well, like a skull bleached in a field for a long time. She was beautiful and terrifying. Slowly she came toward us. One long white hand reached out and nearly touched my hair. I was frightened, but I did not move. Things would be as they must be.

"Once they brought us princesses, the daughters of kings to serve the Lady of the Dead. Now they bring us the daughters of slaves, girls who are too maimed to work. This is not an honor offering!"

My mother did not look away from her eyes. "She is my daughter, and she is all I have."

Pythia looked at me. I saw her eyes fall on my twisted leg. Her brow furrowed, and I saw the paint on it crack in the heat. And I knew it was paint, not her own face. "They will not let you keep her and feed her if she cannot work."

"Gull is a hard worker," my mother said. "She is courteous and quick to please. She could serve you well."

"This is not a large Shrine," Pythia said. "We are not like some others, with handmaidens who have little to do all day. I need a goatherd, not a girl who cannot walk."

"She could weave," my mother suggested.

One taloned hand fixed beneath my chin, tilting my face up. Her eyes were as black as mine. She was an old woman. But there was something else beneath the paint.

I don't know what she saw in my eyes. I can guess, now, these many years later. But Pythia grunted. She turned with something that was almost a shrug. "Leave her here tonight. We will test her. You can return for her tomorrow."

I saw the tension leave my mother's face. "I will. Gull, be good and please great Pythia."

I embraced her, but did not cling. I understood. There was no food for slaves who could not work. My mother was trying to find another mistress for me.

There was at least food tonight. The servant, whose name was Dolcis, brought me a bowl of the same thin porridge they were eating, Pythia and Dolcis both. It was, I thought, the same porridge we ate in the slave quarters by the river, and I said as much.

The old woman looked at me sharply. "The kings used to have some respect for us. They used to bring us fat goats and fresh fish. They used to bring us the first fruits of the vine. Now we are lucky if the country people bring us apples or meal in thank offerings."

"Why?" I asked.

"They are impious," Pythia said. "They make their sacrifices to the gods of bulls and storms, to Athene the keen-eyed. They do not bring their gifts to the Lady of the Dead." She took a bite of porridge. "Who have you made offering to?"

I had never properly made an offering to anyone, but I thought of the libations I had poured in water, or the thin new well-watered wine we sometimes had. "To the Lady of the Sea," I said.

Pythia grunted. "They are sisters, the Lady of the Dead and the Lady of the Sea. Like sisters will, They quarrel, but always reconcile. It is well."

After we had eaten, Dolcis cleared the things away. Pythia sat before me in the light of the brazier. Shadows danced on the walls of the cave.

"Are you afraid of the dark?" she asked.

"No," I said.

"Good," she said, and smothered the fire with ashes until only a few coals glowed. It was very dark within the cave. I had never been somewhere there was not even starlight. I heard her moving in the dark, the rustling of cloth.

"Sit here," she said, and I felt her putting a cushion at my back. I sat up upon it. It raised me so that I sat, my legs crossed, leaning almost over the brazier. She put another cushion behind me so that I might lean back against the wall.

There was more rustling, and I smelled the acrid scent of herbs crumbled over the coals. Rosemary. Laurel. And something richer, like resin, like pine carpets beneath my feet. Something heady, like smoke.

"There," Pythia said. "Look into the fire and tell me what you see."

My eyes itched. It was hard to keep them open. They

watered. The smoke wavered. The tiny glowing lines of coals blurred. I didn't know what to say.

She was still talking, but I wasn't really hearing her. I was looking at the darkness between the glowing lines. At the blackness in the heart of the fire.

"Black ships," I said, and I hardly knew my own voice.

"Where?" Pythia said.

"Black ships," I said. I could see them in the darkness of the coals. "Black ships and a burning city. A great city on a headland. Some of the ships are small, not much more than one sail or a few rowers. But some of them are big. Painted black. They're coming out from land, from the burning city. But there are other ships in the way, between the black ships and the sea."

My voice caught with the emotion of what I saw. "There are so few of them! I can see them coming, rowing hard. The one in front has seven stars on her prow, *Seven Sisters,* like the constellation. That's her name. The soldiers on the other ships have archers. They're shooting at them."

One of the sailors was struck in the eye by an arrow. He screamed and plunged into the sea. One of the ships' boys was hit in the leg and went down with a high, keening sound, his blood spurting across the deck.

One of the small boats was rammed and capsized.

"There are people in the water. They're not sailors, not on the little boats. Children. Women." I could see them struggling. The archers were shooting them in the water.

"One of the big ships is turning back. She's turning around." I could see the dolphin on her prow, white and red on black.

There was a girl in the water, her slim, naked body cutting through the waves like a dolphin herself. She was almost to the big ship. Now she was there. One of the rowers shipped his oar as she reached for it, stretching her arms up the shaft. She got one foot on the top of the paddle, pulled herself half out of the water. Hands reached down to haul her aboard.

"*Seven Sisters* has come about," I said. "She's bearing down on one of the ships of archers, and they're hauling at the oars to get out of the way."

Seven Sisters swung past, close enough that I could see the young man at her tiller, his sandy hair pulled back from his face with a leather thong, lips set in concentration, the wind kissing him.

"They have fire arrows," I gasped. "The blockaders. They're lighting them."

One fell hissing into the sea. Another dropped on the foredeck of *Dolphin* and was quickly extinguished with a bucket of water. A young man with long black hair was hauling one of the children from the fishing boat aboard.

The rest of the fishing boats were either sunk or out to sea, sails spread to catch the land breeze carrying them away.

I heard shouted words, saw the captain of *Seven Sisters* waving.

A fire arrow struck the captain of *Dolphin* full in the chest, his beard igniting. He fell away from the tiller, his face on fire and his chest exploding. The young man with black hair swung the child into the shelter of the rowers' rail and leaped for the tiller. *Seven Sisters* swung away, her course between *Dolphin* and the nearest blockader.

Dolphin's sail unfurled, red dolphin painted on white. It filled with the land breeze. A moment later *Seven Sis-*

ters' spread, black stars against white. Behind them the city burned. Ahead was only open sea.

I was aware of a new sound. It was my own sobs.

Pythia lifted me up as lightly as my mother. "Enough, little one. Enough. You have seen enough and more for the first time."

She laid me on a pallet of soft sheepskins and covered me with her own cloak. "Rest, little one. Rest."

And I did, and dreamed no more that night. I did not doubt that I should stay here.

THE ☉ ORACLE

We were not isolated at the Shrine. Someone came every few days, usually country people with offerings and questions. They brought last year's apples, sacks of grain, fresh-baked bread, and olives packed in their own oil. I had never thought much before about where offerings go. You bring them to the gods and then what? They are subsumed into air?

The offerings were for our maintenance, and we ate what they brought with our goats' milk and the strong cheese Dolcis made from it. There were five white goats on the slopes below. There was a boy from a farm down the mountain who came and tended them. He was twice my age, and did not talk to me, thinking it rather beneath his dignity.

Sometimes nobles would come, in procession with their chariots and fine horses, bronze lances polished to reflect the sun. They would bring salted fish in great jars, amphorae of red wine, and once that summer ten lengths of fine linen, dyed as black as night. I fingered the cloth, wondering if it was flax that I had harvested with my mother and the women of Wilusa.

"Here, let that alone," one of the servants snapped, seeing my small fingers handling his master's gift.

Pythia snorted, "Oh, that is just our Linnea, fascinated with the fine cloth."

Linnea was what she called me, and it stuck, Linen-Girl, the girl from the river of flax. They did not call me Gull in my own tongue, as my mother did.

Often that first summer my mother came up the mountain, but less frequently as the rains began and her work was greater. Also, Aren was bigger, and he had to be watched constantly as he began to walk so that he would not stumble away and drown in the shallows of the river.

When the rains came so did a chariot from the king's own house, to carry Pythia to the rites that marked the Great Lady's return, the weeklong celebrations of the Thesmophoria, the Feast of the Return. She went alone, and did not bring me with her. She said I had not yet learned enough to serve her without shaming her. This should have stung, but it did not. I knew I was not fit to serve before people. I was still clumsy and awkward.

She took me the next year. I had just turned eight, and had grown until I needed all new robes, black, without borders, just turned under in a simple seam. Pythia fussed over it while Dolcis sewed, and I knew that I would be taken with her to the Mysteries.

The robe was long and almost hid my foot.

"Bind it up with a cord," Pythia said, "or the child will not be able to walk."

Dolcis took a fine black cord and bound it around my waist, pulling the fabric loose above it so that it hung in graceful pleats. "There. It must be long for her to grow yet. She's got a lot of growing to do."

"I think not," Pythia said. "She will always be small. She will never have my height."

I had not thought of Pythia as tall. But I supposed her taller than my mother, and said so.

"Ah," said Pythia, "it's the blood of the old shore people, those who were here before my fathers came with horses and bronze. Little and dark, like the islanders. People of the sea, not people of the chariot." She lifted up my long hair, thick and heavy. "You will not need the wig when it is your turn. I've always had it. My hair was as red as Dolcis' face when I was a girl. The wig is heavy and it itches. But you've fine thick hair, as black as a raven's wing. You'll not need it," she said with satisfaction.

"My turn for what?" I stammered.

She turned her blue eyes on me. I don't know why I had thought they were black at our first meeting. "When you are Pythia after I am gone."

"Me? Pythia?"

Pythia touched the side of my face lightly, curled one strand of black hair around her finger. "Do you think we live forever, child? Since before time began there have been the Shrines, some greater, some lesser. And at each there has been Pythia, She Through Whom the Lady of the Dead Speaks. She is always Pythia, though Pythia may age and die. She is the vessel for the Lady, to speak with her mouth and use her hands. For how else may the Lady of the Dead speak clearly to the living, or act above the earth? When I am gone, you will be Pythia."

"But Dolcis..."

She shrugged. "Dolcis does not have the sight. The

Lady marked you as Her own so that you might be brought here where you belong, to serve Her rather than to be a slave all your days."

"Am I not a slave now?" I asked.

"No more so than we are all Her slaves," Pythia said.

"But..." I began.

"Even kings must bow to Death," Pythia said. "Even they, in their fine chariots with their arms so bright must go down into the shadowed lands and stand before Her throne, where She sits with Her Lord, sovereign of the shades. The young warriors with their dogs and bows will go before Her, and She will show them mercy or not, depending on Her will. And Her husband will answer Her pleas for clemency, should She make them, as He did in the case of the kitharist. You remember that?"

I nodded, for I had not forgotten the story of Orpheus, who went to plead with the Lady of the Dead for his bride.

"She has chosen you," Pythia said. "She has chosen you as Her voice and Her hands. You will be dedicated at the Feast of the Return, the Thesmophoria, as is proper. And from that time forward you cannot do as the living do. You cannot shed blood, or watch it shed. You cannot cut flesh with a knife, or wear the colors of the sun. You belong to the Lady, and to the shades beneath."

"But Dolcis kills pigeons," I said. "And she butchered the goat that died."

"Dolcis is not Pythia, nor will be," she said. "These restrictions are for you, not for Dolcis. You will follow them from your eighth year, as I have."

I said what I wondered without thinking. "Does that mean I shall never have a husband or children?"

Pythia's face tightened. "You belong to the Lady, and belonging to Her you cannot belong to any man. For Her vessel to be a man's possession would be the gravest blasphemy. Kings have broken that law before, and even now we see the workings of the curse they called down upon their houses."

Dolcis looked up, startled. I thought she was surprised that Pythia had spoken so plainly, but I did not know of what she spoke. King Nestor had committed no blasphemy that I knew of, and all was well in the palace of Pylos.

Pythia continued. "You will never be a wife, and you will never know a home besides Her Shrine. That is not to say that you cannot know a man, for the Lady is not virgin the year round, but you can never be his wife."

"And children?" I wondered, for this was not so strange to me. Not one of the linen slaves had a husband, though there were a handful of children.

"Any daughters of yours are daughters to the Shrine, or may marry if it is clear that Her hand is not on them. Sons may not sleep beneath Her roof after the third year of their birth."

"What then?" I asked.

"They go to their fathers," she snapped and turned away. "Go on, Linnea. I have much to do."

I dreamed that night that a fair-haired boy like my brother lay at Pythia's breast, that he rode away behind a tall man with bronze-colored hair, leaning over the back of the chariot, crying and reaching for her. I did not tell her of this, though usually I told Pythia all of my dreams.

Instead it was I who stood beside her in the back of the chariot, steadying her on the curves of the road, leaning

against the driver's corded leg. I had not ridden in one before, and it was strange to see the world from so high up.

In later years I have seen many great cities, and I can
say that it was not one of them, but Pylos seemed a great
city to me at the time. In a chariot, it was only an hour's
ride from the Shrine, built about a natural harbor where
the flax river met the sea. The buildings were of several
stories, in the old style of the islands, with tapered columns painted red and black. The palace was beside the
sea, and there was no wall, save a ceremonial one that
kept livestock from wandering into the courtyard. There
were temples and a handsome open one with a broad re-
flecting pool for the Lady of the Sea. It was there that we
stopped.

The priestesses who served Her temple greeted us with
wine and delicate honey cakes, brought a stool for my
mistress, and sat with her under linen stretched against the
afternoon sun. One of them was my mother's age, but had
the look of Pythia about her, blue eyes and sharp nose, red
hair fading to terra-cotta. Her daughter? I wondered. I ate
my honey cake and considered until she called her aunt.

They talked until the evening came, and I learned much
from their words that I had not known before. Pythia was
the half sister of King Nestor himself, by a younger wife.
She had been dedicated with all ceremony when she was
eight, in days when men were more pious and kings gave
their daughters to the gods. Cythera, for that was her
name, was the daughter of Pythia's sister, who was likewise given to the Lady of the Sea.

I licked the last of the honey off my fingers and watched
the mosaics on the floor seem to move, the octopus ten-

tacles shivering like a living thing against painted waves. Like waves moving over the floor. Or shivering in a fire.

"Fire," I whispered. "They will come."

I heard Cythera's startled voice, the clatter as she dropped her cup.

"Peace," Pythia said. "Sometimes it comes on her this way, the hand of the Lady." She knelt beside me, not disturbing my field of vision. "Linnea, what do you see?"

"Black ships," I said. "Fire." Her hand was on my arm, but I hardly felt it. My voice sounded older — stronger and deeper. "I have traveled before, from the islands and the lands that lie beneath the waves. I will not stay here, for darkness is upon the land and the blood of the young doe cries out against the hands of her father, slain to raise the wind!"

I fell forward off the stool, slamming against the cool mosaic.

Pythia raised me, Cythera at her side.

"I'm sorry, mistress," I said. "I sat too long and fell asleep."

"She's bleeding," Cythera said.

I looked stupidly at my hand, where blood welled from a long cut.

"She has cut her hand on a shard of your cup," Pythia said. "Come, Linnea. I will bind that for you and you may go to your pallet in the room there. You are tired from the journey, and the young need more sleep than the old."

I lay down in an alcove off the courtyard, watching the first stars appearing in the autumn sky. Sothis rode proudly in the heavens.

"How did she know?" Cythera asked. "There is little enough said about the sacrifice of poor Iphigenia. Or of the curse her death has called down upon her family, one slain after another. Will that wrath pursue us all?"

"Death waits for us all," Pythia said. "Sometimes as a hunter, sometimes as a mother. We are in Her hands."

İ HAD NO PART in the Thesmophoria that year, except to stand and watch, and to help Pythia prepare for her part. I was tremendously proud that I wore Pythia's black linen bag about my waist, with its brushes of fine horsehair and small silver mirror, twin alabaster pots filled with paint of black and white. Sometimes, in the space between parts of the rite, she must reapply the paint where it had smudged.

I suppose I thought less of the solemn nature of the rites than of the crowd, of being in a city with people I did not know. I shared honey cakes made with almond flour with two of the acolytes of the Lady of the Sea, watched the great procession, and even went into the palace itself when the Old King opened his doors to welcome the Lady. I followed after with the other children, singing the "Anados Kores."

"She rises in beauty. She delights us. Golden maiden! Golden one!" We followed the procession through the wide doors and into the courtyard, where the great round hearth was surrounded by people, the bright warriors multiplied by the ones painted on the walls. Above, the oculus opened to the sky, mirroring the hearth below.

I could not see the king, as I was short and there were many taller people in front of me, but I heard his voice, and it seemed aged but firm. There was another voice after, a clear tenor, which I assumed to belong to his son,

Idenes. "Now is the time of joy," he said. "Let us all eat, and share in Panegia's joy!"

Slaves brought forth great platters of meats, of olives and fish roasted above sweet woods, of the verdant herbs of spring, the sharp young bulbs of onions roasted with rosemary. Like the rest of the children, I stuffed myself.

Later, last year's wine flowed freely and not so well watered as I was used to. I wandered out to find the privy.

Behind the palace were the great storehouses, with their storage bins of clay half as tall as a man, sunk into the ground to keep fresh the peas and grain. I asked a woman for the way to the privy, and she answered me in the tongue of Wilusa.

I stopped. "Mother?" I asked, but it was not her.

"No, little one," she said. I did not know her face, but her hair was light brown and her eyes were blue. Her tunic was the rough one of a slave, and her hands were reddened from the work of the kitchen. I felt the sweetened cakes like a weight in my stomach. "It is that way," she said, and directed me.

Afterward I did not return to the celebration, but walked the other way, the way I had not gone before.

Here the laughter was louder, but a child clad in black mingles with the shadows. The houses along the harbor were lit with lamps, and shadows moved against them, dancing and coupling in the night. It was not the beauty of the Lady they praised, but of Her daughters.

I slid into the shadow of a shed and then looked around.

The moon was rising over the sea, which spread in little ripples, kissing the shore with waves that came only to my knees, smooth as the surface of a mirror.

I walked into the sea. The sand felt good beneath my feet, and the waters splashed nearly to my waist, sweeping against my knees. The moon made a path across the water.

Something filled in my heart, something for which I did not have words. "Great Lady," I whispered, but did not know what to ask. I knew only that something was answered, service given and accepted.

"I will go out from the dance," I said. "I will stand apart. None shall praise my beauty and call me beloved."

Nor would they, in any event, an ugly dark girl with a twisted foot.

"I will walk in the dark places. I will tend the dead." I felt the wind stir my hair like a caress, like a mother's hand.

I went back to the temple and slept soundly on my pallet that night.

The next day I was dedicated, as is proper. I remember very little about it—the ceremony is short, and something of an anticlimax after the great festivals. But Pythia nodded, and seemed satisfied that it was properly done.

AFTER THAT I began my training in earnest. I had to learn all the rites by heart, all the parts, for there is no part of them that is written down. When I asked why not, Pythia looked appalled.

"The language of the islands is for tallies of grain and measures of oil! It is not for the sacred words! If these things were written, then any person might learn them, fitted or not fitted!"

"May I learn then, the writing of the tallies?" I asked.

"You have no need for such things," Pythia said. "They may be useful for clerks and for those who record what measures are due, but if you train your mind you will remember all you need to know. You do not need such laziness!"

And so I learned instead how to remember. Reciting became a pleasure to me, to make the words as beautiful as they might be. The stories themselves were a pleasure to me and beginning a new one was a treat.

I learned how the paints are made, the rendering of fat and its mixing with olive oil, with charcoal and chalk. I learned how the incense that smokes on the brazier is made, and how its most precious ingredients are the resins that come from over the sea and cannot be made here.

"The right trees do not grow," Pythia said. "And while the cypress and the pine have resins that are useful and may be used in extremity, the resins of myrrh are better."

I learned how to watch the people who came seeking the oracle's guidance, and how to understand.

Once a fat man came with his daughter, who was a little older than I. He was the owner of many olive trees, and his land was rich and prospered. He had no son, and his wealth was his daughter's dower. He came to ask of the oracle if there was wisdom in a marriage between his daughter and the son of his friend who had been lately working there, helping him with the harvest.

Dolcis brought them into the cave and spoke with them of farming and weather while I made great Pythia ready. While I painted her eyes, we heard the farmer and Dolcis talking about pressings and speaking of the young man's frugality. And the daughter said nothing. When we came into the room with them Dolcis withdrew; the coals were heaped and the incense scattered. The farmer and his daughter knelt, and I saw that her hair was as golden as the sun, but her face was pinched, and she chewed on her lower lip as her father asked, "Ela, Pythia, is it well that I shall give my daughter in marriage to this man, Elotes?"

I watched her lean forward over the coals. She was silent a long while, but I felt no chill upon me, no sense that She spoke. At last Pythia reached out one long white hand toward the farmer. "The lioness draws down the deer, but the lion eats the carcass entire, and the cubs mew with hunger, and may not even gnaw on the entrails."

The farmer went white.

"I see no more," Pythia said.

Dolcis bustled in and took charge of the two fine jars of first-pressed oil he had brought.

The farmer looked at his daughter, then at Pythia. "Does this mean what I think it does? That my daughter brings all the wealth to this marriage, and she and her children will grow thin while her husband prospers?"

"Her ways are strange," Pythia said. "This I saw. The lion feasted upon the kill, while the lioness and cubs waited in vain."

He went away vowing that there should be no betrothal, and the girl smiled as they rounded the curve of road below, her voice coming back high and clear on the evening air.

I watched them go, and then went back inside to Pythia. She was cleaning the paint from her face with oil.

"Did She speak to you truly?" I asked.

Pythia looked at me sharply. "The Lady of the Dead has given us eyes, so that we might see the truths about us in the world. She does not speak directly save at need, and not for every question that may trouble us. The girl did not wish it. For whatever reason, she feared the man, and she has known him these many months. There is no joy that can come of such a marriage, and the faster it is put from her father's mind, the better."

Pythia took me by the shoulders. "She has given you a gift. You are a true seer. But wisdom is something that comes with age, and you must earn that. It cannot be given as a gift. Sometimes you are Her vessel. But most of the time you must act from the knowledge in your heart, not from Her direction."

But still there were places I did not go. In the back of the cave there was a passage leading down. Pythia had hung a curtain of black linen across it, and Dolcis did not go that way. When once I went to it and pulled the veil aside, Pythia drew me back. "Not yet," she said gently, and I desisted.

In the spring when I was not quite twelve, after we had returned from the Feast of the Descent, Kyla woke me in the middle of the night.

I had seen her rarely since I had left the river, for she had her work and I mine, only when I visited my mother by Pythia's leave. It was hours until dawn, and she was crying.

My mother had been walking beside the road and had stepped upon an adder, which had bitten her heel. I went with her, but there was nothing to be done. My mother took her last breath even before Kyla reached the Shrine. I came at dawn with Kyla and saw her laid out, the women of Wilusa and Lydia wailing about her, as is right and proper. It seemed to me that she had not been more fair, her hair combed and spread around her, though she was nearly thirty.

In the heat of the day Triotes came, and the pyre was laid. He wept and clasped her hand and cut locks of his fair hair to mingle with hers as though she had been a beloved wife, not a linen slave.

I stood there in my black tunic, watching the heat shimmer above the fire, my heart too full for weeping. I did not know what to say, or whom to talk to. Across from me Triotes stood with his arm around my brother, six years old, as small and as fast as a young kestrel.

When the weeping was done and the ashes scattered, Triotes told him to bundle his things, his spare tunic, and whatever he needed. "I will keep my promise to your mother," he said. "You will live in my house, and in a year or so you will be a page to some friend of mine, who can teach you what it is to be an Achaian and a man."

I did not speak, for what should I say? I have known that my brother and I were different since he was a baby. And I thought that Pythia would say that what Triotes offered was just. He would keep his promise, and my brother would be known as the son of Triotes, and he would not be a slave.

I did not stay. Instead, I walked back to the Shrine at night. It was hard going, uphill, with my foot, but I managed it. I realized as I walked beneath the hard, clear stars of heaven, that I could do it more easily than before. My leg was strange and ugly, but the muscles had healed to serve me well enough. I could walk, though I limped. I did not need my mother to carry me where it was steep.

I stopped at the turn in the road where I had first seen the sea and wept.

Then I climbed the rest of the way until dawn, lay down on my pallet, and slept.

I WOKE AT EVENING. Dolcis came in to see if I wanted some of the lentils she had stewed, and I ate them ravenously.

Pythia watched me and chewed upon her bread.

When we were done she took my hand. "It is now," she said, and led me to the curtain in the back.

I didn't want to go, but she held my hand and pulled the veil aside. "What is here?" I asked.

"You will see," Pythia said, and dropped the curtain behind us.

It was dark. It cannot be this dark outside, where even in stormy weather there is some light. It was the utter blackness of the deep earth, where stars have never shone. She took my hand again and led me down.

It was cold. Pythia put my hand on the wall to my left. "You must count," she said. "You must count your steps so that you do not get lost. There are many caves and many turnings, and you must use that memory you have trained to remember your way."

And so we counted. As our steps descended, it seemed very far to me. I could not stop trying to see, my eyes widening and widening in the darkness. "Is this the gate to Hades?" I asked.

"This is a womb," she said. "A gate. A tomb. They are the same thing. We descend and we return. We cross and recross the River. You know the story."

I nodded, though she could not see it in the darkness. "The Lady descends and the land withers. She returns and it greens."

"You have nothing to fear here," Pythia said. "Alone among mortals. Because you are Her handmaiden, and you come and go at Her pleasure."

The floor leveled beneath our feet, and I felt the movement of air, as though the ceiling was much higher. Then my bare toes encountered fur. I gasped. Then I realized that it was a wolf skin spread on the floor of the cavern. My hands encountered it, and then another. They were soft and well cured, put here on purpose, not accidental carrion.

"Stay here," Pythia said. "Stay here and dream until I come for you."

And she left me.

I waited. At first, the darkness seemed to press on me, breathing like a great beast. I could imagine Cerberus waiting not far away, padding toward me with heavy, rending jaws.

When the last faint sounds of Pythia's passage had stopped, and the cold sweat began to dry on my face, the dark seemed less intense. I closed my eyes, and there was no difference.

I could retrace my steps, I thought. I remembered the turnings, how many steps between. There were not so many, only three or four. I could return if I wished, find my way back from the abyss to my own bed. I knew the way back. Pythia had made sure I did.

I stretched out on the wolf skins, and they were soft beneath me. Some hint of Pythia's scent clung to them. She had lain here then. Perhaps many times. She had waited here for some word from her Lady, like a handmaiden who sleeps in the antechamber, always within hearing lest something be needed in the night.

I waited in the dark until I slept, and if I dreamed I did not remember it.

THE AVATAR
OF DEATH

Old King Nestor died at the height of the rains, the winter after I turned sixteen. I had the shape of a woman and my full height now, though I would barely come to the middle of a warrior's chest. My hair had never been cut since I came to the Shrine, and was long enough that unpinned it reached halfway down my thighs. Pinned up, I could make it approximate the fullness of the wig. Pythia was right. I would not need to wear it.

In the palace they were wailing and rending their clothes, as is proper. I walked behind Pythia, with her clothes and herbs, her black bag around my waist, a black mantle pulled over my head. I stood behind her at the funeral rites, which were held in the great courtyard during a lull in the rain.

They had kept the wood for the pyre under shelter, so it caught quick and hard, but the ground beneath was sodden with water and steamed. I looked about as much as I could, hoping to see Aren among the boys, but he wasn't there.

The High King had not come from Mycenae. I didn't wonder why he had not at the time. It was the season of rains, and the roads were very bad. Instead, he sent a kinsman to do the Old King honor, Neoptolemos, the son of their hero Achilles. He was a high-spirited youth some three or four years older than I was, with dark red hair and long limbs that he had not quite finished growing into. His clothing was splendid and his breastplate was worked with silver. During the most sacred parts of the rite he was shifting his feet and whispering with his friends. I thought that a hero's son should behave in a way that was more seemly.

Later, as the feast was ending, I was making my way through the palace corridors to where Pythia was in council with her nephew, Idenes, the Young King. I saw Neoptolemos and two of his friends and would have passed them without speaking, but one of them caught at my arm.

"Come here, girl."

I jerked away, but Neoptolemos blocked me. "Come into the light and let me see you."

"Let me go," I said. If I had been older I would have thought to explain who I was.

One of his friends shoved me back against the wall. "She's not so pretty, but she'll do."

Neoptolemos put his hand around my neck to lift my face to the light. "Yes, she'll do." He was smiling.

I struck his hand away and his eyes darkened. "You should be honored, girl," he said.

One of his friends grabbed my arms. I did not think to scream. I was still too much the slave girl for that.

"I wouldn't do that if I were you," said a mild voice behind them. It was Triotes, who had been my mother's lover. He stood at ease in the hallway, a warrior in his prime, not a boy. "That one is dedicated to the Lady of the Dead. She could shrivel your manhood so you'll never have use of it again."

One of the friends let go immediately, but Neoptolemos hesitated. "I don't fear Death."

Triotes walked up and stood between us. "That's not wise," he said quietly. "When you have seen the ways that Death can take you, you will be slow to offend Her." He glanced at me. "Go," he said.

I drew my chiton up over my shoulder and went. I did not stay to see what he said.

I went back to the Temple of the Sea and said nothing. For in truth, what was there to say?

Soon I had other things to think of. Pythia had taken a chill at the funeral, and she was ill for many weeks. We stayed at the temple while she recovered. Even when she was well enough to go back to the Shrine, she was frail. Her hands were thin and her nails bluish. The veins stood out in the backs of her hands. She was only a few years younger than her brother the Old King, and he had been very old indeed when he died.

We had been back at the Shrine a few days when I asked her if she would go down into the caves with me.

Pythia looked up at me from her place beside the fire.

"I don't think so," she said. Her gaze grew sharper. "Go yourself, if you hear Her calling."

"I…"

"Go," she said. "You can walk in the dark without me."

And so for the first time I took that way in darkness alone, going down into the deep caves without a lamp, with only my breaths and my steps to tell me how far I had gone. I was not afraid. I had been well prepared.

When I returned I sat at her side beside the brazier. It was heaped with charcoal to dispel the chill in the room, but Pythia was still wrapped in her cloak.

"Pythia," I said, "I don't want you to die."

She put her hand on my head. "Was it my death you saw down there in the dark?"

"No," I said. "And yes. I stood on the deck of a ship with the veil blowing out behind me, my face painted white and black. I was Pythia, which means that you were not."

Pythia smiled. "But that is what I want. To know that you will be Pythia after me. That you will keep this Shrine and serve Her faithfully. I have feared…" She stopped, and unwound her hands to warm them at the flame.

"Feared what?" I asked.

Her eyes fixed on the flame, very blue. "That She is leaving us. That She has withdrawn Her favor from this land."

I was horror-struck. "But why? Why would She do that?"

"I will tell you," she said. "Because you must know. But it is a story of kings, and they do not like if we tell it." She stretched out her hands.

"I was born in the palace of Pylos and dedicated when I was eight years old. This you know. In those days kings sought Her favor with the best of their harvest, even to the daughters of their house. There were other princesses who were dedicated this way, even the daughter of the High King, Iphigenia." Pythia sighed. "I knew her. She was younger than I, but we were together at the great festivals, since we were both in Her service and of equal rank.

"This was in the days when her father, the High King, led all of the men of the Achaians against Ilios, that you call Wilusa. They assembled together, all their men and ships, but the wind and the sea were against them, because that city was beloved of Aphrodite, the Lady of the Sea, and She held the seas against them. So the High King called together his priests and advisers, who served Athene and the Lord of the Storm, and asked them what he should do. They told him a terrible thing."

Pythia's blue eyes met mine. "He sent to the Shrine at Dodona, where his daughter served the Lady of the Dead, and ordered her brought forth from the Shrine, saying that she was to marry a mighty hero and cement his alliances. They brought her to Aulis, where the fleet waited, garlanded as a bride, like the Maiden in the Feast of the Descent. And there he sacrificed her living upon the altar and shared out her flesh among his men to eat like a young kid."

I gasped. I clasped Pythia's hand.

She nodded, and her face was stern. "Yes. The Lady of the Dead sent a mighty curse, a curse upon his house and all of his blood that even now is consuming the last of his heirs with madness. And all the men there, everyone who shared in that dark feast, She cursed as well, for they had killed Her Maiden and eaten the flesh of Her servant. All of the heroes, all the princes. Most of them never returned from Ilios, for the Lady and Her Sister made common cause. Those who did return descended into madness, or watched their sons rend their houses apart."

"But King Nestor?" I asked.

Pythia squeezed my hand. "My brother was a pious man. When they dragged Iphigenia screaming to the altar he turned his back and walked away. He had no part in her death, and did not eat her flesh. And thus he escaped the curse, and our house endures."

"But he did not prevent it," I said.

Pythia sighed. "I know. I have asked myself, what could he do, one man among many, and the king of a lesser city, not high in the king's favor? But it remains that while he did not participate in this greatest blasphemy, he also did not prevent it. And while She did not curse him, She turned Her face from him and walked away. It is just."

"Yes," I said. "He had turned his face from Her servant."

"Just so," she said. "But since that time we have been in a slow decline. You have seen the palaces and temples at Pylos, the wealth of my brother and his many ships. But you did not see them thirty years ago, when I was young. My brother has left Idenes six warships. There were twenty that went to Aulis. Idenes can count the jars of olives, the amphorae of wine in his storerooms, but I tell you that they are not the tenth part of what was there when I was young. My brother brought back many slaves to weave and work the flax on the river, as you know, my Linnea. But slaves do not replace the men who went to Ilios and never returned. Those fields have young trees in them now, and will not be planted again. It used to be that in times of peace our ships traded linen out to the islands, even to Krete and Millawanda and the Lydian coast. Now there are too many pirates, desperate men who attack honest merchants, steal their goods, and sell them as slaves in faraway ports."

"What must we do?" I asked.

Pythia patted my hand. "That is the energy of youth. To do something, anything, in the face of the gods' disfavor."

"We must do something," I said.

"What can we do? Can I rid the seas of pirates or raise men from the dead to plow fallow fields?"

I did not answer. I had not thought of these things before.

"Yes," Pythia said. "Now you must think. You must think about the causes of things, about the shape of the world, even though you will never leave this place. You must understand such things if you are to give counsel to kings as well as country people."

"But I will leave this place," I said. "I saw myself on a ship."

Pythia frowned. "Sometimes we are called to come to where the king is to give him counsel. That is it, surely. For once you are Pythia, you may not go forth long from the Shrine where you serve. Surely you do not wish to go?"

"No," I said. "I am happy here with you and Dolcis. This is my home. Why should I wish to go?"

And yet as I said it, there was something that strained inside, some yearning for shores I had never seen, for the songs I had heard as a child in my own tongue. For someone like me. Perhaps, I thought, everyone feels this. But we are all still alone.

"Like calls to like," she said. "And you have the sea in your veins, the blood of the Sea People. Perhaps you would have been better as Cythera's servant rather than mine. But She led you to me, so we take what is given."

"I have never been unhappy here, Pythia," I said. And it was true that I loved her, almost as a second mother, or as the grandmother I had not known. "I would not wish to go to Pylos and Cythera's service if you offered it."

She kissed my brow. "You are a good child," she said. "You are my Linnea, and I die content knowing that you will be Pythia when I am gone."

"You will not die for many years," I said, and knew it was not true.

SHE DIED a year later. In the fall, at the beginning of the sowing season after the Kalligenia, she fell to the ground and a paralysis took her right arm and leg. It dragged down the corner of her mouth and slurred her speech so that Dolcis and I could hardly understand her. It made it difficult for her to eat, so Dolcis cooked grain in milk from our goat and I fed her with a spoon.

"It is Her hand," she whispered, though I could barely understand the words.

Four months later I woke in the night to find her dead. The Lady's hand had touched her again, and taken her in her sleep.

I knew what must be done. I sent for Cythera and her handmaidens, for Dolcis could not go beyond the veil, and I could not carry Pythia to the place she must go alone.

We wrapped her in black, and Cythera held the silver mirror for me while I painted my face for the first time.

White as bone. Black as night. My hair was pinned up with the copper pins Pythia had worn, pinned into the elaborate puffs and curls of the wig, like a painting from the islands that are lost beneath the sea. I did not need the wig. My hair was dark and thick and had no touch of gray.

When I looked in the mirror She was looking back.

I led them into the darkness. I went in front, and Cythera and her two maidens came behind with She Who Was Pythia. Down into the darkness we went. Through the great chamber with the wolf skins, through the narrow passage that dripped with moisture. The sound of running water echoes far in darkness. I could hear that and the choppy breathing of one of Cythera's acolytes, terrified of the dark, of carrying a body to the very. Underworld itself.

The body of Pythia cannot be given to the fire, like these lately come Achaians. It must be returned to Her.

There was no odor in the chamber. Thirty years and more She Who Was Born the Sister of Nestor had been Pythia. Her predecessor was dry bones. We laid her in the chamber. I do not know how many were there. Twenty-seven skulls I had counted, but there may have been more who were crumbled beyond recognition. Twenty-seven lives of women. Four hundred years? More? Since before the bright land people came, with their horses and their bronze. Since before Wilusa burned, or the palace at Pylos was wrought. Before there were High Kings in Mycenae.

Someday my skull would lie here in the darkness.

We laid her with her predecessors, She Who Had Been

Pythia, and in the darkness I said the words that called Her to me. Her avatar. Her voice. As I was meant to be. She came out of She Who Had Been Pythia and dwelt in me.

There is something dreamlike about that winter in memory, as though while the world stirred and grew, I remained in silence and quiet. I had reached for Her and She was silent. Now I waited.

I spent much time in the caves that winter, descending belowground to walk without a lamp in the deep places. I explored passages I had not learned before, counting carefully so that I would not get lost, one hand trailing along icy stones wet with the faintest slick tracks of the rain that fell above.

Only it was not this season's rain. Perhaps last year, perhaps when I was a child, this rain had fallen on the mountains and slowly, very slowly, trickled down into the caverns. Perhaps I would be as ancient as Pythia had been before it found its way to the river and tumbled at last over rounded stones in the green light. Perhaps I would be long dead.

I felt as ancient as mountains, and as still.

Dolcis worried, I know. I hardly spoke, and when I did it was nothing of consequence. Long before the Feast of the Descent she cleared her throat one evening and suggested that we go down to Pylos, to stay at the temple of the Lady of the Sea. "They'd be happy to have us," she said. "She Who Was Pythia used to do that sometimes, before you came to us. There's company there, and any who want to find us will know where to go."

I looked up at her over the fire. "Maybe," I said. "Perhaps later."

Should we leave the anteroom because our Mistress was long absent? I went back down into the caves. I slept on the wolf skins in the great empty chamber. Lying alone in the dark, I felt no hint of Her presence, nothing to tell me what I must do. So, like a dim-witted handmaiden who has not been directed in her work, I simply did nothing. I waited.

Spring came. Country people came seeking Pythia for omens about babies, marriages, good harvests. I told them each what I thought was best according to my wisdom, and hoped that I did not err.

The Feast of the Descent came. Dolcis and I went to Pylos, and I slept beneath the linen awnings of the temple. I had grown so pale from spending time in the caves that Cythera gasped when she saw me and urged me to eat.

"Surely you have been ill," she said, but I shook my head.

The truth was that I could not cast off this silence, this sense of unreality, as though I walked only half on this side of the River, but could not reach the other shore. I hoped to find this missing half in the Feast of the Descent. I painted my face carefully, and Dolcis arranged my hair in the elaborate pins, the thin veil over it all. I sat with eyes downcast waiting to speak, waiting for that coldness along my spine, waiting for Her touch. But it did not come.

The time came, and I spoke my words cleanly and clearly, as She Who Was Pythia had taught me to do, but there was no sense of Her about me. I did not feel Her presence. It was only me, saying the words as I was prepared to.

Afterward, Cythera sat with me in the temple and tempted me with almond cakes. "You have been so long away from town," she said. "Will you stay awhile?"

"No," I said. "We will do the Farewell tomorrow, and then we will return to the Shrine."

"You should stay longer," she said, her keen blue eyes resting on me. "It would do you good."

"I do not know what would do me good," I confessed. "I am waiting, but I do not know what I am waiting for. It is as though everything is still, or that I am still while the world moves around me."

"Are you with child?" she asked. "I felt like that with my first daughter. As though I were a drowsy cow out in a field, sleeping through the summer."

That elicited a smile from me. "I can't see you as a cow. But no, I'm not with child. How could I be? I've never known a man."

She raised her chin. "Perhaps that's the problem, then. You are not forbidden a lover, only a husband."

"I belong to Death, not life," I said.

"You are a young woman," Cythera said. "Not a goddess. You are something more than a passive vessel for Her."

"There is no one I desire," I said. And it was true. I could not think of anyone I had looked upon who kindled any desire in me, except in dreams. And how should I love some Achaian farmer, full of awe for Pythia, or worse yet a man like Neoptolemos, who saw me as nothing but a prize to be taken and discarded at will?

As though she had read my thoughts, Cythera changed the subject. "Neoptolemos is back," she said.

"I had heard," I said wryly.

"He has come to raise an army," she said. "Come to the feast tomorrow at the palace and you will see." I began to demur. "You must come," she said. "It is your Lady's business, and you have every reason to know what passes."

And so I went. I had no part in that feast, or indeed in the Blessing of Ships. That is Cythera's role, and she did it well. I wore my plain black chiton with the mantle, and did not speak.

Afterward there were sweet fruits and roasted pig, the palace doors thrown open so that everyone could walk inside. Last year's wine was opened and amphorae were tilted and the hearth was heaped higher. Musicians played in the firelight.

I stood at the back, watching the warriors.

I could hear Neoptolemos over other voices. "We will raze our old enemies' citadel to the ground!" he said, a double-handed cup in his hand. "We will avenge our fathers, the heroes who fell before the walls of Ilios! And we will return rich in gold!" Around him, four or five young men cheered. "We will win our share of glory!" he continued.

There was a knot of people around him now, young men who had never seen battle. And the Young King, Idenes the son of Nestor, who had much to prove.

It was to him that Neoptolemos addressed himself. "Are we not of the same good bronze as our fathers? Shall we not be fit to stand in the brave company of their shades when we cross the River? Do we not want honors and women of our own? What keeps us then from venturing across the seas as they did?"

I leaned back against the wall. The colors were bright and the wine strong, but I felt nothing except a little sick. No one paid any attention to me. If any noticed me they did not recognize me without the paint. A woman of the town. Or one of the palace slaves.

I edged away, toward the passage that ran to the storerooms. Another was there before me.

Triotes' eyes glimmered in the firelight. There was no joy in his face either. And he knew me.

I felt the faintest touch of a night breeze, Her hand on my sleeve.

"Leave Aren here," I said. "If you take him to shed the blood of his mother's kin the Furies will pursue him all his days. And if you go, you will not return. The fish will eat your flesh."

He looked at me levelly. "Is that your word, Pythia, or Hers?"

"Hers," I said. "And mine. But it is true."

Triotes looked at me again, searching my face for something. "Aren will stay here," he said. "I must go."

"Why?" I asked.

"Because my king will command it," he said. With a last glance at the Young King arm in arm with Neoptolemos, he turned and went down the passage.

I went out through the main gates into the night. I walked away from the revelers, down toward the harbor. The stars were bright and clear over the sea.

The sense of presence was gone. She was gone. I stood under the starlight, watching the waves lapping against the shore, and felt nothing.

"Great Lady," I said. "Why will You not guide me? Why are You not with me? Am I not truly Pythia yet?"

Wait, the silence said. *You must wait.*

"What am I waiting for?" I asked.

The waves beat against the shore and receded. A ship moored against the dock creaked with the rise and fall of each wave. The stars shone in the blackness. And absolutely nothing happened.

I RETURNED to the Shrine. The days lengthened; the harvest was all gathered in. The poppies withered and went to seed.

When the grain was all safely belowground, Idenes sailed. He took six ships and all the men of his house, all the warriors and their arms. He sailed with Neoptolemos and the other ships he had raised. They sailed for Millawanda, where they would meet the men of Tiryns that Neoptolemos had likewise recruited. And then they would sail for Ilios.

Triotes went with his king. Aren, I imagined, wept bitterly at being left behind. He was thirteen, and doubtless thought more of the adventure than the battle at the end.

All was quiet at the Shrine.

Shepherds came with ewes that were ailing—there was some disease that ran among the sheep this year. I recalled something that Pythia said once, about a similar thing in her grandmother's day.

"Take the sheep that are ailing away from the others," I said. "Dedicate them and sacrifice them properly. Share out the flesh among your household, even among your slaves. But do not think you can cheat the gods by keeping them among the others, for if you do this surely all your sheep will be stricken."

And it was so. Those farmers who obeyed lost some valuable animals. Those who tried to cheat the gods lost almost all.

When it was done, and half the land feasted on mutton, I went into the deep caves. I had no part of the slaughter or preparation— I could not shed blood nor see it shed. So I went into the darkness.

The chamber with the wolf skins was silent. The air did not move except at my passing. "Lady," I said, "will You not speak to Your servant? What am I waiting for?"

The caves were silent and gave me no answer.

Wait.

At the height of summer Idenes returned with five ships laden with loot and slaves. One ship was lost on the return, the one that Triotes captained. He was lost at sea with all his men.

Dolcis told me this. I had no desire to go to Pylos and see the captives, to see the men of Pylos celebrating with the wealth of Wilusa.

"Forty slaves," Dolcis said, wiping the sweat from her brow from the long trek up the mountain. "And more that they sold on the way home at Millawanda for gold and silver from Egypt. Idenes is a wealthy man now, a king of some consequence."

She remembered who I was only when I got up without a sound and left the room. I went into the caves where she didn't dare follow me.

I sat on the wolf skins in the dark.

"Lady," I said. "I am Pythia, Your servant. But I was once a girl named Gull."

And I cried there in the dark as I had not since Pythia died. For the captives, perhaps. For my kinswomen I had never known who toiled by the river or in the kitchens of the palace. For my mother. For Aren, now twice orphaned. For myself. I do not know. But I cried until I slept.

THE HEAT SHIMMERED on the land, the air thick and heavy. It was hot, more so than summer expected. Usually there were breaks in the heat, but this lay oppressive on the land day after day.

Even the honeybees were still and the afternoons free of their buzzing.

Three weeks after Idenes came home he sailed again. Neoptolemos had the idea to raid up the Illyrian coast north of Ithaca before the sailing season ended. Pylos had no quarrel with those people, but drunk on victory nobody cared.

I remembered what Cythera said about being like a cow in a field. I felt gravid, sleepy. The heat lay unrelenting. At night, lightning played in the north, but the storms never came here. The heat never broke; the rain never fell.

Four nights later I lay on my pallet beside the hearth. The coals were raked so that there would be little heat. I dreamed.

In my dream I slept beside the river, in the hut I had shared with my mother and Aren when he was a baby. Everything was cool and quiet. I could hear the sound of the river flowing over stones.

My mother came to me and she was lovely, her black

hair combed on her shoulders. "Wake up, Gull," she said gently. "It's time for you to get up."

"But why?" my child self asked.

"I have work for you to do," she said. "Come, little one."

"It's not morning," I said.

"I know," my mother said. "But you must be at the bend of the road when morning comes. Get up, Gull. Come with me." She smiled, and I reached out my hand to her. When she took it I awoke.

I was lying on my pallet in the cave. It was hours yet until dawn. The sky had just begun to lighten. Sothis was riding high in the blackness, as sharp and as bright as a blade, the star that had shone on my birth.

The air was cool.

I stood up.

Dolcis was snoring softly.

Suddenly I was seized with energy. I must be at the bend in the road when the sun rose.

I put on my black chiton and pinned up my hair. I had intended to just tie it at the back of my neck, but the copper pins were in my hand. So I put it up, the high knots and pins intended for feast days. I reached for the alabaster pots. It was dark in the cave, but I knew which was which by scent, and I had no difficulty moving in the dark. I had moved in darkness for years. I painted my face to the whiteness of bone, outlining eyes and lips with kohl. And all the while I felt the urgency pulling at me. *Hurry. Hurry. I must be at the turn of the road when the sun rises.*

I took the black bag and wound it around my waist, as I had no handmaiden. I put in the alabaster pots, the brushes, the little silver mirror. The clay jars that held the herbs for the brazier. As though I were going to Pylos. As though I were going on a journey with Pythia and must carry her things.

Hurry. Hurry.

I took the best and lightest of the mantles and settled it about my shoulders, the veil that I wore only at the Feast of the Descent.

Hurry. Hurry.

The sky was graying when I left the Shrine, hurried across the thick mat of cypress needles and down the mountain. Everything was quiet and still.

I reached the turn in the road before the sun did. The sky had turned to silver. Another scorching day waited.

I sat down at the turn of the road and drank a little from my water skin. The sky lightened to pink behind me, behind the mountains. I watched the dawn come.

Long before it touched the rocks where I sat it cast the mountains as long shadows across the plain, across the shape of the river. Beyond, it kindled the sea like a mirror, silver in the morning.

Making toward Pylos in the bright sun were nine black ships.

İN HER HAND

As I watched the ships making for Pylos in the morning, I did not curse that I could not run. I cursed that I could not fly. It would take me half the morning to get to Pylos, down the mountain and around the road, following the sweeping bend of the river, to the city gates.

My feet were swift upon the track. I had been this way many times, and if my twisted foot did not let me run, it hindered me less than it used to.

The road was dust. The flowers beside the road were gone to seed, yellow and brittle.

Hurry. Hurry.

My mind was flying ahead, as though I had launched myself, swift as a black-winged gull, from the mountain road, soaring over valley and stream. They would see the ships now, less soon than I did, without the height and the sun at my back. Such men as were left in town would rally. Idenes was not there. How should he be? He and his warriors were up the Illyrian coasts, harrying people who had never harmed us.

The shade was welcome where the road passed beneath the trees along the river. I was hardly conscious of my body.

My gull's eyes could see the black ships beaching, the quick and furious fight along the wharf, the blood staining the stones of the harbor, pouring out like the libation at the Blessing of Ships.

Hurry. Hurry.

That ragged sound was my breathing. The sun was climbing up the sky. The track was rutted from animals and chariots. Here, just here, one had rolled over my leg so long ago.

Hurry. Hurry.

Now I could see a column of smoke rising. Something in Pylos was burning.

A gull could turn on the ocean breeze, see the fight moving toward the square, uphill toward the palace, slide through the rising smoke on tireless wings.

Hurry. Hurry.

The landward gates were open. Just inside lay one of the youngest warriors of Idenes' house. He had taken a sword thrust to the stomach, and his entrails were spilled in the dust, mangled where he had rolled in his agony, but his eyes were open.

I cannot spill blood nor see it spilled, some part of me that was Linnea whispered in my head. I ran to him and knelt in the blood.

His eyes widened, and I knew what he saw — Death, with Her white face and long cool hands. He tried to speak, but he could not. I put one hand against his forehead. "Let go, sweet boy," I said, and he died.

I closed his eyes.

I could hear the shouting. They were near the palace. A long column of smoke rose from the market stalls near the harbor.

I rose and I was wind. She filled me like a vessel brimming over. I ran down the street.

A knot of defenders had drawn back before the palace gates, which were open and broken. They had breached them, then, and the men of Pylos had counterattacked. There were bodies in the street, soldiers, and two of the palace menservants who had taken up swords. Shouts, curses, the ring of sword upon sword. The screams of the wounded.

A boy in a blue tunic stood beside the wall, where the vines overhung in flowering abundance. There was a sword in his hand, but he handled it awkwardly. I knew him. It was Aren.

His opponent had the better of him, a young raider with long black hair, shirtless in the sun, his shoulders gleaming with oil. He was inside Aren's guard. His sword rose, knocked Aren's sword to the side, returned for a swift upward stroke.

In a whirl of black like the flurry of wings I was between them, the blade tip almost grazing my stomach.

"Stop!" Her voice burst out of me, pitched for festivals, to carry over musicians or screaming warriors. "Lay down your swords!"

The raider's eyes widened. The sword slipped from his hand into the dust. Behind me I heard the *thunk* as Aren's dropped as well. The raider sank to his knees beside it. "Great Lady," he said.

"Lay down your swords!" I shouted again. A burly

raider with a cut bleeding across his cheek threw his down, fear and awe competing.

"On your knees to Death!" I shouted, and they went down like a wave, warriors of Pylos and raiders alike, all across the square before the palace, across to the Temple of the Lady of the Sea, like grain before the wind.

There was no sound except the moaning of the wounded, the slapping of my bloody feet on the stones as I walked forward.

Wild elation filled me, fury and power.

His head was bent, light brown hair pulled back in a leather thong. He wore a leather breastplate such as fighting seamen wear. His sword was worked with silver and laid by his hand. "You are their king, Captain of *Seven Sisters*," I said, for I knew him. I had seen the stars on the prow of one of the beached ships, and I had seen his face in dreams before. "Why have you come to Pylos?"

He looked up, and he flinched. "I am not a king," he said. "But I am their captain. We have come for the captives, for our wives and children taken in slavery, for the women of Wilusa. We have come to raze Pylos as they razed Wilusa."

And I realized that I was speaking his tongue, the first one that I had learned with my mother's milk. He was not surprised. Does not Death speak every language?

I reached out my hand, stained with the blood of the young guard, and touched his hair. He recoiled, then stopped himself. "You have come for the captives?"

"Yes," he said. "For those women brought here by Idenes, King of Pylos, from the sacking of Wilusa."

I pitched my voice so that it would carry, speaking first in the language of Wilusa, then in the language of the Achaians. "Enough blood has been spilled here today. The Shades are satisfied, and the dogs of the Underworld have drunk their fill. You have pled your case before the Lady of the Dead, and She finds merit in your claim. You, boy!" I turned to Aren, who knelt still by the wall, eyes as blue as the sea. "Go to the place where the women work flax beside the river, and tell the women of Wilusa to come forth, all the women of Wilusa with their children, bringing food and whatever belongings they have. Tell them that I command it."

Aren leaped up and ran, his feet pounding in the dust. It would not take him long to reach the river, as young and as swift as he was. And he knew well where to go.

One of the palace servants knelt nearby, trying to stifle a moan as he held a long cut down the length of his arm. Across the square, in the high seaward gallery, I could see the women of the temple looking out, Cythera's white veil stirring in the breeze. "You," I said to the servant. "Get up. Go into the storerooms and kitchens of the palace. Fetch out the women of Wilusa. And tell the others to come, that the injured might be tended."

I turned to the captain of *Seven Sisters*. "You will have your kin, and no more blood will be shed in this town. Tell your men that."

"We have not touched the temple," he said. "We are Her people."

"It is good that you remember that," I said.

The captain stood. "We are to have our kin," he said. "We are under truce, by Her will and in Her hand."

Behind me I heard a lapping noise. The buildings behind the palace by the harbor wall were burning, the rooms of the clerks who kept the grain tally, the work-shops where pots were made.

I turned to the men of Pylos. "Put out the fire," I said, "before it spreads to the storehouses, for all the grain is harvested and belowground."

They did so with alacrity. Those storehouses contained clay jars as tall as a man, sunk into the earth, and also jars of lentils and olives, dried fish preserved in oil or salted, fresh olives in their own juice, new wine. Food they would sorely need.

Two of the raiders were attending to their wounded, the burly man with the cut on his face helping another to stand, when I heard a shriek behind me. A young girl in a stained tunic came running through the gates and threw herself about his neck, crying incoherently.

Tears were running down his face, salt mingling with the blood. "Ah, sister," he said. "Little sister. You live. Ah, Tia." He buried his face against her hair.

I turned away.

The doors of the Temple of the Lady of the Sea opened. Some of the townspeople looked out, women and children who had taken shelter at Her altar. With unaccustomed haste, Cythera and her two acolytes came forth, water skins in their hands, to tend to the wounded and the dying.

WHEN ALL WAS ORDERED, it was not such a great slaughter. Ten men of the town dead, and two of the raiders. Another twenty or so with wounds but who would live. I watched. I ordered the men of Pylos to go and bring out the olives and wine in the storehouse nearest the potter's shed, because the bright sparks were leaping that way in the brisk ocean breeze. They could not bring the heavy floor jars, but could at least bring out the small ones of brined fish and wine. The breeze caught and tore at my veil, sending it flying behind me like a flag, my twisted foot brown with blood.

I heard a step behind me. It was the captain of *Seven Sisters*. "You are a woman of Wilusa," he said. "And yet I have never met you before."

"I am Pythia," I said.

There was a stir at the gates. The sun was midsky, and the women from the river had arrived. There were thirty or so, dark-haired and confused, and some five or six of my mother's generation. They paused just inside the gate, pointing and speaking, looking at the ships, at the raiders engaged in loading jars of olives aboard. I had not told them they might take food saved from the flames, but it seemed cheap enough, that they might leave the rest in peace.

Then one woman started forward. "Husband? Nicos?"

A young man lifting jars of olives shoved the jar he was holding into the hands of another man and ran across the square.

Then they all started moving. Crying, searching. There were many who did not meet the eyes of the one they sought, raiders catching at women's hands, asking after other names, after children. And the women of my mother's generation hung back, children at their skirts. Could they hope that any of their kin would be here, after eighteen years?

At last one woman I had known in childhood reached

out a hand, plucking at the sleeve of a warrior in his prime. "Anati? Is that you, grown up?"

His eyes went wide. "Aunt? Aunt Lide? It can't be! You were dead in the great fire."

She shook her head, tears brimming over. Two little boys watched speechlessly, the children of her captivity, younger than Aren.

I turned away. My mother was dead.

The fire was under control. Two of the storehouses were lost, but the rest survived. The men of Wilusa were loading the last of the amphorae into their ships, lifting women over the high rails and preparing to run out the ships.

The sun was sinking. A high pall of cloud spread from the mountains, alive with lightning. I could feel the wind on my face, moist and cool. The storm would break tonight.

I had been everywhere, laying out the dead of the town for their kin.

The captain was beside me again.

I turned and looked at him, veil pushed back and held by copper pins that were burnished by the slanting light.

"How is it that you've come here?" he asked. "Who are you?"

"I am Pythia," I said. "And I am of the People too."

He looked seaward, then back at me. "We are loading the ships," he said.

"Where will you go now?" I asked. "Will you return to fair Wilusa with her people?"

The captain shook his head sharply. "Wilusa is no more. Surely you know that. This time they have burned it all, and killed everyone who was not taken as a prize of war. There are none left to rebuild, and the men of Tiryns winter on the ruins before they raid the Lydian coast."

"But you and your men?" I asked.

"The fleet was at sea," he said shortly. "We are all that is left."

"Nine warships," I said, remembering my dream of the burning city, "and three fishing boats. Some capsized running the blockade and some burned in the water. *Seven Sisters* and *Dolphin, Pearl,* and *Lady's Eyes.*" I saw them again in my mind's eye, the ships I had dreamed as a child in Pythia's lap. "*Hunter* and *Swift* and *Menace. Winged Night* and *Cloud.*"

The captain looked at me. "We have none such as you. The Shrine at Wilusa has never been rebuilt, not since the Achaians razed it and dragged Kassandra from its altar. The women of the Lady of the Sea were taken as prizes, and we don't know where they have been taken. We hoped that one of them at least might be here."

I shook my head. "No, I would have heard if there were. Cythera would have known and told me." I glanced up toward the temple. There was a glimmer of white on the steps, Cythera watching me. "You have no priest or holy man of any kind?"

"We have an old man who takes the auspices, who is clever about wind and sea. There is none other. We have no Sibyl."

"You do," I said, "for I am coming with you."

He was at a loss for words.

"Am I not a woman of Wilusa, as you said? You have come to free the captives. I was born a slave here, but my mother was born in the Lower City, in the shadow of the Great Tower." I touched his arm, Her hand within mine,

Her voice in my throat. "She was born to do this. And surely you know that I would not let My servant come to harm."

He inclined his head. "Great Lady," he said.

"Make haste," I said. "Idenes will not tarry long in the north, and if you wish to be off without a fight you must hurry." I turned away, then looked back over my shoulder. "You must be at sea before this storm breaks."

In the gathering wind I crossed the square to the steps of the temple. Cythera was waiting for me. "I know," she said. "You are going with them. I have seen it in you all day."

"I am," I said.

"You carry Her within you, like an unborn child, to places I cannot see," she said. "I do not understand why, but perhaps I understand better than you do."

"Perhaps," I said. "I can see this journey's beginning, but I cannot see the journey's end."

Cythera raised her hands above my head. "May the blessings of the Lady of the Sea, Silver Aphrodite of the Fishes, rest upon you and follow after you all of your days."

I bent my head beneath the weight of her blessing, surprised to find tears starting in my still-mortal eyes. "Look after Aren," I said.

"I will," she said. "He's a brave boy, and while he doesn't understand what happened here today, in time he will, when he is grown to the manhood you have given him."

I hugged her and walked away, down to the last ships beached in their place. I did not look back toward the Shrine, or toward Dolcis. She would serve Cythera, or wait until another should be called to the Shrine, though I doubted that would happen.

My Lady did not mean to return.

The captain was talking to the young raider with the long black hair. "I am ready," I said. I felt suddenly light-headed, as though the freshening wind was lifting me with it. I had not eaten or drunk all day, except for the water at the turning of the road that morning.

"We will run *Dolphin* out," said the captain. "And then *Seven Sisters* last."

I turned. Pylos was smoking sullenly under the spreading cloud. The world spun suddenly, Her power draining out of me. I felt myself falling.

"Catch her, Xandros!" I heard the captain say, and then I knew no more.

THE SEA PEOPLE

I dreamed that I slept at my mother's breast beside the river. I could feel the gentle rocking of her breath, hear the sounds of the water and voices speaking in our language.

I woke.

The rocking was real, and the sound of the water. I lay on a pallet in the front of the ship, my head forward to the point of the room, which widened to perhaps my height a little beyond my feet. The ceiling was very low. I could just sit upright without bumping my head. There were no windows, but some faint light leaked in through the chinks in the boards overhead.

I could hear the slapping of the water against the prow, the voices of people on deck. I did not hear a rower's chant. Perhaps we were under sail, then.

There was a water skin beside the pallet. I drank greedily. It had been dawn when I last drank. Now it was...when?

I splashed my face and hands as well, wiping off the

residue of the paint with the inside of my mantle. Then I crawled out and went on deck.

I had not lain there long. The mainland lay behind us on the horizon, wreathed in storm clouds that stretched out over the sea. It was those winds that carried us, filling the white sail painted with a red dolphin. The oars were shipped, their ports blocked with wooden pieces fitted closely so that the seawater that splashed up her sides would not come in. *Dolphin* rode before the storm, leaping the waves like her namesake. White foam flew from her bow and the sail strained full with wind.

Some thirty men were on her deck, fore and in the pit where the rowers sat, along with ten or so of the women and children. On the afterdeck, broader and longer than the foredeck, the captain was at the tiller. He was the black-haired raider. The pious one, I thought, who was first to drop his sword.

When I came out of the shelter of the prow the wind hit me, lifting mantle and robes like wings, as though it wanted to hurl me into the sky. I made my way along the deck, to where the captain stood at his work.

"Are you well, Great Lady?" he asked.

I climbed the four rope steps to the afterdeck. The movement of the ship was wonderful, faster than a chariot. "I am well," I said. "And you don't need to always address me as Great Lady. I am Pythia. When it is only me."

He nodded, but did not speak as he attended to a minute correction of course, changing the tiller just a bit as the wind shifted a little.

I looked out over the sea. Eight other ships bounded along, spray flying in the gathering night. Already Pylos was indistinct behind us. Nearest to us, *Hunter* leaped, barely a rope's length away, her white sail painted with the archer, his bow drawn and his arrow ready, just as he hunts the skies. Beyond her I could see *Swift,* her sail painted with the sharp-winged bird she was named for. Behind us, last from the coast, was *Seven Sisters,* the bright Pleiades picked out on her sail. I could not see the people on her deck at this distance.

"Where are we going?" I asked.

He took one hand from the tiller and pointed ahead. "There," he said. "That smudge on the horizon is a small island."

"I thought those islands off the coast had no water," I said. "That is why the men of Pylos do not stop there."

"They don't," he said. "But that's where we've left the rest of our people."

"The fishing boats," I said. "You did not bring the fishing boats into Pylos."

"No. Nor the women and children that we had with us. We will beach the ships for the night there and continue in the morning. Also, *Dolphin, Hunter,* and *Pearl* have stores from Pylos, which must be shared out among the ships."

I nodded. I wondered how much they had brought aboard. I had been busy with other things in Pylos.

I looked up at him, and realized I was not looking far. Like me, he was small and dark, light but well muscled. "What is your name?" I asked.

"Don't you know?" he said with a wry smile.

"Death knows everyone's name. But I am not Death now, only Pythia."

"Xandros," he said. "Xandros the son of Markai."

I did not know the name of his father. "Are you a prince of Wilusa?"

He laughed, and adjusted the tiller again. "No, Lady. I'm a fisherman. Neas is a prince."

"Neas?"

"Prince Aeneas. The captain of *Seven Sisters*. He's our commander now. He's the only one of the royal house left. Well, him and his son, but the boy's not but four."

"How did you survive?" I asked.

His eyes darkened. "We were away up the coast when the Achaians came. We came back as the city was burning."

Xandros looked out to sea, to where the foremost ships were coming about, their sails lowering, as they turned the end of the island. "We landed and did what we could. There were a few fishing boats in the Lower City that had not burned, so we got everyone we could onto them and ran out, just as Neoptolemos got back from chasing some Tyrian merchants who had escaped. We got five boats away, but one foundered the next night, and one was so badly damaged we had to leave it on one of the islands. We've overloaded the warships, but they're seaworthy."

He looked ahead. We were not yet abreast of the island, but he saw something that I did not. "Stand by to drop oars!" he yelled. "Make ready with the sail!"

Men scrambled up from where they had been talking and resting. Two went to either side of the mast, to the bottom of the sail. The others went to the oars, removing the blocks from the ports and lifting out the oars.

Now we were nearly abreast of the island. Ahead of us, five ships had turned. To our left, a flurry of activity on *Hunter*'s deck told that she was doing the same thing.

The oars went out through the ports, held parallel to the surface of the sea, the narrow side of their paddles to the wind.

"Your pardon, Lady," he said, and gestured me out of the way. I stepped aside, against the railing on the right side. It was almost full dark now.

"Bring in the sail!" he shouted. The great white sail collapsed downward, the men fighting it into restraining ropes. Our momentum suddenly checked.

"Left side on the count of three!"

Down among the rowers another man's voice took up the rower's chant.

All the left side oars swept forward and bit as one, blades flashing as they turned in the air.

"Hard over!" Xandros yelled, and put the rudder as far as it would go, the muscles in his arms straining against the water.

Dolphin turned neatly to the right, slowing and bouncing a little as she crossed the wake left by *Swift*.

"Right side on the mark!" he called again.

As the left side oars left the water and then bit again, the right side swept forward and joined them in perfect time. We continued on, a full quarter turn off our original course. Behind us, I heard the rower's chant start on *Seven Sisters* and knew they were about to do the same.

Xandros grinned at me. "Not seasick, are you?"

"No," I said. "Should I be?"

"Ever been on a ship before?"

"No," I said.

We were gliding into the island now. It was low, just a sandbar above sea level, with some scrubby trees clinging to life and providing some shelter. On its white shores were three old fishing boats, drawn up with their nets spread to dry. Above them, at the edge of the trees, there were people and shelters, awnings spread to catch the dew and fend off the midday sun. A fire leaped and shadows moved around it.

"On my mark!" Xandros yelled.

We glided toward the shore, sand glimmering ahead.

"On three, ship!" The oars lifted from the water at once, droplets falling, and turned in the air, side on.

"I'd hang on if I were you, Lady," he said.

I grabbed the rail behind me as *Dolphin*'s prow slid onto the beach with a shock. I didn't fall. Oars were brought in as the two men who had handled the sail jumped over, guiding the ship a little farther up the beach. A stone's throw away, *Seven Sisters* glided into her place.

Now the oarsmen leaped down, pulling the ship farther up the beach with each incoming wave. Xandros jumped over the side, crossing around the prow and back, assuring himself that *Dolphin* would not drift off.

I went up to the side and looked over the rail at the oar ports. It was a drop of nearly my height. Xandros was below. "You'll have to jump down, Lady." He was standing thigh deep in water.

I swung my legs over the rail. I had not noticed that my feet were crusted with blood.

"Jump," Xandros said encouragingly. He reached his arms up. "I'll steady you."

I jumped. The cold sea water was a shock, splashing nearly over my head, as clear and as light as rain. It felt wonderful. Xandros grabbed me about the waist. "Careful," he said. "Do you swim?"

"I swam in the river when I was young," I said. "Never in the sea."

A wave came in, splashing me to the chin. I scrubbed my dirty feet in the clean white sand. Then I followed Xandros up the beach. Already men were swarming back onto *Dolphin,* passing down jars and amphorae from Pylos, the stores to be shared out.

A child came running down the beach and caught one of the women who had been a captive in Pylos about the waist, a boy of nine or so. The woman went to her knees in the sand, clutching him to her, her words incoherent.

"He was one of the fishing boat children," Xandros said, and there was a catch in his voice. "Some of them drowned when the boat capsized getting out of the harbor. That one was a good enough swimmer. He made it to *Dolphin.* But he had no family."

"Do you have a family?" I asked.

I couldn't see his face in the dim light. "They're dead," he said. "Killed for the pleasure of watching them die." Xandros turned and walked back to the ship to help with the unloading.

I walked up the beach. It seemed odd to hear so many people speaking the language of Wilusa. Then I realized what was strange. Until today I had never heard it spoken by a man.

Their prince saw me walking and came over to me. "Pythia, I must talk with you."

"I am here," I said.

He drew me a little ways from the others. "We must light a pyre for the two men killed today. We have brought their bodies from Pylos, but we must pay them honor to-night, because tomorrow we must sail. We are too close to Pylos to remain once Idenes' fleet returns. I will need you to do what is proper." He stopped. "Today has given us hope that some of us may be reunited on this side of the River, and it will help if you can do this. It will do people good to see these rites done as they should be, not in the haphazard way we have since we sailed."

I nodded. "Of course this can be done. I will need help building the pyre, and it will be hard to find enough wood on this island. But it can be done. And I will say the words that are right and proper. You will address their shades, Prince Aeneas?"

He nodded. "I will do it. I have done it before."

Three men gathered wood and we heaped it for a pyre, across first one way and then the other to build a proper bier. The two men would lie on it together, like brothers. I arranged their limbs as well as I could, for the stiffness was setting in. It was well to do it now, given the heat of the days. There was wine to pour out in libation, the best of Pylos' vintage, but I had no herbs or resins except the ones for the brazier that induce visions. We would have to do without. I went apart a little and straightened my dress, and repainted my face with the white and the black. I had enough paint for a while, but I should have to make more. The charcoal is easy to find, but the chalk must be rendered with fat carefully. It would be difficult to replace.

While I was apart they had assembled around the bier, quietly, respectfully, for the most part. There were four hundred or so in all, all the people left of Wilusa. When I appeared beside the bier some of the men stepped back. They had seen me in Pylos, but did not know that I had come.

I spoke the words that are right, the Calling of the Descent and the Lady's Greeting. Sothis rose clear and bright out of the sea.

Prince Aeneas cleared his throat and leaned forward. He touched the torch to the wood. It took some little while to catch. Then he addressed their shades, telling them that they had fulfilled all their oaths in life, that they were revered and praised by their People.

He looked out at the crowd, this ragged bunch of pirates, and I saw what he saw. "My friends, your sacrifice has brought back two score of our blood, reunited our families, given these women back into loving arms, restored these children's mothers. If you are waiting beside the River, may the ferryman be swift, knowing that he carries heroes who have given their blood for the blood of the People."

I saw their faces in the firelight. So many young and so few old, so many men and so few women. Clothes that were tattered and could not be replaced without looms. And how can one weave on a ship? Where would the flax and wool come from? How long could we live on stolen food with no fields to plant? We could not live on fish alone.

The fire leaped. I raised my hands in praise and farewell. Two of the rowers started with their drums, a steady beat that got faster. There were flutes then, and the other drummers joined in. I stood still while they began a long, slow dance about the fire, the acrid smoke rolling over us with the smell of burning flesh. I had not seen this dance before, majestic and slow, yet as wild as the storm. Faster and faster, whirling their pain and feeling away, under the wheeling stars. Sparks flew and vanished in the air. I felt dizzy again, and sat down on the sand at the edge of the trees. Faster and faster. Sparks whirling up into the air.

"What do you see?" Aeneas said gently. He had sat down beside me.

"Sparks," I said. "Sparks flying from an altar. You will raise an altar at the other end of the world, at journey's end beyond the sea. There are many roads between here and there, and not all of them are kind. But some of them lead to this city you must build."

"A new city?" he said.

"You have said it yourself," I said. "Wilusa is lost. We cannot live upon the sea. So we must build a new city far from our enemies."

I shivered. Her hand on me was too much. I had not eaten since yesterday evening, and She had worn me like a cloak.

Aeneas drew his own mantle around me. "You should rest," he said. "I do not know what battles you have fought today."

"I am all right," I said. "Though perhaps you are right that I should eat something, Prince Aeneas."

"Come to the fire where they are cooking," he said, drawing me to my feet with his hands. "There is fresh bread from Pylos, and a stew of lentils with greens in it. And fresh fish roasted above the coals."

My mouth watered at the sound of it. Behind me, some of the dancers were lamenting, their cries mingling with the drums, calling encouragement to the two men who must find the River.

"I should stay until the fire dies," I said.

"You can come back," he said.

I was a little unsteady on my feet. "As you say, Prince Aeneas."

"Call me Neas, as my men do," he said. "And give me your hand. How will it look for the Avatar of Death to fall flat on her face?"

I stifled a laugh. "Not so well, in truth." I took his hand and let him lead me to the fire.

⊙∏ THE WAVES

We slept on the beach that night. I woke cold and cramped and went to join the knot of women who were tending the fire. They drew back from me and did not speak, and I did not know what to say. I had never been much in the company of women except for those of the temple, and since the accident that broke my leg, I had not really had friends, girls who were my age. Perhaps it was because I was set apart by my dedication. Perhaps it was because I would never be a wife or the mother of a family, and since those things are women's life, we had little to talk about. So I did not know what to say and sat there silent and still.

At last one who had known me in childhood reached out and gave me some of the bread from yesterday that they were eating. "She was Gull," she said. "Her mother was a boatbuilder's daughter in the Lower City. I remember her well. She died of a snakebite several years ago. Her mother gave her to the Shrine when she was a child."

Several of them shifted then, looked at me less suspiciously. I took the bread. "Thank you," I said. "I remember you from when I worked the flax as a child. Your name is Lide. You had a little boy."

"He is here," she said. "He's nine years old now. And I have a younger son too. I never thought our people would come."

"They have come too late for my mother," I said. "And for so many. Eighteen years is a long time."

"Are you so young then?" one of the women asked, a light-haired girl younger than I. "I thought you were very old."

"She is very old," I said. "I am not. My name was Gull, but now it is Pythia."

"Is it true that you called down winds from the sky and struck the Achaians dumb? So that they didn't resist our men at all?" she asked.

"Not exactly," I said. "There was a truce."

Lide nodded. "That was well done. Otherwise many more men would have died before it was over, and we by the flax river might not have been saved, because who would have known where we were or how to send for us?"

"Did everyone come?" I asked.

She shook her head. "There were four who wanted to stay with men they have there. They stayed, and their children too. But all the women who were taken in the war this summer came."

That did not surprise me.

WE SAILED at full morning, leaving the ashes of the pyre on the beach. As we were preparing to leave, Aeneas came to me. "If it suits you, Pythia, it suits me well for you to remain on *Dolphin*. Space is tight on the ships, and Xandros is the only one with a private cabin for you. He has given you his cabin in the prow, and he will sleep with the other sailors. I should give you mine on *Seven Sisters,* but..."

"I know," I said. "You have your son aboard, and you must have a place for him."

He nodded. "Is that well, then?"

I agreed, thinking it easier to continue on *Dolphin* rather than start over on some other ship.

We went south along the coast all that day, passing villages I knew the names of, villages that owed arms and service to Pylos. Before darkness we crossed the gulf and the shores beyond were lands I didn't know.

Much as he disliked it, Aeneas brought us in to land on the mainland. There were no islands that were suitable, so the best we could do was a stretch of beach that was sandy and not right next to a town.

This night was very different. The fires were kept low, and the men took turns in arms around the camp, watch and watch alike, all night long. The men of *Hunter* had the first watch, and did not sit down to eat. After moonrise, when everyone was stretching out on the sands to sleep, the men of *Lady's Eyes* took the watch. *Pearl*'s crew would relieve them before dawn.

I wasn't sure where I should be, so I stretched my mantle on the sand near the others from *Dolphin*. I lay on my back and looked up at the moon, still waxing and growing brighter each night. It was strange to sleep this way, on sand under the open sky. The ocean was very loud, and all around me were the noises of a great crowd of people, snores and the occasional cry of a child, whispers, shuffles. I had slept for years in the darkness of the caves, and to sleep like this under the sky was both bright and strange. I rolled over, trying to block the moonlight with my mantle.

Xandros was a few feet away. He was not sleeping either. I could see the bright gleam of his open eyes. "You're not tired?" I whispered.

"It's hard to sleep on a strange shore," he said. "When any minute the men of this place might fall upon you."

"So why don't we sleep at sea?" I asked.

"It's dangerous," he said. "We can't anchor except in shallow water, and if we don't we might drift apart in the night. We can't have fires except in the braziers on the warships. There's no water for washing. And people need to move about, relieve themselves. But we're vulnerable on land."

I heard the soft shuffle of *Lady's Eyes'* men patrolling slowly around the edge of the camp. "Wouldn't it be hard to attack a camp like this with the moonlight this bright? The sentries would see you. Wouldn't a moonless night make more sense?"

"It would," he said, "but people don't always make sense." There was something in his voice that was amused. "Did they school you in war at the Shrine?"

"No," I said. "They taught me how to look at the world and see what is plain before me."

"I meant no offense, Lady."

"Were you schooled in war, then?"

Xandros shrugged, as much as one may while lying down. "I was a fisherman, and I went to sea with my father when I was old enough to be a help, not in the way. When I grew from boy to youth, my father talked to his friends and kinsmen, and they found a·place for me on one of the warships, a rower's bench on *Lady's Eyes*. After a few years I moved to *Dolphin* and became the chanter."

"The chanter?"

"The rower who sets the pace with the song. It has to be with the ship's movements when she's maneuvering. Otherwise the drum is fine, if it's just going forward in a straight line."

I remembered the differing songs, the way they wove in the orders for turns. "I see," I said. "And how did you become captain?"

Xandros shifted. "The same man can't stay at the tiller all day. It's too tiring. I learned the orders for maneuvers and when to use them, so I took a turn at the tiller so the captain could rest. He was killed."

"Getting out of the harbor," I said, remembering my dream. "He was hit with a fire arrow."

"Yes. I took the tiller, and later Neas made me captain." His voice dropped a little. "I can't imagine what my father would say, that I'm the captain of a warship. The last resort, of course, if the sons of fishermen captain ships like *Dolphin*."

"She's a beautiful ship," I said.

"The most beautiful ship in the fleet," he said. "One of the newest. She's alive."

"Yes," I said. Everyone knows that ships have spirits. "Tell me about her," I said. And he did, until he and I both slept.

THE NEXT DAY was hot. We continued southeast along the coast, a little farther out to sea because here the beaches were rocky. By midday the sun was scorching, and the reflection off the water hurt my eyes. There wasn't a breath of wind. The sailors rigged the sail flat over the forward deck to give the rowers some shade, and the children played listlessly in the shadow of it. Xandros had the rowers alternating benches, so that only half the oars on each side were in the water at once. It cut our speed in half, but half the men could rest at a time. They could not go on, hour on hour, in that heat.

My black robe seemed to trap the heat. I pulled it up in the belt, so that my legs were half uncovered, and pinned my hair away from my neck, but still the sweat crawled on me.

Xandros took turns at the tiller with another man, the burly man with a healing cut across his face, whose name was Kos. When Kos took the tiller, he came down and sat in the shade a moment. His shoulders were brown with sun, and like everyone else he reeked. I handed him the dipper for one of the water barrels lashed along the inside of the rail, and he drank thirstily.

"It's hot," I said. This was more than obvious.

He nodded shortly, the water dripping off his chin. "And we need to stay close in to land, so we can put in if we need to. Neas doesn't like it either."

"Doesn't like what?" I asked. I had heard the shouted conversations a while ago, but there were always shouts back and forth between the ships when we rode close together like this.

"The sea," he said. "Look there."

I saw nothing and said so.

"There is no wind," he said, "and yet the sea is disturbed and the waves are running a hand span below the oar ports. And there is a haze on the horizon. A storm is building where we cannot see it, and we must be able to put into a good shore before it breaks. See, there is *Seven Sisters* ahead and farthest in shore. Neas is looking for a place. But these beaches are too rocky. We will tear the bottoms out if we run in."

He was right. An hour or so later, before the sun had begun to dip, we saw the clouds piling up on the horizon, white and billowing and deceptively far away. Shoreward, cliffs marked the edge of the land.

Dolphin was meeting each wave, but the spray was flying up and soaking my feet fully the height of a man above the surface of the sea. The air seemed thick.

There was a shout ahead from *Hunter,* as far ahead as *Seven Sisters* but to the seaward of her. I squinted, holding up my hand to see what they had seen. White on the sea. Like a gull's wings.

Ships. Several at least, some that I knew. I had seen them often in Pylos at the Blessing of Ships. And one in front with her sail set, running toward us on a wind that did not touch us yet, the *Chariot of the Sun.* "Neoptolemos," I said.

I turned, yelling as I went. "Xandros!"

By the time I reached the stern, *Seven Sisters* had seen them too and was turning away from the shore, falling in line beside *Hunter.* Xandros had the tiller back, and Kos was on the prow.

The sail was unstretched from where it had been, and two men were hurriedly putting it back to the mast.

"All oars in on the stroke," Xandros shouted.

The second pairs of oars hit the water, and *Dolphin* surged forward.

"Pick it up," Xandros yelled. "We need to catch *Seven Sisters*."

The drumbeat increased, like a racing heartbeat.

One of the women smothered the cooking fire in the brazier amidships. The children leaped about like startled birds.

Dolphin gained on *Seven Sisters* and *Hunter*. Kos shouted across. I couldn't hear what Neas said, but Kos did.

"He says pass the word back that the fishing boats are to set all sail and run before the wind, putting as much distance between them and the Achaians as possible. *Swift* is to go with them for escort, since she's the smallest of the warships and the closest back in the line. We are to go forward between *Seven Sisters* and *Hunter*. *Pearl*, *Menace*, and *Cloud* are to be behind us, and *Winged Night* and *Lady's Eyes* are to spread out to the seaward to come down upon them to ram."

Xandros shouted the orders back to *Pearl*, three ships' lengths behind us, a fragile link in a chain across the ocean.

Then he looked at me. "Get the women and children under cover in the stern or bow before we get in bow shot."

I went forward and did so, sending most of them into the larger cabin at the stern. Kos' sister, who was the thin girl from the kitchens at Pylos; the boy from the fishing boat, and his mother crammed into my cabin. We would all just fit. It was stifling hot.

The sound of the oars, the creaking of the ship, the drum, and the voices above were almost paralyzing.

Two days ago I had felt no fear. Now I felt it. I was shut

in this cabin with nothing to do, while Death bore down upon us. I had no doubt that the men of Pylos had come to pay us for the raiding of their shores. Neoptolemos did not even need that pretext.

The ship shuddered. We were coming about. I could hear the shouted order for left side double quick.

Those men had been rowing in the hot sun all day. They must find the strength to row twice as fast, to stay with the drum. Quick thunking noises and a scream. They had peppered the foredeck with arrows. Those thuds were the arrows striking the boards above our heads, the scream meant someone was hit.

Splashing. Shouts.

Kos' sister huddled in the very point of the prow, her hands in her mouth to stifle a scream. The other woman bent over her son, as though putting the fragile barrier of her body between him and the arrows above.

"Do you hear what they're doing?" I said.

"I heard the captain just now," she said. "We're to pass close between two ships."

Thunks again. Another volley of arrows all down the side of the ship. *Dolphin* bucked. Had we crossed someone's wake? There was no way to make sense of the battle from down here.

A scream and a whimpering cry from almost outside the door. One of the rowers in the first tier, I thought. I had seen those men this morning, but I did not know their names.

It was only a little distance, not even the height of a man, from the cabin to the first tier. I could pull him inside in a moment and see what could be done. Kos' sister was near. I met her eyes. "We can get him in," I said.

You must not shed blood nor see it shed.

This time it was easier to disobey.

I opened the door and we darted out.

It was the first man on the right side, with an arrow through his shoulder. He had fallen in the space between the benches, his oar hanging loose in the port, fouling the one behind it on each sweep. His face was set, his teeth clenched.

I grabbed his right arm, the one without the arrow through the shoulder. "Get his feet!" I shouted. She did.

"No," he whispered.

"Be quiet," I said. "We'll get you inside and you'll fight another day." The girl dragged him and I half lifted. It must have hurt awfully, but it took only a moment to get him inside. The young boy's mother looked up, the rower's head falling almost in her lap.

"Here, now," she said, lifting his head up and turning his shoulder so she could see it.

I started back to the door.

"Where are you going?" the girl said.

"The oar has to be moved. It's fouling the stroke," I said. "There are no men with hands free to do it."

I darted back out, low in the shelter of the rower's rail, but still the wind hit me. It had picked up, cold and laden with rain. The storm was almost on us.

"Left side on the mark!" Xandros yelled. The left side oarsmen pulled their oars out, causing a turn to the right. He was completely exposed up there at the tiller, not even a shirt between him and arrows, or a leather breastplate such as Neas wore. In the shelter of the rail I couldn't see what he saw, could see nothing of the battle or the sea.

He saw me moving and nodded fractionally. The oar

was fouling the stroke, and the left turn was awkward and slow, with two oars out of ten not pulling. I crawled across the deck and closed my hands around the handle. I had no idea they were so heavy. It took both hands to pull it up, dripping through the port, and ship it in what must be its usual place.

We met a wave head-on, splashing up over the prow and the rail. The seas were getting high.

There were shouts out on the water. I didn't know the voice, but the tongue was Wilusan.

Xandros nodded. "On the mark!" he yelled. "Prepare to set the sail! Right side on three! Left side skip the beat!"

The chanter took up a different song, and the clouds reeled overhead as we turned sharply again, the wind behind us now, blowing straight down the ship. There were no arrows. We must be temporarily out of range.

On Xandros' mark the sail went up. It caught and filled, billowing out white against the black clouds behind us, the dolphin leaping red on white.

The ship surged forward.

"Keep the stroke!" Xandros yelled. Under oars and sail both? That would be our maximum speed.

I turned and went back in the cabin.

The boy's mother was drawing the arrow while Kos' sister held his arm still. Her face was white, but she was crooning, "Be still. Just for a moment. Be still."

The arrow came out in a great rush of blood. The man moaned and his head rolled to the side.

"Is he dead?" the boy said in a hushed tone.

I put my hand to the side of his neck, felt the strong

beat pulsing there. "No," I said. "He's passed out from the pain. Let me see the wound."

"Salt water," said the boy's mother. "Salt water to clean it."

The girl went and got some.

I looked at the wound, washing the blood away where it welled. Skin and muscle torn, a whiteness at the bottom and one sharp chip of bone. I pulled it out. "It's chipped his collarbone," I said, "but I don't think the bone is broken through. He's breathing well, so it's not in the lung, and too high for that I think. If we can stop the bleeding, he should mend."

"Pressure," the boy's mother said. "Clean cloth and pressure till the bleeding stops."

We took turns holding it tight against him while the ship tossed and bucked. The light was gone. It was dim twilight in the cabin, too soon for natural twilight. There was a surge of sound, like a great roaring. It was rain.

I went to the door and looked out, then slid out and shut it behind me.

The rain beat down in sheets. The sodden sail held the wind and strained at the ropes. The oars were all shipped now, the drum silent. When I stepped out of the shelter of the prow the wind lashed at me, and it was hard to stay on my feet. I made my way down the ship between the rowers. Some of them were nursing minor hurts. Most sat with their heads down, like horses who have run their race and worn their hearts out in sight of the finish line.

Kos and Xandros were both at the tiller. I clung to the rope steps to the afterdeck and climbed up, ignoring Kos' hand.

All about us the horizon had closed in, leaving us alone

amid mountains of green water. Each wave splashed up over *Dolphin*'s prow, sending a plume of foam into the air, but she shed water like her namesake. In the back, three men were bailing.

Far out to our right I could see another ship. It was *Winged Night*. I could see the black wings painted on her spread sail.

"Is Bai all right?" Xandros shouted.

It took me a moment to realize that Bai must be the rower. "The arrow was in the shoulder, not the chest," I said. "I think he'll make it."

"Good," Xandros said. It was taking two of them to keep the rudder straight.

"Where is everyone else?" I asked.

"I don't know," Xandros said. "Neas told us to pass straight through and take their worst, then run on with the wind behind us. The storm came up fast. Any prayers you have right now to the Lady of the Sea would probably be appropriate."

The clouds gathered down like omens, like the anger of the Lord of Storms.

THE ISLAND
OF THE DEAD

The storm and night both came down on us. Bai, the wounded rower, woke dazed with pain and vomited in my lap. The girl was seasick as well, and it wasn't long before the cabin stank. I couldn't blame them for their illness. The ship rose and fell so violently that sometimes I bumped my head on the down swell. Night came, and we huddled there in the dark. We did not dare a light with the movement of the ship, even if one of us had been able to go all the way aft to get fire. If there was still a spark in the brazier, which I did not know.

Sometime after full dark two of the rowers came in to join us, dripping with rain and shivering.

"The captain told us to get some rest so that we'd be fresh later in the night," one of them said. "How's Bai?"

He was sleeping, or perhaps passed out again, but there was no fever.

Six of us huddled there in a cabin that tapered from a hand span at the front to the height of a man at the back, a cabin only a little longer in length than my height, and only tall enough for me to sit upright.

We did not speak. The only one who could lie down was Bai, and that with his head in my lap and his feet at the point of the prow. The child fell asleep on his mother's lap. He, at least, was not sick.

One of the rowers smiled. "He's got a sailor's stomach. The captain will promise him a bench at this rate."

His mother didn't quite smile. I could hear her thought as clearly as if she'd spoken it aloud—that at this rate we would be putting children to the oars soon enough.

Kos' sister was shivering. She came and sat next to me, and I put my mantle around her. "Are you all right?" I asked quietly.

"Just cold," she said. She was shaking, but her body shrank from contact with mine. She was only a few years younger than me and very pretty. I had no doubt she'd received a warm welcome in Pylos.

"What is your name?" I asked.

"Tia," she said. "Daughter of Iaso, the boatbuilder. Kos is my older brother."

I closed my eyes for a moment in the dark.

It is like this always in Her service. Things swirl around and sometimes we can see the patterns, like Her hand on my sleeve, the faint whisper of the future, the past.

Sometime in the night the rowers changed their shift. Two more wet, exhausted men came in. One of them was Bai's friend, and took over his care. Bai wakened and took some water. There was still no fever as far as I could tell, and the bleeding had slowed to a seepage beneath the bandage when his arm was moved.

The night would never end. I thought that I would never sleep, but I did, slumping half sideways against Tia.

I dreamed that I stood on a hillside with a brown river beneath me, young olive trees sleeping in the sun on the slope below, vines stretched in orderly rows. A girl stood beside me, her hair like flame, her black tunic blowing in the breeze. Her skin was fair, but her eyes were as dark as caves beneath the earth. I knew Her.

"Great Lady," I said. "I do not know Your purpose. And I have seen blood shed against Your laws."

"You have obeyed Me," She said. She stretched out one white hand, skin flecked golden in the sun. "You have answered My purpose."

"To carry You within me to where You wish to go. But Lady," I faltered, "this burden is too great. I do not know the things I need to know. I can't carry You alone."

She turned and smiled, lips as red as pomegranates. "You aren't alone."

I woke to the tossing of the ship. It seemed a little lighter than before.

I extricated myself from the others and slipped out the door.

The rain was falling in squally patches, and the sail strained at the mast. Dawn was coming, and I could barely see the length of the ship. I could see enough to know that Xandros was still at the tiller, tied on with a length of rope. Living or dead, he could not leave it.

I thought about crossing the deck, but a great wave came onboard, nearly sweeping me off my feet. I fell beneath the rower's bench. Salt water broke over me. I dragged myself back up and back into the cabin. There was nothing I could do.

Midday came, and the storm was worse. We were tossed about. Each time we wallowed deep into a wave I wondered if we would rise again. Water dripped in from the chinks in the boards above, and we began to bail some out the door to where three of the rowers were bailing, lashed with ropes to the rail. All the food was aft except for some olives, but no one wanted anything enough to go aft. There was water in my water bag still. The girl could not eat, and Bai did not want anything but water. I wished for bread but there was none.

Someone banged on the door. It was one of the rowers, calling the two who were resting. "Come out. We've got to get the sail in. The captain says it's useless, and it's going to tear away in this wind."

"What does it mean to be without a sail?" I asked.

He looked at me. "It means that there is nothing to do but go where the storm takes us, and hope he can keep us pointed into the waves."

They were gone.

I leaned back against the door and closed my eyes. I had worn out my entreaties to the Lady of the Sea already, as had everyone else. I closed my eyes. *Please, Lady, mercy on Your people,* I thought. *Mercy.*

Night overtook us. One of the rowers came in with a jar of wine and a fresh water skin, with brined fish that did not need cooking to eat. Tia took one look at them and was ill on my feet. Bai ate them. He still had no fever, and I was beginning to hope that he might mend, if we didn't all drown.

Sometime after midnight it seemed to me that the pounding of the rain was less. The ship still rolled violently, but the roaring of the wind seemed to have abated a little. I climbed over the others and looked out.

The rain was indeed less. It spattered unevenly across the deck now, which was swimming under a hand span of water. Still *Dolphin* met each wave. Kos was at the tiller.

I made my way aft. The water in the bottom was over my ankles, and the ship was still pitching.

The wind swirled around me as I reached the steps. The stern cabin door opened and Xandros came out. He checked as he saw me, caught my arm as a roll of the ship threw me off balance. "What's wrong?" he shouted. "Bai?"

I shook my head. "He's fine," I shouted back. "I wanted to see what was happening. The rain seemed less."

Xandros climbed the rope steps. "Kos, you should go below. Your turn." He untied Kos from the tiller.

Stiffly, Kos tied him in his place. I climbed up the ladder. The wind hit me and I held on to the rail. Two lengths below, the sea churned white with foam, lashing at the ship. Ahead, down *Dolphin*'s side, I could see a patch of sky between the clouds, the faintest hints of stars.

"That's where we're steering," Xandros shouted. "You should go below. You could be swept overboard."

I thought of that reeking dark hole, and shook my head. "I'll stay here a few minutes," I said.

Xandros shook his head. "You know if your Lady calls, I suppose."

I held on to the rail. I was not foolhardy.

The wind felt good. The waves seemed more regular somehow. We rose and then fell, leaping forward, without the side to side motion that there had been earlier. I said so to Xandros, leaning close to him to speak into his ear.

He nodded. "These are more like regular rollers. We're coming out of it. And no real damage to the ship that I can see. We've been more than lucky. We've been in Her hand."

We were heading east. I could see the sky lightening a little ahead of us. "I wonder where the others are," I yelled.

Xandros shook his head. "Scattered all over the sea," he said. "If they've ridden it out."

An hour or more passed. I held the rail and felt the last rain spatter over me. The stars were ahead, the last tatters of storm cloud flying behind us.

Lady, I thought, *thank You for Your mercy on Your people. Mercy, and dawn.*

Pink streaked the far horizon. The great green waves lifted us and rocked us.

Xandros cleared his throat. He had untied the rope. "There's a water skin just there," he said. His voice was hoarse from shouting, and I could hardly hear him. "I think there's still some in it."

I brought it to him and unfastened it. He raised one eyebrow and held it out to me. "Do you want it, Sybil?"

"We can share it," I said. I took a small sip and gave it to him, watched him drink, his throat moving with each swallow.

Everyone else was below or sleeping. It was like being alone on the vast sea, dawn and flying stars. His sodden hair clung to his shoulders, one perfect drop of water standing on his browned skin. His face was remote, quiet as though silenced by the sudden, unexpected beauty of the morning.

Something touched me, something unfamiliar.

I had not put a name to it when the door below opened and Kos came out. "Xandros? Do you want to set the sail?"

He handed me back the water skin. "Yes," he said. "Let's take it halfway up the mast to give us some steerage. We need to figure out where we are."

I looked out over the waters in the gathering dawn. On the horizon behind us something lay dark on the waves. It looked like another black ship, her sail drawn down. "Xandros, there!"

We kept her in sight while the sail was set, then Xandros maneuvered a little to bring us ahead of her and cross in front of her. Before long we could see that it was indeed one of our ships.

"Is she a hulk?" Kos wondered. "I don't see anyone moving on her deck."

"Can you see who she is?" Xandros asked. I noticed that both Kos and I saw things sooner than he did.

The next lift of a wave showed her prow to both of us at the same time. "It's *Cloud*!" Kos shouted. Now we could see her tiller engaged, a white streak behind her. There was still someone at the helm at least.

The sun rose red out of the sea.

I stood on the stern deck while Xandros gave the orders to drop the sail and maneuver with oars to come alongside *Cloud*. As we got closer we saw that she was half awash, and that everyone was bailing. There was a shouted conversation across the water that I caught only half of, but deduced from Xandros' part that *Cloud* had taken a rogue wave amidships over the deck. Three rowers had been swept into the sea. Though they had heard them calling and yelling in the sea, they were unable to turn and get them, so they were lost. They had been near *Winged Night* through the first part of the storm, and she had been riding it well, but they had not seen her since twilight the night before. They had seen two other ships far out, but ours, Achaian, or random merchant traffic they didn't know.

"We were near *Hunter* until the worst of it yesterday," Xandros said. "And late in the day Kos saw something he swears was *Seven Sisters* ahead of us."

I thought about the fishing boats in the storm. A dozen men, eight women, and fifteen children. The warships might ride the storm out, but the fishing boats were much smaller.

Full morning came. The sea was still rough, but not heaving as it had. Everyone came out and set about cleaning up and bailing. We rode close by *Cloud*.

The young boy from my cabin was up on the prow. "Look there!" he cried.

I did. Xandros shaded his eyes and squinted. "Please, Lady, not Neoptolemos."

Three warships rode together, their sails folded and their oars out.

Kos ran forward to join the boy. "No," he shouted back, his face split with a grin. "It's *Seven Sisters, Hunter,* and *Pearl!*"

We came up to them and a cheer ran from ship to ship as they recognized us. Aeneas waved from the tiller as we came alongside. "Xandros, you lucky bastard!"

"That would be you," Xandros yelled back. "The Sea Lady takes care of her own, and we're glad of it!"

Neas laughed.

We came close enough for ropes to be thrown between all five ships, and pulled us side by side like a giant raft.

Cloud had the worst of it, though *Pearl* was hurt from the battle. Too close a pass down one of the Achaian ships had broken half the oars on her right side, and she was now running with only five to each side.

Xandros leaped lightly across the gap to *Seven Sisters*. He reached back for me. I looked at him skeptically. "Prince Aeneas needs his oracle, Lady," he said.

I took his hands and jumped.

The captains of the other ships had come aboard as well, and we all crowded onto the afterdeck of *Seven Sisters*. There was also an old man who I realized was Aeneas' father, Anchises. He looked at me with something between shock and horror.

"My son," he said. "You cannot have a woman at your council." Two other men's faces set in stern lines.

Aeneas looked up with a mild expression. "Father, is it not fitting and proper that I should have the counsel of Sybil and hear her words?"

"Throughout the ages, kings have taken counsel of Sybil," Anchises said, "in proper place and at proper time. They have gone apart to her dwellings in deserted places, and asked their questions of her in darkness. And she has replied in such verse and length as the gods use when they veil their mysteries from men. Kings do not invite her to open council, where her words are no more than others and where she may hear politics and policy and openly speak of the strategies of men."

Aeneas looked annoyed. "Father, do you see a cave where we may go apart? We are on the open sea, storm battered. I would have counsel here and now. And I am not a king." He turned to me. "Lady, you are the only representative of the gods among us. I would ask you to stay."

"I will stay if it pleases you, Prince Aeneas," I said.

Anchises snorted. I could see that not all of the men were pleased. I kept silent, though in truth I had nothing to add. She did not touch me, and I knew little enough of sailing.

The crux of the matter was this: We were five ships in the middle of the ocean. Where the other four warships or the three fishing boats were none of us could say. Two ships had seen *Winged Night* during the storm, so it seemed certain that she at least had survived. One had seen a ship they thought was *Lady's Eyes,* but she was the oldest of the warships and not as sound as she had once been.

"She's stoutly built," Xandros put in. "And Jamarados is a good captain. I wouldn't give her up yet."

We did not know where we were. In a day and a half with the storm at our backs we could have been blown far. Also, none of the ships had adequate water.

"Our casks are fouled with seawater," Xandros said. "We have three or four water skins, and the amphorae of wine, but that's it."

One of the other captains had not even that, so plans were made to send some wine over to his ship.

"We've plenty," Xandros said. "More than a hundred jars."

I noted to myself that I had not kept careful watch on him in Pylos at all.

While we were at council, a shout was heard from the prow of *Seven Sisters.* "Land!"

We all went forward.

It was a smudge on the horizon, a low semicircular island.

Two captains jostled each other, naming islands they thought it might be.

"That's too far," one said. "That's clean up north of Lazba."

"Well, it's not Dana," the other said. "We can't be as far south as that."

Anchises gripped his son's shoulder. "This is our punishment for not pouring a libation to Aphrodite Cythera when the storm ended. That is the Island of the Dead!"

"We cannot be there," one of the men protested. But it seemed as though we were.

"The Island of the Dead?" I asked Neas.

He nodded. "In my great-grandfather's boyhood there was an island that had everything that men might want—green pastures and olive trees, a fine town, a strong defensible location on the trade routes, a high mountain that rose out of the sea and could be seen from afar. There was a mighty kingdom there, allies of Krete. They had many ships and sailed all the seas there are. But somehow they angered the gods. The mountain exploded and destroyed it all, groves and pastures, town and fair people."

His voice was very quiet, his eyes focused on something I could not see, as if he remembered. "The sea rose up in great green waves and drowned the cities all along the coast. A quarter of the people of Krete died on that day, and all the ships that were at sea. Only the palaces and towns on high hills survived. And when the seas calmed, there was nothing left of the island except two crescent beaches low on the sea, which churned with bodies and ruined trees."

"That was here?" I said. "I have heard the story of the Drowned Land, but I didn't know where it was."

"It was here," Neas said. "Thera That Was, the Island of the Dead."

"It is accursed," Anchises said. "We must steer away."

"If it is Thera," *Hunter*'s captain said, "then there is not another island near at hand where we can get water."

"We must have water," *Cloud*'s captain said.

"We cannot set foot on the Island of the Dead," Anchises said. "Or the curse will come upon us."

"Is there water there?" I asked.

"We do not know," Xandros said.

"It's large enough to have water," *Hunter*'s captain, Amynter, said. "All those fair pastures that Neas spoke of must have had some springs."

Anchises pursed his lips. "That Prince Aeneas spoke of."

"Father," Neas said.

"We need water badly," *Cloud*'s captain said. "I think we should go ashore and look for a spring."

One look at Xandros told me he was not the one who wished to go.

"Anyone who sets foot on the Island of the Dead trespasses in Death's realm," Anchises said.

"That is not to be taken lightly," *Pearl*'s captain, Maris, said. "Danger on the seas is one thing, but the wrath of the gods is another."

Xandros nodded in agreement.

"I will go," I said.

Neas whipped around to look at me.

"I am not trespassing in Death's realm," I said. "I am Her handmaiden. I have nothing to fear in Her holy places."

"What will you do, Lady?" he asked.

"I will go and find a spring, if there are any. I will ask Her leave for us to take Her water, and make whatever propitiations are necessary." Anchises scowled, and I looked straight at him. "To inquire further about Her sacred rites is unseemly."

There was no answer possible to that, so he held his tongue.

"I will come with you," Neas said. "I must speak for the People. It is fitting and fair. Besides, there may be snakes."

IN THE END, *Seven Sisters* came in close, nearly beaching at the end of the larger of the two semicircular islands. Neas jumped down into the water and reached up for me. The water was cold and the waves still running high, but not dangerously so. We waded in.

"The beach is broad and sandy," Neas said. "We could bring the ships in if we wanted."

I nodded. He took my hand to help me to the top of a dune. We looked over at the lagoon between the islands.

The water was as clear as glass, lapping over white sand, turquoise near the shore and then deepening to cerulean quickly, as though there were a very deep place in the midst of the island. On the bottom I could see walls, the foundation of a building, what looked like a dock, all underwater lapped by the waves. I saw a movement, and for a moment I thought it was a woman in a dark cape poised in one of the empty doorways, but then it moved and I saw it was an octopus. It flowed into the darkness.

Neas still held my hand. "This was a mighty city once," he said.

"And now it sleeps," I said, "beneath the waves. It is the Sea Lady's city."

"It's not deep," Neas said. "Three spans or less. Two even. I could dive."

"And do what?" I asked. "Disturb the dead?" I reached down and picked up something from the sand beneath my feet. It was a piece of broken pottery, worn by the waves, but with still the whorls and border visible. "If you must have something of them, take this." I pressed it into his hand and led him away from the water, toward higher ground.

He turned it over and over in his hand.

I climbed the rocks, as black as night, new and as sharp as bronze. I was very careful, for I am not sure-footed.

He was looking still at the water. I called him and Neas climbed up to me. There was a look in his eye I had never seen on a man.

"What do you see?" I asked gently.

"A city," he said. "A ship with an octopus on her prow. Palaces with red columns and painted roofs. A great wave." His blue eyes were unfocused, the stubble on his chin golden in the sun.

"Things that were," I said. "In your great-grandfather's day."

"Yes. I cannot remember."

"We cross the River," I said. "And dwell in the fields of undying grain under the sun that never sets. And when the time comes, we cross the River that is Memory, Lethe.

We return to this changing world, and remember nothing of what came before."

"Not our loves? Not our dearest companions?"

I turned his hand over, caressed the shard in his broad palm. "Not unless something recalls it to us."

He looked at me now. "Do you think she has forgotten me, beyond the River?"

"Who?" I asked.

"My wife, Creusa," he said. "She was lost when the city fell. And my world is darkness without her." He ducked his head, choking off the last words.

"You can cry, my prince," I said. "Tears for the honored dead are honorable indeed."

He sank to his knees on the black rocks, clutching a broken piece of pottery to his chest, his shoulders shaking. I knelt beside him. "Cry, my prince," I said. "You are carrying us all. You can cry on a deserted island where there is none but me." I stretched my black sleeves over him like dark wings.

I did not catch any words he said, except "Creusa, my beloved." I clasped him about with my arms, and held him until he ended. Above, the black-winged gulls whirled on the sea wind. *I am Gull,* I thought. *I am the granddaughter of a boatbuilder in the Lower City.* Even were I not Pythia, I could not look so high as Aeneas, the last prince of Wilusa.

At last he moved. "Your pardon, Lady," he said, and did not meet my eyes.

I touched his face, the warm rough line of his jaw, lifted his eyes to mine. "It is nothing. She is used to the sweet tears shed at the foot of Her throne."

He nodded sharply. "It is so?"

"It is," I said, and smiled at him. "All is well, Prince Aeneas."

"Neas," he said.

"Yes," I agreed.

Neas turned over the shard in his hand, then slid it into his belt pouch. He stood. "I've been foolish," he said. "These islands are low and rocky. There is no water here."

"There is," I said.

"Why do you say so?"

"Because the gulls are nesting," I said. "See? They will not nest where there is no fresh water to be found."

We climbed up together. There was a tumble of stones, old ones, worn and shaped, with bits of shell in them. Some looked as though they had once been squared. Nearly at the top, there was a green hollow, and a small spring that trickled from between the stones. The gulls screamed at me and beat at us with their wings.

"We will not disturb your nests," I said aloud, "or anything of this island that does not belong to us. We know you are the creatures of the Lady of the Dead." I knelt beside the water. "Great Lady," I said, "this water comes from Your holy places beneath the earth. Grant that we may fill our casks and have water for the People." I took a sip. It was sweet and fresh and cool as a mountain stream, as sweet as Her assent.

"We will fill our casks here, Neas."

HER MERCY

In the end, we were three days on the Island of the Dead.

At first, most of the men were reluctant to set foot on the island. Even when Neas came back to the ships and explained that there was water, I saw the eyes rolling and the motions to avert evil.

"I spoke to the Lady of the Dead," I said, "and asked Her for water. She sent Her birds to show us where it was, a sacred spring as clear and as pure as any in the world. We may fill our casks as long as we disturb no living thing on the island that is Hers."

After this there were some who would come ashore, and they began loading water for *Hunter* and *Seven Sisters* first.

By the end of the first day we had just begun loading clean fresh water onto *Dolphin* and *Pearl* when a sail was sighted. There was a flurry of movement, oars unshipped, sailors recalled from the island. *Seven Sisters* and *Hunter* ran out, preparing to meet and delay the newcomer as long as possible. We heard their cheers coming back over the water. It was *Winged Night,* and she had all of *Menace*'s people aboard.

As twilight came the three ships returned to the island and we heard their story. *Winged Night* had ridden out the storm, seeing other ships in the distance, but essentially alone. At dawn on the second day, as the storm was abating she had come upon *Menace,* near foundering with her decks awash. She had closed on the sinking ship and lying alongside had taken all her people off with ropes, except for one woman who had fallen in the sea and drowned. *Menace* was lost, but twenty-one sailors, five women, and four children were saved. The loss of the ship was hard.

"Ships may be replaced," Neas said, "but the blood of our People is spread thin. We cannot spare even one, even the smallest child, and you have rescued thirty who would otherwise have been lost. Tonight we will honor the crew of *Winged Night.*"

Amid the reunions, he drew me aside. "We will have to be several days here. Is that well with your Lady?"

"It is," I said. "If She had not meant for us to find refuge here, She would not have let Her sister bring us to Her doorstep. I have seen no sign that She is displeased."

"The beaches are broad and the water shallow over a sandy bottom. There is water aplenty. No man comes here. We must stop a day or two, heal our hurts, and find room for *Menace*'s people on the other ships. Also, perhaps *Lady's Eyes* and *Swift* will join us." He did not mention the fishing boats. One doesn't speak of ill, as that may invite it, but as time passed it seemed more and more likely they were lost, especially since *Menace* had been overwhelmed. She had been one of the newer warships, if not the largest.

So we stayed. That night Neas lit a bonfire, and the men paid tribute to the courage of *Winged Night*'s crew with the best wine of Pylos. Drums and flutes were produced, and before long there was singing beneath the almost-full moon, the long line dances weaving around the fire, singing familiar songs of home. In their rhythm I heard the echo of the flax slaves. This was where they had come from, the songs they had sung as they worked, sounding of sorrow and loss. I heard them now outpouring relief and release.

Tia did not dance, but she stood near the fire clapping the dancers on, a wine flush on her face. Kos pirouetted in a circle and then threw his arm over Xandros' shoulders, shouting out the words at the top of his voice. Bai could not dance. He took a few steps and nearly fell. Tia saw and helped him sit, near enough to the fire to sing, but not to be trampled on. He spoke to her. Words of thanks, I thought. Her flush rose higher. He looked up, patted the ground beside him. She hesitated, then sat down on his left, the width of a man still between them. But she smiled.

I turned away. *I will go out from the dance,* I had said. *And none shall call me beloved.* It had not seemed hard at the time.

And now what should I dream of? A prince's courtesy, smiles and trust that were for his oracle, not for me?

Instead I found myself thinking of a lean, smooth form darkened by sun, of Xandros' still, deep eyes.

I walked away from the crowd on the beach, drawing my mantle about me, walked down toward the inner lagoon with its dark water and secrets. No one followed. I followed the lagoon around until I found a place where a tumble of rocks spilled down into the water, perhaps part of the fallen wall of some great palace that Neas remembered. I sat there on the rocks under the moon, wrestling with my heart.

Great Mistress, I said, *it is not that I do not love You more than life. Or that You are not mother and father both to me. But as Cythera said, my body is a young woman's. Is it so odd that I should be moved by a man of my people?*

There was no answer except the quiet lapping of the waves. The reflections of moonlight on the water rippled across sunken doors and windows. No bones remained, just the skeletons of houses waiting underwater, reminders of what had been. The water was shallow. The houses were deceptively close, as though you could simply wade out and walk those streets, step into the Land of the Dead.

What had I forgotten when I crossed the River? Had I lived in those houses, slept behind those windows? I could not help imagining a palace with red columns, a great soft bed where I lay entwined with warm arms, golden stubble against my breast, my hands against his shoulders, doomed lovers on the last day of the world.

But the world is not ended, She whispered in me. *The world ends, and begins again. That is the Mystery, if you have courage to follow it.*

I belong to Death, not to beginnings, I said.

Ah, She said.

I heard then the scattering of small stones, as though someone else was climbing up the rocks. I waited to see who it would be, not certain which I wished it to be.

It was Tia.

I sighed.

She startled when she saw me and almost fell. "Lady! I didn't expect you to be here."

"You didn't expect anyone to be here," I said. "You have walked apart, and wanted solitude. I will go."

"No," she said. "Stay." Tia looked away, out over the sea. "There is something I…"

"Sit beside me then," I said.

She folded up next to me, her knees hugged tight to her chest. "I know that there are things…I mean, if you think…"

I looked at her, waiting for her to go on.

"There are things that can stop a baby, yes?"

"Ah," I said.

"I don't…I can't…Kos doesn't know yet, but he'll wish me dead when he does."

"Kos will do no such thing," I said. "You are blameless in this, as are all captives. He loves you dearly. He risked everything to find you and rescue you. Kos will never turn away from you." I had seen enough of the man to know this, the love and relief on his face in Pylos when he saw his sister alive against all hope.

"I dishonor him," Tia said.

"You do not," I said. "Are you certain it is so?"

"I think. It's been a long time since my courses."

"Let me see," I said. "Lift your tunic. I will touch only your stomach."

She flinched, but did as I asked.

"Lean back a bit." Tia was so thin that her hip bones were sharp, but there was a little pouch of flesh that should not have been there. Under my hand it was firm, as hard and as solid as muscle, rising four finger widths above the bone of the pelvis. I pressed gently, and it was firm. "Yes,"

I said, "you are with child. How many moons since your courses?"

"I don't know," Tia said. "Since I was on the boat to Pylos, I think. Three, maybe four moons? Can you stop it? My mother once said that there are herbs?" Her voice was hopeful.

I shook my head. "There are, but I have none of them. And even if I did, I could not give them to you now. You are too far along. They could kill you." I moved my fingers, pressing a little, and felt it, the faint flicker of movement, almost imperceptible, the movement of a child with many months still to go before breathing air.

Tia bit down on her lip. "That might be better."

"It would not," I said. "Tia, look at me."

She did, and I did not see what I feared, the real desire to die. "I can't tell Kos," she said. "But sooner or later even he will know."

"He will know," I said. "And it will be well. Kos would never do you harm."

She bent forward over her knees. "Everyone will know. I want to just be rid of it. And you are telling me I must bear it."

"All these women here know what it is to be prizes of war, even the few who escaped from the City. There are many who have borne the child of their captor. None will blame you or consider you without honor. You remember what Prince Aeneas said earlier?"

She looked up at me and shook her head.

"Every life of the People is valuable. Is irreplaceable. Including yours."

"Even the smallest child," she said. "But Sybil, I do not want this child! I will look at it and hate it. I will cast it into the sea. I will wish it never born, or dead. Tell me that when it is born I can leave it in some deserted place."

"No," I said. "You cannot." And it was Her implacable mercy that spoke through me. "Her hand is upon it."

"It will die?" she said.

I reached forward and put my hand on her stomach again. "The child is a daughter," I said. "And if she lives, she belongs to the Lady of the Dead."

I had dreamed on the boat, sitting next to Tia, of a girl in black with long red hair, a place with young olive trees, of Death speaking to me through pomegranate lips. Those, perhaps, were always Hers, but not the freckled hands, thin and fair like Tia's, but spattered with gold. Those belonged to a real girl. "She is the granddaughter of Iaso the boatbuilder, and when she is weaned you will give her to me to be my acolyte. I will raise her as a daughter to the Shrine, and she will be Sybil when I am gone."

"You will take her?" Tia said. "Really?"

"Yes," I said. I drew her tunic down. "I will take your child. She will have honor and a place. It is so."

You are not alone, She had said. I did not carry Her alone. There was also this tiny scrap of life with the capacity to hold Her, She Who Would Be Pythia after me.

"You'll tell Kos this?" Tia asked.

"I will tell Kos," I said. "I will help you tell him if you wish. But he will not be angry at you, no matter how much he curses the Achaians and vows dire vengeance upon them."

IN FACT, he didn't. Tia and I sat with him on the rocks the next day, while *Dolphin, Winged Night,* and *Pearl* spread nets behind them and fished offshore as though they were little fishing boats, not warships. Feeding this many people took a lot of food, and if we were forbidden the gulls' eggs on the island, we were not forbidden the fish offshore.

What Kos did was cry and beg Tia's forgiveness that he had not protected her. He had been away at sea. Their parents had been killed, and a younger brother still at home. Tia's baby nephew had been taken from her arms and killed in front of her. She had been watching him while his mother was at the market, a sister older than Kos who was missing and whose fate was unknown.

"I should have been there," Kos sobbed. "I should have died rather than let this happen to you."

"If you were dead," I said gently, "who should care for Tia now? Who should support her and the child she carries? She needs her living brother."

"It is my fault," he said. "Tia, dear sister." He cried against her neck while she held him and cried too.

"It's not your fault, Kos," she said. "I know you'd have done anything to keep this from happening. It is my fault. I should have run. I should have done something else. I dream it over and over. And every time I stand there frozen and do nothing."

"There was no place safe," he said. "Where would you run to?"

I let them cry before me, alone on the rocks with the wheeling gulls. "You are together," I said. "There is nothing you can do now for your family, except live. Live as your parents would have wished, and take care of each other."

"That's all any of us can do," Kos said. "Take care of each other."

"We are all one kindred now," I said. "Sea people and horse people, Lower City and Citadel. We must act as one kindred, bound in honor and love."

Kos wiped a tear from his sister's face. "This baby is the last of our line. Promise me you'll take care of yourself and not do anything foolish. Mother wanted a granddaughter so badly. Remember how she was when Kianna was pregnant? Everyone kept wishing her a boy, but Mother kept wishing for a girl?"

Tia was laughing and crying at the same time. "She did. That's exactly what she did."

"I promise I'll take good care of both of you," Kos said. "Until it's time to give her to the Lady, as Sybil says."

"She will be my acolyte," I confirmed. "She will be a daughter to me."

WHEN I WAS DONE with them the sun was high and I was thirsty. My head was aching. I did not go back to the camp. There were too many people who needed something, who wanted a word just now. I went apart, toward the spring, my head hurting so badly that all I wanted was to lie down in the shade of the stones, in the dark.

"Sybil?" Neas said. "Where are you going?"

"I am going to pray," I snapped.

"Oh." He drew up short. "I didn't mean to disturb you."

"I'm sorry," I said, remembering my duty. "How may I help you, Prince Aeneas?"

He came up and stood before me. "That was well done," he said.

I shrugged. "These are not hurts I can heal. Only time, and the favor of the gods. And some of these breaches will never be mended."

He looked down at me. "What if the child is a boy?"

"We will cross that bridge when we come to it," I said.

Neas raised one eyebrow. "You do not know?"

"I think," I said. "I think that I have read Her signs rightly. But one can never be certain."

"You seemed certain in Pylos."

"That is the kind of holy mystery that comes on one perhaps once in a lifetime, to be the vessel for Her will so completely. I cannot hope for that guidance again." I looked out across the sea. "She Who Was Pythia taught me that we must ask for Her guidance, and use our eyes and our hearts when Her will is not plain. I do as best I can and hope that I do not err, or fall into folly and hubris."

"More or less like being a prince," he said.

"Perhaps, Prince Aeneas."

"Neas."

"Yes."

"Go apart, then," he said. "I will see that no one disturbs you at the spring."

"They will disturb you instead," I said. "Is there no one in whom you confide? Xandros?"

Neas looked away. "Xandros is my friend," he said. "A good companion, and one whom my heart trusts. But this lies between us now—that my child lives and his are dead."

I caught my breath. "I did not know that he had children," I said.

"He had two daughters. A little girl who was three years old, and a baby just learning to walk. They were killed because they were too young to be useful slaves. His wife put up such a fight when they went for the girls that they had to kill her too, even though she would have been a valuable prize."

I turned my head away. "But your son lives," I said, it catching in my throat.

"He was four, not three," Neas said, and his voice shook only a little. "He hid while they raped and killed his mother. My father found him and got him from the house before it burned over his head. I was too late returning to Wilusa with the fleet. If we had been there, it would not have been."

"Now you sound like Kos," I said.

"Kos was not in command. I was." His voice was harsh. "The responsibility is mine."

"No," I said tightly. "That rests with Neoptolemos. He is the one who raised a fleet in Pylos, who incited young kings to war. He is the one who was greedy for gold and the women of other peoples. I watched him. I saw him at the feasts, speaking of glory and treasure, kindling ambitions and desires. I stood as close as I am to you, and I watched him. I know precisely where the responsibility lies."

I took the prince's hands. "He wanted slaves to sell in Millawanda, the Free City. They stopped on the way back to Pylos and sold many slaves. That is where many of our people are. Others were taken to Tiryns, but if you have seen Tiryns of the Mighty Walls towering over the plain of Argos you will know that there is nothing we can do to assail them. But in Millawanda we may yet find some of our lost people and free them somehow."

"We raided Pylos because it was what I could think to do," Neas said. "There were men of Pylos who burned Wilusa, and we knew that it did not have great defenses. I could not think what else we could do, besides try to restore some of our folk, and to give us vengeance for so many things." Neas dropped my hands. "But I am a man of twenty-two, not a boy to run aimlessly from place to place. And my desire for blood is not so great that I would take us all out in a blaze of glory to restore things that cannot be restored."

"Nothing can restore the dead to you," I said gently, "not this side of the River."

"I know," he said. "Yet I feel like Theseus, running madly through the coils of the labyrinth, with horrors following at my heels, and every twist bringing me a new dreaded sight. I dream, and it pursues me. I am sunk so far in horror heaped upon horror that I cannot taste wine or see the sun above. The world has ended. And I don't know why I yet live."

"You live," I said, "because you are fortunate, because you are clever, because some god favors you. You live because these people need a leader. Because the world ends and then begins."

"If it is the will of the Lady of the Sea," he said, "it is a bitter kind of favor."

"The favor of the gods is often thus," I said.

"I think we must go to Millawanda," he said. "While we cannot assail the place, we may be able to buy the freedom of some of our people with the plunder of Pylos."

Which in turn was plundered from Wilusa, I thought.

A vast chain of piracy across the sea, where honest mer-
chants do not dare to go, as they did when She Who Was
Pythia was young. Each year more fields will lie fallow,
fewer boats fish the sea, fewer children grow healthy and
strong. How am I to raise up dead men to plow fields that
are fallow, to strip brush and plant young olive groves? I
am a woman of seventeen. I am ten years in Her service,
but if She Who Was Pythia had no answers to these ques-
tions, how am I to find them?

"Also, I had spoken of this to Jamarados and Livo, who
is *Swift*'s captain. If they cannot find us on the seas and
they aren't foundered, perhaps they will take *Lady's Eyes*
and *Swift* to Millawanda."

"Then it is to the Free City we must go," I said.

"But after that, I know not," he said. "I can see no farther than the next curve of the labyrinth."

I smiled. "Then you must do as Theseus did and follow
Ariadne's thread. For there are passages through the dark
places that are well known to us who are raised in darkness and have nothing to fear there."

Neas looked at me. "That is what that story is about,
isn't it?"

"Yes, my prince, it is," I said. "All kings must make
that descent before they are crowned, all true kings in the
old stories. Sometimes it is omitted today, in houses that
have offended Her. But I should not speak of that."

The blood of Iphigenia spilled at Aulis did not touch
him, and he needed no new horrors today. Of that, at least,
his house was clean.

"To Millawanda, then," he said. "But I think we should
wait one more day here and rest. We can hope that *Swift*

and *Lady's Eyes* will come, and even if they don't the men need rest."

"Rest and hope," I said. "We will pour libations to the Lady of the Sea and thank Her for Her grace, and to the Lady of the Dead, who lets us squat on Her doorstep."

"A day of rest," he said. "We will eat the fish that Xandros is catching and have games on the beach in honor of the Divine Sisters. Footraces at least we can manage. And contests of swimming."

"On the ocean side," I said. "Let us not disturb the Dead City by diving for its treasures."

"No," he said. Then he smiled at me. "Thank you, Lady. My heart is lighter."

"Burdens shared are halved," I said, and smiled at the old saw, still true enough. It was true that my headache was better.

THE PİRATE CİTY

We were three weeks on the way from the Island of the Dead to Millawanda. The last, dreamy, drowsy days of summer were on us, hot and still. Most of the time there was no wind, and we had to go under oar. In the afternoons, thunderstorms often came up and we ran into the nearest beach so that we would not have to ride out the worst of them, though if there was no island at hand we would run before the storm, letting the winds hasten our way to the Free City.

One afternoon like this Kos was at the tiller and I stood at *Dolphin*'s prow. The wind of our passage washed over me, cooling me after the heat of the day. The sea was turquoise. In the distance, far off to our right, some island I did not know glimmered like a jewel in the Aegean.

Xandros came up beside me and leaned against the rail, bending over. "Ah, there he is," he said, smiling.

I looked down. A shadow raced just below, more than the length of a man. A dolphin was riding in our bow wave.

In a moment his nose broke the surface, an old dolphin, his face seamed with scars. He seemed to smile up at Xandros.

"He's been with us for four days," Xandros said. "The same old fellow."

"He looks like Kos," I said, "with the scar."

Xandros laughed. "He does, doesn't he? Perhaps he looked like Kos before."

"Before?" I asked.

"In Wilusa and in the islands they said that dolphins were the souls of sailors lost at sea. That's why they escort our ships. And that's why they must never be harmed. They might be our kin or our friends."

The dolphin made a long leap out of the wave, gleaming over the surface and plunging in just ahead of us. In a moment his shadow was beneath us, riding on our momentum across the sea.

"I didn't know that," I said. "I do not know the mysteries of the Lady of the Sea." I watched the dolphin rise and fall, always within our slipstream. "Xandros, why do people call Neas the Beloved of the Lady of the Sea? Why does he say he's under Her protection? And why is he a prince and our leader when his father is living and here, and he's not?"

"The first part's easy to answer," Xandros said. "He's Her son. Neas is the son of Aphrodite Cythera. Of course She looks out for him. What mother wouldn't? The last part's more complicated. It's a long story."

"Tell me," I said. "While you are resting from the tiller."

Xandros smiled and leaned on the rail, then sat with his legs dangling toward the water. Droplets of water splashed up on his feet. "Sit down, then. It's a long story."

I did.

"In my grandfather's day, when King Priam was young and his reign was still uncertain, he married a girl of the old nobility, a girl of the shore people who were here before Priam's house ever came to Wilusa. She bore him three daughters, and died of the third. He remarried, this time a niece of the Hittite emperor, who brought a great dowry and cemented the alliance. She had many children, including Hektor; Alexandros; and the twins, whose names are known to many. The daughters of his first wife were honored, but obviously were not going to be mothers to Priam's heirs with so many sons of Hekuba. The middle daughter died of a fever when she was a child. Kassandra, the youngest, was given to the Shrine of Apulion, the Lord of the Bow, who favored Wilusa above all other places. She was our Sybil, like you."

Xandros glanced at me. "I have heard of her," I said. "And how she was brought to Mycenae as Agamemnon's captive."

Xandros nodded. "The oldest daughter was called Lysisippa. She was given to the Shrine of the Lady of the Sea, the most holy Shrine. There is a sacred place where the river flows out of Mount Ida. It's a grotto five times the height of a man, where passages go back into the very roots of the mountain, glittering with water and shining stone."

"A very great Mystery," I said.

"A very holy place," he said. "Where the waters of the world are born, and sacred both to Aphrodite and to Her Sister."

"A womb," I said. "And a grave. No wonder this is the most holy place of the People."

Xandros agreed. "It is the most holy place. And it is at the feet of Mount Ida, a day's walk from the City. Anyway, it was to that Shrine that Lysisippa was given, as it is the oldest and most honored, and she was Priam's eldest child."

The dolphin rose out of the water again, his head nearly brushing Xandros' feet.

"Since you've never seen Mount Ida, Lady, let me tell you that it is very green and rich, with pastures wide and lush enough for every horse in the world. When the rains begin and the land greens, before the foaling season, the houses of Wilusa take all the horses, especially the broodmares, up onto the slopes of the mountain, where the grass is new and tender, and the heat and flies will not disturb them. Thus the Horse People have done since they came to Wilusa. Anchises was a younger son of one of the noble houses, and went with the horses and cared for them, because the great horses of the Troad were the source of all our wealth."

"Ah," I said.

"In that day they say he was very fair to look upon, tall and straight, a young man of sixteen. Lysisippa was ten years older, and already Cythera by then. So she had all the majesty of her rank, and all the beauty that Aphrodite spends on Her priestesses. Anchises looked upon her, and his heart was moved. From that moment on there was no woman in the world save Lysisippa."

"As sometimes happens," I said.

"He was not of rank to have had her, Priam's eldest, and himself the younger son of a lesser house. And in any event, she was Cythera and could be no man's wife. But he wooed her anyway. He composed songs to her that he sang in the pastures at night while the horses grazed. He made a vow to Aphrodite that he would be forever true to her, and never so much as touch another woman while he lived. And at last, Aphrodite Herself was moved by his prayers. Lysisippa came to him at night as he watched his horses, and lay with him on the slopes of the sacred mountain."

"Surely that is permitted to Cythera," I said.

"It is," Xandros said. "When the time came for Anchises to return to the City, not a day passed that he didn't speak of Lysisippa, to the weariness of all about him. And when foaling season came again he returned to the Shrine like a swallow to its nest. He kept this up two years. By now his father wanted him to marry. But he told them all that to do so would be the gravest blasphemy, as he had sworn an oath to the Lady of the Sea that in his life he would touch no other woman save Lysisippa."

"What did his family do?" I asked.

Xandros shrugged. "What could they do? He remained unmarried, and spent as much of each year as possible at Mount Ida, until the war came. Neas was born to Lysisippa the summer after Prince Alexandros brought the Achaian queen as a prize of war, so when the time came for him to go out from the women and live with his father, the City was besieged. He did not go that year. I was born then, when my mother was gone to Kaikus as a refugee. The Lower City had already been taken and burned, and those who could go had gone."

"Is that far?" I asked, knowing nothing of the area.

"Far enough." Xandros looked at me and smiled. "Far enough for a woman nearly ready to give birth, with her home burned and Achaian raiding parties everywhere.

But she did not die. Nor did she speak of it much. I was born when she had been only a few days in Kaikus."

The dolphin rose again, nearly under my feet this time, flirting with the ship's prow, a knowing expression on his face.

"So Neas remained at the Shrine all that year. And all the next as well. The City fell, and all the children of the royal house were killed, even the infants who were thrown from the walls." His voice was tight, and I knew that he thought of his own daughters. Xandros did not look at me. Instead he fixed his dry eyes on the sea. "After that, for months there was no rule, and little food. Some who escaped the siege starved that first year. Lysisippa kept him at the Shrine, and he escaped that fate."

"Long past the age when he should have gone away from the Mysteries," I said, and I understood better.

"Yes," Xandros said. "But the Lady of the Sea loved him as Her own son. He played in the sanctuary at the foot of Her throne. He had no fear of Her displeasure, any more than any well-loved son fears his mother. He was more than six years old when he came out of the Shrine and went to his father in Wilusa and was known as the son of Anchises."

And how should she send him out? I thought. *It is proper and fitting, but to send a young child into war and starvation is not in any mother. And clearly the Lady did not object.*

"Since then, he has always had the favor of the Lady of the Sea," Xandros said. "No man on any ship he captained has ever been lost, and no ship under his command has foundered, unless you count *Menace,* which was far from him at the time. He is lucky. Blessed. If it can go well for him, it does. If She can stretch forth Her hand and help him, She does."

"To lead him through the storm and to the Island of the Dead," I said.

Xandros nodded. "Or wherever else. When he came to Wilusa, everyone knew he was Lysisippa's child, and that he was the last of the line of Priam. But he was six years old. The People could not be governed by a child at a time like that. So the lords and captains who had survived formed a council, and it ruled in Wilusa until now. He was known as Prince Aeneas out of respect, but he made it very clear when he was a youth that he had no desire to overturn the rule of the council and make himself king, and that instead he would abide by their wisdom."

"That is wisdom indeed from a youth," I said. "Especially one who is favored by the gods and has every advantage of beauty and courage. Most would not resist the temptation of power and the blandishments of people with something to gain."

"Neas is not like most men," Xandros said. "He is the one who has always done everything right."

And yet it has availed him little, I thought. *He was away with the fleet when the City was burned. He could not save his wife, whom he loved. His son looks at him out of great haunted eyes, like the rest of the children here. He cannot fight without losing men who cannot be replaced and there is nowhere to run. He cannot keep honor with his father and yet guard the lives of the People. There is no choice he can make that isn't wrong. The favor of the Lady of the Sea is little enough to go on in this labyrinth.*

"You will follow him, whatever his choices may be?" I asked.

Xandros looked up, surprised at the question. "To the ends of the earth," he said.

I looked away, out to sea. No man had ever looked at me the way Xandros looked when he spoke of Neas. And why should he not? Whether they were lovers in truth, or if it had merely been the kind of friendship that develops between youths and dissipates when bridal beds and children come between, the feeling was there. Love cannot be controlled any more than the sea can be. Now and forever, his heart was given.

SEVERAL DAYS LATER we came to the Pirate City, Millawanda, that the islanders call the Free City. Three generations ago it had won its freedom from both the Hittite emperor and the Great King of Mycenae, that Atreus who was Agamemnon's father. Since then it existed between, keeping its sovereignty from all nations, a city-state allied with neither power.

All the nations of the world traded here. Coming into the great bowl of the harbor, surrounded by the square Hittite fortifications with their heavy towers, we saw ships from every land. There were Kretan ships, many oared and swift, Achaian ships from half a dozen places, the swift dark ships of the islanders from Lazba with the eyes painted upon their prow that were like to the Wilusan ships, broad-beamed Tyrian merchant ships with two sails, and even the slender Egyptian ships, their lateen sails looking odd to me.

In the bow, Kos gave a great shout and Xandros and I looked to see where he pointed.

At one of the great wharves that jutted out from the

land rode *Lady's Eyes* with *Swift* beside her. In her shadow were tied all three of the missing fishing boats.

From *Seven Sisters* a mighty cheer rose, cutting through all the noise and bustle of the harbor. It resolved into words. "Ae-Ne-As! Ae-Ne-As! Ae-Ne-As! Aphrodite Cythera!" The luck of the beloved of the Lady of the Sea had held again.

Our ships came alongside the wharf, and our people rushed together in a great wave, embracing and calling out to one another. Jamarados, the captain of *Lady's Eyes,* clasped Xandros in a great hug. I remembered that Xandros had served there, before *Dolphin,* as Kos now served with him.

Neas leaped onto the wharf, clasping the fishing boat captains about the waist, embracing them like brothers.

"We had thought you lost," Jamarados said to Xandros. "We thought we were all that was left."

"We thought you lost as well," Xandros said. "And I'm glad we were both wrong."

IT WAS NIGHTFALL before we had sorted out everything, and Neas had paid the port fees so that we could dock with the other ships. They are careful about things like that, in the Free City. In most places merchants would think twice about demanding payment from a man with eight warships, but in Millawanda they do not. If you do not pay, then the port is closed to you. No man will sell you stores or trade with you. If your crew decides to take things into their own hands, the city has a watch maintained by its prince and a council of merchants. At need they can call forth some hundreds of men all sworn to protect the property of the city, so they have no need to fear any but the most well-armed war expedition. Several adventurers have discovered this to their loss. Even Neoptolemos would not be foolish enough to try the patience of Millawanda.

Jamarados had rented a large house in the harbor quarter, one of many such owned by merchants and rented out to foreigners. He quickly cleared out his own quarters for Neas, and everyone set about fitting in there. Neas ordered that half the crew must stay on each ship at night rather than ashore. I wasn't certain whether this was for space or safety, but it was prudent either way.

I was jammed in with ten women in a large room off the main courtyard, an airy frescoed room that was obviously intended for the wives and children of the household. It was a big room, but not so much so for eleven of us.

Still, it was cool and pleasant, with a small fountain in the courtyard and a tiled floor done in blue and white in the Hittite fashion. The frescoes were in the style of the isles, however, with deep blue fish swimming inside geometric borders. It was very pretty.

It was strange to be with the women in a civilized place this way, to not be summoned to council. After a while I pinned up my hair with the copper pins as She Who Had Been Pythia had taught me, put my veil in place so that it covered my hair but not my face, and went in search of the men.

I found Neas in a room on the other side of the courtyard. They do not have one central room with a hearth, as I was accustomed to, but rather a series of rooms off square courtyards in the style of the islands. Neas was mixing wine and water in a plain copper krater and serving it out to his guests. Xandros was there, and Jamarados, and *Hunter*'s captain and Anchises. Two of the other men I did not know.

One was a man of Anchises' age, with a neatly trimmed pointed beard in the Hittite style that was laced with gray. The other was twenty years younger, but so closely resembled him that it was obvious he was his son. They were both richly dressed in embroidered robes, though those of the son were shorter and slashed at the sides for greater movement.

I checked in the doorway. I did not know what the customs were, and I felt Anchises' eyes upon me, warning me away. Neas looked to see what his father was glaring at and saw me.

"Gentlemen," he said, "this is Sybil. She serves the Lady of the Dead, She Who Is Called Ereshkigal in your tongue."

I inclined my head.

The older of the gentlemen looked up and almost smiled at me. "I am Hattuselak, and this is my son, Elaksas. In kinder days, long ago, I was the guest-friend of Lord Anchises in fair Wilusa. Indeed, Elaksas' mother was his distant kin."

"The granddaughter of my father's great-uncle," Anchises said.

"It is my pleasure to welcome you to Millawanda," Hattuselak said to Neas. "I hope that you will honor me with the tale of your voyage."

They talked far into the night. I excused myself after some little time and went to make sure that the women knew about the guests and were preparing some food.

Then I lay down in a room that wasn't rocking and slept.
I knew that I should hear what had happened in the
morning.

NEAS AND XANDROS sought me out together while I was
spreading my hair to dry in the sun. I had washed it in
clear fresh water from the fountain and at last gotten all
the salt out, then combed it and tugged free every last tan-
gle. Clean and combed, it fell nearly to my knees. I sat in
the sun beside the fountain, my head inclined and my hair
spread to dry, my eyes closed. It was peaceful in the sun,
with the sound of the fountain nearly drowning the noise
and the chatter of the People.

Still, I heard their footsteps approaching and knew who
it was without looking. "Yes, Prince Aeneas?" I said.

He sat down beside me on the fountain rim. Xandros
hovered.

"There are slaves," he said. "Neoptolemos brought
some fifty or sixty women and older children here. They
were sold, and some of them have been taken from the
city, though most are still here. Unless we wish to break
the laws of Millawanda and take them by force, it will require hundreds of deben of gold to trade for them all from
the owners who have them now."

"I don't think taking them by force is a good idea,"
Xandros said. "We'd have to get out of the harbor afterward. Did you see the forts?"

"And we would have to take dozens of people at once
in dozens of places, from what you say," I said. I lifted my
head and let my hair fall back. "Then fight and flee with

them through the streets to the ships before getting out of the harbor. Gold may be a better solution this time."

"The problem is..." Neas said.

"We don't have hundreds of deben of gold," Xandros finished.

"Why did I see that problem coming?" I said.

"Because you stopped us from stripping Pylos bare," Neas said.

"Oh, it's my fault now?" I asked. "If you had waited to strip Pylos you would have run straight into Neoptolemos."

"A lot of it wasn't portable," Xandros said.

"I know," I said. "You grabbed everything that wasn't solid bronze or sunk in the earth."

"I'd have gotten those if you'd given me more time." Xandros grinned. "Those big pots full of lentils, as tall as a man..."

"Where would you have put them on *Dolphin*?" Neas asked, also smiling. "Did you have room after the hundred amphorae of wine?"

"Perhaps he should have just tied them on behind and towed them," I said.

"That would be very seaworthy," Xandros said.

Neas shook his head. "You're both as silly as children."

"And you're not?" I asked.

"I am a very serious man."

"Indeed," said Xandros, pulling a long face that almost but didn't quite look like Anchises.

Neas rolled his eyes, but he was still smiling. They both looked better for a night of real rest in real beds on land. "The problem still is that we don't have hundreds of deben of gold. And we haven't got anything we can sell or trade that's worth that amount."

"Except the ships," I said.

"Except the ships," Xandros agreed with a pained expression.

"But if we sell one of the ships, where are we going to put fifty more people?" Neas asked. "We're already jammed in on the warships, and it looks like that's going to get worse. One of the fishing boats is barely seaworthy, and we may have to scrap her and move everyone onto one of the warships."

"None of the three of them are in good shape," Xandros said. "I wouldn't really like to take any of them out, not out of sight of the harbor."

"Well, they've got to go out of sight of the harbor. Wherever we go," Neas said.

"Are we going?" Xandros asked. "Why not stay here? It's not home, but it's not so far away. Plenty of people speak our language. It's not Ahhiyawa."

"And do what?" Neas asked. "We've got four hundred people. Fishermen, farmers, horse breeders. Only no farms, no horses, and three leaky fishing boats. We have no way to earn our living. And the merchants of Millawanda will not extend credit lightly. We'd be selling ourselves into slavery."

"What will we do somewhere else?" Xandros asked.

Neas looked at me. "Found a new city."

"A new city? You can't be serious! We've got only four hundred people."

"Xandros, we're all that's left of the People. We have to stick together," Neas said. "We can't just scatter to the eight winds in Millawanda."

"Neas..."

"Xandros, I need you at my side. I need you on my side when I talk with the other captains." Neas leaned forward.

Xandros let out a long breath. "I'm with you. You know that. I don't have the slightest idea what you're doing, though."

"Neas is right," I said. "If we stay here, we have four hundred separate fates, and the People will no longer exist. We will vanish into the Free City, three hundred men with debts they cannot pay. And that will be the end. We must stay together and go on. And somehow we must find the gold to trade for the slaves."

Neas leaned back against the fountain. "And that's the trick."

I leaned back next to him. "It certainly is."

Xandros sat on the ground and leaned back against the rim between our knees, his hands clasped around his own. "This is going to be dangerous, isn't it?"

TRADES

N eas was in a fine temper. I could hear him shouting all the way across the courtyard. I hurried
over to see what was happening.

Xandros was escorting two young boys out the door.
They were clean, but wore nothing but breechclouts, and
looked to be ten and twelve years old. "Come on, boys,"
Xandros was saying. "We'll find a place for you to sleep,
and then we can go down to the harbor." He raised one
eyebrow at me as I passed. I didn't know him well enough
yet to know if it was a warning or not.

I went into the chamber that Aeneas was using as a
workroom. "What is the matter, Prince Aeneas?" I asked.

"He's an idiot," Neas said.

"Xandros?"

"Not Xandros." Neas paced across the floor. "Amynter,
Hunter's captain. He's gone and sold himself into slavery
to get his boys back. He traded himself to a merchant for
them."

"The boys who just left?" I asked.

"Yes, the boys who just left." Neas picked up a cup on

the table and put it back down. "So now I have no captain for *Hunter*. And two more children."

"Prince Aeneas," I said in my most reasonable tone, "what father would not do the same upon learning that his children live? What father would not trade his servitude for their freedom? Amynter traded nothing that was not his own to give."

"Yes. Well. I still have no captain for *Hunter*." He was calming down, but kept pacing. "I would have found a way to trade for the boys if he had but waited on me. Now I have lost one of my best men, an experienced captain who cannot be replaced. And who knows if the merchant who bought him will be willing to trade him again? An experienced man-at-arms is worth a great deal."

"So would those boys be, to a brothel," I said.

Neas stopped in his pacing and looked at me. "You think?"

"Of course that is what Amynter thought," I said. "When he reckoned his sons' worth in gold."

"Well," Neas said.

"It is a hard thing," I said, coming and sitting on the edge of the table, "to reckon our lives and those of our loved ones in gold. To say to oneself, baldly, what am I worth? What can I do that is worth anything?"

"That is what I have been asking myself," Neas said. "What can we do to get hundreds of deben of gold?" He turned and picked up the cup again. "What am I worth, the prince of a people that are no more? I have nothing that is mine except this sword."

"You have eight warships and the men to sail them," I said. "That is the asset we have. No horses, no farms, no lands or crafter's workshops. The question that we must ask is, what can we do with that?"

"I can think of only one thing to do," Neas said. "Turn pirate in truth. There are merchant vessels still, richly laden this late in the season. There are villages along the shore and in the islands with few defenses."

And that is the way of it, I thought. *Seize other vessels about their business and enslave their crews. Raid fishing villages with no wealth except their women. Trade those people for our kin. Sell them into slavery to buy our people free.*

It seemed to me for a moment that I heard the voice of She Who Was Pythia behind me. *Can I rid the seas of pirates or raise men from the dead to plow fallow fields? You must think about the causes of things, about the shape of the world. You must understand such things if you are to give counsel to kings.*

We should trade our lamentations for theirs, and other women would weep, other cities burn, other parents seek their children in vain. And so it goes on, spiraling downward into the dark, deeper with every year.

Neas was looking at me. "Can you think of anything better?"

"No," I said slowly. "I do not see what else to do either. But perhaps before making such a weighty decision we should seek guidance of my Lady. Isn't that what oracles are for?"

"You can do this here?"

"I can," I said. "It is better in a holy place, but I can seek Her in any darkened room."

*   *   *

W<small>E CHOSE</small> an inner room with only one window. I covered it in three falls of cloth and set up the brazier. I felt oddly keyed up. It had been weeks since I had tried to see anything, since before I left Pylos. Carefully, I painted my face white and black. Neas sat quiet in the corner as a suppliant should, considering the question he would ask Sybil. We were almost ready when Xandros knocked on the door.

Neas answered it.

"Sorry," Xandros said, "but Hattuselak is here, and he says he needs to talk to you immediately, Neas. He says it's important."

"A moment," Neas said, and looked at me.

"Go," I said. "I am not quite ready yet."

He left, closing the door. I stirred the coals on the brazier and knelt beside it, looking into the fire.

Wait, She whispered. *It is changing as you wait.*

I could feel eddies of it around me, the shape of the future changing. Like the octopus shimmering underwater I had seen on the Island of the Dead, or the painted one seeming to shift on the floor of the temple in Pylos. I focused on one glowing coal. Shifting in the flames.

This city will burn too, I thought. *Not this year, but next, or the one after. The walls and towers will not save it. There is too much gold in Millawanda. It will go down in fire as well.*

The door opened. Neas was back, a delighted expression on his face. Relieved, I thought, as though something lay before him unexpectedly.

He came and knelt across from me. "I'm sorry for the interruption, Lady."

"I have seen what there is to see," I said. "We cannot

stay here. This city will fall as well, and we will have fled one sacking for another."

"We are leaving," Neas said. "Hattuselak has shown me how." He could not contain his good news any longer. "The merchants of Millawanda have talked together. For many months none of them have dared send trade ships forth to sell goods across the sea. There are too many pirates this year. In the spring, when the sailing season began, the first three ships to sail were all taken within hours of leaving port. Since then, none have sailed. But Milla-wanda depends on trade. If the merchants dare not send their ships forth, the city will starve, even though Egyptian and Kretan ships come in."

"What has this to do with us?" I asked, though I was beginning to see.

"They will pay us richly to use our eight warships to escort a merchant convoy south along the Lydian coast and down to Byblos. Hattuselak has vouched for our honor with the merchants, and swore upon his own life that we would not plunder their trade ships ourselves, but rather see them safely into Byblos with all their cargo. In return for this, we will have those slaves Neoptolemos brought from Wilusa."

"The slaves are very valuable," I said. "But if their ships cannot go out without being lost, it does not matter how many slaves there are in Millawanda."

"Yes," he said. "That is the argument Hattuselak used. He said that it was an opportunity that would not come again—eight strong ships manned by honorable men, commanded by the son of his guest-friend. We can see them safe to Byblos."

"That is far," I said. "Have you been there?"

Neas shook his head. "Not that far around the coast.

I've been as far as Rhodes and the Lydian coast. Jamarados has been to Byblos, and south of there as far as Ashkelon. We used to trade in Ugarit before it was sacked and burned."

"When was that?" I said.

"Five years ago," Neas said. "The spring I married Creusa. It was a great city, an ancient city. And now it is no more. I was not on that last trading mission, but Jamarados and Xandros were, when Xandros was a rower on *Lady's Eyes*. They arrived, and the city was nothing but ashes and the unburned dead."

I shivered despite the stuffy heat of the room. The brazier was warm. *What is happening?* I asked. *Why, Great Lady, are all the cities and works of men falling one by one? Even so far away, where the curse that Agamemnon invoked has no sway? What is happening to Your people?*

Neas looked at the brazier. "Does this course bring good to us? That is the question I would ask of Her."

"Yes, Prince Aeneas," I said. "It does." She answered his question, but not mine.

W E SAILED from Millawanda a few days later. Neas had gotten rid of the fishing boats because they could not keep up, traded instead for food and other stores, as well as the freedom of Amynter, *Hunter*'s captain. With the fifty slaves we had recovered from the merchants of Millawanda, we were crowded in very tightly on the warships. Fifteen merchant ships joined us, so with twenty-three ships we were a very great fleet. It took half the morning to get out of the harbor.

Dolphin was on the seaward flank of the convoy, half-way down the line. Xandros was nearly frantic trying to keep the merchant ships together, rather than straggling out under sail all over the place, like a dog with a flock of unruly geese.

It was a beautiful sight. Twenty-three sails spread on the deep blue sea under an azure sky, the sun golden and the air balmy. Standing on the prow alone I caught sight of a shadow in our bow wave. It was the old dolphin again, seamed face smiling, escorting us back out to sea.

I bent down. "I believe," I said, "that you are some friend of Xandros, some old sailor who accompanies us out of love." The dolphin rose in a long leap, playing with the foam, and sank beneath us again. "And you are a flirt," I said with a smile.

I looked back along the length of the ship. Xandros was at the tiller. Kos was helping our newest rower. Bai couldn't take his bench back until his collarbone healed, so we had a new rower in his place, the eldest son of Amynter brought out from Millawanda. His name was Kassander, and he was trying very hard. At twelve he was old enough to start learning the trade, but he still couldn't keep the rhythm very well, and was constantly fouling the oarsman behind him. Kos was fairly patient. Xandros kept looking forward and grimacing with every foul, but he said nothing and let Kos do his work.

We were nearly four weeks on the way to Byblos, and the sailing season was ending when we arrived. We had stopped nine times on the way, trading at great cities and small. Our first was Halicarnassos, hardly two days' trip down the coast, then Cnidos on its cape. Then we turned out to open sea, crossing to the island of Rhodes, the greatest of the islands. Kamiros is a great city indeed, fortified like Millawanda, but to a lesser degree. This was the last place where the tongue they spoke was like enough to that of Wilusa for everyone to make themselves understood. After that, we relied on those like Jamarados who had learned some of the Lydian or other tongues.

After Kamiros, we crossed to Patara on the Lydian coast, and then to Myra. Then we cut across the great bay to Korakes in Karia, and then across to Soli, on Kyrenia, where the copper comes from. The merchants traded wine, salt, olives, and oil for great ingots of raw copper. These are smelted by skilled men and mixed with tin, which is how bronze is made. The ratio differs, and it is a mark of skill to know how much to mix to make swords that are sharp but do not break easily. Neas explained these things to me while the merchants were ashore, trading.

From Soli we went five days at sea along the shore of Kyrenia and across the sea to the east, striking southward when we cleared the treacherous cape and came into the port of Paltos, just south of where Ugarit had been. From there we followed the coast south to Arkah, and then to Byblos.

By now the weather was turning. The sailing season was ending, and we must wait until spring to sail again.

"We will stay in Byblos," Neas decided. "We can winter over here and perhaps escort other ships back in the spring. I will arrange a place where we can haul the ships out and mend them. They will need to be retarred at least."

"There are some rotting planks too," Jamarados said. "Is there anyone who has a boatbuilder's skill?"

Kos shifted back and forth. He was not accustomed to

speaking in Prince Aeneas' council, and I wondered why Xandros had brought him. "My father was a boatbuilder. I wasn't brought up to the trade, but I was around it all my life. I can have a look."

Xandros nodded. "I've done emergency repairs. I know how the planks should lie, though I don't have the skill of seasoning them and preparing them. And seasoning them takes months at least. A couple of years is better."

"Where will we get the wood?" Amynter asked.

Neas looked out at the coast, at the busy port. "They are known for their woods here. Cedars that are the finest in the world."

"Indeed they are," Jamarados said. "That is the chief wealth of these parts, besides trade. In Ugarit we used to buy cedar that was seasoned and ready for building. Surely we can trade for it here, though it was expensive."

Neas blew out a long breath. "Everything is expensive. And we have months to make our trades last, until spring comes and we can put to sea again."

"Is that what we'll do?" Amynter asked. "Hire out again next spring?"

"It is beneath the dignity of a prince of Wilusa to trade like an islander," Anchises said. "Better that you should make your way with a sword, as befits a nobleman."

"Better that I should think about the good of the People before my own honor," Neas snapped.

"Better that you should think of the scraps of honor left to you by your noble uncles, by your noble grandfather, and think too well of yourself to grub like a merchant," Anchises said. "Great Hektor would never . . ."

"Father," Neas said, "Great Hektor is not here."

"Great Hektor had the honor to die for his city," Anchises said and held Neas' eye.

We all stood in stunned horror, not sure what to say.

Neas turned away. "I'll check on the stores," he said, and walked across the plank to *Seven Sisters*.

Anchises looked after him, then about the silent council as though daring someone to speak. No one did. Each captain looked at his feet, or at the sea. And then they parted with few words until only I and Xandros were left.

"We are all without honor," Xandros said, looking in the direction Aeneas had gone. "Only Neas feels it most, as he had most to lose. Lord Anchises speaks what we all know."

"There is no point in speaking it," I said hotly. "Can't he see that it doesn't matter? What is honor next to survival?"

Xandros stared at me. "Lady, do you know nothing of the hearts of men?"

"I see that we must survive," I said.

"And it does not matter how we do that?"

"Of course it matters," I said. "And I am not suggesting that we break faith with these merchants we have promised to protect. But we must do something, or else just sit and wait for the deluge to wash over us. Xandros, this is not just about us. This is not just a misfortune that has fallen upon the People. I know this."

Xandros pushed his hair back from his face. "What is it, then?"

"I don't know," I said. I leaned back against *Dolphin*'s rail. "I can't see the shape of it. Like seeing a storm and not knowing how big it is, or trying to draw the shape of the coast."

"Drawing the shape of the coast?" Xandros said. "How can you draw the shape of the coast? And how can you know how big a storm is? It's too big to see."

"But if you could," I said. "If you could then you could understand what you needed to do."

"You need to find a beach to run up on, or get as far out to sea as you can to ride it out," Xandros said.

"Yes," I said, "but the gods can see."

"We aren't gods," Xandros said.

"How much less than gods are heroes?" I asked. "Surely heroes are but a little less than gods."

Xandros shook his head and he was smiling. "Lady, you are speaking to me of Mysteries, things that are far beyond my understanding. These things are not for me to see."

"They aren't beyond your understanding," I said. "They are beyond your learning, as they are beyond mine."

He cocked his head. "What do you mean?"

"Can you learn to replank a ship?"

Xandros nodded. "Yes. I mean, I don't know how to do it, but if Kos can teach me, of course I can learn it."

"Can any man here?"

He leaned back against the railing of the deck. He smiled. "Well, no. Not every man. Amynter is very set in his ways, and Kassander doesn't know enough about seamanship yet to understand what needs to be done. And there are several who are just too slow. Boatbuilding's a skilled trade."

"Could I learn?"

"You're a woman."

I crossed my arms. "If I were to try, Xandros. Could I learn?"

"Yes," he said. "If anyone would teach you."

"How did the first boatbuilder learn?" I asked.

Xandros put his head to the side. "I don't know. How should I know? Maybe the gods taught him."

"And if the gods taught me the shape of clouds and how they moved, I could understand the storm," I said. "There are things we can learn that we don't know. It's not that we can't, it's just that we don't know how."

"And maybe the gods don't want us to know all their Mysteries," he said.

"How do we know what is their will?" I asked. "We don't know unless we ask them. Perhaps the first boat-builder sat beside the sea with an old log and shaped it, and the Lady of the Sea smiled upon him and was glad to have him ride on the waves. Perhaps that is how it was. Perhaps She whispered in his ear all the secrets of the deep."

Xandros shook his head. "Lady, you are leading me too far from shore."

I smiled. "And you are following," I said. No one had ever gone so far before. I put my hand on his arm.

Xandros froze and I pulled my hand away before I saw that he was looking over my shoulder.

I turned. Ten ships were coming into the harbor. The foremost ship was painted with the Chariot of the Sun.

"Neoptolemos," I said.

YOUNG GODS

The princes of Byblos are strong rulers, and they do not allow brawls to break out in the streets because it would hurt trade. The prince was a man called Hiram, the fourth or fifth of that name. He was young and energetic, some five years older than Neas.

We had not been long in the city when he sent for Neas to see him in audience. Jamarados went with him to translate and Amynter and Xandros to bulk up the party. Also, Xandros knew a little of the language from past trading trips to Ugarit, but looked as though he didn't, something that can be an advantage in diplomacy.

It seemed that Prince Hiram told Neas in no uncertain terms that whatever blood feuds existed between him and Neoptolemos, they must be suspended within the walls of Byblos, or both of them would be his guests in the dungeons below the citadel for far longer than they wished.

I was glad, when I heard this, that Neas had not taken Anchises to the audience. I didn't think Hiram's tolerance would have been improved by a long recitation of Neas' lineage.

And so we rested in the same harbor as our enemies. Somehow I doubted that Neoptolemos liked Hiram's peacekeeping any better than Neas did, but perhaps he too had little choice. The weather turned bad. Autumn was upon us.

It was time for the Feast of the Return. On a squally day, the sky leaden with rain clouds, I approached Neas about it in the courtyard of the house we had rented with the profits of our journey from Millawanda.

Neas sighed. "I wish that we could keep the customs of our People. There are rites of all peoples here, and Prince Hiram seems not to object to such things, particularly if they are kept private."

"The Egyptians have a Shrine here," I said. "Surely no one can object to rites within a private house." I gestured to the high wall and sturdy gate. "Especially as no one can see. What concerns me more is how it can be done. There can be no procession unless we go round and round the courtyard, and I do not know what I can use for the gate."

"There is a storage pit around the back," Neas said. "It's used for grain and beans. It's raw earth, not stone, and is only about as deep as my waist with boards over the top to keep animals out. Would that do?"

"It will have to," I said, scuffing my foot in the dust. "This ground is hard packed and there is probably stone beneath it. There is no way to dig anything deeper." We went and looked at it. It was rough, but it would do.

More troubling was the question of who would do the other parts. I should do Demeter, of course. She has the most lines, and her part is the one that keeps the entire rite flowing. I had done it twice in Pylos, since She Who Was

Pythia died. Some of the choruses could be dispensed with, but I would still need a strong singer for the Lord of the Dead. His part is one of the hardest, and indeed that is one of the most coveted parts for a priest, with range and emotion that goes from rage to fear to grief to understanding of the way the world must be. I should have to cut it down, in any event, for no one could possibly learn all of it in a short time, unless he were a priest with a trained memory. To teach the part to someone uninitiated is almost blasphemy, but I could see no way to do this without the Lord of the Dead.

The Maiden is rather easier. Her lines are short and largely repetitious, with only one section that needs a good voice. After all, she was going to spend most of the rite sitting in the grain pit waiting for an entrance while the Lord of the Dead and I sang at each other.

After some little thought I settled upon Tia.

"Me? I can't!" she said, pushing her hair back behind her ears. "I'm not dedicated."

"You don't have to be," I said. "The Maiden is usually sung by an acolyte. I sang the Maiden for years in Pylos, but sometimes she's sung by any girl with a true voice and a lovely face."

"I can't stand up in front of all those people," she said, but there was a light in her eyes. Once, before this war, I thought, she had been the kind of girl who knew her beauty and who loved to sing for her kindred. That beauty and love was in her still, under her grief.

"Tia," I said, "you must do it for the People. We all must do what we can to the best of our abilities now, whether or not we were trained to the task. This is what is needed of you."

One hand curved down to the growing swell beneath her tunic and she looked down. "I'm not a maiden," she said.

"Neither is the Kore," I said, and sat down beside her. "All through the heat of summer She has ruled over the parched lands beneath the earth with Her hand in Death's. She has lived in a dark place as the Queen of the Dead, abducted from Her kindred and taken as His dark bride. And now Her mother has come to ransom Her. She has won Her daughter back from Death. And so Persephone puts off Her black robes and begins to climb. She waits naked in the earth in the darkness. And She forgets. All that has passed before is behind Her. She waits while Her mother sings to Death. And then She comes forth robed in white, innocent as a newborn baby, enfolded into the arms of Her kin." I paused and took her hand. "Tia, you are the right one to do this. I know."

And so she agreed.

There was really only one choice for the Lord of the Dead, one man with sufficient presence and a sense of timing. Besides, Neas had seen enough rites he ought not have in childhood. The inner workings of one more wouldn't make a difference. He had a strong voice too, a little light and pleasant for the Lord of the Dead, but resonant and flexible. We spent hours while I taught him the part from memory, and I was glad indeed that She Who Was Pythia had made me learn each and every part completely.

If he had been a priest, I thought, we should have been well matched. We were too well matched for comfort as it was, our voices blending together, light and dark, like fire and shadow. But he was not a priest, and I had best remember that.

At last the night came. I awoke Neas at midnight, though I let Tia sleep a little longer, and he helped me with the last preparations of the pit, with placing the torches around the empty animal pen behind the house where people would stand.

He fidgeted in the cool predawn air. "Isn't it time?"

"No," I said. "We must wait until the stars begin to pale. Otherwise you will have to stretch your part out waiting for the dawn, and you don't want to do that." I rearranged the folds of his cloak. Neas wore a dark tunic belonging to Amynter, which was a bit short on him, and my black cloak folded double and pinned with gold at the shoulder to make a short cloak like men wear. With his sword at his side and his hair combed he made a passable Lord of the Dead. I had my long black tunic, which was getting old and shabby enough to look as though I had been seeking my daughter in the wild for months.

Tia came out a little later, when the stirring in the house became obvious. She was clutching a loaf of bread. I stared at it. "Am I not supposed to eat?" she said with horror.

"No, no, it's fine," I said. In truth, she should fast, but at her point in pregnancy she might pass out cold if she had to wait in a strung-up state for hours on an empty stomach. "It's almost time," I said. "Go ahead and get in the pit."

Clutching her bread, Tia climbed into the pit and Neas put three of the four boards back on top. Sitting on the ground, she could look up and see us but not be seen by people settling down to sit in the animal pen.

When most of them were there I started the lament,

soft and quiet, from one corner. Kos went round and lit the torches as I had asked him to, and gradually the curve of the animal pens came into light. All of the People were sitting on their cloaks on the ground or leaning against the fences in back. Someone had dragged two benches outside for Anchises and the men who had been wounded to sit on. I could see the children's enormous eyes shining in the torchlight. Neas' son sat on his grandfather's lap. Amynter's two boys were still for a moment. I let my voice grow in the gathering light.

This is a song that has no instruments, just the raw pain of a mother calling for her lost child.

Xandros sat cross-legged toward the front, and I saw him put his head down in his hands. I hoped Neas would not choke with tears, but I could not turn my head to look. I held the last note, willing that he would not.

And then he came in true and strong, the same tune but different words, how he loved this wife he had taken from her people, how she had lit the darkness of his eternal tomb and brought summer to the lands below. Where she walked the flowers bloomed.

Now at last I could turn toward him and I saw that there were tears in his eyes, but there were none in his voice. His turn exactly matched mine, a quarter turn, so that he was still three quarters to the People and only the extreme left could not see his face. What a priest he would have made, I thought, had he not been a prince! His sense of timing was absolutely perfect. As my arms rose, starting the invocation, his rose in perfect mirror, leaning toward me so that it seemed that we pulled at each other without touching, only our voices accusing and counteraccusing, then reconciling, life and death tugging at each other.

The stars were gone. The sky was streaked with pink and with white wisps of cloud. The sun was just below the horizon. A breath of wind brought the sweet smell of baking bread from the ovens.

Neas stepped back. Now the lament was his. Now the loss was his. He would dwell in darkness half the year, return to the caves of bone and sorrow. He slid the third board away with his foot.

Tia rose from the darkness, her white robe shining, her long hair spread across her shoulders in the morning breeze. I could well believe that flowers sprang up where she trod. Her clear, high voice cut across the stillness, warbling on the first note like a child's, then catching true.

I looked across to Kos and nodded, and he started the hymn that the entire People sing, the "Anados Kore." "She rises, Golden One, blessings strewing. Golden One, we adore You! Joy You bring us, joy and light..."

I embraced her, and there was that light in her face that told me there was much more there than her, that she was transported by love, as I had hoped. "Welcome, dear daughter," I said. "Blessings bringing." Pressed against her, I felt the child jump within her and knew that there were three of us in this rite, me, Tia, and Pythia to Be.

I knew that Tia felt it too, because she flung her arms around me, murmuring, "Thank you, thank you." I am sure that to those watching it seemed a very convincing reunion.

Afterward there was fresh-baked bread and honey. The children ran round and round, laughing and dancing. Even Anchises seemed in a good mood, and Neas took ribbing about being the Lord of the Dead very well indeed.

He was his mother's son, I thought. He should have

been a priest. Had he been, we should have been a perfect match for each other. Resolutely, I shoved that thought out of my mind.

Kos hugged me, his other arm around Tia, who was chattering and eating more bread. I did not need to go apart for this prayer. Silently and with a full heart I said, *Dear Lady, thank You.*

FOR DAYS AFTERWARD a holiday spirit prevailed. The rains came, and between the paving stones new grass sprouted. The air was cool and the breezes off the sea wafted away the city stench. Tia rounded out, as she should now, and seemed less drawn and thin.

Neas and Kos were often at the harbor, making the trades of lumber to repair our ships, and overseeing the work that was done. In the end, Kos needed help. We paid a local boatbuilder to join Kos in the work and bring his three apprentices. Kos brought three likely boys as well, so that they should learn something of the trade.

Meanwhile, Jamarados made good bargains of some of the things we had brought from Millawanda. He and Xandros went often to the markets, and gradually some of the others began to venture out into the city. One day, when it was warm and not raining, I decided to explore on my own. While I do not serve the Lady of the Sea, it seemed to me wise to visit Her temple, since I was now one of Her people, and on the sea at Her mercy. Moreover, I was curious.

The great temple of the Lady of the Sea, whom they call Ashteret in Byblos, was not a single building. There was an entire quarter given over to it, with a vast marketplace inside. The streets were paved with blocks so finely hewn that the seams were almost invisible, and several wells were bounded about with stone so that one could draw water easily and cleanly. In this marketplace were all the goods of the world—doves and lambs for sacrifice, traders in precious metals and gems, food, ivory, and horn, alabaster, even cloth made of fine Egyptian linen. Last and most costly was the papyrus for writing things on that Byblos gives its name to.

All this trade was carried on under the eyes of the gods, and the priests took a tenth of the profits here, fees taken out in a deben's weight of silver or a young kid. Her sanctuary was roofed in fragrant cedar and the roof beams were as broad as a man, such was the wealth of the place.

With my black cloak drawn about me and my plain robe, I looked like a servant doing the shopping. Well-bred women of Byblos did not go on foot, but in elaborate litters with curtains of fine cloth, attended by bearers and slaves, and I certainly did not look like a priestess of Byblos.

I don't know what I expected. Something like the temples of the isles, I suppose, not this vast echoing hall, the altar with the smell of blood still clinging to it, though it was midmorning and not a feast day. People strolled among the columns. Some were seeking shelter from the already strong sun, others loitering just off the market-place, or talking with the temple girls. I had not understood before that for the price of an offering one can keep company with Ashteret's servants, going aside with the slave girls who belong to the temple. For that reason the temple is exceedingly well lit in the evening, and offerings are made constantly by sailors of every land.

At midmorning the oil lamps were not lit and the torches had burned down to ash, great streaks of soot staining the carved columns. I went up the middle of the hall. My footsteps echoed in the vastness.

The effigy was carved of fine stone and stood nearly twice a woman's height, with painted staring eyes looking toward the sea. Her arms were raised stiffly, one holding a sistrum and the other a sheaf of grain, for in Byblos She reigns over more than the sea. A painted sacred snake curled around the bottom of Her skirt, as stiff and as lifeless as She was. There was power here, but it did not rest in the statue.

I knelt at Her feet and waited.

Nothing happened. I heard the sound of footsteps coming and going, the sound like the waves of the marketplace outside. And nothing more. If She had words for me, I did not hear them.

After a time I stood up and made my way down the left side of the room. The walls of the temple were courses of stone to just above my head, then planked with cedar above. The roof beams were cedar as well, and the high ceiling.

The stone walls were covered with carving. Some of them were the scratch marks that the people of this coast use to convey words, but I could not read them. She Who Was Pythia had thought I had no need to read or write the language of the isles, and this was infinitely more complex and difficult, with marks that looked so similar it would take practice to tell them apart. I could see a pattern, but only that — marks repeated frequently that must be common words in the language of Byblos, a language I did not speak. Without the words, the pictures above were pretty and nothing more.

I had turned to go when I heard a voice I knew.

"Wait a moment longer," Xandros said. "Please."

I thought he had spoken to me until I turned. In the shadow of the column across the way, almost beneath Her effigy, Xandros stood with his back to me.

"I can't," she said. She drew her hand away, and I saw her as she stepped into the sun that came in through the doors. She was fifteen or so, the first blush of womanhood, small breasted and slim. Her hair fell in oiled curls halfway down her back, her arms were banded in bracelets, and the cascading ruffles of her skirts were embroidered with scarlet and gold. Her skin was warm ivory, her lips and nipples stained red. She was very beautiful.

"One more moment?" he asked.

She hesitated, her feathered brows drawn together. "Only a moment," she said, and stepped toward him, her arms going up to wreath about his neck, her pale skin against his black hair. He kissed her, and I should have looked away. I should not have watched the way his mouth moved on hers, tender and demanding, the way his hand caressed the curve at the small of her back. But I could not look away, even though my heart rose in my throat.

"Can I see you?" he asked, pulling back, their noses almost touching, hers fair and straight, his darkened by sun. "Later?"

"Yes," she said. "Later. Again. I promise." I heard the slap of her gilded sandals on the stone as she hurried away.

He had not seen me in the shadow of the column. I waited until he had left.

With my twisted leg and dusty black robes I looked like a slave doing the shopping. And why shouldn't I? Was I not born a slave? What should it matter to me what Xandros did? He was not my kinsman or my lover. He was scarcely my friend. He was simply the captain of the ship that fate had put me upon.

I walked back to the harbor, and a towering fury was on me. Why should I care? Didn't I know better? What cause had I to expect that Xandros was not like all the other sailors, who rutted and took their pleasure in ports with no thought of tomorrow? Why shouldn't he be like all other men, who seek nothing but beauty?

Well, I have little of that, I thought as I stalked through the doors of the house, black cloak billowing behind me. *Little enough. Oh, enough to terrify and bring men to their knees from the fear of me. Enough to reach for them in the end with Her white hands.*

I will go apart from the dance, I had promised, *and none shall call me beloved.*

I lay down upon my pallet on the floor and stared at the ceiling dry-eyed, and it came to me that I could take this with bitterness, or not. I could imagine that Xandros had betrayed me, when he had promised me nothing, when there was nothing but friendly words between us. Or I could know that it was my fate, not his, that intervened here. I was the one who had promised to go apart from the dance, to need no love but Hers.

I had spoken no word to him, nor he to me. He did not know that I had seen him at his tryst. And I would never speak of it.

I rolled over on my pallet and buried my face in my robe. No, I would not speak. I would not let this poison all friendship between us. After all, I had always known that I would be alone.

THE DAYS OF WINTER passed. Kos seemed satisfied that the work on the ships was well done. But peace could not last. When the men of many nations are confined in port together, words are spoken, insults exchanged. Moreover, I knew Neoptolemos, and I should have known that he would not heed Prince Hiram's warnings forever, or at least that he should get around them by treachery.

I was awakened by shouts and the sounds of men running, and dashed into the courtyard in time to see the sturdy gate opening, Amynter with his sword in hand at the door. Jamarados was shouting, and in the light of a single torch I saw them coming in through the gate. Kos had blood on his long knife, and he was half dragging Neas. Blood stained Neas' tunic and he clasped his side while it dripped onto the ground.

"What happened?" Amynter demanded.

"Close the gate," Jamarados ordered. "And put out those torches. Put men on the walls with bows." He turned and shouted again. "Put out the torches, I say! Our archers will be backlit!"

Men leaped onto the walls. The one nearest me was Bai, who grimaced as he climbed but scrambled up nonetheless.

I ran to Neas, calling for Lide, the woman with the most healing skill. She came running. I saw now that there were others hurt, though none so much.

"What happened?" I asked Jamarados.

"We were coming back from the ships when some men

fell upon us in the dark," he said. Jamarados grimaced. "Neoptolemos."

"Where is Xandros?" I said.

"He wasn't with us," he said. "He was at the temple." Jamarados looked up at the walls. "We'll keep careful watch, but I don't really think they'll follow us back. Assaulting this place would cost them men and bring Prince Hiram down upon them for breaking the peace. As it is, we can't prove that Neoptolemos had anything to do with it. It might have been common thieves."

"Common thieves attack a group of armed men?" I said incredulously.

Jamarados shrugged. "They were Achaian. But we can't prove it. And they went for Neas first."

I followed Lide and Kos into Neas' room. They had his tunic off, and I could see the great bloody gash in his side.

"Water," Lide said. "Clean water fresh drawn, and cloth. Now." Kos hastened to do her bidding.

I went to the door and tried to keep out the dozen or so people who all wanted to crowd in. "Prince Aeneas is hurt," I said. "Let Lide tend him, please."

"Is he dead?" one man asked.

"No," I said, moving aside a little so he could see Neas propped up with Lide cleaning the wound, knowing that if I did not let him see the rumor would spread. "He's hurt; now give him peace."

They did eventually begin to disperse, reassured each and every one by me. When there were no others left I went back inside. Lide was wringing out a bloody cloth, and the bowl of water was all blood. Neas lay quiet, white and drawn, bandages wrapped around his middle.

"He's lost a lot of blood," Lide said quietly, "but as near as I can tell it sliced skin and muscle and turned on his last rib. It didn't go in his stomach or bowels. Prince Aeneas was very lucky." A stomach wound is almost always fatal, though it may take many days to die.

"He's feverish and weak, but if it clears he should be up and about in a week or so," she said. "I'll watch over him tonight. He needs sleep and rest now."

I left him with her. I walked back into the courtyard, where men still watched upon the walls. In the corridor I saw a small bundle. I thought someone had dropped something until I realized it was a child.

Wilos looked up with eyes as blue as Neas'. "Is my father dead?" he asked very quietly.

I knelt beside him. In all the fuss he had been entirely forgotten. "No," I said. "Your father will be fine. He was hurt in the fight, but he's sleeping now. When he wakes up you can come and talk to him."

Wilos bit his lower lip and said nothing. I picked him up and slung him on my hip. He was small and light for a child nearly five. "Come, then," I said. "We'll go see him now."

We went in, and Lide stood up. "Just a moment for Prince Wilos," I said, and put him down beside the bed. There was a glint of bronze at Neas' throat, one of the marketplace charms from the Great Temple. "You see?" I said to Wilos. "He's sleeping."

Wilos reached out and touched his hand. "Papa?"

Neas' eyes flickered. "Wilos? I'm fine, son." He opened his eyes. "I'll be fine soon."

Wilos worked his mouth, but no sound came out.

"I'm not going to die," Neas said. "I'm going to sleep

because it's nighttime. Lide is going to put you to bed, and you're going to sleep too."

I looked across at Lide. "I'll stay with him."

"Come, Prince Wilos," she said. "It's long past your bedtime. Let's go back to bed now."

They went out and Neas closed his eyes. "That was well done," he said.

"Sleep, Neas," I said. "Just rest. I will stay."

IT WAS THE COLD HOUR before dawn, when even in a great city it grows still. No dogs barked, and the city was silent. I dozed in the chair beside Neas' bed. The lamp burned low. The only sound was his breath, and I watched the rise and fall of his chest. His fever was no better and no worse. I did not feel my Lady's presence at all. Which under the circumstances was a relief. If his fever left him, he would live.

With each breath the sword amulet rose and fell on his chest, the bronze glinting in the lamplight. I dozed and woke with a start.

Someone had come in without my hearing. He sat in the chair behind the door, his hair bleached by the sun, a young man with a tired face. He wore plain stained leathers, and I would have mistaken him for a man of Byblos if not for the shadow of folded wings.

"Who are You?" I asked, for I have seen the gods before.

"You aren't afraid," he said with a half smile.

"Should I be?" I asked. "I serve the Lady of the Dead and rest under Her protection."

"Most people fear the gods," he said.

"Most do," I agreed. "But I fear men, and what they do."

He smiled again. "You're brave. I like that. I come only for the brave."

I looked down at Neas sleeping, the sword at his throat. I kept my voice steady. "Why are You here? Have You come for him, then?"

"Not in the way you mean," he said. "I am not Death."

"I know that," I said.

"It was I who turned the knife from him," he said, "so that it scored along his side. If I had not shouted he would not have turned, and it would have taken him in his kidney. And then he would have died."

I looked down at Neas' face and kept my eyes unblinking. "Why did You do that?" I asked. "Neas is not of Your people."

He almost shrugged. His shoulders didn't move, but His wings shifted restlessly. "He's a brave man. And he wears My sword."

"Xandros bought it for him in the temple quarter," I said. "He said it was for luck."

"Well, it's brought him luck, then." He smiled a little sheepishly.

"Who are You?" I asked again.

"I am Mik-el, one of the warriors who waits upon Baal."

I shook my head. I was used to Her awesome majesty, mysterious and beyond understanding. "You are not like any god I have ever met."

"I'm a very young god," he said, and this time he did shrug.

"Gods can be young? There can be new gods?"

"There could hardly be gods of war before there were warriors," he said. "Or gods of grain and harvest before men learned to plant seeds and till the soil. There was a time before that, not so long ago."

"But my Lady..." I said.

"Your Lady is old," he said. "She was old when the first man looked up from where he knelt in the long grass and wondered why his brother had fallen and would run no more, when the first woman wrapped her dead child and placed her in the earth like a womb. She was old when I was born."

"How were You born?" I asked.

Mik-el's wings shifted, as though he settled in his chair. His eyes were far away. "I'm not entirely certain. I know what I seem to remember. But I'm not sure whether it is true, or if it happened to Me, or to some other I've known."

"Tell me," I said. "If You will. The night is long."

He looked at Neas sleeping. "It is long," he said, and shrugged. "Why not, then?"

"Once, long ago along a great river, there was a young man who killed a hippopotamus that was mad, that killed men and toppled boats. He killed the beast in the reeds along the river. His people were glad and made him chief over them. For many years he led them, and they grew in number. His children grew strong and his people prospered. But then there was a crocodile. It was twice the length of a man. At first it ate their goats and then it ate their children. People went to the chief and said, 'When you were young you killed the mighty hippopotamus. Go now and kill this crocodile that eats our children!' So the chief went with some other men, and they found the place where the crocodile was, and it was twice the length of a man, with teeth longer than a man's hand. And there was a battle in the mud of the riverbank, and the crocodile lunged and with one great blow bit off the chief's foot. With his last strength the chief drove his spear into the beast's brain, and it died. His life blood pumped out on the riverbank. The people were delivered from the crocodile, but their chief was dead."

I smiled, for I felt that I had heard this story before, somewhere or other.

"They buried him at the edge of the desert with every honor, and they made songs about him. They set up a stone and carved a picture of a king with his spear through the crocodile, and they laid flowers and figs before it, praying that they might always have a king who would give his life for his people. His sons and grandsons called upon his spirit to help them when they hunted. Soon others did as well."

"And what happened to him?" I asked.

Mik-el put His head to one side. "He didn't pass on, cross the River, as you would say. He stayed and watched over his people and listened to their invocations. As his sons grew old he whispered in their ears, and did not know if they heard or not. Sometimes it seemed they did. So he stayed. Soon all those he had known and loved had grown old and died, but there were new people, children of his children's children who hunted along the riverbank. And it seemed to him that there were still young hunters who needed his help, and who whispered his name as they hunted birds in the reeds along the river. So he stayed, and decided he would stay as long as there were those who needed him."

"That was long ago," I said.

"Many lives of men," he said. "Before ships sailed the seas or fields were plowed. When all the men there were in the world would fit into one of these great cities."

"Why is the world ending?" I asked. "One by one the cities are falling. Like the island that was Thera is sunk in the sea."

Mik-el sighed. "It's a thing beyond your understanding. I'm not sure I entirely understand it Myself. You see, there are these great stone plates that float on a sea of fire like icebergs on water, and sometimes they run into each other..."

"What's an iceberg?" I asked.

Mik-el blinked. "It's a big... Never mind. It's not because of the gods or anything like that. It's like waves on the shore. It's the way the world works."

"But the gods created the world," I said. "Didn't they?"

"And the world created the gods," he said. Mik-el leaned forward. "In the beginning there was nothing, not even time. And then there was something. A word. A thought. And then in an instant there was everything. Brilliant light everywhere. Stars and starstuff all spinning out in the firmament. And there was Everything and Nothing."

"Day and night?" I said.

"Evening and morning," he said. "And time. Because now there was before and after. There was earth and water and air and sun and fire. And the waters came together and rained down on the earth and there were oceans."

"And from Gaia and Kronos, from Earth and Time, were born the other gods," I said.

"Exactly!" he said. "At least sort of. I think that's probably the best I can do explaining."

"So why are the cities falling?" I asked. "And why did You help Neas?"

"I'm not sure I can explain the first part in ways you'd understand," he said, "but as to the second, I helped your captain because he's a brave man and shouldn't be taken from behind by treachery. He's wearing My sword."

"Because Xandros gave it to him," I said.

"He's the one I've seen before," Mik-el said. He smiled, and His face was light. "There was a young man of My people, the son of the son of My son fourteen times. He wanted to know where the river went. And so he sailed a ship of reeds along the riverbank and through the tangled channels of the delta past places where someday there would be cities, until he found the sea. He looked out on the ocean where the water goes to the horizon, and he knew how big the world was. Then fear woke in his heart and also great longing, to know everything and see every shore, to go to the ends of the earth and understand the tracks of the winds. And when he lay on the beach that night while the stars turned over his head, he wondered what they were made of, and if the darkness around them was just another ocean. I knew that if it took ten thousand lives of men, he would sail to every corner of the universe. He comes and he goes, passes over the river and back, and I help him when I can. I find him when I can. He is the son of the son of My son fourteen times, one of the sons of My heart."

"Xandros is a good man," I said. "I'm glad to see that he is beloved of some god."

"Even a young one," he said, and his mouth twitched with not quite a smile.

"Even a young one," I said, "Mik-el Who Waits Upon Baal."

Behind me Neas stirred. "Sybil?" he said.

I turned. "Neas? How do you feel?"

He raised his head a little. "Thirsty," he said.

I put my hand to his forehead, and it was clammy and cool. The fever had broken. "I will get you some water," I said.

"Who was just here?" he asked. "I thought I heard you talking with someone, but I don't see anyone here."

"I was praying," I said as I poured water from a jar, for it was true that the room was empty.

BYBLOS

I awoke at dawn when Lide came in. She checked Neas'
bandages and seemed satisfied, so I went off to bed
while she stayed. At midmorning I was awakened by
Kos. Groggy, I half sat up, wondering if something was
wrong with Tia.

"Jamarados says Neas wants you. Come on."

I ran my fingers through my hair and stood. My head
felt leaden.

Jamarados, Amynter, Anchises, and others were
crowded into Neas' room. I came in. "What's happening?" I asked. From the fact that Neas was sitting up, it
didn't seem that he'd taken a turn for the worse.

"A messenger from Prince Hiram just arrived," Amynter said. "He says he requires Neas' presence in audience
immediately."

"It's about last night," Neas said. "It must be."

"You can't go," Jamarados said. "You're not in any
shape to."

"Prince Hiram does not have the authority to issue orders to the Prince of Wilusa," Anchises said loudly. Everyone ignored him.

"If you don't go," Amynter said, "then what does Hiram do? Forget it?"

"He can't lose face that way," Neas said. "No prince can. No, then he sends his men to bring me by force."

"You shouldn't be up today at all," Lide said from beside the bed. "If you move about too much you'll tear that open again and bleed. And you've no blood left to spare."

"What if I go in your place?" Jamarados said. "That might satisfy Hiram."

Neas looked around the room. "Where's Xandros?"

"He was here a little while ago," Amynter said. "But I think he's gone out again."

"It will hardly satisfy Hiram for you to go," I said to Jamarados. "Brave as your offer is. He wants Neas, and he's going to get Neas one way or another."

"I'll have to go," Neas said, pushing back his blanket.

"You can't walk as far as the Citadel," I said. "You'll fall flat."

"He doesn't have to walk," Jamarados said, "if Sybil comes too. Wellborn ladies travel in litters. Order a litter for her, and since he's the highest-ranking man he can share it with her. That's what the Egyptians do."

I went to put on a cleaner tunic and to comb out my hair while they ordered the litter and got Neas ready. Amynter came with us, but Jamarados was ordered to stay. In case we were Prince Hiram's guests for some time, Neas wanted someone with good judgment left in command.

*   *   *

THE CITADEL was large and imposing, as one might expect. Prince Hiram received us in his audience chamber, a great room paneled in cedar and decorated with gilded caps on the beams. It was not painted, and the floor was plain, rather different from the chambers I was used to.

"At least he's got only a couple of guards," Amynter said under his breath.

Neas nodded but didn't speak. The effort of getting from the litter at the door to the end of the hall was enough.

I agreed with Amynter. This looked more like a threat than an arrest.

Hiram was a handsome man a few years older than Neas, with a close-trimmed black beard and bright eyes framed by swooping brows. He did not rise from his chair, or offer us one. "Prince Aeneas," he said in Achaian, and I did not know if he meant the title as respect or irony. But I did know why Jamarados was not necessary as interpreter this time.

"Prince Hiram," Neas said, inclining his head.

"I understand that there was a brawl last night, between you Denden and the Achawoi. I believe I had warned both you and the prince of the Achawoi that I would have no feuds between you that break the peace of my city."

Neas raised his eyebrows. "I have heard of no brawl. Some men were set upon by common footpads and defended themselves. The thieves fled. This has nothing to do with any blood feud."

"Perhaps it is as you say." I could see that Hiram did not believe him.

"My prince, I am not aware of any quarrels with the

Achaians," Neas said. "My men know not to break the peace of this city."

Hiram looked at him and his eyes narrowed. "Do not think that I am ignorant of your plans. Because I am not Egypt's pet dog and do not inform them of your works, you should not think that I support this foolishness. Byblos tolerates you pirates, not welcomes you. And we will not be part of your confederacy. When Pharaoh cuts off your foreskins for trophies and you go to a life of labor in Egypt, remember that I warned you."

"I do not understand your words," Neas said, but I saw that Hiram believed this no more than he had believed Neas before.

"There shall be no more brawls," Hiram said. "I hope that is clear."

"It is clear," Neas said, inclining his head. And the audience was at an end.

AMYNTER LEANED CLOSE as he walked beside the litter on the way home. "What was that about?" he asked.

"Wait until we are within walls," I whispered. There was still Hiram's escort about us, and the slaves who bore the litter.

We came in through the gate, and I thought Jamarados was half faint with relief. He helped Neas into his room and brought him clean water, and we told him what had transpired.

"I do not understand his warning," I said. "Do you know what plan he means?"

Neas shook his head. "Where in the world is Xandros? I could have used him there."

"No doubt with his girl," I said bitterly.

"Girl?" Jamarados looked up. "Oh, you thought… At the temple? That's not a girl; that's one of the temple eunuchs."

"The what?"

"In these lands," Jamarados said, "the priests are gelded, like bull calves. They aren't men or women either. They serve Ashteret, like the girls do."

"Ah," I said blankly. I had never imagined such a thing. I supposed it might be done, though I could not see what Xandros would want in such a thing. Or perhaps I could, I thought. Perhaps I could see all too clearly.

Neas looked at me keenly and changed the subject. "Well, when he gets back, send him to me. But the thing that's more important is what was Hiram talking about? We're looking to escort merchant ships back to Millawanda in the spring. If there is some plot against Egypt, we have no part in it. But it makes me wonder what Neoptolemos thinks to do in Byblos."

"I don't know," Jamarados said grimly, "but I think we'd better find out."

IN THE END, it was Xandros who found out.

Winter deepened, and the seas were stormy. Nonetheless, new ships kept arriving in Byblos, rowing hard against the winds. The sailing season was long since over.

I stood with Neas and Jamarados on the wall one day, where we could see a tiny part of the harbor around the buildings farther down the hill. We could just make out several ships rounding the breakwater under oar.

"Lydian, Karian, Achaian, Kretan, everyone but the Egyptians," Jamarados said. "Even some people I've never heard of, the Shardan, who say they live on an island three weeks' sailing to the west of Pylos, beyond Illyria. I've never seen this many warships abroad in winter before."

Xandros had come up behind us. "About the Shardan," he said. "I've got an idea."

Neas didn't ask Xandros where he'd been. We were used by now to his going abroad in the city. He was beginning to speak the language like a native, and his knowledge of local trade rivaled Jamarados'. However else he spent his time was none of our business.

"Let's have it, then," Neas said equitably.

"My friend has talked with a Shardan captain," he said. "They're from so far away almost nobody speaks their language and they don't have any idea that we're not friends of the Achaians." He forestalled the obvious question. "My friend is good with languages." *As is Xandros,* I thought. *He's quicker of mind than he thinks he is.*

"Then what are the Shardan doing here?" Jamarados asked. "They don't usually trade in Byblos."

"They were invited to join in an expedition that would make them all rich, to have a share in sacking cities if they would come and bring their warships."

"Whose cities?" Neas asked.

"Who isn't here?" I said. "Egypt, of course. Who else has wealth enough to make it worthwhile?"

"Egypt," said Jamarados. "That makes sense."

"It does," said Neas. "That's what Hiram meant. He thinks we're part of this plan too."

Jamarados whistled. "I wonder if they can carry it off.

There must be nearly two hundred ships here. And if they don't sail until spring, more can come in then. There's a lot more gold there than convoying merchant ships back to Millawanda."

"And a lot more danger," I pointed out. "From everything I've heard, Egypt is powerful beyond imagining."

"Not more so than the Hittites," Jamarados pointed out. "We were their allies, and they were mighty friends."

"Not mighty enough to keep the city from being burned," Neas said. "They were mighty in my grandfather's day, but not so much anymore." He turned to Xandros. "Do you think that your friend can arrange for you to drink with the Shardan captain and find out what you can? What cities? When? How do they plan to deal with fortifications?"

"And what about the Egyptian fleet?" Jamarados asked. "True, they're not seamen like the Kretans, but they do have a fleet, and I'd not laugh at it."

"I can do that," Xandros said. He didn't look happy.

It was a week later, well after the turning of the sun, that Xandros came in late and woke the three of us. He smelled of stale wine and cheap incense, but he was stone sober. I rolled out of bed and went to hear what had happened.

"The plan is this," Xandros said. "They're sailing as soon as the season opens, and they're going south along the coast. They're going to sack Ashkelon and the Egyptian garrison there, and then fall on the cities of the Delta after the harvest is gathered in. They think that when the Egyptians hear that Ashkelon has fallen, their fleet will put to sea and go to its aid, and that Pharaoh will send his army north through Gaza, leaving the Delta clear of troops as far as Memphis."

Jamarados let out a long breath. "That's ambitious."

"And tactically sound," Neas said. "Whose plan is this?"

"Guess," Xandros said.

"Neoptolemos," I said. "This is the same trick."

Neas nodded. "The same trick that lured us away from Wilusa. He's a good captain, I'll give him that."

I felt Her cold hand on my back. More cities burned, more lands destroyed. Where would this end?

"He wants to be Great King," I said, and hardly knew that I said it. "Orestes son of Agamemnon is dead, and all of his house. The son of Achilles wants to be king over the Achaians."

"What is that to us?" Jamarados said. "Who cares who is king of the Achaians?"

"He is cursed with the blood shed at Aulis," I said. "He and all his kin lie under that dark curse. The Furies pursue them and all who sail with them."

Xandros looked up, startled. "We're considering sailing with them?"

Jamarados nodded. "It's a possibility. We're either with them or against them, and with two hundred ships I don't think we're against them. And there is gold in Egypt. We should think on this."

Xandros was pale. "I will not sail with the men who murdered my children for sport," he said, and walked away.

Neas looked after him. I waited.

At last Neas shook his head. "We will not sail with

Neoptolemos," he said. "There is blood between us that cries out for vengeance, and there is not enough gold in Egypt to satisfy it."

"This is our chance of peace between us," Jamarados said. "I'm just pointing that out."

I remembered that face in torchlight, urging the Young King of Pylos to sail against Wilusa, his smile and his shadowed eyes. "Neoptolemos is treacherous," I said. "He tried to murder Neas in a dark street. There can be no peace between us. He has everything to lose from such a peace, and nothing to gain."

"We have much to lose as well," Neas said. "All this winter I have restrained any man who wanted to collect his blood debt from the Achaians because the People could not afford it. We are few and without a homeland, vagabonds and wanderers on the sea. We are little more than the pirates Hiram named us."

"Yet we are more," I said. "We are women and children as well."

"And it is for their sake that I have restrained any who talk of honor," Neas said, looking at me. "It is for their sake that I have restrained myself." His lips tightened, and I knew that it was so.

"My prince," I said, "that is courage greater than any other."

He smiled. "I'm glad you think so. But there are more who will call me coward that I haven't met Neoptolemos face-to-face. If we go tamely back to Millawanda, there are many who will."

"I am telling you," Jamarados said, "we will not be allowed to go tamely back to Millawanda or anywhere else. Do you think that when the sailing season begins they will let any ship leave this port that might warn Pharaoh? Do you think that in their hundreds they will not fall on us and kill our men, taking our ships to be part of their expedition? If we are not with them, we will be against them. Neoptolemos is not fool enough to leave us free in his rear."

"Then we must leave now," I said.

Jamarados looked exasperated. "Lady, you are an oracle, not a sailor! It is the dead of winter, and storms pound this coast one after the other. We cannot return now. The winds are foul for Millawanda."

"And fair for Egypt," Neas said.

We both jerked around to look at him.

"Oh no," Jamarados said. "You're not thinking what I think you are."

"Pharaoh will pay well for the information we have," Neas said. "And if he's about to be attacked from the sea, perhaps he needs some sea raiders of his own. If we must fight, I would rather it was against Neoptolemos than beside him."

"Do you see how many ships there are out there?" Jamarados said, pointing toward the harbor.

Neas grinned like a boy. "Aren't you the one who was telling me how powerful Pharaoh is? How big his fleet is?"

"How are we even going to get out of the harbor? I tell you, they're not going to just let us go."

"For that we need Xandros," Neas said. "I have a plan." He clapped Jamarados on the shoulder. "Don't worry. It will all be fine," he said, and left in search of Xandros.

Jamarados and I looked at each other.

"I hope you know what you're doing," he said.

* * *

FOUR HUNDRED PEOPLE cannot keep a secret. For the moment, then, no one knew that we were planning to leave Byblos soon except the five of us. We brought Xandros and Amynter into the secret, because they must plan for our departure, but otherwise all the People thought we should wait out the winter in Byblos and then return to Millawanda. The other captains would have to be told, but Neas preferred to wait until the day before. We knew that once people started being told it would be a very short time before everyone knew.

The dark moon was five days off. That night, and the one before and after were our best chances of getting out of the harbor undetected. In the meantime, Xandros found out what he could about the ships that went out regularly, mostly fishing ships of Byblos that went out before dawn on clear days and returned at midday.

"It's our best chance," Xandros said as we stood in counsel together. "Yes, our ships look wrong in the water at a close look, but if we're under sail with the oars stepped, we could manage on a dark night, if we answer them fair if they challenge us."

"That's up to you and Jamarados," Neas said. "Do you think you can manage so they don't suspect?"

Xandros nodded gravely. "If I don't have to have a long conversation. I can manage the accent if I don't have to talk a lot."

"Keep it short, then," Neas said. "*Dolphin* had better go first. The first ship is the most likely challenged as they pass the warships."

"And the last is most likely caught," said Amynter.

"That's why the last is *Seven Sisters*," Neas said.

"*Lady's Eyes* will be second and you'll follow her with *Hunter*. Then *Winged Night, Cloud,* and *Swift*. Have archers ready in case you need to silence someone."

Jamarados shook his head. "I'm not sure we've got anyone keen enough to silence someone in the dark from the deck of a moving ship. And if we start shooting and only wound someone, they'll yell and bring the whole place down on us. I think playing dumb is a better choice."

"Take it as it comes," Neas said. "If you have an archer that can make the shot, fine. If not, then play dumb. You'll have to take it as you see it. I trust your judgment."

Lady, I thought, *we need a cloudy night with a land breeze and no rain or bad weather out to sea. I realize this is asking a great deal, but it's for Your son, so perhaps it could be managed?*

THE FIRST NIGHT of the three was pouring rain. The waves in the harbor splashed up waist high on the breakwaters, and the wind was gusty and out of the south. Neas was edgy because he had told the captains to have their men ready, and not to let them out to the taverns and drinking places and temples.

"We can't go in this," he said. "Not under sail. We could do it under oar, but they would see that we aren't fishing ships."

"Then we wait," Jamarados said. "It may clear tomorrow."

IT DIDN'T. All the next day it rained.

At nightfall Neas was pacing back and forth around

the courtyard when Amynter came in. "There's a group of Achaians sitting under an awning down the street. They're watching us."

"Are they armed?" Neas asked.

"Of course," Amynter said.

Neas paced over to the corner. His steps were still a little hesitant, though the wound in his side seemed to be healing well. He turned and looked at me. "What do you say, Lady?" he asked formally. "What are the words of our Sybil?"

I spread my hands and felt the faint tremor of power along them. "It is in your hands, Prince Aeneas. The Lady of the Sea trusts Her son."

"Then we go tonight," Neas said. "I know. The weather." He forestalled Jamarados and Amynter. "But it may not be better tomorrow night, and then the moon will be waxing. And each night we wait the chance is better that Neoptolemos will find out what we're doing." He turned to Xandros. "I want you to go make ready at the ships. Tell the men to stand ready. I'll be there soon."

Xandros nodded and hurried away.

"What about the Achaians?" Amynter asked.

"We may have to take care of them the hard way," Neas said. It almost seemed like he was looking forward to it.

ASHTERET'S HAND

Four hundred people cannot sneak anywhere. Four hundred people sneaking through the streets of Byblos is a procession, not a quiet departure. No one, not even the Achaians, could fail to notice.

It was decided that we would make our way to the harbor by ship's company, in order of our sailing, one ship at a time, in hopes that night and rain would cover us somewhat. *Dolphin*'s people were to go first. With us would go Neas and five or six picked men who would take care of the Achaians who had been watching the house, if they were still there when the first of us were ready to leave just after midnight.

By midnight it was pouring. The rain fell in sheets, and the streets were tracks of mud and filth. It was completely dark. With my heaviest mantle pulled over her head, Tia was all but invisible from a few steps away. She shivered faintly.

I put my hand on her arm. "Are you all right?" I asked.

She shrugged. "I just don't feel well. There's nothing wrong."

"I hate to drag you out in the weather," I said, "but it's just a short walk down to the ship, and then you can get into the forward cabin and rest. From then on the work is up to Xandros."

"Ready?" Neas asked, coming around the corner. He was wearing his leather breastplate, and his sword was at the ready.

Xandros nodded. "We're ready."

Dolphin's people stood silent, carrying as little as possible. Almost all of our goods and food had been taken down to the harbor already and packed aboard.

"Then let's go," Neas said. He and his picked men eased the gate open and went out in the rain.

Xandros waited beside me, counting softly under his breath. He looked up at me, his black hair already plastered to his skin with rain. "He said to give him a count of five hundred," Xandros said. "That's a hundred five times." He reached over and squeezed my hand. "Don't worry," he said. "It will be all right."

Ahead, we heard a muffled shout, almost lost in the rain.

"Wait," Xandros said. He finished his count.

Then Xandros rolled the gate open again, and we piled out into the driving rain, my hand under Tia's elbow on the slippery street.

Neas came back to us. In the faint light I could see that his sword was dark with blood. He leaned close to Xandros, but still had to yell to be heard over the rain. "Go," he said. "We've taken care of their watchers. None of them got away. But we don't have time to waste, not if we're going to move in small groups."

Xandros nodded, turning to Kos. "Come on then. Straight down to *Dolphin*."

I hurried along with Tia right behind Xandros, the others behind. There were three or four bodies at the end of the street, where it met the main road down to the harbor. One of them was still moving.

A young man lay in the contents of his stomach and bowels, trying to retch from a stomach he no longer had. A sword had opened his entire abdomen, and the blood pooled around him, spreading in the rain.

"Go," I said to Tia, and turned to him.

I bent down so he could see my face, white even without paint beneath the black hood. I put my hand on his forehead. "Depart," I said in Achaian. "Find your way safe to the River, and to the lands of undying sun."

He could not speak, but I saw his eyes widen, then move in assent as Xandros came and stood beside me.

"Xandros?" I said.

He nodded tightly, drawing his bronze knife from its sheath. With one stroke he cut the young man's throat. I jerked back, the fountaining blood spattering my robe. My foot slipped and I fell down in the muddy street.

Xandros took my elbow and hauled me to my feet. His mouth was set. He said nothing. There was no need. We followed the rest to the ship.

WE WERE THE LAST to reach *Dolphin*. Kos had helped Tia aboard. Xandros boosted me up and turned back to keep watch, I supposed. I went below in the forward cabin, where Tia was with the nine-year-old boy and his mother, Polyra. Bai was there too, moving our bundles around to make a comfortable place for Tia. She was soaked to the skin and shivering. Bai opened up one pack he'd brought aboard earlier and pulled out a fine warm wool cloak to wrap around her. "I'm fine," she said, but she smiled rather than flinched at his touch.

He went back out on deck and I knelt down beside her. The boy was changing into a dry tunic while his mother scolded him. It was very cramped in the cabin with all our things, as well as six big sacks of lentils that were packed into the very point of the prow and the dozen or so big jars of green olives packed in brine that were in the corners.

And then we waited. After a while, I went back on deck. The rain was still falling hard, and there was no sign of dawn. I saw a movement down the dock. A child was being handed up to *Seven Sisters'* deck, while several others waited to board. It was Wilos, I thought, from the stooped back of the man on deck who reached down to get him, probably Anchises.

I went aft. Kos was standing at the tiller, one hand on the rope that tied us to the dock. "Where is Xandros?" I asked.

"I thought he was forward with you," Kos said.

"No," I said. "He never got onboard. I thought he was keeping watch."

"I haven't seen him," Kos said.

"He might be on the dock," I said. "Or talking to Neas. I'll find him." A nervous energy gripped me. I could not simply sit below, huddling among the stores, waiting for someone to hear us leaving. I slid back over the side and onto the dock, making my way along the planks toward *Seven Sisters*. They had almost all of their people aboard.

Neas was helping the last woman over the rail. He turned to me.

"Where is Xandros?" I asked.

"Here," Xandros said. He was coming along the dock, bareheaded, a cloaked figure behind him. It was a youth with honey skin and black hair pulled back from a high, clean brow, beautiful even in the rain.

"Oh no," Neas said. "Xandros, no."

"This is Ashterah," Xandros said, "and she's coming with us."

"She is not," Neas said. "We have enough mouths to feed as it is."

"I can't send her back to the temple now," Xandros said. "She knows where we're going. We have to take her with us."

The youth's eyes flicked from one to the other. He did not speak Wilusan, not much anyway. Even soaked, even without the gorgeous clothes, he was almost unbearably graceful.

"We could dump her in the harbor," Neas snapped, "and then she'd not tell anyone."

Xandros' hand moved toward his belt, tightened. "You wouldn't do that. But the Achaians would, if we leave her."

Their eyes locked.

Neas looked away, grimacing. "You're a damn menace. Fine, put her on *Dolphin*. And get moving! We're all aboard, and you're the first ship out!"

The rowers were on their benches. I scrambled over the side. Bai had to reach down to help Ashterah up. It was clear Ashterah had never been on a ship before. I took his elbow and steered him aft, between the rowers' benches. "There," I said, pointing to the aft cabin and speaking slowly. "There is where you should go."

I went back forward, passing Xandros. Bai was back at his bench, his shoulder healed. Kassander, Amynter's son, stood ready between the banks of rowers to pass orders up and down in a whisper. The rowers could use neither the drums nor chants as we moved in the dark, so all the orders must be passed by runner. He looked nervous. I thought he must be twelve or so, a few years younger than Ashterah.

I put my hand on his shoulder and leaned close. "It will be well," I said. "We are counting on your skill, and you will not fail. It is so."

"Thank you, Great Lady," he said and moved aft, where he could hear the captain.

Bai grinned. "He's a good boy."

"Yes," I said. "Will I be in your way if I stand here?"

"No, but you'll want to get down if they start shooting."

Kassander came back down the row, speaking to every second man. "The captain says to unship every other oar and get them in the water as quietly as you can."

I felt *Dolphin* move as they complied, saw Kos casting off in the stern. We swung away from the pier.

It seemed very loud to me, but I suppose the sound was muffled by the rain and the slap of the water against the dock. Or perhaps it was not so loud at all.

We began to move. Even though the rain was beating down and the wind freshening, I felt a slow exhilaration rising. We were moving, we were going back to sea, we were escaping Neoptolemos and the Achaians, we were in Her hand once again.

"Aphrodite of the Waves, watch over us," I whispered, and felt the wind like Her breath against my face.

She Who Was Pythia had been right, I thought, as we met the first waves, mounting each roller steady and sweet. Like calls to like, and the blood of the Sea People was in my veins. I had never been seasick, not even in the storm that took us to the Island of the Dead, and my sea legs were as steady as Xandros'.

I heard the guards on the breakwater call out, but did not understand the words. They had seen us. I guessed from their tone that they had not recognized who we were, but wondered what we were about.

Xandros answered them, a little hesitantly.

They called back, a man's voice with authority this time.

Xandros gave a one-word answer.

Another reply, closer and more preemptory. They were not reassured. I could hear that from the tone.

Another voice answered from our aft deck, a boy's voice, high and clear. It sounded innocent and perplexed, rattling off words in the language of Byblos. Ashterah.

"Aphrodite Cythera, Ashterat of the Sea, I didn't expect You to answer my prayers quite so immediately!" I whispered.

Ashterah was chatting with them. There was a laugh from the breakwater. We slid past, the oars held above the water on the left side on Xandros' order.

And then we were past them, out of the harbor into the open sea. *Dolphin* pitched, rearing like a horse scenting his freedom. We leaped forward as the sail spread, catching us on the rising wind, speeding us southward to Egypt.

* * *

THE WEATHER didn't improve. Dawn found us running south under low scudding clouds over a choppy sea. From the shelter of the rowers' rail I could see three other ships spread out, running with the storm as we did — *Winged Night, Hunter,* and *Lady's Eyes.* The others must be behind or ahead, too far apart to see. I went aft and climbed up on the deck with Xandros, who was at the tiller. The wind gusted and threw me hard against the rail.

"Careful," Xandros yelled. "It's rough."

"Are the other ships here?" I asked.

"They all made it free of the harbor without any trouble. But I haven't seen any of the others since then. Impossible to stay close together in this weather," Xandros shouted.

Kassander came weaving his way along the deck, spray flying. He looked frightened. "Lady, Kos said that you need to go forward right now. That Tia needs you."

I hurried forward to the cabin, knowing what I would find.

Tia curled on the sacks of lentils, her robe soaked below the waist.

"Her water has broken," Polyra said. "And her pains have just come on her hard."

I drew her back toward the door. "Isn't it too early?" I whispered.

She nodded. "A full moon, I think. We need Lide. She's the most skilled midwife among us."

"Lide is on *Seven Sisters,*" I said. "We are too far apart. I couldn't even see *Seven Sisters* when I was on deck. And if we were within sight, there's no way we could come alongside and get her over in this weather."

Polyra let out a long breath. Then she drew one in. "Have you ever assisted at a childbirth?"

"Me? No. I am forbidden to shed blood or see it shed. I've never been anywhere near a childbirth."

"I've had two of my own," Polyra said. "And I was about when my mother was delivered of my younger sister when I was a maiden. That's something. I know how it should go, at any rate."

"I will do as you say," I said. "I will help in any way I can."

Polyra drew a deep breath again. "Take my son aft to the rear cabin. It's not seemly for him to be here, as old as he is. And get Xandros' knife. I'll need a sharp blade when the time comes."

I took the boy aft and put him into Kos' keeping. Kos gripped at my arm and invoked every god he could think of. "You'll keep her safe, won't you?" he pleaded.

"Polyra and I will do what we can," I said, detaching his fingers from my sleeve and pressing them. "Tia is young and strong. It will go well."

I did not speak for the baby. I could feel Her wings hovering near. A full moon early, born on the tossing seas to a girl scarcely a woman herself, in a place with no warmth, no fire, it had little chance.

I made my way forward again, past the rowers with their heads down, dripping in the rain, the salt spray flying and soaking me. *Gracious Lady,* I prayed, *I knew Your hand was on this child. I pray that I was not wrong in divining how.*

I felt Her like the pulse of my own heart. *Blood has been shed in the Sea Lady's city, the blood of Her people. Death must answer for death.*

I said none of this, and hoped it did not show in my face when I opened the door. I sat by Tia and said soothing words, brought her sweet fresh water to drink. There was time between pains.

Day came, gray and fitful, as we ran before the winds, the seas heaving and fighting.

Each wave of pains racked her, her back arching, her lips bloody where she had bitten them. And then subsided, like waves on the sea. I could not tell if they were closer together or not. They seemed endless, and yet there was time between.

Night came, and the storm was worse. The wind blew an eerie song through the gaps in the planking overhead.

Tia drank and dozed a little between each crest, dropping into a stupor with her eyes half open. Polyra shook her head. "It has been nearly a whole day since her water broke. She must deliver soon if she is to deliver a live baby."

And still these waves of pain crested and broke.

It was hard to check the progress in the darkness. There was nothing but Tia's ragged cries, her hands clutching at mine, scrabbling in pain, climbing up one wave of darkness after another.

Time stood still. Out on the sea our ships might founder, the People might drown. Xandros would be tied to his tiller, shivering with cold and exhaustion, keeping our bow into the waves.

Tia and Polyra and I fought as though the entire future of the People lay in this one child. The entire ship might sink at any moment, but we would not think of it. This one life was the only one worth thinking of.

In the first gray light of dawn, Polyra checked Tia

again. "Look," she said, drawing me down to see as Tia gasped in the wake of a wave. Between those stretched lips was something pale and hairless.

"It's the crown of the babe's head," Polyra said. She knelt up and took Tia's hand. "Next time you must begin to push," she said. "Do you understand? We are nearly there."

And push she did, screaming. I didn't see that it moved at all. I didn't see how anything could fit through. Once more. Twice more.

"Give me the knife," Polyra said.

I had cleaned Xandros' blade in seawater. It was bronze, and very sharp. Polyra wrapped most of the length of the blade with her cloak, choking up on it so that only a finger's length of tip remained.

Tia started up the crest. "Push, push," I said, holding her hand. "Now, Tia."

The blade flashed, the tip cutting the flesh at the corner of the stretch. Blood spattered, and the head moved. A small bloody face dark with exertion, a strangely elongated head.

"That's perfect!" Polyra said, putting the knife at her side. "Perfect, Tia. One more push, on the crest, to get its shoulders free."

Tia was sobbing, and she bit down on her lip.

I saw the ripples of the contraction coming across her stomach. "Now, darling."

She gasped, pushing down on her elbows, and I saw it slide free into Polyra's arms, shoulders and torso and long legs. Polyra lifted it, blowing into its mouth, her own breath clearing its throat and nose. And then it cried, a high mewing sound like a seagull.

The bronze knife flashed again, and she cut the cord.

"One more push for the afterbirth," Polyra said.

Tia was trying to push up on her elbows. "Let me see!"

Polyra handed the child to me and bent for the afterbirth.

It was light and incredibly tiny, arms and legs like sticks under translucent skin, bald and without eyelashes or brows, but the tiny legs were kicking and she was screaming.

"Tia," I said, handing her the child, "you have a beautiful daughter."

The tears overflowed her eyelids and she took the baby to her chest, tiny bloodied hands against her breast. "Oh," she said. "Oh, come here, come here. Tiny so tiny." I think she hardly even noticed the afterbirth. She winced when Polyra washed the cut she had made with salt water, but she did not even look up from her crooning. I sat back against the lentils and let the tears run down my face.

Polyra rearranged things, cloth to absorb the blood, and the warm woolen cloak around Tia and the babe. "You must keep her against you," Polyra said. "She is very thin and can die of cold. There is nothing here to warm her but you."

She had quieted now, against Tia's heart, her eyes closed perhaps in sleep. Tia closed her eyes too, the cloak tight around them.

Polyra crawled away, and I with her. Carefully, she cleaned the knife.

"Will she live?" I asked.

Polyra looked at me. "You ask me? You're Death's handmaiden. What does She tell you?"

"Nothing," I said, and realized that was what I felt. The pulse of Her wings was gone. The crisis, whatever it was, was past.

"She will live if she can eat," Polyra said. "And stay warm. These very young ones sometimes can't eat, and thus die. Or die of cold. But I think Tia will keep her warm. Sometimes they don't breathe, either, but this one seems to have no trouble crying, and she seems strong enough."

"That is well," I said, trying to find some of my ancient dignity again. "She is to be Pythia after me."

"Born from death," Polyra said. "Stolen from it, really."

"All children are stolen from death," I said. "That is the Mystery. I have not understood it until now."

Polyra patted my shoulder, and there was something almost motherly in her eyes. "Go and tell Kos," she said. "He's probably ill with worrying."

I went out on deck. It was early morning, and the storm was beginning to abate. Through the rain I could see Xandros at the stern, lashed to his tiller. Kos came stumbling toward me, sloshing through knee-deep seawater. Half the rowers were bailing. None rowed. The spread sail gave us way.

"Tia? How is she?" His face was gray and his eyes were bloodshot. The blood on my clothes must have looked frightening indeed.

"Tia is fine," I said, embracing him. "She is young and strong and already she mends. She and the babe are both sleeping. It's a little girl."

Kos lifted me in a mighty bear hug. "Praise to your

Lady and Cythera Aphrodite and all the other gods! A little girl and Tia well! Ela, Ela, Cythera!"

He put me down with a splash.

"And the ship?" I asked. "We seem to be out of the worst of it. It's not rolling as it was."

"Not too much damage," Kos said. "This water's all coming in over the rail, not from a leak below the waterline. We're staying ahead of it, and it's getting better as the seas aren't running so high as they were. Still, there's a reason that men don't sail in this weather. And we lost the boy."

"The boy?" I asked, thinking for a moment of Polyra's son.

"Ashterah," Kos said. "He went overboard in the worst of it, during the night."

"Oh," I said. I looked aft. Xandros' ashen face, bound to his ship, told me everything. That, and the beating of Her wings that I had felt. One life begun, one ended.

"He thinks it's his fault," Kos said. "He's half mad with it and won't let me take the tiller. Still, we're riding the storm, and I thought it best not to cross him."

I went aft. "Xandros?"

He said nothing. The ropes had raised weals around his waist, splashed with salt water. He did not ask me about Tia and the child.

"Xandros?"

He said nothing. I stood beside him as the sun broke through the clouds. Morning wore on. Out to sea I could see *Seven Sisters, Hunter,* and *Winged Night.*

"Will you take some water?" I asked, offering him a full water skin. He shook his head and would not drink, would not look at me.

It was full afternoon when we saw a low, long shape on the horizon, and the sun was hot overhead, the soaked decks steaming in the sun.

"Land!" cried Kos in the bow.

I looked and heard a sound behind me. Xandros had fainted in the traces. I used his knife to cut the ropes and lowered him insensible to the deck while Bai caught the rudder.

We had reached Egypt.

THE MOUTHS
OF THE NILE

I do not remember how we came to the mouths of the Nile. I do know that it was three days that we plodded along the coast after our first landfall, but I was on deck for very little of it.

Tia took ill with a fever. Sometimes, Polyra told me, fevers come on after the child is safely delivered and the mother may yet die. With such a tiny infant, there would be no chance for her either, if Tia were to die. I was terribly worried and sat by her, bathing her face and breasts with cool water.

On the third morning Tia woke with her brow cool and damp, and the fever brightness had left her eyes. Whatever its cause, the fever had passed.

Xandros, however, seemed worse each day. He did not eat, and took only a little water. On the third day I crawled into the bow cabin to find him lying awake, staring up at the sunlight streaming through the chinks in the deck above. I sat down beside him.

"Xandros," I said, "you must leave off this grieving."

He looked at me, eyes fierce in a face that was too thin, too honed. "It is my fault, don't you understand? I took her from her oaths. I led her from the place she was vowed to be. I brought the curse of the Lady of the Sea down upon her, and upon me!"

I looked at his face, and I saw that he believed it, but I felt no shadow upon us. Whatever wings Death had wrapped us in on the deeps, Her presence was gone now. "Ashterah's death was not your fault," I said.

"If I had not taken her from Byblos..."

"If you had not taken her from Byblos, the Achaians would have slain her for what she knew," I said. "This is what you told Neas. Was it a lie then?"

"No," he said, and looked away. "They might have. I shouldn't have told her anything."

"Perhaps not," I said, folding my legs and sitting beside him. "But if you had not asked Ashterah's aid, how would we have questioned the Shardana captain and found out what they planned? We needed her help. None of us speak Shardan."

Xandros rolled onto his side so that all I could see was the line of his ragged hair, his dirty chiton. "I don't know. All I know is that I have stolen Her priestess, and the Lady of the Sea has cursed me. Everyone I love..." He broke off, facing away from me, and I understood.

Xandros had been the one who did not grieve, who did not drink or fight, who did not weep or lament, who did not fling himself at his foes seeking death. Xandros was cool, steady. Xandros was reliable. Xandros was the one who never gave way to inconvenient emotion, piloting his ship through whatever weather, faithful to Neas in all things. And yet in less than a year his wife and daughters had been killed, his city lost, his friends gone. All that he had known before was gone forever. Kos had his sister and she him. Neas had his father and his son. Xandros had no one, save a foreign priestess met in a temple brothel, and even she had been taken.

I put my hand on his shoulder, and it was warm under my fingers. "Xandros, my friend," I said. "There is no curse upon you. Ashterah served the Lady of the Sea. It is the prerogative of the gods to stretch out their hands to their servants when they will, to call their handmaidens when they wish. If Ashterah was called by the Lady of the Sea, that is between Ashterah and Her Lady. You cannot take that upon yourself. It is not yours."

He was quiet.

"I know this," I said. "I know this as I know my name. And if my Lady should call me, it would have nothing to do with anyone else."

In Byblos they make the sacrifice with blood, I had heard. And it is not always the blood of a bird or a lamb. Ashterah knew this. And perhaps she did hear that call. Who can know such things?

I rubbed the tight line of his shoulder, hard muscles under sun-browned skin. I wanted to keep touching, far, far too much, but I stopped. "Come, Xandros," I said. "Come on deck in the air."

He shook his head, but I drew him by the hand. When he sat up, his eyes were wide and he clutched at my sleeve.

"Are you light-headed?" I asked.

He nodded.

"I shouldn't wonder," I said. "You haven't eaten in

nearly four days, or drunk more than a little. Come on deck, in the light, and drink some water."

"I don't..." he said.

"You must come," I said. "Kos is going to name and accept the baby. You are his captain, and must stand in for his kin as witness. You will offend the truest man of your company if you do not." I was harsh, but he frightened me. It had been too long with only a little water.

I thought he would refuse, but he did not. I got him out onto the deck. The winds were blowing fresh and cool, and the sun was warm on the weathered planks. The sail was furled and we floated calmly among the other ships like so many seabirds resting on the waves. Southward, a green mass waited.

Under the high sun, Kos lifted the child high so that all might see her. It is a father's task, but one given to closest kin if there is no other. Tia stood beside him.

"Her name is Kianna," Kos said, and drew her down against his chest.

For their sister, I thought. *The one whose fate would be forever unknown.*

Kos held the baby in one arm, and his other arm went about Tia's shoulders. Xandros crossed the deck in a few steps, only a little unsteady. "Congratulations, my friend," he said, clasping Kos' hand. Then he bent and kissed Tia's brow in a gesture that seemed oddly like Neas. "Your daughter is beautiful. May the sun rise many times on her long and happy life."

I knew then. I had a word for the thing that leaped inside me, pure and sweet. I thought my heart would break at the grace of him, black hair shining like a raven's wing, bending with a gentle smile over this little girl who lived while his own daughters were offal for the kites. I knew. And I knew what was not mine.

Unobtrusively, I went and fetched water. I brought it to him while he talked with Kos, and he drank without thinking, only looking around at the second swallow.

"Sit," I said, gesturing to the rower's bench. "Sit while you talk."

The baby was squirming, and Tia sat down too, so that she could put her to the breast. In the bright sun I could look at the child more clearly. She was not, in fact, entirely bald. Her head was covered with soft faint fuzz that might be reddish gold when it grew. Her eyes, now squinched up with bliss as she nursed, were a cool gray-blue, like storm clouds far out to sea. Her fingers where she kneaded were long and white, and without much baby flesh on her, the line of her jaw was sharp and clear under skin like cream. Xandros was right, I thought. She is indeed a beautiful child. And if we can get her there, a beautiful woman.

I remembered the dream I had had, huddled with Tia in our first days out of Pylos. The slope of young olive trees with the river beyond, My Lady speaking to me from a face framed by red-gold hair, a girl with long freckled hands. *But where is that place?* I wondered. *Lady, help me find the place, and I will find You the priestess.*

At nightfall Neas went ashore with some of his men. He was back before dawn. I came on deck in the gray light to hear him talking with Xandros. "We must go somewhat to the east," he said, "to the harbor of Tamiat. The peasants who live among the reeds say that is where the great lords are."

"We need a port," Xandros said.

Although our ships did not require deep water, they

were not meant for the meandering channels and mudflats of this coast. Even standing off a bow shot, I could smell the dank rich greenness of it, the thousand mouths of the Nile making their way into the sea through thick stands of trees and reeds. There must be some larger channel where the river was broader, I thought. And a port.

Neas gave his captains orders, and as Jamarados and Xandros hastened to carry them out he beckoned me to the rail. He looked out toward the lowering coast and did not speak.

"My prince?" I prompted.

He was quiet, as though putting off some difficult question. "Strange, isn't it?" he said.

"Yes," I agreed, propping my elbows on the rail beside his. It was like nothing I had seen before. Somewhere in the predawn darkness was the call of a bird I did not know.

"And yet not strange," Neas said. He was silent for a long moment, and we watched the stars of night setting into the sea. "I do not speak of these things to the others, because they will think me god-touched, which isn't always a good thing in a captain." He looked at me sideways and smiled.

"They do not mind calling you the Beloved of the Lady of the Sea," I said.

"Ah, but that's different," he said, "when they mean it for a luck piece. But you know how that story ends, Her beloved, Her son." Neas raised one eyebrow.

"No, I can see that's not a comfortable comparison. Their touch can be both a blessing and a curse."

"Speaking of curses," he said, and I knew he was finally getting to the heart of the matter, "Xandros has told me that he lies under a curse. That the Sea Lady has condemned him for taking Her priestess."

"There is no curse!" I exclaimed, dashing my hand from the rail. "Xandros is sick with grieving, but there is no immortal hand in this."

"Are you certain?" Neas asked. "You know I cannot afford a captain who lies under Her displeasure, not with so many lives entrusted to him."

"There is no curse," I said. "Does it take a curse, my prince, for a boy who has never set foot on a ship to fall overboard in a storm?" I looked him squarely in the eye. "Are not men lost in severe storms all the time, without a curse involved? And they are sailors, men who are accustomed to the movement of the ship. For a boy who has never been afloat before, a misstep hardly requires divine intervention."

I saw the set of his shoulders relax. "That is true. She should not have been on deck at all, but Xandros said she wanted to see."

And she had not the blood of the Sea People in her veins, I thought, the steadiness that has been mine from the moment I set foot on a ship. It requires but a moment's inattention to lean on the rail, perhaps nauseous or dizzy, and be swept overboard. Perhaps it was merely an accident.

Neas smiled. "Well then, if there is no curse, then Xandros must do his duty. He has offered me his sword back. I will not take it. I need him on *Dolphin*, where he belongs. And we will run up the coast to Tamiat and see how Pharaoh will appreciate our news."

*   *   *

Pharaoh was not in Tamiat, of course. Egypt is a mighty kingdom, many times vaster than all of Achaia together, and the great Nile cuts through it south to north. From the mouths of the Nile it is several weeks' journey upriver to where the Nile rises from the vaults of the Underworld at Elephantine. Pharaoh, who was the third Ramses by name, ruled from the city of Thebes a long distance to the south. Tamiat was ruled by a vizier, who spoke in his stead.

This vizier seemed an able man to Neas, and grasped the situation immediately. Either Neas spoke the truth, in which case the kingdom stood in peril, or he was a false messenger, sent by these same sea raiders to cause Egypt to move the fleet and open a path for the pirates who would follow. In our favor was the condition of our fleet, and the number of women and children who would not, in the course of things, be a part of any raiding party. To our detriment stood that none knew us, and why should we not be part of this conspiracy we claimed?

The vizier took a middle path, neither believing nor disbelieving us. He sent fast scout ships hurrying north to Ashkelon, there to wait and see if there was indeed a pirate fleet. Other ships he held in readiness in Tamiat, while some others he sent south with us to the great city of Memphis. They would escort us up the Nile to the capital of Lower Egypt, where we might carry our news to Pharaoh's most trusted deputy, the Princess Basetamon, his sister. There she would hear what we would say, and there, not incidentally, we would be far from the coast and unable to break free if it turned out that we were treacherous.

So it was that we began to sail up one of the greatest

mouths of the Nile in company of ten Egyptian warships. At first, the river was narrow and shallow, flowing between overhanging trees and vines, choked with reeds along the edges so that it was impossible to tell where the water ended and land begun. Lotus blossoms scented air already thick with swamp smells. Now and again a startled duck would erupt into flight, and herons fished in the shallows.

So too did the crocodiles. One passed by *Dolphin*'s side, fully as long as a man, eyeing Tia and her child at the rail with one reptilian eye. I was reminded, suddenly, of Mik-el's story. I could easily see why evil would take the shape of a crocodile to these people, and I wondered if this was where he had been born, long ago in the dawn of the world.

On the second day the river broadened and the growth along the banks thinned. We saw farms now, men working in fields of barley, getting the harvest in, women bent over picking beans from bright green vines. There were no olive trees. There were no almonds either, or any kind of tree that I was used to, except figs that grew close beside houses, planted for their fruit. Fishing boats scurried out of our way on the river, too numerous to count. Barges waited to carry the harvest.

At a time when Kos had the tiller, Xandros came forward to stand with me at the prow. "Do you see what I do?" he asked, nodding toward a village beside us on the bank. A boy mother-naked was tending geese, staring out at our fleet, his stick in his hand. Behind, smoke rose from the village bakery, spiraling up into the still sky.

"See what?" I asked.

"None of them are walled," he said. "Not so much as a mud brick. It's not just the meanest villages that are unfortified. Look at the towns. They have no walls between their houses and fields, and the fields come right down to the river."

"That must be what Neoptolemos heard," I said. "No wonder he thinks it ripe pickings."

"Who has heard of such a thing!" Xandros said. "Towns without walls? Children who stare at strangers with no fear that one of us will put an arrow to the bow?"

"People who have known peace," I said. "Long years of peace. Long enough that war is something you go to, not something that comes to you." I leaned forward, looking out over the river. "There is strength in this land like I have never seen, its vastness and its quiet. Their gods are strong. And their people have not been afraid in many lives of men."

Xandros shook his head. "Then may their gods help them if Neoptolemos comes! I doubt there is a good sword among these villagers, not one among twenty men."

I felt Her hand at my back like a whisper of wind. *This is what peace looks like. You cannot find it if you have never seen it, child of war, child of the People.*

And so I watched them. I rose with the sun and watched them begin their day. I saw the priests of small temples raising their arms to the sun, the laborers going about their work, the women coming down to the water to fill their jars. Some paused to watch our craft go by, black painted among the light, lateen-sailed river boats, not brightly painted like the Egyptian war galleys. But none ran in fear to hide their families and their goods. They were curious, not afraid.

This is peace.

*   *   *

ANOTHER DAY and the mouths of the Nile rejoined, and I saw why it is called the mightiest river in the world. From one bank the other retreated into distance, almost as though we were at sea. Broad and smooth and flawless between its banks, it flowed unceasing, without any of the hitches or rocks that had been in every other river I had seen. Sometimes there were shallows, where crocodiles lay on sandbanks a hand span beneath the water, only the bumps and ridges of the tops of their heads showing.

The river traffic increased—reed boats like circular baskets big enough for one man only, poling along the banks, barges under fifty oars, galleys moving swiftly upstream, their slanted sails tilted to catch the following wind. It was the custom for southbound traffic to hug the right-hand side and northbound traffic the left. It seemed strange to me at first, until I realized that if we were all intermingled there would surely be accidents and larger craft overrunning lesser ones. As it was, the smaller boats stuck close to the bank, while the largest and fastest took the center of the river.

And so we came to Memphis.

If I had thought Pylos great as a girl, I had been disabused of that notion when I saw Millawanda. If I had thought Millawanda busy, I had not yet seen Byblos. And if I had thought Byblos fair, it was only because I had never looked on Memphis. I tell you that there is no more beautiful city, nor will be to the world's ending, though Egyptians swear that her beauties are nothing besides those of Thebes, with the vast Great House of the God and the Great House of Pharaoh vying for pride of place. I have not seen Thebes. Yet I find it hard to imagine how any city could be as lovely as Memphis.

Her streets were broad and paved with white stone, tall date palms waving in every breeze. Beyond her broad houses and bright temples the fields were green with harvest, every crop ripe and ready. As though divided by a knife, the greenery ended in desert, so that one might stand with one foot on irrigated fields and the other on sand. Yellow hills rose gently, and beyond some little way what appeared to be the shadow of three perfectly even mountains, all beneath a sky of such piercing blue that I knew what the artists were thinking of when they colored blue faience. It was a pale copy of the sky.

We were lodged very courteously in longhouses of mud brick that belonged to the soldiers of the Division of the Ram. Unlike all peoples I had met, the Egyptians had men who did nothing but soldier, season after season, year after year, as though it were a trade they had taken up. Villagers and craftsmen knew no more of the sword than fishermen knew of the plow. Rather than have the great lords, the Nomes, bring men of their household to war, they all paid taxes to the maintenance of the soldiers of the crown, who were organized in groups with various names.

Just then the Division of the Ram was away from Memphis, ordered to some place or another to help with the harvest. It happened that way most harvest times, I heard. They should be ordered where there was surplus, so that food did not go to waste, and they returned with provision that was then set out for public use, either to feed the army or some other town or village where the crops had failed.

The barracks were one story and built of sturdy mud brick, cool in the hot days and warm at night, with well-dug privies and a broad courtyard that looked upon the river and a dock. Our ships were moored there. We came ashore at last and we divided ourselves out among the buildings. It did not look like home, but it was clean and cool, and it seemed the best we could do.

Lide washed out Neas' finest clothes as soon as we landed. "He'll need them soon," she said, spreading them to dry in the sun. "He's to have an audience with that princess." She sniffed, which showed clearly what she thought of a woman about men's business.

I took off my black tunic and washed it out, and the veil as well. If there was to be an audience, I must be ready as well. If Pharaoh's representative was his sister and thus a woman, perhaps the Egyptians would not object to my presence or find it strange, as indeed men did in Millawanda and Byblos. As I spread them to dry I looked at them with some embarrassment. The dye had faded from true black to a rusty brown, and they were rent and torn with hard wear. I should look like a beggar, but there was no better among us. But at least I still had my paints.

Before the afternoon was out, Neas was calling for his clothes and for me. The Princess Basetamon had sent two litters and required Neas to wait upon her immediately. I went, and Xandros and Jamarados, the two captains who were the most capable in dealing with foreigners.

I sat beside Neas in a litter of cypress wood, looking out through curtains of linen drawn so fine that they were almost sheer, carried by four tall dark-skinned men so alike in appearance they might have been brothers. Their heads were all shaved alike and their bodies gleamed with scented oil.

I exchanged a glance with Neas. Either he was being

received as a prince indeed, or these people were simply wealthy beyond our imaginings.

It was the latter. When we reached the palace we were made to wait in an antechamber for some while, as there were many people on business with the princess and this was some sort of court day, when she heard petitions. The chamber where we waited was five times the height of a man, and every inch of walls and massive pillars were alive with carvings and with the beautiful colored writing that they make in Egypt. Above, the ceiling itself was bordered with dark blue, and in the center the sun rode gilded with real gold. There was a fountain of clear water, and a maidservant who came and washed our hands and arms with a golden ewer lest we bring the dust of the street into the royal presence.

After some little time a man came to us. His head was bald and he was quite old, dressed in a long skirt of pleated linen, with a staff in hand and a leopard skin draped across his left shoulder and wizened chest. To our astonishment he greeted us in the tongue of Wilusa.

"Be welcome to the Great House of the Black Land, Prince of the Windy Towers," he said, his voice only slightly accented. "I am Hry, a Priest of Thoth, who is master of all learning. In a few moments you will go before Princess Basetamon, She Who Speaks with Pharaoh's Voice in Memphis, Beloved of Amon. I will speak your words to her in Khemet, which is the tongue that the Gods have given to the people of the Black Land."

"You speak our tongue well," Neas said. "I have not heard it so well spoken in any land."

The priest's dark eyes twinkled. "Many years ago I traveled the world, seeking knowledge as Thoth himself did. I traveled in many lands and came at last to Wilusa, the City of the Windy Towers, where I sat at the hearth of Priam and heard new tales. Are you his kin, Prince Aeneas?"

Neas' hesitation was so brief that perhaps no one but I would have seen it. "I am his grandson," Neas said, "and the last of his house. My mother was Lysisippa, his oldest daughter."

Hry smiled. "I remember her indeed, Prince Aeneas. She was a beautiful young girl, a maiden intended for the service of some goddess. She had your eyes and your hair, yes, the same look to her face, though not your carriage and she was not tall."

"My father was a tall man," Neas said. "Anchises the son of Capys. He is here with us, and lives yet."

Hry shook his head. "I do not believe I knew him."

And how should he, I thought? Anchises is ten years Lysisippa's junior. He should have been a crawling child on the floor when Lysisippa was a maiden.

"I shall also instruct you in how things are done in the court," he said. "As you are in our land, we shall expect you to make due reverence."

Neas nodded. "We should not wish to offend in any way. It is wise for travelers to heed the laws and customs of their hosts, and to honor the gods of that place in due fashion."

"Ah, you are indeed Lysisippa's son!" Hry said, the corners of his eyes crinkling in his ancient face. "I have never seen a child so hungry for stories of other places, so full of interest in the gods and customs of others! Were she a daughter of Egypt she should have been a dedicant at the Great Temple, but her gifts were recognized there and she was to be sent to service at a great shrine, so did the worth of her shine forth! That is one of the maxims of Thoth, if you did not know." He thought for a moment, translating the words in his head. "A lamp shines out like the sun if you put it under a basket."

"If I had a lamp," Neas said, "I should not put it under a basket."

Hry looked at him for a moment and then laughed. "I see that you should not, Prince Aeneas. For is this not one such that you have brought with you?" He looked at me and I truly saw him, old man of an old people, and the ibis shape that surrounded him, eyes as keen as the skies.

I lowered my head in reverence. "Holy one," I said. "We wait upon your grace."

He raised my chin with one crabbed hand, and I heard Neas shift his feet nervously. "You I would talk to further, Maiden of Nepthys."

"Nepthys?" I asked.

"That is what we name the wife of the Lord of the Red Land here," he said.

"The Red Land?" I asked.

Neas cleared his throat. "The audience?" he said. "The fleet that's planning to burn Egypt? Perhaps the two of you can talk about the gods later?"

Hry laughed. "A true son of Horus, this one! Very well, we will leave off talking of our trade."

He led us into the audience chamber in due turn.

It was a very great hall, with pillars carved in the shape of lotus blossoms to hold up the ceiling. Nobles stood among them, bright as flowers in a field, their dyed linens and starched white skirts gleaming, gold glinting at their throats, on their arms, at their ears, and even on the thongs of their sandals. At the end of the hall was a stone dais, and on a chair of carved ebony wood sat the princess. Her gown was green, caught up beneath her breasts, and a massive collar of gold and malachite covered her chest and her breasts. Her hair was black and held in many plaits, each one dressed with beads of gold and malachite. At one side stood a slave with a plume of great iridescent feathers, and on her other side stood another with a cheetah on a chain. It was the first time that I had seen one of those great cats. It waited patiently sitting on its hindquarters, and could have been carved and painted except for the faint twitch of its ears.

Then I saw no more, for we bowed low, Jamarados and Xandros behind us. Hry was talking, translating Neas' words into Khemet. The princess spoke, and her voice was melodious. "You may rise," Hry said.

Her eyes were on Neas' face, and I saw that beneath the green paint over her brows they were brown, a faint wrinkle beginning between them. A woman of twenty-five or more, old enough for the responsibility her brother entrusted to her.

Hry was translating her questions, how many ships and of what kinds, sailors from which lands, how many oars to each. As Neas told her what we had seen in Byblos, she gestured to the side. A heavy middle-aged man wearing nothing but a white skirt and gold bracelets came forward and sat on the steps to her chair, bringing forth papyrus and a stylus that he dipped in some dark liquid. Straightaway he began scratching on it, and I realized that he was recording the numbers Neas gave, the descriptions of ships and their men.

The princess asked many questions. Neas answered

them all. I could see that he was impressed with her thoroughness, with her knowledge of war. She did not look at me after that initial glance, nor toward Jamarados and Xandros. We were not important. We were a part of Neas' trappings, as the patient cat was part of hers.

It seemed long that she questioned him, and the papyrus was traded for a second piece before she ended.

Hry turned to us. "The Beloved of Amon, She Who Speaks with Pharaoh's Voice in Memphis, bids you to return to your folk. You are all guests here, and you have Pharaoh's gratitude for your good service. She will speak with you further in a few days. In the meantime, the Royal Guard shall provide you with fresh rations, and you have the freedom of the city. However, your ships must stay moored, as I am sure you understand."

"I do," Neas said. "And tell Her Majesty that I appreciate her benevolence." He inclined his head, and I saw her brown eyes follow him. Then we left the hall with Hry. And thus we came to Egypt. But whether we were guests or prisoners remained to be seen.

THE BLACK LAND

That night I slept on land, or rather tried to sleep. It had been so long since Byblos, since I slept without *Dolphin*'s rolling beneath me, that when I lay down on my pallet in the barracks near Tia and her child I could not sleep. It seemed that the floor moved oddly beneath me. When I opened my eyes it stopped, but as soon as I closed them again it moved. I realized what else was missing—Xandros' quiet breath, sleeping or not sleeping as he brooded on the curse. I had not dared to leave him alone with the humor that had been on him.

Perhaps I was wakeful because he was alone now. I sat up.

But surely he would do nothing foolish. And he was sharing a room with half a dozen men. It wasn't as though he could cut his wrists with no one noticing.

Ah, but surely Xandros would not try such a thing in a room with his men, some other part of me said. If he got up and went out they would merely think he went to the privies. No one would follow him.

I got up and went out into the cool Egyptian night. I crossed the courtyard, the white stones still warm from the day's sun, walking toward the dock. The moon was high, making a path across the river. And I was not surprised to see Xandros there.

He turned when he heard my steps and waited. There was no knife in his hand or anywhere else I could see. He simply waited, as though we had arranged to meet.

"Can't sleep?" he asked.

"No," I said. "It feels strange to sleep on land."

"For me too," he said.

Downriver a little ways the docks of the palace were bright with torches, and several painted boats sat ready, their oarsmen visible in the light of the lamps on their prows. They waited, dicing and eating, for the great nobles to come out and be rowed home from some royal banquet or other. A little farther on, a swift scout ship was being prepared. It pushed off from the dock and started off downriver, back toward Tamiat, toward the sea.

"Did she believe us, do you think?" Xandros asked.

"I think so," I said. "But I do not know. It's hard to know the inflection and tenor of questions in a language I don't know. If I spoke Khemet, I would know. Perhaps I had better learn."

"You could learn Khemet," he said.

"I could." A thought half formed wormed its way to the surface, bursting into flower as a desire as though I had always wanted it. "I could learn to read."

Xandros looked at me. "I believe you could," he said slowly. "I hadn't thought a woman could, but if any could it would be you."

"It would," I said.

We stood there in silence awhile longer, watching the moon rising white and clear. It cast our shadows behind us, two of a kind, dark against the pale stones.

I glanced back to the rooms where Neas slept. I wondered if he sprawled in sleep, abandoned as a child, or if his discipline held even there, the knowledge that he must behave as a prince. I did not know, and of course I never would.

"Ah," said Xandros softly. "You too."

I looked at him quickly. His face was still and thoughtful. "Yes," I said. "And you?"

He gave me his own rueful sideways smile. "Always."

"For how long?" I asked.

"Forever," Xandros said. "Since we were boys together."

"Has anything ever come of it?" I asked gently.

"He's a prince and I'm a fisherman," Xandros said. "Of course not. But he is my captain, and will be as long as I live."

"He is a prince, but you are the captain of a warship, his most trusted captain," I said carefully. "And you are his friend. Surely that makes a difference."

"Do you think so?" Xandros said. "I don't. We both know who we are." He looked out over the river. "We should sleep."

"We should."

"It's not so easy with Kos snoring," he said. "Or Bai rolling around and mumbling."

"I see that," I said. The night was living and strange. Xandros had said enough, and he wanted to say no more.

"I was going to go sleep on *Dolphin,*" he said. "Do you want to come? If sleeping on land is difficult, I mean."

"I could," I said. We stepped over onto the familiar planks, went below to the bow cabin, quiet and tiny and empty. I rolled up in Tia's good wool blanket, left here no doubt in the heat of the afternoon when a wool blanket seemed really unnecessary. Xandros lay down behind me. I could almost feel his warmth against my back, and I wanted to curl against him. I knew better, but I could not make myself move away. So I lay there, not quite touching him.

I heard him move, hesitantly. I almost felt his hand brush against my hair. Would he touch me? And what would I do if he did?

Xandros stilled. I listened as his breathing grew slow and steady, drifting away into sleep with the soft lapping of the river at the posts of the dock, the faint creak of the ship.

At least one question was answered this night, I thought. I knew that I wanted him to touch me, wanted to sleep against him, as near as breath. No man had ever desired me, no man that I would have. It seemed more than cruel to desire Xandros son of Markai above all other men.

I lay awake listening to him sleeping as long as I could.

WE WAITED and we waited. No word came from the palace. Neas paced up and down the dock, Jamarados beside him, counting days upon his fingers.

"Listen, Neas," he said. "It's at least four days from Tamiat to Ashkelon, and probably more with the wind dead foul. They'd have to go under oar the whole way, so a week or ten days more like. And then four days back to Tamiat, and four more up the Nile to Memphis. That's if they found Neoptolemos in Ashkelon when they came, and we know he didn't sail straight on our heels. They were waiting on more ships and on a break in the weather. So eighteen days from when we left Tamiat at best. That's still two days to run. And probably we won't hear anything for a week or two beyond that."

Neas sighed. "I know."

"We wait," Jamarados said. "That's all we can do."

I could not. On the second day after that I went alone to the Temple of Thoth. It is part of the complex of the Great Temple, one small part of that vast section of buildings and courtyards. The temple here was as large as many cities.

I wandered through the public courtyards, trying to find my way. At last I saw the statue of ibis-headed Thoth, and thought I knew where I was. Two door wardens stood before the gates, staves in their hands. I went to them and tried to ask for Hry with gestures and his name. They shook their heads gravely at me.

A young man with a shaven head came to the gate, and they opened it for him while he began some conversation with them, presumably asking what I came for. "Hry, Hry," I said.

He nodded and again made an incomprehensible response, then went inside. In a few minutes he returned with another man, this one wearing a white skirt and a leopard skin across his chest as Hry had. He spoke some words to me with Hry in it.

I gestured again, trying to indicate Hry's height and manner. Surely they must know him, as old and respected as he was.

The young man said something to the elder that I did not understand, save one word, "Wilosat."

"Wilosat?" I said. That must be Wilusan, either the person or the tongue. I patted my throat. "Wilosat?"

The elder priest spoke again and went back inside. In a moment Hry returned with him.

"Ah, the Maiden of Nepthys!" he said, a smile splitting his face. "I am pleased that you have sought me out!"

"I'm sorry, Hry," I said, "if I have inconvenienced you. I wasn't very good at making myself understood, though I asked for you by name."

The old man laughed. "Hry is not my name, child. It's my title. I suppose in your language the nearest words would be He Who Reads. I am one of the priests who have charge of the texts, both sacred and secular, and we are all addressed as Hry. My own personal name is He Who Walks with the Sunlight of Amon." He took my arm. "Come, let us go in out of the sun. There is a shaded courtyard within that is a better place to talk."

It was, in fact, a lovely place. Four date palms surrounded a rectangular pool. Lilies floated on the water. A stone bench stood at each end, where the shade of one palm would cover it in the morning and the shade of the other would do the same in the afternoon.

Hry sat down beside me and stretched out his legs

with a sigh. "So why have you sought me out, Daughter of Wilusa?"

"I want to learn to speak Khemet," I blurted out. "And I want to learn to read."

He looked at me and all laughter was gone from his face. "Why do you want these things?"

"Because it is useful. Because it will help my prince. And because I want to know," I said. "Is it forbidden?"

"No, surely not," Hry said. "In the Black Land there are many women who read. And how could we forbid sailors to learn our language?" He looked at me keenly. "So that is the plunder you would have of Egypt."

"We do not seek plunder, as Your Reverence knows," I said.

Hry smiled. "Everyone who comes to Egypt is seeking some treasure. Everyone who sees our wealth wants some part of the beauty that is ours. Some, like this Neoptolemos you name, want to steal gold and ivory with his sword. Some, like your prince, I think, do not yet know what they seek. And you? You have come searching for the greatest treasure of all. What is it you really want, Maiden of Nepthys?"

I met his eyes, and answered as though he were She Who Had Been Pythia, the words tumbling from my lips. "I want to know everything. I want to know how the clouds move and why islands fall into the sea. I want to know how to plant almond trees and how to make children grow up straight and healthy. I want to know how princes should govern and why people love. I want to understand the stars in the heavens and all the words that were ever made. I want to remember every story that was ever told."

"You want," Hry said, "to be a god."

"No." I was startled. "No, I don't mean…"

He nodded. "Yes, you do. You yearn after knowledge as our *ba* yearns after the sun, following it beyond the western hills into the world below. These are things we know in sleep or in death, that dream that is beyond awakening. Knowledge sits at the foot of the throne of Isis, where beside Her husband, Osiris, She judges the dead."

"I am Death's handmaiden," I said. "I serve the Lady of the Dead."

"Isis then," he said. "Not Nepthys. Do you know Her story?"

"No," I replied.

Hry shifted on the bench. "I will tell it to you then, you who want to know all the stories ever told. I will teach you Khemet. And reading. This is the House of Thoth, who is master of all learning. No one who desires knowledge as you do is ever turned away, for we reverence all learning, no matter its source, even if it comes clothed as the maiden of a foreign goddess in scraps of black linen."

I looked down at my threadbare tunic and felt the color rise in my face. "Master Hry," I said, "I would not come before you clothed in rags except for the dangers of our journey. It is not disrespect, only that I have nothing else."

He raised an eyebrow. "Has the princess not sent clothing to you? Or anything else that you might need?"

"She has sent some food," I said. "A generous amount of grain and beans. I think she is waiting to see if we are lying or not."

"You are not lying," Hry said. "I know Wilusa of old, prideful and bold. If you come in such desperate straits it is because you are in desperate peril. I believe Prince Aeneas."

I felt tears start in my eyes. I had not realized how afraid I was that we were not believed.

"She is cautious, as befits a ruler. When word comes from Ashkelon, she will believe and you will be honored," he said.

I did not say that in other lands caution was not much respected in a ruler. The People love above all else boldness, even above courage and honor. It is the fleet of foot, the daring, the impulsive we love—Prince Alexandros who carried off the Achaian queen and gave insult to her husband's powerful family—this same prince who was Neas' half uncle. We should rather go down in songs than live, I think. And perhaps that is exactly what we have done.

Egypt was not like that. Egypt was old. And caution was much valued, caution and deliberation. I feared that this time it would not serve them, not against the swift and the jealous.

I understood now why Neoptolemos wanted to raid Egypt. So much wealth so lightly defended is a tremendous temptation. But more than that, I could see why men's hearts would be moved to jealousy, the envy of things they did not understand, of luxuries they had not imagined. I had seen the markets. Ordinary women shopped unveiled, their ears adorned with bronze posts washed with gold. Ordinary shops sold mirrors, scented oils, even the expensive myrrh resin that She Who Had Been Pythia had treasured most of all. The streets were clean and swept. The markets were full of fish, grain, fruit, and every good thing, and even the meanest seemed to have bread.

Hry was twenty years Anchises' senior, and he was hearty and hale. He told me that in Egypt it was no great thing to live three score years, and that there were many men who lived a decade beyond that. We reckon a man old at forty, and Anchises was not fifty yet. Who would not want to seize the treasures of Egypt—long life, plentiful food, luxuries that we reserve for kings in the hands of common folk?

I heard Her at my elbow then. *It is easier to destroy than to build, easier to harvest than to sow and tend. The work of generations can be destroyed in an hour's fire, the building of a century destroyed in a summer's war. A child takes ten moons to come into the world, fifteen years to raise, and can be killed in a moment. They cannot steal the treasures of Egypt because they do not understand how to keep them. What use to steal the harvest, if they kill those who plow the fields? There will be no grain next year. What use to fire the olive trees? Will they then fruit for the conquerors?*

"Maiden?" Hry said, touching my arm. "Are you all right?"

"How shall I raise dead men to plow fields that are fallow?" I said, and they were the words of She Who Had Been Pythia. "How can I restore what is lost? So much is lost, and we are so few."

Hry took my hand. "My dear girl, I do not know. That is in the hands of Mighty Isis, not in mine. But I promise you this, for the sake of my guest-friends in windswept Wilusa, for the sake of Lysisippa and Priam as well, if there is any knowledge in Thoth's halls that will help you, it will be yours."

I looked at him and saw that his old eyes were watery. "Thank you," I said. "Thank you so very much."

AND SO I began what seemed to be my second apprenticeship. Each morning I went to the Temple of Thoth from sunrise until the sun stood straight overhead and I learned. Hry taught me words of Khemet, showing me how to hold my mouth to shape their sounds. As he did, he showed me the symbols that they draw and how each might sound—word and symbol together, ox and ox, water and water, life and life.

And he told me stories. He told me how Osiris and Set were brothers, and how Set betrayed His brother and killed Him, how Isis searched through the swamps of the Delta for the scattered parts of His body, searching by moonlight in the dark waters.

Hry took me into the temple, into the parts that were permissible, and I watched them robe the statue of Isis in clean linen and anoint Her with oil. Afterward, I knelt with the others during the hymns, and came forward to touch my forehead to the hem of Her skirt.

Later, sitting beneath the date palm with Hry, I rubbed the scented oil from my forehead. "What is this fragrance?" I asked, breathing deeply between my hands. "It's the most amazing thing I've ever smelled. It's like all the flowers in the world."

Hry smiled. "It's the essence of roses. They are flowers that grow in the Land of Two Rivers, in what was Mittani and the Hittite lands. They use it there to anoint kings. We use it to anoint gods."

IN THE AFTERNOONS I returned to the barracks where the People lived. There was food enough, but little to do. Neas paced and had the same conversations with his captains over and over. Jamarados went abroad in the city, making trades as he could. Xandros did not, but I was not surprised. At night, I slept beside him on *Dolphin,* chaste as a child beside its mother, chaste as though he were my kinsman. Even so, it was something to listen to his breathing, to talk quietly when sleep did not come. If I wished for more I knew better than to ask for it.

ON THE FOURTEENTH DAY after our audience a messenger came for Neas, bidding him to attend on the Princess Basetamon immediately. We went, Neas and I, Jamarados and Xandros, with Hry to interpret, in the same state as before.

In the litter I could feel the muscles in Neas' thigh jumping with nerves. He smiled at me grimly. "If it goes badly, stay behind me and Xandros. We'll try to fight our way clear."

"You are mad," I said, thinking of the massed spearmen and archers.

Neas grinned at that. "Yes," he said, and bent and kissed me.

His lips were warm and soft, tasting of olive oil and bread, brushing against mine for one long, endless moment.

And then I looked up at him in utter shock. I had not thought, I had not dared imagine such a thing. Well, perhaps I had, months ago, but with the grief for his wife on him I had put it from my mind. I should have said something. I should have reached for him, perhaps. But I did nothing.

His smile faded. "I don't know why I did that," he said.

"Nor do I," I said. In trying not to sound giddy I sounded instead peevish.

"Mad, I suppose," he said. "You told me so." His blue eyes flicked to mine, then away.

"I did," I said. Warm, so warm, soft golden stubble on his chin. The closed curtains of the litter gave the illusion of privacy.

"I should know better," he said. "I won't do it again."

"No, I expect not," I said. I hoped he did not hear the disappointment in my voice.

Outside the bearers shifted, lowering the litter in the courtyard of the palace.

"Luck?" Neas said.

"You don't need luck," I said. "The gods know you were telling the truth."

"Truth needs twice as much luck as falsehood," he said, giving me a cocky grin as he opened the curtains and stepped out.

WE CAME INTO THE HALL immediately this time, and there were no other petitioners. Hry walked before us, and he gave me a grave nod.

Kneeling on one knee to the princess' left was a young

man about Xandros' age, clad in a short white skirt and the striped head cloth that soldiers wear over his shaved head. His upper arm was encircled by a broad band of reddish gold.

Hry began to interpret as the princess spoke. "Hear now the words of Ephi, Captain of the scout ship *Greatness,* which took up Pharaoh's commission to investigate the truth of the words of these Denden."

In pieces we heard the story. The vizier of Tamiat had sent three scout ships under the command of his youngest son to go to Ashkelon and see if we told the truth. They reached Ashkelon after nine days of poor weather and saw nothing out of the ordinary, whereupon the vizier's son said that if he were commanding a pirate fleet he would certainly not be out in this weather, but rather waiting still in Byblos for the weather to break. It seemed to be clearing, so he ordered them to sail up the coast toward Byblos. Two days later they sighted a hundred ships at sea, some of them still setting forth from Byblos, all of them warships and southbound. The fleet of the Sea People saw them, and ten heavy warships separated immediately to engage them.

At this the vizier's son knew that all we had said was true. He shouted to his captains to make all possible speed and run downwind as quickly as possible, running for Ashkelon or for Egypt. This young captain had commanded the last boat, the one farthest in the rear. He had immediately put about and run. He had seen first the other ship, then that of the vizier's son overtaken. One had been hit with fire arrows and burned to the waterline. The ship of the vizier's son had been rammed and boarded.

"We rowed with all our might," he said. "The wind was at our backs if we turned out across the sea instead of hugging the coast, fair for Tamiat. We did not try to make Ashkelon, just ran straight for Egypt, leaving our friends to die." I heard the note of grief in his voice, even in Khemet, heard his voice choke in his throat. "We have brought Pharaoh word, as we were ordered. The Sea People are coming upon us with two hundred ships or more, with all the people of the isles."

I understood enough Khemet now to understand some of what the princess said as she turned to her scribe, though Hry spoke her words that we might understand.

"Take this message for the Son of Ra, my brother, Ramses the Lion of Egypt. The Sea People have made conspiracy in their lands, the Akiawasha, the Meshwesh, the Peleset, the Tjekker, the Sheklesh, the Shardan of the Sea. All of them are in arms against us. They will come down on Egypt like a plague. I shall ready such ships as we have here and send them to Tamiat, where I shall go myself, and we shall await Pharaoh's arrival."

She turned then to us, and her eyes met Neas'. She spoke and waited for Hry to translate. "Prince of the Denden, you have done us great service. You have the gratitude of the Black Land. You say that they are enemies of yours who have already burned your homeland, leaving you with nothing but your ships. If we give to you all that you need to repair them, will you take service with us? Will you join us in battle against the Sea People? If you will take service with us, we will reward you generously, and give refuge to all your people. Surely strong and brave men such as you will soon earn much praise in Pharaoh's service, and I tell you that my brother is generous indeed to those who serve him well."

Neas did not hesitate. Though he spoke through Hry, his eyes were on the princess' face. "Great Lady, nothing would please us better than to take up arms against the Achaians and Neoptolemos, for the blood that lies between us is bitter indeed. We will do so with great joy, and will slay them in Pharaoh's service as well as for our own honor."

She rose then from her seat, the beads on her braids chiming softly as she moved, for they were wrought of pure gold. In her hands she lifted a broad gold armband, four fingers in width, chased with pictures of a lion hunt. She stepped forward, and taking Neas' left hand in hers, drew it onto his arm. "Take this, then, as token of your commission."

"I shall be faithful to your charge," Neas said, and he smiled into her eyes. "We will sail for Tamiat as soon as we may."

THEY SAILED in two days. In between there was constant running back and forth. Egyptian slaves brought vast quantities of rations, water, and beer. Most was for the ships, but much was for us on land as well. All of the women and children of the People, as well as a few old men like Anchises, would stay in Memphis, in the barracks of the Division of the Ram. We would not go into battle. Instead, the warships would be equipped as they should be, with fighting men.

The second day four score of archers arrived, lean dark men from the south of Egypt, armed with bows of wood and horn. Their arms were strong and well muscled, and their heads were shaved and gleamed in the sun. They moved as one man at their officer's command, bows at rest before them, each man the same distance from his neighbor. I had never seen such a thing.

Jamarados looked at them and smiled. "They're Nubian archers," he said to me. "Some of the finest fighting men in the world. They come from the great deserts, where a man is not reckoned such until he can shoot a vulture on the wing. They're going into battle on our ships, to stand on the decks and shoot at the enemy while we maneuver."

"Do they do that always?" I asked, as they stacked their bows in unison, each placing his quiver of arrows propped against it to the left. "Do everything together?"

"They're soldiers," Jamarados said. "They've trained for this since they were boys. Each morning they practice at butts in the hills above Memphis. I went to watch them a few days ago. They can fill a target the size of a man full of arrows in less time than it takes for me to take a breath. I suggested to Neas that he should ask the princess to let them come on our ships. They're spoiling for action, after all, and they can't swim to Tamiat."

I had thought that some men might object to Neas selling their swords, and said as much to Jamarados.

"Lady," he said, "you do not know fighting men. It was all Neas could do in Byblos to keep men from pursuing their honor fights with the Achaians, and none more so than Xandros. Do you think we forget our wives and families? Do you think we forget what we've lost? I don't think there's a man among us who isn't relieved to finally have a chance to get some back against the Achaians."

"Didn't you get some back in Pylos?" I asked. "Surely that counts for something."

"It does." He nodded. "But not enough. Neas knows the temper of his men best. Escorting convoys in exchange for goods is all very well, but this suits us better. I would ten times rather sell my sword to Egypt than be less than what we are. And when we've had some back, then we'll see what's next."

"I imagine you could remain in Pharaoh's service," I said.

Jamarados nodded. "We could. And not a bad thing. Better than Millawanda, certainly. The pay is better, and I hear from the Nubians that they award bonuses well. Good service and a fair master. Ramses is young, but he's well thought of. We could do worse than good service with a good king."

"We already have a king," I said. "Neas is our king."

Jamarados shrugged. "Neas says he's no king. And what has he got to be king of?"

What indeed? I wondered. As long as we had no city, we were not a kingdom, just a bunch of wandering ships searching for a refuge. Now that we seemed to have found one, what did I have to complain of?

Except perhaps being left behind.

I watched them sail at sunset on the second day. *Seven Sisters* went first, Neas at her helm, hair held back with a leather thong. He raised his fist in salute to the People on the dock, the westering sun glinting off Princess Basetamon's gold bracelet on his shoulder. A great shout rose, and my throat closed. Beauty beyond measure, glory beyond price. Whatever there was belonged to Neas, now and to world's end.

Dolphin was last. I stood with Tia, while Kos walked down the ship, singing the chant. Bai looked up from his oar and would have waved if his hands had been free. Xandros was at the tiller. His hair was loose on his shoulders, and his eyes looked far ahead, down the river.

Great Lady, I prayed, *if he goes seeking You I cannot stop him. I cannot stop him this time. I must leave him in Your care.*

Great Lady, protect these men I love.

☉N LAND
AND SEA

Three days later ten bearers arrived from the palace, bringing things for the People, part of the price of our lives and ships. They had copper pots for frying fish, heavy clay pots for cooking stews and pottages, a bag of salt and other foodstuffs, and ten bolts of linen. Most of it was white and of a moderate weight, but there were two bolts that were printed, one with a green pattern of fish, and one in brown with a pattern of lotus flowers. There was also one small bolt that was black, and I knew it was meant for me.

I was with the women in the courtyard beside the empty docks, watching as they divided up the foodstuffs and cloth, some seventy women and forty children, with five men who had remained because of age or infirmity.

Suddenly Lide's son came running along the riverbank, yelling at the top of his voice. "Look! Look!"

I ran to the dock.

Coming down the river from the south was a great

fleet. Egyptian galleys painted red and green crowded the river, their oars sweeping in perfect time. In their midst, painted with blue and gilded with gold, swept the largest ship I had ever seen, a great galley of sixty oars. Her sails were of white linen, and on her decks Nubian bowmen stood as though they were carved of wood. The sound of the drums came over the water, and the high sweet wailing of flutes. All along the shores of the river, people had run out to watch. As the ship came even with the city a great cheer went up.

Lide's son bounced up and down beside me. "Who is it?" he said. "Is it a god?"

"Almost," I said, my hand on his shoulder. "It's Pharaoh."

By now a procession had hastily assembled on the palace docks, nobles vying with one another for the best places. When the great galley came alongside the docks I could just make out the figure of Princess Basetamon before the press of the crowd intervened.

Ramses himself was impossible to mistake. A painted plank descended to the dock, and a dozen Nubian archers came down in single file, making a space between them at the bottom. I saw the sun flash on the golden serpent he wore bound to his brow, the uraeus, the symbol of kingship. Beneath the circlet that held the uraeus he wore a gold and blue head cloth rather than the twin crowns, a warrior king, like the second Ramses, or the legendary Thutmosis. The crowd cheered wildly.

Princess Basetamon came forward and bowed deeply. He raised her by the hand, and together, surrounded by the archers, they made their way into the palace, followed by all the multitude that had traveled on the king's ship.

Beside me someone sniffed. I looked and saw that it was Anchises.

"Aeneas was meant to be such a king as this," he said quietly.

"He does not wish to be a king," I said.

Anchises gave me a long look. "He was born to be king," he said. "It doesn't matter whether he wants it or not. The gods chose it for him, and chose him for us. Sybil, do not tell me that you of all people do not see it."

I looked away, out toward the river and the city. "I do," I said.

"I know that you do not like me. But remember this," he said. "All that I have done, I have done to make him king, for without him the People will die. And before I cross the River I would know that it has not been in vain."

The sunlight made streaks of fire on the river, glancing off ripples and flashing like flying sparks, as though one could strike sparks from water, cold and warm at once.

"He will be king," I said. "He will found a mighty house. A son yet unborn will rule a great city, and out of his line will come kings of men and nations. Many years will pass before these things happen, but it is so."

"It will not happen in Egypt?" Anchises said.

"No," I replied. The light on the water made my eyes tear, and Her hand was cold on my back. I could see the sparks flying upward, souls rising from the bottom of a deep well, rising into a golden sunbeam plunging through the dark. "It will be far from here, in a different land. He will carry the gods of Wilusa to a new home, and in that place they will bless him. He will plant young olive trees and plow fields that are fallow."

I staggered and almost fell. There is a reason why Sybil is supposed to sit.

Anchises caught my arm. When I looked in his face there was for the first time respect there. "Sit," he said gruffly. "Sit on the railing here."

I did. He brought me a cup of water. I looked at it. So simple, really. Fired clay, holding plain river water, a bit of sediment swirling in the bottom. The light flashed off the surface in the sun.

"You will not see this place," I said. "You will die on the sea."

"I don't need to see it," he said quietly. "I have seen it in your eyes."

I looked up at him, and saw for a moment what Lysisippa must have seen, a man fit to consort with the Lady of the Sea. It was not entirely from his mother's kin that Neas got his kingship.

"Thank you," I said.

He shrugged. His eyes were blue, and when he looked away from me for a moment he looked like Neas. "I'm too old to fear a prophecy about being lost at sea. Such things happen. It is my son and my grandson I fear for. You said that a son unborn would found this city."

I thought for a second, listening, though Her voice was faint to me again. "I do not think anything ill will happen to Wilos," I said carefully. "I don't see that. But I do see a brother. And what will come of that I do not know."

"That is in the hands of the gods," Anchises said piously, tipping out some water into the dust in libation.

*   *   *

THE NEXT DAY Pharaoh and all his fleet sailed northward, and the Princess Basetamon accompanied her
brother. With them went all the soldiers in Memphis. If
they did not engage the enemy, if Neoptolemos and his
men won through and came upriver, they would meet little
resistance. All the great lords had gone, the Nomes with
their chariots and their spearmen running beside. In the
few days that followed we saw them marching hastily
along, spending one night in Memphis with their men and
then going northward, southern lords coming after their
king from distant estates, late to the battle that was surely
by now joined in Ashkelon or on the sea. For ten days
they passed, company after company, and then they were
gone. All the men who would answer Pharaoh's summons
already had.

And the days passed.

It was spring, and the sailing season was begun. The
days grew longer, lengthening toward high summer. It
grew hotter still.

In the lands of Achaia or Wilusa the Feast of the Descent was past, and the Lady dwelled beneath the earth
with Her dark Lord. The olives would be ripening, the
grain would be cut.

Here, in Egypt, the harvest was over. It was the heat
of the year, and the fields were empty, baking in the sun.
The river ran low and sluggish. A hush lay over the city.
The white houses baked in the sun. Whatever was happening, whatever would decide their fates, happened far
away on the great green sea I knew so well. And I abided
in Memphis.

Hry found me distracted at our lessons. One morning

he put down his tablet and said, "Let us go into the garden and drink melon water."

Gratefully, I got up and went with him. We sat under the trees sipping water with slices of sweet melon in it, water from the cisterns below the temple, where deep in the earth they stayed cool even in summer.

There was some sound in the street outside and I started up.

Hry put his hand on my arm. "It is nothing," he said.

I listened. He was right. It was only the porters letting in a kitchen slave whose arms were laden with pots.

"We wait," I said, "and can do nothing."

"That is often the way of it," Hry said. "Why don't you tell me a story?"

"I tell you?" I asked. "But you are the teacher and I am the student."

Hry took a sip of his melon water. "You have traveled on the sea and seen islands I have not. You know stories I do not. Tell me a new one as I have told you, for thus is knowledge accumulated."

I thought for a moment. There was something about the stillness, about the hush of waiting that reminded me of Neas' eyes when he stood on the haunted island, speaking of a great green wave rising and rising. "Let me tell you then of the Island of the Dead," I said. And I told him.

Hry listened and did not ask questions until I came to the end. He leaned forward and his eyes were very bright.

"How long ago was this?" he asked.

"Neas said that the island was lost in his great-great-grandfather's day. That it burned for many days and the sea was littered with bones and pieces of trees."

Hry smiled, which seemed incongruous. "You have

told me a wonderful story indeed, Maiden of Isis," he said. "As the pieces of a broken pot fit together, so does the tale of our lives. You have given me a piece that fits perfectly."

"I don't understand," I said.

"Come," Hry said, and led me inside with great excitement. We went through one corridor and then another until we came to the vast archives, where scrolls lined the walls from floor to ceiling, each tied with linen with seals upon them. He puttered up and down the rows, examining one seal after another. "Just a moment, my dear. I will find the right one."

At last he found the one he sought and, sitting upon a stool, spread it upon his knees. I looked over his shoulder, but I still could not read most of the words.

"This happened," Hry said, "in the reign of Ramses the Great, the second of that name, in the twenty-second year of his rule." He began to read. "And there appeared in the north, clearly visible from Gizeh, a vast pillar of smoke. Along the Sea of Reeds the water rushed out, so that fish lay flopping on solid ground, and the seabed was exposed to its foundations. It was a very great wonder, and many came to see. Pharaoh ordered a body of his men to investigate, and they rode in their chariots on the bottom of the sea as if they had been on land. And then at once the sea rushed back in with a great green wave as high as the roofs of a mighty city, and all those who had ventured out on the sea bottom perished. The sea returned to where it had been. Yet for many days the conflagration in the north remained, a pillar of smoke by day and a pillar of fire by night."

"It's the same story!" I exclaimed.

"It is indeed," Hry said. "And now it seems to me that the pillar of smoke and fire that they saw must have been from the island, even though it was far away across the sea. But such a great calamity must have been visible even over the distance, if the smoke stretched deep into the sky."

I looked up, as though I could see the sky even though we were indoors. "How high is the sky?" I asked.

"How deep is the sea?" Hry replied. "I have lived in lands where it rained often. I think the sky must be very deep indeed, because great clouds float on it like ships on the sea. And like fish, they swim at different depths and at different speeds. Sometimes they move very quickly, and sometimes not. Sometimes you may see two clouds passing, one below the other."

"The sky is the opposite of the sea," I said.

"Not the opposite," Hry said. "The inverse. It follows many of the same rules, but depth is from here up, not from here down. One goes deeper as one goes higher, until one reaches the place where the moon and sun are. And then beyond that much farther are the stars, like shells on the sea bottom."

"...and if the darkness around them was just another ocean," I whispered. Something pushed at my mind, like a dream I had almost forgotten.

"What?" Hry asked.

"That was what a man I met in Byblos said," I explained, coloring. I was not sure it sounded well, to hear that I had thought that I talked to a god.

"A scholar?" Hry asked.

"A warrior," I said carefully. "A warrior named Mik-el, who had once lived in the Black Land."

"Ah!" Hry sounded pleased. "Then he had some learning, clearly."

"Yes," I said. "I think He was curious." I thought of the slow channels of the Delta, of the great crocodiles along the banks, of the young warrior with His shabby leather and bronze, His dusty folded wings. "He has all the time in the world to learn."

Hry looked at me and smiled. "And that is what you want, Daughter of Wilusa. But only the gods have all the time in the world."

"I know," I said. One life could hold so little compared to all there was in the world.

FIFTY-SIX DAYS had passed since Neas and the People went to war. I was doing some little thing when Tia came to me, the baby in a sling across her chest. "Look," she said.

On the river there was a white sail, one scout ship beating hard against the current, sail spread as well, making upriver with all possible speed. As she came nearer I saw as Tia had seen the smudges and smoke on her prow, the burned spot on her rail where a fire arrow had hit and been extinguished. Tia's hand went to her mouth.

"It's an Egyptian ship," I said. "A messenger."

"But the news..." she said. "Bai..."

"She's coming into the palace dock," I said, watching her turn in the water, the right-side oars coming out of the water as one. There were eight ports, but only six oars sweeping on each side. She had lost men as well.

"I am going to see," I said, and ran from the courtyard

toward the palace as fast as my foot would allow me. I
waited for no one. Half the city would try to get there.

I ran. My breath caught in my throat. I pushed through
the people crowding toward the dock, shoved halfway
back into a stall full of pottery. I could not push my way
out.

I climbed up on the greatest of the pots, clinging to the
pole that held an awning above the stall. I could see over
the crowd, but could not hear what the young man said
who leaped to the dock and began to speak.

What I did hear was the roar of the crowd, beginning
at the front and rolling backward like a wave. I pounded
the shoulder of the man before me. "What?" I screamed
in Khemet. "What happened?"

He turned to me. "A victory! A very great victory!
Thanks be to Isis and Horus Her son! A great victory!"

"Truly?"

"Truly!" And he grabbed both sides of my head and
planted a wet kiss on my nose. "A great victory!"

I elbowed my way closer to the dock. The young captain had stepped down, gone to report in the palace, most
likely, and a scribe had taken his place, reading a piece of
papyrus out to the crowd over and over. I did not understand it all, but I understood much of it, because the words
were simple.

"Hear the words of Ramses, Pharaoh of Egypt. We have
met the enemy on land and sea, and he has gone down in
blood and tears. The sons of the Black Land have van-
quished the enemy, though he was as numerous as stars in
the sky. We have taken many slaves and much wealth, and
many of the enemy are slain."

"On land and sea," I whispered. There had been a sea

battle then. Which meant our ships had been in the midst of it. But of them Pharaoh's dispatch said nothing.

Initial joy began to turn to whispers. We had won, but nothing was said of this division and that, nothing said of this man or another. We must all still wait to find out what we truly wanted to know.

On the seventh day our ships arrived. I was at the Temple of Thoth, and did not know until I came home in the afternoon. As I approached the barracks of the Division of the Ram I heard many voices, and then I saw above the flat roof the peak of a mast. Again in the settling heat I ran.

There were only five ships beside the docks, five of the eight who had sailed. Who was missing? I came closer.

Seven Sisters rode at her mooring, her deck scarred and blackened in places. Behind her was *Pearl,* and Amynter's *Hunter.*

I came in sight of the courtyard, and there they were, the men of the People, and all of the rest, reaching and touching and crying.

Winged Night and *Dolphin* were down the dock, and my heart leaped into my throat. The ships were here. Where were the men?

I began to push my way through the throng, when Kos caught me about the waist and lifted me up in a huge hug. "Thank you for taking care of Tia and the child," he said.

"Where is Xandros?" I asked, and was surprised to hear my voice catch so.

Kos put me down and looked into my face, as though he had thought of something for the first time. He smiled.

"Don't fear for him; he's right over there by Neas. Not a scratch on him, for all that we boarded two Achaian warships."

Somewhere a wail went up, from some woman who had just heard worse. Lide was bustling around, helping men lift down the wounded from *Pearl*'s deck, slung in linen stretchers between two poles. There were nine or ten who could not walk, and Lide was everywhere among them, pushing the bearers and telling them where to go.

Neas stood near them. As one boy came past, carried between two men, Neas leaned down and took his hand, clasping it wrist to wrist as a kinsman and a friend. It was Kassander, Amynter's eldest son. The wrappings around his leg were brown with dried blood. Lide all but pushed Neas away and took charge of him.

Xandros looked up across the crowd as though I had called his name and smiled. Our eyes met.

"Sybil?" a voice said at my elbow. "Will you come? One of the wounded has died and we need you. He is a man of *Winged Night*'s crew named Harmos."

"I will come," I said. I followed him into the room where Lide had laid out the wounded and went about my office.

HE WAS BURNED that night on the banks of the Nile, as the others who had died in the battle had been burned on a great pyre at her mouths. The Egyptians thought this horrifying beyond belief, but they did not prevent it, as long as it was only the dead of the People we burned.

There were so many. Neas spoke their names over the fire with Harmos. So many men I had known so little, so many lost. Three ships were gone entirely. Beside the fire, Neas told us what had happened in a voice as good as any bard's.

"When Pharaoh came to Tamiat," he said, "he sent us on to Ashkelon with twenty Egyptian ships. He had more than a hundred ships in all, but the others had close to two hundred. When we got to Ashkelon it had been sacked." He looked out over the People, the faces limned in firelight. He did not need to describe it. They had seen a city sacked, and what comes after.

"We turned back to Egypt, because we knew now that the fleet must be between us and the main Egyptian fleet at Tamiat. And it was so. We sailed for a full day, and at morning on the second day we saw them before us."

And a feat of seamanship that was, I thought, to find so small a thing as a fleet on the sea. And no small feat of diplomacy, to bring the Egyptian ships with them as though Neas commanded them, not the other way around!

"They had just begun to engage the Egyptians. Fire arrows were flying, and the Egyptian ships moved in under oars, while the wind was behind the great flotilla." Neas smiled. "But we were behind them."

Some of the faces stirred in the firelight. Tia held Kianna to her breast, Bai's arm around her shoulders. I had thought perhaps they might at last come to some understanding. She leaned against his scarred shoulder, and the baby was quiet.

Neas' voice was clear and rich, his face burnished with fire. "We came down upon them like a wolf upon sheep. We were in their rear with twenty-eight ships before they knew we were there. It was in that first melee, as they turned to defend themselves, that *Swift* was rammed

by a big twenty oarsman from Lydia. It overran her, and
she sank. Many of her men swam to safety, though, for
she was close by *Winged Night* and *Cloud*. These are the
names of the ones who did not." And he named them all,
reciting each with a pause between. With each name there
was a collective groan, for each was someone's friend,
someone's brother.

"*Dolphin* came alongside the Lydian ship," Neas said,
"and the Nubians and our men boarded her. Karosanas
was killed, and Kassander was wounded."

Karosanas, I thought. The big, silent oarsman in the last
row below the stern, with his thick beard and broken nose.
And Kassander, the messenger boy. I looked across the
fire, and Xandros' face was calm, calm as resting underwater. I could see him in my mind at the tiller, black hair
flying. He would have used his sword, if they were so close
to the stern, leaped down among the rower's benches, lithe
and swift and deadly.

"The Lydian ship sank," Neas said. "And she would
have taken *Dolphin* down if she had not backed her oars
and gotten free."

Kos, I thought. I could hear him shouting the count,
Xandros at the tiller again. "Left side on two. Right side.
All back!" And somehow they had responded. Against
all hope, *Dolphin* had backed away from the wreck that
would have pulled her under the green water.

I had lost the thread of Neas' narrative. *Lady's Eyes*
and *Seven Sisters* had driven forward into a storm of fire
arrows, driving straight for Neoptolemos' *Chariot of the
Sun*. They had caught *Lady's Eyes'* sail alight, and she
had rammed *Chariot of the Sun* with her decks blazing.

"Jamarados fell on that deck," Neas said quietly. "He

fell to three Achaians, and two he took with him into the Underworld. He was a brave captain, a wise friend, and a dear counselor. All of the People shall miss him. As I shall." He stopped and his throat worked, and for a moment he was silent.

"But Neoptolemos did not fall," he said. "He leaped to the deck of another Achaian ship that came near, and *Lady's Eyes* burned to the waterline and sank. These are the names of the men who died, for only two of them came to *Seven Sisters*." And he told out the names of Jamarados' crew, all but two men. The other twenty-eight were dead.

The Nubian bowmen had done well. From the decks of *Cloud* and *Pearl* they had peppered the Shardan ships with arrows, until at last one of them managed to close with *Cloud*. The fight was fierce and sharp on her deck, the bowmen aboard *Pearl* afraid to shoot into the melee for fear of hitting *Cloud*'s men. Twelve of the bowmen fell aboard *Cloud* and ten of her crew before the Shardan were thrown into the sea. Her oars crippled and her tiller crushed, the remaining crewmen from *Cloud* were taken aboard *Pearl*, along with eight men who were wounded. *Cloud* sank into the sea.

All in all, more than eighty of the enemy ships were sunk, and Egypt lost nearly forty.

"All about this middle sea," Neas said, "women are weeping and children are fatherless. All about this world we know, men will never return. But we, the men of the People, have returned!" He lifted a great pottery bowl full of wine, drank and smashed it. Around us, a shout went up. Bai breached a great amphora of wine, and Tia and Polyra began passing it about.

Neas stood up. The pyre burned on. "The honored dead!" he shouted.

"The honored dead!" came the shout back, then "Ela, Son of Aphrodite! Aeneas! Aeneas!"

Xandros' face was flushed as he shouted. "Ela! Son of Cythera!"

One of the rowers began a beat on the drums, and in a few minutes the snake dance began winding its way around the fire. Harmos, I thought, was having a funeral like a king.

I stepped away from the dancers, into the cooler air away from the rippling fire. I did not dance.

In a moment I looked up. Neas was standing behind me. The firelight glinted golden off his hair, off the great golden armband that he wore.

"Welcome home, Prince Aeneas," I said formally.

"Sybil," he said.

I sat down on the stone railing that separated the courtyard from the dock. "You have done well."

Neas sat beside me. "As well as I might," he said. "We have lost so many men. But I do not think there will be another battle like this for an age. On land Pharaoh's army met the raiders who had landed and those who had come overland from Ashkelon. They say he killed thousands. It will be a long time before they come again."

"Perhaps the isles will know some peace," I said.

Neas shook his head. "How will that be? There are fewer men still to fish and to farm. There are more people desperate. I think there will be more pirates rather than less, more people driven to desperation as we are."

"But for now we are safe," I said.

"Yes," Neas said. "For now." He stretched his hands

out, and in the light they looked gloved in flame. "He's a good king. Young Ramses. That's what his men call him. Old Ramses ruled forever, they say. He's a fair man and an honorable one. And he knows what he owes us for falling on the enemy's rear like that."

"Did you win the battle for him?" I asked.

"No, but it would have been a lot more expensive. He's the kind of king who counts his men's lives." Neas glanced up toward the fire, toward the dancers.

"As are you," I said.

"I do not want to be a king," Neas said.

"So Jamarados said," I said, before I thought.

His lips tightened. "I will miss Jamarados," he said.

"So will I," I said. And I meant it.

"We will stay here a time," Neas said. "The ships are in bad repair, all of them except *Pearl*. And we all need rest."

"We do," I said. He seemed content not to dance, but rather to sit by me. Perhaps rest was the bounty Neas sought of Egypt. Rest, and an end to the turnings of the labyrinth.

DESİRES

The next morning I went to the Temple of Thoth. When I returned, Neas was waiting for me.

"A messenger has come," he said, "bidding us to a feast in six days' time. Pharaoh is holding a great banquet to celebrate the victory. I am to go, as well as four men of my choosing and as many as five women. One should be you, but I do not think that there are others who should go. Egyptians are not as we are, and do not understand that we do not display our women in public."

I glared at him. "In Pylos," I said, "women attended public festivals, if not private dinners."

Neas colored. "Have you...em...seen what Egyptian women wear...at feasts...? I mean, I did in Tamiat and..."

I almost laughed. "I have seen what they wear in the temple, and what they wear in the markets. Honestly, Neas! Have you not seen breasts before?"

His face was scarlet. "Not rouged," he said. "And they...er...paint their nipples."

"You must have been looking rather closely, then," I said.

He ducked his head, and I thought with a pang that perhaps he had been.

"I will certainly go," I said, tossing my hair back. "I see no reason why I should not attend as the Egyptian priestesses do. And I will see if there are any other women of the company who would care to make up the number. Who are the men to be?"

"Xandros," he said promptly, "and Maris, *Pearl*'s captain. Amynter, though he's not likely to enjoy it."

I thought not. Amynter was rather conservative and set in his ways, for all that he was an excellent sailor. He had a suspicion of foreigners, and had never learned a word of any other tongue, something of a trick for a man who must trade. Jamarados would have been better, but Jamarados was dead.

"The last should be my father," Neas said. "Of course."

"Of course," I said, thinking that Anchises and Amynter could keep each other company. Maris had a young wife, Idele, one of the women recovered in Millawanda, so she should come if she wished. I thought that she was clever and curious, despite her slavery. She had miscarried right after we had come to Egypt, but with her husband home safe she seemed to have brightened.

In the end, there were only three women, not five. Many of them did not want to go, whether afraid of mixing with the Egyptians or careful of their good names. Tia could not go, because she must nurse the child. Idele did want to come, and so, to my surprise, did Lide.

"It's not often I'll have the chance to see a royal Egyptian banquet," she said. "If I have to go stark naked I will!"

"I don't think we're actually to be naked," I said, but I had no idea what was proper to wear.

So I asked Hry.

His eyes crinkled and he smiled. "Oh, you will look well," he said. "All of you. You should all come to the temple and dress. I will find suitable clothes for each of you."

I tried to demur, but he stopped me. "Consider it my gift. Consider it hospitality repaid for the generosity of Priam in Wilusa. And tell that to your prince. He, especially, should look fine. I will manage it all!"

And so at noon on the sixth day we all came together to the Temple of Thoth, Xandros and Amynter with the air of men expecting their execution.

Lide and Idele and I were ushered into a long bathing room. It was open to the sky, but stood in shade at this time of day. The spaces between the columns were filled with palms and other plants in enormous pots, making a green screen that entirely separated us from the bathing room of the men nearby.

A maidservant stood by me with a pot of scented oil and a razor. "As the priestesses do?" she asked me.

"Yes," I said. "Definitely. Everything as you do. Except for my hair."

I had already learned that in the Black Land most women of rank shave their heads entirely. The lovely intricate braids they wear are wigs.

"I must keep my hair, as it is part of my office," I said in Khemet.

She nodded, and set about oiling and shaving everything else. When she had done, I plunged in the pool and washed it all away. It was very strange, seeing my body in the water, naked as a child's. Not a hair on my legs or arms, even my pubis nude, as I had not seen it since I first began to change into a woman.

Lide splashed in after me. She too looked odd. Lide gave me a sideways grin. "I can see how it would be cooler. You know, the maid says that some Egyptian women bathe twice a day? And they pluck their hair out so it will never grow back. Men too. They start plucking their beards as soon as they begin to grow."

"So that's why all those smooth faces," I said. A thought struck me. "How did you and the maid understand each other?"

Lide snorted. "And me in the market every day? Trading those endless fava beans the princess sent us for a little variety? How long should it take to learn enough to chat? I picked up the tongue in Byblos while we were there too."

I smiled. "Amynter never picks up a word."

"Amynter never talks to a native." Lide swam a couple of strokes in the pool, and I was reminded suddenly of the flax river. Lide had held me up in the water when I was a child just learning to swim. I had forgotten that. Suddenly I missed my mother.

Lide must have seen it in my face, or perhaps she too was reminded of the river that had been our home. "Ah, child," she said. "Your mother would be proud of you now, were she here to see you. I set your leg, you know, when the chariot hit you, but you would have died without her nursing. She was a stubborn woman. That's where you get it."

Her arms floated out from her sides in the clear water,

her eyes far beyond me. "She was on the ship with me from Wilusa, when we both fell to King Nestor's lot. She was a pretty girl, and she'd had a lot of attention. They'd hurt her pretty badly. Some of us died. But not her. She had a spirit in her that wouldn't break. By the time we got to Pylos it was clear she was with child. One of the other girls who was that way threw herself overboard in the night and drowned. After that I made sure to sit close by your mother at night."

She looked at me, raised one eyebrow. "She guessed what I was about. She looked at me with a gimlet eye, just like you do, and said, 'Lide, I'm not going to kill myself. I'm going to raise a son who will cut their balls off!'"

I laughed, and then stopped. "But I wasn't a son," I said.

"No, you weren't," Lide said. "And you've done more than she could ever have imagined you'd do. You've gotten us all safe to our kinsmen, and led us to a safe port. Your mother would be very proud of you."

I burst into tears, standing waist deep in an Egyptian bathing pool.

Lide came and put her arms around me. "There now, child. Never a word of complaint from you, strange and god-touched as you are. You're a solitary creature, but even so you need some people of your own."

I didn't say anything, just cried on her shoulder.

"Come now," she said. "Come and let the girls make you pretty. That's something you've never done, I imagine."

"No," I said, still sniffing a little. "It doesn't matter if Death is pretty."

"Tonight you aren't Death," she said.

*   *   *

I DRESSED in the twilight. Hry had told the maids that I should dress like their own senior priestesses, and the girls had taken that seriously. There was a gown of sheer white linen, so thin that I could see the outlines of my hairless limbs quite clearly beneath it. The skirt was crimped and stiffened into dozens of folds the width of my finger, and it fastened beneath my breasts with a girdle of gilded leather. Above, my breasts were rouged and each nipple painted dark and lovely. Over my shoulders went a short cape of thin linen, dipping to my waist in front and back, pleated in elaborate folds. Over that went a collar of gold and glass, set with hundreds of tiny pieces of red and blue. On my bare arms went bracelets of gold, and a pair of gold hoops hung from my ears.

The maids were uncertain what to do with my hair, but at last they braided it in twelve sections, securing the ends of each one with gold wire. Then they painted my face.

I had never had anyone do it for me. It is not proper to wear Pythia's paint until you are Pythia, and I had not taken an acolyte. Kianna, I thought, would have this office someday, but it would be long years before her little hands would be steady enough to paint my eyes.

They painted my eyelids lapis blue and outlined them in kohl. My cheeks were stained with rouge, and my lips tinted like my nipples. When at last they held a burnished mirror up for me to see I hardly recognized myself. Looking out of the mirror was a dark-eyed Egyptian girl, small and light, with curving breasts and eyes that flashed fire, and a long, secret smile.

"You are beautiful," one of the maids said. "This is what we call beauty in the Black Land." Her hand traced my cheek lightly. "You have good bones. You will be beautiful in death."

"I am Death," I said absently, turning the mirror. For a moment I almost saw another face there, crowned with the uraeus, the sacred serpent of Egypt.

"Ah," she said, "but in the Black Land, Death is beautiful. When you stand before Osiris' throne you must be careful, for the beauty of Isis is blinding, like the beauty of the moon when you have been long underground."

And I felt Her, like a whisper at my side. *This is My face too,* She said.

"This is my face too," I said, touching my lips with wonder.

Outside the room I heard Hry. "Come on, Daughter of Wilusa! Bring the women and come! The litters are waiting in the courtyard, and the hour is here!"

We came out into the torchlit courtyard. Neas was waiting beside the first litter, where he would sit with Hry. He too had been shaved, and he wore a knee-length skirt of fine linen, pleated like mine and stiffened. On his arm shone the princess' bracelet. Beside him was Xandros.

His black hair was held back with a clasp of gold, and his linen skirt fastened with a belt of gilded leather. His limbs were shaved, and his smooth brown chest gleamed with scented oil, myrrh, and rose and something else besides. When he saw me his mouth dropped open. He dragged at Neas' arm.

Neas turned, and his mouth dropped open too. But he was a prince, and faster on the recovery than Xandros. "Sybil?"

"Prince Aeneas," I said with great dignity, coming and

standing beside him. If I moved slowly my limp was hard to see.

"You look different," Xandros said.

Neas smiled. "You look beautiful." His eyes said that he meant it. I was not used to men looking at me that way, and somehow to have Neas look at me like that was oddly disconcerting.

"Come, come!" Hry said. "We cannot be late. Everyone, please get in the litters!"

He gestured Neas to the first one. I dropped back and got in the second with Xandros. I did not want to ride with the look of scorn I had seen on Anchises' face, or the dismay on Amynter's. I almost smiled as I saw Lide get in the litter beside Anchises. Let him try to lecture her!

The litters were lifted by the temple bearers. Boys went ahead carrying torches. Xandros was silent. At last he ventured a sideways look. "You look nice," he said. He kept his eyes carefully above my neck, but I saw when I turned my head how they glanced down to my breasts and stomach, half bared in the fine linen.

"Thank you," I said. "I think you look nice too." And that was all we said until we reached the palace.

On ordinary days the Egyptians dine on stools about a table, or perhaps just sitting on the floor. For banquets, however, cushions were spread about long, low tables, and guests sat or reclined as they wished. On a dais at the end of the hall were three tables facing outward, where Pharaoh and his highest officials would eat. The center one was for the king himself, and no one shared it with him. The one to his left was for the Princess Basetamon.

She wore pure white tonight, but the great collar of lapis and gems she wore was so large that it reached almost to her waist. Her hair was dressed high and laden with jewels. Rings glittered on her fingers attached to pieces of gold mesh that fastened about her wrists, so her hands were covered in gold. Beside her, her brother watched out of dark Egyptian eyes, the double crown upon his head.

We were escorted to cushions at the far end of the hall, with ships' captains and lesser priests. We had barely begun to recline before the musicians struck up a song on harp and flute, and servants came around with the first of the meal.

I was served stuffed duckling with tender hearts of palm, seared fish upon a bed of melokhia greens, olives from Achaia, and mussels from the deeps of the sea. There was wine as well, sweet and dark red, from Byblos and the lands that border it, cakes made with almond flour and iced with sesame paste.

We were eating and talking, looking about, when a servant came to Neas. "Prince Aeneas," he said respectfully, "the Princess Basetamon requires you to attend her."

Neas looked up. "Oh. Well. Then." He got up and followed the servant. I watched him bow almost to the floor as he greeted her, then prostrated himself to Pharaoh.

"He shouldn't do that," Anchises said sharply.

"Be quiet," I said.

"It's important," Amynter said. "If Pharaoh thinks well of us, then perhaps we can stay in his service. We fought well enough."

I was surprised to find an ally in Amynter, and I looked at him. He shrugged. "I want to stay here. Good food, good king, good weather. And plenty of everything a man might need." He picked up a duck wing and took a thoughtful bite. "I've had enough. My sons need somewhere to grow up where they won't be slaves. If Neas can fix it with the Egyptian king, I'm in favor of that."

I watched.

Pharaoh said something to him and he replied. Whatever it was seemed to please the princess. She patted the cushions beside her and then drew him down to sit, their shoulders almost touching. She laughed at something he said, and picked up a piece of almond cake and gave it to him.

Neas took it with a faint courtly nod, his eyes never leaving her face.

Amynter looked where I did and shrugged. "Whatever it takes."

Anchises was livid. "That painted whore!"

"Are you trying to get us killed?" I hissed at him. "They are our hosts, and we owe them the very clothes on our backs."

"My son is not—"

"I'll take him out," Lide said, rising. Maris rose too, and with an apologetic nod to his young wife, helped Lide take a still-sputtering Anchises from the hall. No one noticed. There were too many servants coming and going, and a dancing troupe began with youths tumbling down a polished strip in the middle of the table.

Neas was laughing at something Basetamon had said, leaning near her, his arm almost touching her breasts.

"He doesn't seem to have a problem with her breasts," I said under my breath.

Xandros followed my gaze and grimaced. "He's drowning in her eyes. You should have seen them in Tamiat.

When they thought that we foreigners did not understand there were jokes and bets about how long it would take the princess to try out her new barbarian hunting cat." He shrugged. "In Egypt women are as free as men to take lovers. And he's something new, something different."

I looked down the table. Hunting cat indeed. Neas looked like a young lion. "Something splendid," I said. It was true that I had never seen a man as beautiful as Neas. Dressed like a prince, how should any woman not turn toward him?

Xandros nodded. There was something mocking in his tone, though he himself was the butt of the joke. "What do we have against that? Against the glories of Egypt?"

"We are his friends," I said.

"I am his friend, while life and breath last. And I will not risk that for anything." Xandros lifted the cup to his lips. His dark eyes were serious. "And it is enough."

"I am his friend too," I said. "And his Sybil. That is all the gods have meant for me to be." I knew this. I should not desire more. He was my prince, and I his oracle.

Xandros looked at me sideways, as though he wanted to say more.

I lifted one of the heavy cups and held it out to him. Neas might be entranced by Basetamon, and I could hardly complain if he were, but Xandros was not. No matter where we voyaged or what befell us, Xandros remained himself, curious and clever and true.

With half a smile, Xandros held the cup to my lips, and I drank wine from his hand, as though we pledged. His eyes were dark and warm on mine, like to like. "Friends," he said.

"Always that," I said, and knew I would mean it down the long fall of years.

WE WERE a much smaller party coming back than we had been going to the palace. Anchises, Maris, and Lide had already left. Aeneas stayed. It was just Amynter, Idele, Xandros, and me returning. Amynter was drunk, and he staggered off the moment the litter set down at the barracks of the Division of the Ram. Idele hurried off to find out what had happened to Maris. I walked down beside the dock.

The starched pleats had fallen out of my gown, and the earrings were heavy on my ears. My hands smelled like roasted meat, and it had been so very hot, the air thick with incense, perfume cones, lamp oil, food, and the scents of two hundred guests. Beside the river it was cool.

I heard a step behind me and knew it was Xandros. He came and stood beside me and we watched the lights going out at the palace. After a moment, he sat down on the quay and took off his gilded sandals. I took mine off as well and sat beside him, dabbling my feet in the water. In the white moonlight my twisted ankle was grotesque, a parody of smooth flesh, blue veined in the light. Drops of water flashed on my skin.

Our shoulders did not quite touch.

One by one the lights winked out over the water. One of them was in the princess' bedchamber, where she drew Neas down to her on sheets of scented linen. Or perhaps she kept one lamp lit, to see his golden skin above her.

I wondered if Xandros was thinking the same thing.

Probably. "I will return all we borrowed to Hry tomorrow," I said.

"That's good," Xandros said. We sat in silence for what seemed like a long time. Xandros splashed his foot back and forth in the water. "Are you learning a lot? From Hry, I mean," he asked.

"Yes. So much," I said. "So many things I didn't know I didn't know, if that makes sense."

"It does," he said. "You like it."

"Yes," I said. How should I not? My hunger was not for banquets and rich foods, but for all the knowledge the Temple of Thoth had accumulated, all the knowledge in the world.

Xandros sighed. "We can't stay here," he said. "Not without becoming like the rest, the Nubians and the Libyans in Pharaoh's service."

"What do you mean?"

"They have no gods, no people of their own. They aren't slaves, but they belong to Egypt. And Egypt will never let them go." Xandros splashed his foot in the river. "I saw them in Tamiat. Barbarians. Foreigners. Stepchildren of the gods. People not fortunate enough to be born in Khemet." His tone was sharp, and he glanced sideways at me. "People talk in front of me. I look like a dumb sailor, I suppose."

I smiled. "They don't realize how fast with languages you are." It was true that at first Xandros did not seem as clever as he was, because he was quiet and not quick to speak in company.

"They're happy enough to let us serve them. They'll even break bread with us. But we're not the same as them. We're children of lesser nations, lesser gods. No one is really worthy except people born in Khemet. The worst of them despise our barbarian ways. The best of them feel so terribly sorry for us."

"Perhaps they have reason to," I said. "Look at the land they have built. What do we have that can compare?"

"Our honor," Xandros said. "Our manhood. It's not what the gods give you at birth that matters, but how you bear it."

"Sometimes what you're given at birth matters a good deal," I said, thinking of the children of slaves, born of rapes.

"It's the dreadful pity that gets to me," Xandros said. "Pity us, not born in Khemet! But with a little work we might learn to be civilized!"

"It's not like that," I said, thinking of Hry and the temple, the maidens who had taken such pains to make me beautiful, Hry who had listened to my stories like a colleague, a fellow servant of the gods.

"Isn't it?" he asked. "Do you see them coming here, eating our food? Celebrating our festivals?"

"Hry did," I said. "He was the guest-friend of Priam."

"Maybe he did," Xandros said. "But there are exceptions to everything. Most of them don't care what happens outside Egypt. They don't know where our lands are and they don't care. It doesn't matter. Anything that really matters happens here."

"Xandros," I said, "who but Egypt could have stopped Neoptolemos and the great fleet? Who else has that power?"

"Nobody. But it's not going to make anything better for us, or for people in the islands. Neas is right about that."

"It would have made things much worse if Egypt had

fallen," I said. "Xandros, do you envy them their peace and prosperity so much?"

"No, I resent their smugness," he said. "I resent that they don't have to worry as we do. That they can't be bothered to work to keep their children safe, just rely on men who do nothing else but soldier and foreign mercenaries to do what they won't dirty their hands doing! Do you think I like killing? Do you think I like doing this work?"

His eyes were blazing and I searched his face. "All I ever wanted," he said, "was to be a sailor. The rest of it... it's better than death. And it's what Neas needs from me. So I do it. But I'm not like him. I don't want to kill. And I hate it every time."

"You do it so well," I said, thinking of the young guard in the street in Byblos. That was not bloodlust, the heat of battle that takes one and leads one on, but horrible cold compassion.

His mouth tightened. "Yes."

I searched for words. "Xandros, this is not forever. We will be done with this. There will be fields to plow and trees to plant, and yes, seas to fish. We will come to the end of this, and there will be peace."

"Do you really believe that?"

"I do," I said. "I have foreseen it for Neas."

Xandros searched my face. "Then we must leave."

"We will," I said. "Our destiny is not in Egypt." Much as I might wish it otherwise, I thought. I could dream of the archives and the long slow days, the orderly rhythm of the temple, the stately service of the gods. I could be so happy here. I could find everything I sought. I could need no other love but Hers, here in the quiet of Her service.

I stood up. "We will leave Egypt," I said. "You will have your wish." And I went in, before he could see me cry.

NEAS DID NOT RETURN the next day until afternoon, and I did not see him then. Amynter told me with great satisfaction that Pharaoh had promised to keep us on for good wages, and that Neas had agreed. He whistled as he went about his work. For all that he didn't speak the language, Egypt was quite good enough for him.

As it was to me.

I went to the Temple of Thoth and my heart was heavy. There was nothing I could say to Hry. What could there be? He had shown me nothing but kindness. And now it seemed that Neas meant for us to stay in Egypt forever.

He was always gone to the palace, and I knew what that meant. He came back to us laughing, smelling of myrrh and precious resin, his white linen skirt kilted like an Egyptian prince. He even trimmed his hair and wore it beneath a soldier's head cloth, like the bright, beautiful warriors limned on the walls of the Temple of Thoth.

And I, I was seized with restlessness. My lessons gave me pleasure, but when I returned from them I thought I would go mad, sitting with Tia and Polyra cooking endless fava beans on pots above the fires in the barracks courtyard.

Hry sensed this in me. One morning he asked me to return at nightfall, rather than staying by day.

"Why?" I asked him.

"It is time for you to learn the stars," he said.

My first impulse was to refuse. Why should I do his

bidding and come at night? And then I thought better. Our ships navigated by the stars. The more I learned of them the better I could help Xandros.

I stood beside Hry on the roof of the Great Temple while he pointed out this one and that, and I learned their names in Khemet that I had known only in Wilusan. As night drew on the fires of the city were banked and dark, and the sky above shone in the clear desert air brighter than I had ever seen. It was so black that it seemed to have depth.

"You see?" Hry said softly. "It is an ocean."

"I can almost see distant shapes," I said. "A little blur here and there, like something too faint to see. Like something too far away."

"When I was a boy," Hry said, "I could see much more clearly. Now the faintest stars are lost to me."

A pale sheen in Andromeda, like a vague circle of light. "If I could see more clearly..."

Hry chuckled to himself. "If you could see more clearly, you would know the shape of the stars. You would navigate the skies."

"I would," I said, and in the black depths could almost see it. "I would build a ship of moonlight and silver, and Xandros would pilot it for me." I smiled at Hry. "And we should sail beyond the baths of the stars and far away, to strange islands in that ocean where men have never walked."

"And the wind that would fill your sails is desire," Hry said. "It is desire that gives our *ba* wings. To yearn with such might must come to something."

"Must it?" I asked.

Hry patted my arm. "You must learn to be patient. It is not time yet for you to sail."

And I did not know if he meant to sail the stars, or the much more mundane seas that lay between the Black Land and the world.

SOTHIS RISING

A few days later I was leaving the Temple of Thoth when Lide came hurrying up to me on the steps. "There you are!" she exclaimed. "You must come right away. And bring the priest with you."

"What's happened?" I said. "Kianna? Has something happened to the baby?" But if so, what possible use could Hry be?

"No, not the baby," Lide said. "Get the priest. I'll explain on the way."

I ran back inside and got Hry, whom I had just parted with. We came outside together.

"Come," Lide said. "It's important."

"Is someone ill?" Hry asked. He was panting a little in the heat.

Lide was taking us through the city, to the outskirts where the Nubian bowmen practiced at their barracks on the edge of the desert. "You could say that," she said.

I struggled to go faster, but I lost them in the streets. I could not really run well, even after so long.

Nubian barracks? What in the world could Lide need

Hry for there? As we got closer I realized it was not just the Nubians who were there, but that they guarded the camp of slaves taken in the great battle, though that camp grew smaller by the day as the slaves were sent all over the land in small groups.

The sun was blinding, and this far from the river there was little breeze. If there was any, it was bone dry and smelled of the far deserts, not of the sweet green banks. The prisoners had some tents against the sun, just ragged blankets propped on sticks, and nothing else. Lide stood beside one tent some little distance away, while Hry knelt and looked inside. I came up to them as quickly as possible.

"Achaians?" I said. And then I did not need to ask. The boy who lay inside was my brother.

Aren was curled up on his side, shaking with fever in the heat of the summer. He was taller than I remembered, with long fair hair clotted with sweat. *Thirteen,* I thought. *He is thirteen now, a young man, not a child.* There were bloodstains on his chiton, and he curled tight.

I turned to Lide. "Has he been castrated, then?"

"Circumcised," she said. "All Egyptian men are, even their slaves."

Hiram had said as much, I thought, in Byblos, but I had thought that he meant it figuratively that Pharaoh should take the foreskins of all the captives. Apparently not.

"The cuts have gone bad," Lide said. "As sometimes happens with cuts of any kind. He's got a terrible fever." She knelt down and lifted a pot of water, but he turned his head from her, his eyes clenched shut.

One of the Nubians had come up behind us, presumably asking us what we thought we were doing. Hry stood up, and I saw the man straighten perceptibly as he saw the priest.

Lide dipped the hem of her tunic and began to sponge Aren's face. She had birthed him, I remembered. I remembered that well. She had washed the blood from his baby face and laid him on my mother's breast.

Hry turned back to us, speaking in the tongue of Wilusa. "I have told the captain here that this young man is not Achaian, but Denden, and one of your people who went overboard during the battle. He must have been taken prisoner by accident. I have told him that the boy is the honored lady's brother. I will arrange that we may take him to the temple, where our doctors can tend him."

I grabbed Hry's hand. "Will you really do this?"

Hry smiled, and the sun beat down on his old bald head. "Of course. He is your brother, isn't he?"

"Yes," I said. "He is my brother."

It took some little while for Hry to order bearers and a litter. It was sunset before we carried Aren into the Temple of Thoth and gave him to the care of that doctor that Hry trusted most. Hry then led me and Lide into the courtyard with the pool and sent for cool water. "Come and sit," he said. "My friend will do what he can, and we must give him room to work. He will have to trim the cut that was made and take the bad skin off. And then there are medicines he will try. But it is better if we are not in his way."

We sat down in the cool evening and sipped water. The stars were coming out.

Hry patted my hand. "You must love your brother very much."

"I hardly know him," I said. "He was two years old when I went to the Shrine. I have barely seen him since."

"Except in Pylos," Lide said. "When you sent him to find us and bid us to come to the harbor."

"That wasn't me," I replied. "It was Her. I kept Xandros from killing him, though." In my mind's eye I saw them once again, against the broken gates and the wall covered in flowering vine, Xandros with his hair flying loose, his sword coming up in a backhand stroke to open his stomach, Aren with his borrowed sword responding too slowly. I had thrown myself between them and all of Her power had filled me.

"Will he live?" I asked Hry.

"We will have to ask the doctor," Hry said. "There are no more skilled physicians anywhere in the world than here. He is in good hands."

We sat in silence in the starlight.

After a while we went in and sought the doctor. Aren lay in a bed in a cool room open to the river breezes. His manhood was bandaged and lay beneath a linen drape, and his eyes were closed.

The physician was washing his hands. He turned and dried them on a cloth. "I have cleaned the cut," he said. "I have trimmed the bad skin and washed it well, then seared the cuts with a knife dipped first in boiling water and then passed through a flame. I have treated it with honey and bandaged it in clean cloth. And I have given him a tea to help his fever. He will need to stay here and be tended for some days, but I am hopeful."

I looked at him. Aren was sleeping, and the sweat stood upon his white forehead. He looked nothing like me, I thought. Nothing like my mother. He looked like Triotes.

"We have apprentice healers who watch through the

night," the physician said. "You need not fear for his care."

"I don't," I said. I knew the thoroughness with which everything was done in the Temple of Thoth.

"Go home," he said, "and rest."

LIDE AND I WENT, but I could not sleep. I rose and returned before dawn.

They knew me now at the temple, and the sleepy door wardens let me in. There was a lamp in the hall of the chambers of healing, but the apprentice on duty did not try to stop me from going in. I went in and sat.

Aren seemed less flushed. I put my hand upon his brow. The fever seemed less. My hand looked strange there, or perhaps it was just that his was so much a stranger's face, a young man, not the child I remembered. His nose was straight and strong, his jaw jutting and still too large for his face.

Aren opened his blue eyes. He looked at me. "Mother?" he said, still half asleep.

"No, Aren," I said. "It's me." I did not realize that he, too, missed her still.

His eyes widened. "Pythia?"

"Yes," I said, and felt my eyes fill with tears.

"How did you get here? Where am I?"

"You are in the Temple of Thoth," I said. "In the care of physicians. And I've been here."

"The last time I saw you, you were leaving Pylos with a bunch of pirates," Aren said. "How did you get to an Egyptian temple?"

"It's a long story," I said.

"Tell me."

And so I did.

By the time I had reached the part where we were in Byblos, the physician had returned with a bowl of barley porridge for Aren and another cup of the tea. "You look better, young man," he said in Khemet.

Aren looked at me. "He says you look better," I said.

"How is it that you speak their language?" he asked.

"I've been learning," I said. "It's not so difficult."

"Tell him I want to look at his cut," the physician said. "And perhaps you should go out. It's not the sort of thing I'd want to show my sister."

I translated for Aren and his face went hard. "It's the Egyptians that did this. They've cut off my manhood."

"Not all of it," I said. "Just the foreskin. All Egyptian men are so. Most of them have it done when they come of age."

"I'll never..." he began, then flushed to the roots of his hair.

"Yes, you will," I said. "It doesn't stop all the Egyptians, does it? It's not your foreskin that makes you a eunuch; it's your balls."

"I don't really want to talk to you about my balls," Aren mumbled.

"I'll go out then," I said. "And come back later this afternoon."

I went back to the barracks and slept.

OVER THE NEXT FEW DAYS Aren mended, and I began to wonder what would happen once he was well. I would not send him back to the slave camp.

It was four days before I caught Neas, as he was always at the palace. I found him in the courtyard wearing white linen, with a new gold collar around his neck that matched the lion hunt bracelet on his arm. His skin was smooth and oiled, but he looked tired.

I did not wait, but told him all that had happened. "You see why I had to take him to the temple," I finished. "He is my brother."

Neas looked at me with the same expression he'd had for Xandros on the docks in Byblos when he'd brought Ashterah to the ships. "I see that. But he's also an Achaian, one of the men we fought against."

"He wasn't at the sacking of Wilusa," I said. "I made sure of it. His father would not take Aren. He never sailed before this last expedition with the great fleet."

"That's good," Neas said, and I knew that he was considering fairly. He would always consider fairly any matter I brought to him, no matter how much it might vex him or create trouble where there was none. "So no man will have a direct blood feud with him. But he is still Achaian, one of their people."

"He is my brother, born of the same mother, a daughter of Wilusa," I said. "If I am of the People, so is he."

Neas sighed, and I knew that I had won. "What is it you want?"

"To bring him here," I said. "I cannot leave my brother to be a slave."

"Very well," Neas said. "But the boy will have to look out for himself. I am not going to run around protecting him from anyone's ill will."

"If you greet him," I said, "it will be enough. No man will risk your displeasure."

"I wish that were true," Neas said. "There may have been a time when it was, but it is not this time." Neas sighed. "I need your counsel, Sybil," he said, leading me away, to the riverside. I knew what he meant, then. I hadn't really expected him to speak of it, was not even sure if he felt it as I did, since he was so often gone.

"There are two factions," Neas said. "I would be a fool not to see it. Those who want to leave Egypt and go somewhere or another, like my father, and those who are content with the bargain I have made with Pharaoh and will stay here." He looked at me. "I know you love Egypt and that you have made many friends. You understand why I have made the bargains I have made."

"Yes. I understand," I said. And I did, at least in part. As mercenary contracts go, this was a good one, better than escorting convoys. But I could not tell from his face if he meant other bargains as well, if he thought her part of it, a bargain for his people that he must seal with his flesh.

I put my hand on his arm and he did not flinch, but he did not warm to me either. He was courtly and distant, Prince Aeneas. "Neas," I said carefully, "there are bargains and bargains."

He met my eyes. "She is a beautiful woman. I have nothing to complain of." He turned and sat down on the quay, where Xandros and I had watched the moon the night of the banquet.

"Neas," I said and sat beside him. We did not touch.

"I am a prince," Neas said. "I have known all my life what that means. Princes do not choose. They know their duty to their people and what honor demands. I was fortunate when my father chose Creusa as a wife for me. She was kind and lovely, and I would have chosen no better when I was seventeen and she fourteen. I came to love her."

"That is the blessing of the Lady of the Sea, Cythera, whom we call Aphrodite," I said. "You are beloved of Her, and She has given you everything She could."

"Yes," he said. His gilded sandals trailed in the water. "But every man knows that there is a time when you can rely no further on your mother's gifts. You must do things for yourself. You cannot expect your mother to solve everything, for your mother to make you whole."

"That is true of women as well," I said. "The first time I wore Pythia's paints and knew that She Who Was Pythia would not be there to guide me, I knew that I was alone indeed. And that I would never again be safe."

Neas looked at me sideways. "Were we ever safe?"

"No, but we believed we were. Doesn't Kianna think she is safe, with Tia and Kos to guard her, Bai and Xandros and all the rest?"

"And me as well," he said. "She is safe here, and there is food for all of them to eat. I have made my bargain. And that is how it is." He clapped his hand on my shoulder as though I were one of his men, stood up, and walked away.

"My prince," I said, knowing he did not hear me. "You are worth so much more than all the grain and fava beans in the world."

And so Aren came and stayed with us. Xandros took him into the ships' company and gave him the task of tending to Kassander as he mended. They were of an age, and Kassander was still having trouble walking. I did not fear they would quarrel, for I knew the messenger was a quiet boy made even more so by the pain of his healing leg. Like me, he would never be fleet of foot, but a rower does not need to be. It was his back and his arms that must do the heavy work.

ONE NIGHT not long after, I came at night to view the stars with Hry.

It was a long time before the lights of the city began to disappear, and there seemed many more people in the streets than usual. I asked Hry about it, and he smiled.

"Do you see there?" he asked, pointing. "Do you see how on the eastern horizon that group of stars is just rising above the distant hills? Tonight they will come no higher, but tomorrow night Sothis will rise clear and cold out of the desert, and he will blow his hunting horn among the skies. The sound will be heard from one end of the Black Land to the other, and Hapi will open the great vaults of the Nile at Elephantine and let loose the flood. For forty days the river will rise and cover the fields, bringing life to Khemet. Tomorrow night when Sothis rises there will be great celebrations, and the next five days are the birthdays of the gods."

"I was born on the night of Sothis' first rising," I said. "Lide told me so, and she birthed me."

Hry's face split in a wide grin. "That's wonderful! We know here in the Black Land that children born on the night of Sothis' rising are beloved of the gods, that those who share the gods' birthdays are their chosen. It was not misfortune that marked you as Hers, but clear starlight."

I looked at the horizon where Sothis would appear. It had shone bright and cold before dawn when the black ships had come to Pylos, bright as on the night of my birth.

From the docks of the temple came a great shout and men spilled into the courtyard. From where we were on the roofs I saw other priests like Hry in their robes of office hastening to a small stone building at the end of the quay.

"What is happening?" I asked.

"The river is rising," Hry said. "The priest had gone to measure it on the stones, and it has begun. Hapi has loosed the waters!" His voice caught, and I realized what great joy this brought him. "The miracle has happened again, and the gods have renewed their covenant with Khemet!"

Hry put his hand on my head. "Tomorrow, Daughter of Wilusa, you will see rejoicing such as you have never seen. Make feasts with your people, for you will share in the bounty of the Black Land as you have shared in her risks and travails this year! I will send fish and wine so that you can honor the gods!"

THIS CELEBRATION is not our celebration. We do not honor the gods at the rising of a star. On the other hand, the People love to celebrate, and do not lightly turn down the gifts of wine and fish. And doing so would indeed be a grave discourtesy to Hry and to our hosts.

Neas, of course, was bid to the great feast at the palace. He left before sundown, oiled and shaved, his skirt worked in many pleats and his belt studded with gold. He gave me a smile as he left, while I worked with Polyra to set up the skewers to roast the fish over the fire. They should be basted in oil to make their skin crispy, and there were sweet melons to eat and bread smeared with honey, melokhia greens chopped and folded into beaten eggs cooked on a flat stone and sprinkled with goat cheese. I wore my new black tunic, made like my last one only not ragged with wear.

"Good night, Prince Aeneas," I said.

"Good fortune, Sybil," he said. A smile passed between us, and he was gone.

An hour later bearers arrived from the palace with six great pots of beer, each as high as a man's waist. "Gracious Lady," they said, "we are servants of the palace and we met Prince Aeneas as we came in. He told us to bring this beer here, that his People might share in the feast."

"Trust Neas to remember the beer," Xandros said. He opened one of the pots and dipped his cup in, draining it in one gulp.

I looked at him speechless, then thanked the bearers and told them to go.

"Xandros," I said, hurrying back, "did it never occur to you that Neas might not have sent this? That something might be amiss?"

"Of course it did," he said levelly. "That's why I drank right off. It will be hours yet before the pots are opened and served out and all of the People drink. By that time it will be obvious if I am all right or not."

"And if you're not?" I demanded.

"Then you know to pour it out," Xandros said. "And what to tell Neas."

"By all of the gods," I said, "I wish I could dump you in the Nile."

"And who would you have me order to drink it? Bai?

Kos? Kassander? I am under the curse of the Lady of the Sea, so it matters less what happens to me."

I clenched my teeth. "Xandros, for the thousandth time, there is no curse!"

"So you say," he said.

My retort was swallowed up in other people coming up with details about cooking and such things. When I looked for him a few minutes later I saw him sitting with Kos, who had Kianna in his lap while Tia stirred a huge pot of fava beans. "Boiled beans, baked beans, stewed beans," I mumbled to myself. "The Land of Beans."

By the time dinner was ready it was clear that there was nothing wrong with Xandros, something he made a point of as he came and sat by me with his bowl. "I feel so very good tonight," he said pointedly, taking a huge bite of bread.

I ignored him completely.

Night fell, and the stars faded in clear and bright, covering the vault of heaven. And the river as well. As night came up and down the Nile people came to the water's edge, and soon tiny points of light were sparkling all across the expanse of the river. I walked onto the dock and looked out at the blue distance in the east, the winking dots of fire on the water.

"What's that?" Xandros asked, coming to stand beside me.

"Hry told me that they make little clay lamps in the shapes of boats to honor Isis, and that people set them to float on the river. It's good luck and honors Her if they float a very long way before they go out. The ones we're seeing must have been launched upstream here in Memphis, but before the night is over I imagine we'll see ones from far up the river."

"They're beautiful," he said softly. "Like stars on the water."

"They are," I said. He of all of them saw the magic too, felt it in his bones, felt the touch of Mystery. He and Neas, of all the People.

Sothis rose above the horizon in the wake of the evening star, Cythera's star. The lights twinkled on the river as they rode up and down on the ripples. Somewhere upriver a barge was lit on the water, the sound of music coming clear to us. A soft breeze tugged at my hair.

Behind us, I heard Kos getting out his drum. A few moments later he started, and the clear male voices of the rowers came in, one soaring young boy high and far above in descant. It was Aren. I had not heard him sing in a very long time, but he knew all of the words. The voices of the People, singing the songs we sing in exile.

The song changed, and it was a merry song, a courting song, Kos' strong, deep voice leading it. The next voice was Tia's. I turned around and saw that she stood in the firelight, the glow of the bonfire turning her white dress to flame, a beautiful clear voice with depths like the sea. She was looking at Bai, who sat watching her, Kianna on his lap. The baby was sitting up with Bai's help, her great gray eyes as dark as the skies, round and bright.

The song ended, and some other drummers started, and I saw the dancing line begin. Not the snake dance yet, but a bright whirl of clothes and limbs made fleet by the beer.

Xandros took my hand. "Come and dance," he said, and his hand was warm on mine.

"I don't dance," I said. "I don't know how."

"I'll teach you," he said. He smiled at me, dear and bright, as familiar as a brother, as strange as the sea.

I closed my eyes for a moment so that I would not see that smile. "I can't," I said. "My leg won't."

"I'll carry you," he said, and put one arm around my waist and whirled me into the dance. My foot hardly touched the ground.

Light and shadow and the dizzying circles of the round dance, Xandros' bare arms around me, my arms against his chest. I could spin off him on my left foot alone, and he would catch me at the end of each turn, reeling me back to him like a fisherman's net. Every face I saw was smiling.

At the end of one long turn I came face-to-face with Kos, who was dancing now. "Little priestess!" he said. "I knew Xandros could get you to dance!" He picked me up, smelling like beer and sweat, and spun me around. "Be with us in our joy, Sybil!"

Be with us in our joy. It ran under my skin like a prayer, like the throbbing beat of the drums. *Be with us in our joy. Be with us in our joy.* Kos was beautiful, every hair of his head precious, every callus on his rower's hands.

And more beautiful still was Xandros, claiming me back, a big pot of cool beer in his hand. I took it from him and drank deeply. His hair was escaping from the leather thong that held it, and his chest was slick with sweat.

"You can dance," he said.

"Yes," I said, and put the beer down. "Dance with me."

Be with us in our joy. In our joy. The drums rose wilder and faster, the snake dance began, Xandros' hands on my hips, moving in time to the music.

He caught me out reeling after six or seven rounds, and

we drank again. Sothis gleamed clear and cool over the star-strewn water. I leaned back against his arm and we sat on the rail.

"Tonight is the night of my birth," I said. "I am eighteen years old tonight."

"So young," he said, his brow slick with sweat, "I'm twenty already."

"So old," I said, "to be a maiden."

"We can do something about that," Xandros said, and kissed me.

It was warm and sweet and he tasted of beer and I wanted it to go on and on. My hand rose and caressed his hair, the line of his chin, holding him against me so he could never stop, like there was something starving inside me that I had never imagined. The drums and his mouth, my arms around his bare torso, his hands on my back. Starving. Never letting go.

I don't know how long it was that we sat like that, locked together. The heavens spun over us and the fire died down. The music stopped and Kos put away the drum. We finally broke apart when Aren leaned over the rail next to me and threw up in the river.

"Too much beer," Xandros said, surfacing.

"Yes, sir," he said, looking a little green. If he noticed what I was doing he didn't care, compared to his state.

"How many tankards?" Xandros asked.

"About five, I think," Aren said.

"Drink some water and go lie down," Xandros said. "You won't feel better in the morning, but you'll feel better sometime."

"Yes, sir," Aren said, and stumbled off.

I felt my head clearing. I hadn't drunk nearly as much as Aren. I looked around.

The skirt of my tunic was halfway up my legs, where Xandros had been stroking my thigh. Around the fire, no one was left except two or three people who seemed to be sleeping. A moving mass farther down the dock looked like Maris and Idele in a shadow, doing something that didn't seem at all like my business, but that involved a great deal of groaning.

Xandros touched my chin with one finger, turned my face to him. "It's not forbidden, is it?"

"No," I said. "I am forbidden a husband, not a lover." I looked in his eyes, and I wanted to kiss him again.

I stood up and I saw the hesitation, saw the moment of indecision in his face. I took his hand as he had taken mine to draw me into the dance. "Come with me."

I led him onto *Dolphin,* into the bow cabin, and we sank down together in the darkness, his warm skin on mine. "Love me. Love me," I whispered, and he laughed and kissed my throat.

He got my tunic off over my head, and I unfastened his skirt and it was a different kind of dance, one I did not know.

I ran my hands over him, learning the shape of him, the soft skin and hard muscles, the dimple at the end of his spine. When I stroked just there with my finger he groaned and buried his face in my hair.

"Do you like that?" I whispered. My fingers ran down his back again and then paused, a breath, and then a moment more, before I stroked just there again.

He pressed tighter against me. "Yes, yes, I like it." He rolled off me, lying beside me. "But unless you want it to end right now, you'd better wait a moment on that." His face was strained. It was the oddest power, to see him flushed and hungry, to see him wanting me.

Xandros smiled. Gently, he traced the shape of my nipple, round and round, watching my face.

"Harder," I said.

He bit his lower lip, smiling, not a nice smile, not gentle at all. "Like this?" He snapped it between his fingers, pulling and stretching.

I squeaked in surprise, but it felt good. "Yes, that," I said, reaching for him. "Everything."

It hurt a little at the end, but the longing was greater, my hands clasped behind his hips, pushing and grinding him against me, as though there were something I wanted more and more that I couldn't even name.

He groaned and bucked and I held him until he slid off me, pulling out and leaving me still yearning. I moaned and arched against him.

Xandros laughed deep in his throat. "I know what you want," he said, and slid his hand between my legs, rubbing and touching while I pushed against him, almost in a frenzy. There was something I wanted and I was going to have it.

And the world went dark and light and dark again, my hips shaking against his hand, and then I lay in darkness, his head pillowed on my shoulder, his arm around my body.

Our breathing was loud, loud as the muttering of the river against the dock.

"I want this," I whispered.

"So do I," he said. One hand made a lazy circle on my

stomach, gentle and quiet. "I didn't know at first that you were so beautiful," he said.

"I'm not," I said, and ducked my face behind the curtain of his hair.

"You are to me," he said. "Do you think your leg matters lying down?"

And suddenly I was laughing, though tears started in my eyes. "I suppose it doesn't."

I ran my hands through his long hair, as soft and as dark as mine. "You are beautiful, Xandros. You are everything that is good and true."

I felt him smile against my skin. "Oh, praise me more."

I bent my lips to his brow. "I've always thought you were handsome. Even the first day I met you. When you nearly killed Aren."

"I didn't think you were you the first day you met me," he said.

"I was me and Her both," I said.

He was very quiet and I thought he was dozing when he said, "I thought you were beautiful too. I hadn't thought Death was beautiful before. I mean, it's almost blasphemy, isn't it? To see Death walking, Her feet soaked in men's blood, and find something beautiful in Her."

"The gods are beautiful," I said. "Always."

He kissed me, soft and deep. "But when I carried you onto *Dolphin* after you fainted, I realized you were a young woman too, younger than me, not a crone. A young woman with a face that could have been my sister's, under the paint."

"We are alike," I said. I stopped. I had never spoken of this, since I was dedicated. "My grandfather was a boatbuilder in the Lower City," I said quietly. "My mother was his only daughter, before she was taken. She grew up in the shadow of the Great Tower, in the sound of the sea."

Xandros stroked my hair. "My father was a fisherman, and my grandfather before him."

"Do you think...Do you think you could have loved a boatbuilder's granddaughter?"

There was a smile in his voice, as though he told a secret too. "I could have loved a boatbuilder's granddaughter. A girl who grew up with me in the Lower City, a beautiful smiling girl who loves to dance and really knows how to clean fish." I pressed my face against his shoulder. "I might have married a boatbuilder's granddaughter, my dear friend, the sister of my heart."

Suddenly there were tears in my throat, and I tried to keep my voice from shaking, so I whispered instead. "I could have married a fisherman. If none of this had ever happened, and we were in Wilusa."

He kissed me, so I didn't need to say any more. The gods willed otherwise, my mother had said. But they had left us something still.

Xandros snuggled closer, as warm and as close as my shadow.

I lay half drowsing against his arm, ran my hand down his body to his manhood. "You know," I said sleepily, "the only problem with all this shaving is the stubble."

Xandros snorted. "It's kind of a problem on my end too, you know."

And we laughed and dozed and curled together under the blanket.

*   *   *

I WOKE BEFORE DAWN and knew from his breathing that he was awake. In a moment I heard him get up and go on deck, heard the stream as he made water over the side. Then he came back and lay beside me.

I shifted back against him.

"Are you awake?" he whispered.

"Yes," I said. "But we don't need to be."

"No, not yet." He burrowed his face into my hair.

Somewhere out over the river the first water bird called.

"Xandros?" I said.

"Yes?"

I laced my fingers with his. "Before I was Pythia, before I was Linnea, my name was Gull. My name is Gull."

I felt his breath against me. "Gull," he whispered, "is a beautiful name. You are Gull."

And we fell asleep again in each other's arms.

INUNDATION

I woke in the morning to find Xandros watching me. Bright sunlight poured in through the chinks in the boards above, making little warm patterns on our skin, like the spots on a cheetah, only in reverse, bright on dark. I saw him and I smiled.

He relaxed a little, and I saw that he had been afraid that I would be angry. "Hello, Xandros," I said, and stretched one cramped arm.

"Good morning," he said. He looked down at my side, where the light made patterns. "You're absolutely certain..."

"...that it's not forbidden? Absolutely. Completely. I am very, very certain that it's not forbidden. I would not have done it if it were."

He raised one eyebrow. "No, I suppose you wouldn't."

There wasn't much to say to that other than the brutally honest — I would not break my vows for you — but I didn't want to say that, so I said nothing. Instead I stretched against him. Skin on skin was tremendously

sensual, stubble included. And it was quite some time before we got up.

WHEN I FINALLY WENT to help Tia and the other women
clean up it was nearly noon. I held Kianna while Tia was
scrubbing out one of the big pots, wishing my mouth
didn't taste like stale beer. Kianna made gurgling sounds
on my shoulder and pushed at my lap with her little feet.
Her legs were getting stronger. She didn't crawl yet, but
she could inch forward on her belly like an earthworm,
making little hooting sounds as she did.

"Are you going to marry Bai?" I asked.

Tia didn't look up from the big pot. "Yes," she said.
"I was afraid to even think about it at first because of
Kianna. I mean, babies are a lot of trouble when they're
yours, and you know, expecting him to put up with every-
thing when... I was worried that it wouldn't work. And so
I thought maybe I should wait to think about getting mar-
ried to anybody until she's three and goes to you. Kos says
I don't have to get married right now."

"You could," I said. "I promised you that Kianna
would be my acolyte, and she will be." I rubbed my cheek
against Kianna's soft face, her soft hair as she climbed
against my shoulder. "I will take her when she is weaned
and she will be a daughter to me."

"Perhaps by then you will have a daughter of your
own," Tia said.

"I could have more than one daughter," I said. I looked
down, horrified to find myself blushing. "Are you surprised?" I asked.

"The only thing that surprises anyone is that it took

you so long." Tia grinned. "You and Xandros are well matched. Kos says they've been friends a long time, and that he's always needed someone like you. And it's been coming for months, hasn't it?"

"I suppose," I said. I had never really talked about a man, certainly not with a woman friend near my age. I wasn't sure how to begin.

I was spared from finding something to say by Neas arriving. He ambled in through the gates looking well pleased with himself and came up to us. "Where's Xandros?" he asked.

I colored again, but Tia answered before I could. "He and Kos went fishing," she said. "In one of the little basket boats."

Neas looked irritated. "I suppose they'll be half the day, then. I wanted to show Xandros this." He held out a sword.

It was longer than our swords by a hand span and more slender, with a leaf-shaped blade that curved gently. It was sharpened on both sides and the hilt was wrapped with stiff wool dyed dark reddish purple and fastened with gold wire. Other than that it was unadorned, and the sleek bright lines of the blade shone in the light, beautiful and lethal.

"Where did you get that?" I asked Neas.

"From one of the Nubians," he said. "He gifted it to me. He had several that he took off prisoners from Byblos and the cities of the coast."

"It's lovely," I said. "I've never seen one like it. Can I?" I asked.

Neas raised an eyebrow, but handed it to me. "I thought you were forbidden to shed blood?"

"I'm not planning to kill you with it," I said. "I can hold it, can't I?" It was heavy, solid as a full carry-measure of grain, but beautifully balanced so that I could hold it in my hand without strain. It was much thinner than our swords, and the point was sharp. You could slash with it or use the tip, and yet it was strong enough to block a spear thrust. And I said so to Neas.

His eyebrows went up even farther. "Our Sybil knows something of swords?"

"Neas," I said, "I can see what is plain before my eyes. It's better than anything we have. With it you could get inside a man's guard while he still could not reach you, and against a spearman you would be able to block."

"I could," he said. "And if I had a shield I could withstand archers long enough to close." He looked at me and his eyes were as bright as the blade. "Sybil, with swords like this a man could rule the world. There is nothing that can stand against them, not even chariots. And if you put together swords like this and men trained to fight in close order like the Nubians, rather than running as skirmishers as we do, not even chariots could break the formation. That's the problem the Nubians have now. They can't fight in close if the chariots come in. But with these swords you'd cut the horses to pieces and the drivers would be in too close for their javelins to work very well."

"With swords like those and men trained to fight in close order, a small group of men could hold off much greater numbers," I said slowly. "We could win, even though we are few."

"Yes." Neas looked down at the blade and he swallowed. "But no one is doing that. The Shardana have some of these, and the men of Tyre and Ugarit That Was, but they fight the same way we do, each man rushing in for honor. The Egyptians have the Nubians, and you have seen how they fight like one man, but they cannot stand against chariots." He looked up at me. "Do you see? With swords like these, the day of chariots is over. These are the swords that destroyed Ugarit, and these are the swords that nothing can stand against."

"Except," I said, "a group of men with swords like those, and shields, who know how to fight in close order."

"The enemy could run forward seeking honor even with swords like these and break off them like the sea off rocks."

"We could stand against anyone," I said.

"You see it," Neas said, and clasped my hands. There was something light about him, something that reminded me suddenly of Mik-el. "Sybil, you see it! The Egyptians do not!"

"You have brought this up to the Egyptians?" I said, taken aback.

"They have the swords already," Neas said, "taken from prisoners or given as gifts in trade. And they don't understand. They all just blink at me and say, 'This is not the way it was done in our grandfathers' day. This is not the Way of Maat.' They have taken one of the best-balanced blades and gilded it for ceremony, but they don't understand what it can do."

"Perhaps they do understand," I said. "But it doesn't matter. Things must be done according to Maat, the Balance. Things that are well done should never be changed."

"But the world is changing," Neas said.

"I know that," I said. "My prince, we are a young people with young gods. If there is a new way to do something we will try it. It might be silly, or there might be some advantage in it."

"How can we know until we try it?" Neas asked.

"That is my point, Neas. You see every reason to try something, and they see no reason to. There's a saying they have: Don't fix it if it is not broken."

Neas shrugged. "We have every reason to, all right. We're on a knife's edge, and anything that gives us an advantage may be the difference between our survival and the deaths of all the People." He took the sword back and hefted it experimentally. "I've been looking for the thing. The gods know that I have been praying for the thing. This is it."

"But not the sword alone," I said. "The other piece is you. You must teach them to fight in close order like the Nubians. And no man has done this before."

"Then we will learn," he said. "That's why I'm hunting for Xandros. He'll see."

"He will," I said. "Of all the men here he will see." Xandros had the quickest mind, and he saw straight through the how of things.

Neas looked out at the swollen Nile, dark with silt and life-giving soil. "We are not like them," he said softly. "For them safety lies in the old ways, in things that are unchanging year after year."

"And for us the world is changing," I said.

Neas nodded. "If we had kept to the old ways, Citadel and Lower City, horse people and sea people, each caring for our own, bound only by ties of kinship, we would die. You did not grow up in the City, Sybil. You don't know how far we've already come from our traditions. The fishing boat children with no kin are cared for by others."

"There are so many women," I said, "who have lost their children, so many with no bonds of kinship. Is it strange that they should take an orphaned child of the People?"

"It would be in the City," Neas said.

"You learn differently in captivity," I said gently. "It does not matter what your station was once when you are all slaves together, and it does not matter whose child it is if it is one of ours. You said it yourself on the Island of the Dead, Neas. Every life of the People is valuable. Even Kianna. Even Aren. Was it not so in the City?"

"No." He shook his head. "We were like everyone else then. There were some with much more than others, and some children were wanted and some were exposed." He looked me in the eye. "The child of a rape would have been left on the hillside for the beasts, and you would not be Sybil."

"And Bai would not marry Tia," I said.

"Tia would live all her life in Kos' house, unmarriageable and pitied, eating from his charity."

"That will not happen," I said.

"No." Neas smiled. "The women of the People are too few. There are three men for every woman, and a young woman who is pretty and well spoken, able to bear healthy children, can choose among her suitors, rape or no. If she picks Bai, it is he who has gained, not her."

"We must take care," I said slowly, "to keep the good that has come from this when we are in our new city, to keep the People we have become. Perhaps that is what the gods intended all along."

Neas looked away. "Our new city. Do you really see it so, or was that encouragement spoken to me in a dark time?"

"It is true," I said. "I know it as I know anything. We will not stay in Egypt, Neas. That is not your fate."

I wasn't sure if he looked troubled or relieved. "Where should we go? We can't return to Byblos or the cities of the coast. Every hand there will be raised against us for the blood of their men lost in the great fleet. I see no choice besides staying in Egypt." Neas looked at me sharply. "And besides, I thought you liked it here."

"I do," I said, and I meant it with all my heart. "But it is not your fate to die here. You will found a new city in a distant land. That is what I have seen."

"And you, Sybil?" he asked. "Where will you die?"

"I do not know," I said. "No more than any other mortal."

I would that it were here, in this ancient land. I thought I would that it were here, when I had passed four score years in useful service. I would lie here, under this sun, in this quiet place that called to me with deep voices of peace. I do not know why I loved the Black Land so, or why it filled me with a deep thrill like the sound of a great drum at a distance to know that I had played some little part in preserving that peace. I suspect, looking back. I imagine that I had loved this land before. Love is without end.

AND so our life fell into a peaceful rhythm, merging for a moment with the deep tides of the Black Land. The flood rose and descended. Tia married Bai, left the room she had shared with me for one with him.

The flood waters subsided, and the planting began, big sleepy black oxen in the fields working the rich soil. Somehow Xandros found his way into Tia's place. Some nights we just lay quiet in the dark, listening to the soft sounds of the river, of the People sleeping. Other times I would turn to him and in the darkness discover unknown worlds. I would go to sleep with his hair against my face listening to the firm, steady beating of his heart.

In the fields of Egypt the first beans began to sprout, two green leaves unfolding to the sun. By day, Neas taught his men the skill of close-order fighting. As he had predicted, Xandros was the first to understand what Neas wanted. Day after day they sweated, shields made of bulls' hide in their left hands, swords in their right. Not all of them had the new swords of course, but there were more and more among us. Many had been taken from captives or those slain in the great fleet, and as Egyptian soldiers learned that we would trade beer for them, they were glad to trade us their trophies.

I watched them in the courtyard. Neas shouted out the orders, like a captain to rowers, with Xandros and Maris to pass them on. Indeed, it was the rowers who did the best, accustomed as they were to moving in unison and answering chanted directions. They stood in lines three men deep, shields on their left arms, each man covering the right of the man next to him, each boat's rowers forming up as a company. Xandros would shout to *Dolphin*'s men, and they would turn on Kos, the front man on the right, facing first one way and then another, advancing at the same pace, swords drawn. In the dust that rose from their moving feet I saw endless shadows. Standing by the cooking pots I thought I saw other feet moving, not bare and tanned as theirs, but shod in leather sandals studded with bronze, medallions stamped with eagles.

Like the leaves opening in the sun, two fragile sails pale green and trembling, I felt the beginning of something.

WHEN THE PLANTING was done, Pharaoh ordered the ships down the Nile to Tamiat because there was the rumor of raiders. We waited, and the men sailed. This time Xandros had a breastplate of leather and a fine new sword, and he gave me a sideways smile as *Dolphin* slid away from the dock, his hands on the tiller.

They were gone forty days, and came back without having seen an enemy, much less engaged one. Xandros came eager and happy to my bed, and I kissed his throat and chest as though we had been parted a year.

Afterward, we lay replete, murmuring sweet things in the warm night.

"There is no great fleet," Xandros said. "What there was is shattered. There are a few ships left, but they are scattered and hiding, for the most part. This winter there will be few raids, and nothing that can assail Egypt."

"That's good," I said. I was not entirely thinking about ships.

"The sailing season is ending," he said. "We are wintering here."

"And I suppose Neas means for us to stay on," I said.

Xandros gave a short laugh, as though it wasn't really funny. "Well, he's certainly not going anywhere! The princess told him that she had hardly been able to stand it while he was away with the ships. Next time we're supposed to go without him while he stays in Memphis."

I pushed myself up on one elbow. "He's supposed to stay in Memphis?"

"Yes."

"With the women and children and old men while his ships patrol against raiders?"

Xandros nodded. "That's what the princess says. She's completely entranced with her barbarian prince. And she says he must never be allowed to leave her side again."

"Allowed?" I raised one eyebrow.

"That's the word she used," Xandros agreed.

"Will Neas stand for this?" I asked.

Xandros shook his head. "I don't see that he has any choice. If he doesn't do what she says, what then?"

"Our contract is with her brother, not with her," I said.

"Her brother is in Thebes," Xandros pointed out. "And the sailing season has ended. In any event, we aren't going anywhere until spring."

THE DAYS were at their shortest, and the fields of Egypt greened. Anchises sought me out as I returned from the Temple of Thoth.

"Sybil," he said formally, "I would speak with you."

I went aside with him, though I looked on him with trepidation. My dealings with him had never been what I should call pleasant. "How may I assist you, my lord Anchises?" I asked.

"I want you to talk to my son about leaving Egypt," he said, his mouth twisted as though it hurt him to ask me. "He may heed your counsel as he does not heed mine."

I thought carefully. "Why do you wish me to do this?"

"If it is not done soon it will never be," Anchises said. "Already four men among the People have taken Egyptian wives."

That much at least was true. And it was to be expected. Half a year we had been here, and there were three times as many men as women among the People. Our men, coming home with spoils and bonuses from the battle, accounted heroes who had helped Pharaoh preserve Egypt, were not unattractive to Egyptian women. Four had married so far, and I was certain that before the winter ended there would be more.

"Are you afraid it will be five, my lord?" I asked.

His mouth tightened and for a moment he looked very like his son. "It will never be five," he said. "My son is not reckoned an appropriate husband for Pharaoh's sister. And he never will be. Though in the old days his grandfather took to wife a niece of the Hittite emperor!"

"Those days are gone," I said carefully. "And even in the days of Wilusa's power the Great Kings of Egypt did not send their daughters to marry the lords of other lands. No, I think that you are right. Aeneas will never marry Basetamon."

"Is that what we are to be?" he asked, and his blue eyes met mine, a little watery with age or light. "We are to be no more than the concubines and hired men-at-arms of a foreign nation?"

"Some men would say it is better than slavery," I said. I would say so, if he asked. But he had never asked me before what I thought.

"Is that all we hope for? To avoid the lash? What has become of our pride, our sovereignty?"

"My lord, if you had tasted the lash you would not disdain avoiding it," I said a little tartly. But then I sighed. He was right. And though I hated to agree with him, I must. "You are right that this is not our destiny. I will speak with Neas when I may."

"I will not," he said, and almost smiled. "If I say more to him of it he will only get his back up and heed you less."

"Then we are in agreement," I said. "I will do as you ask."

I FOUND NEAS ALONE a week later, when we were celebrating another wedding. One of Maris' rowers was marrying an Egyptian widow, a woman with a fishing boat and two young sons, and no man to help her fish the river. They broke a jar together in the Egyptian way, and then we did the snake dance, some of her relatives jumping into the festivities too.

I found Neas by the fire, clapping in time but not dancing. His hair was cut to no more than a finger's length, and his face was shaven.

"My prince," I said, standing beside him.

"Sybil."

"My prince," I said, "I do not think I will dance at your wedding to Basetamon."

He looked into the fire instead of at me. "No, I don't think you will."

"And when she tires of you, my prince?"

Neas shrugged. "We will be a fighting force her brother reckons valuable. He will not cast away a sword to his hand as easily as she will cast away a pastime. There will be no peace next year. There will be raids and war on the western border. The Libyans were emboldened by the great fleet, and they will make trouble."

I took both his calloused hands in mine, made him look at me. "Neas, is this the best we can do?"

"I can do no better," he said, and his eyes were full of regret. "What would you have me do? Steal away in the middle of the night with the People stuffed aboard ships, hoping that Basetamon doesn't pursue? And go where?"

"If we can't go east to the cities of the coast we must go west."

Neas shrugged. "To the Libyans? The Shardana?"

"Think on it," I urged. "That is all I ask."

"I will think, Sybil," he said.

Across the fire, I watched Amynter dancing with the bride's aunt, a plump, smiling woman of thirty-five or so. Yes, I had heard right when she arrived. She was also a widow with several half-grown children. She looked like the sort of woman to take Amynter's sons under her wing, cozying them to eat without treating them like children. He spoke little Khemet and she spoke none of our tongue, but they seemed to be getting along well enough.

THE HARVEST TIME CAME, and the first of the crops were gathered in, the green beans and the spring fruit. The year had turned. The days lengthened again.

I counted the captains. Xandros would go, and most of the men of *Dolphin.* Maris would go with *Pearl,* and so would his young wife and most of their men, though not the man who had married. Amynter and *Hunter* would not go. He was courting the widow, and he was plainly content with his lot. *Winged Night* and her captain would likely be reluctant. We had begun with nine warships and three fishing boats. If we left Egypt, it would be with three ships. Anchises was right. Many would not leave now, and that number would be more each day.

And I, I had one more reason to stay.

In moments of terror I wondered what Xandros would say, and then I told myself that it mattered not at all. The daughters of Pythia belong to the Lady of the Dead, daughters to the Shrine. I could keep my child as well as Kianna with no fear of starvation. The children of Egyptian temples are well provided for, and Hry had made it very clear that I would be welcome indeed in the service of Thoth. If I wished to stay I should not lack a place, and neither should the child.

And yet.

I felt Her path leading me on across the sea. *Carry Me,* She had said, *like an unborn child in your body to a new place. Carry Me with the People.* If I stayed, I should leave Her service. I should lose Her as well as Xandros.

I did not even need to wonder what he would do. He would follow where Neas led, even to the ends of the earth.

THE HARVEST was gathered in. The dry season began. Soon the seas would open and the ships of all nations set forth.

On a hot day when the sun stood straight overhead Kianna took her first steps from her mother's hands to mine, then fell back on her fat clouted bottom in the dirt and laughed. Her hair had come in thin and red, shining like copper, and a sprinkling of freckles showed across her nose.

When we had laughed and cuddled her Tia looked at me meaningfully. "They will be sisters," she said.

I nodded.

"Have you told Xandros?" she asked.

"If he doesn't notice it's because he doesn't want to," I said, and I did not meet her eyes. "It's not as though he's never seen a breeding woman before." And I wondered about them too, my child's older sisters that the Achaians had slain. Someone had killed a child Kianna's age. Some man I had blessed at Pylos had cut her little body to pieces with a sword, a child that Xandros had loved and cuddled and walked with at night, a child he had talked to while still in her mother's belly. Small wonder he did not see. He could never bear another loss like that.

"He will see when he wants to," I said, and held Kianna when she clung to my hands, the sweet baby scent of her against my face.

Or he will not. He will go far across the sea with Neas, and I will stay here in Memphis, I thought. *He will not know, but the child will be safe.*

THE NEXT DAY Amynter came in from the palace with news. Our ships were ordered to Sais in the western delta, to be ready lest the Libyans make war. Our ships would sail, and Neas would stay in Memphis.

That night I lay in our bed, but Xandros did not come.

I waited and I turned and thought. The sounds of the People quieted. And still he did not come.

At last I uncurled and got up. Perhaps he was ill. Or

perhaps one of the men was. There were many good reasons for his absence. I did not go to the door out of concern. I just wondered where he was.

He was standing with Neas beside the river. Behind them, the rising moon made a ribbon of light across the water, shining on Neas' hair, their heads inclined close together, talking in low voices. I started to duck back inside, but Xandros saw me and beckoned.

I went to them.

"I'm glad you're awake," Neas said, and his eyes were troubled. "I have need of your counsel."

"In the middle of the night?"

Xandros looked solemn. I wondered what they had been talking about.

Neas nodded. He turned, looking out over the river, his back half to me. "Sybil, it is time to leave Egypt."

"Leave?"

"Have you not counseled me before that it was not our destiny to stay?" I could not see his shadowed face and looked instead at Xandros.

Xandros shook his head almost imperceptibly, and made some grimaces that I had no idea what he meant by. Did he mean that I should urge him to go, or that some strange mood was on him that I should discourage?

"I need to know how we are going to get all of the People to Sais," Neas said, his back still to me.

"Why Sais?" I asked.

"Because Pharaoh is there," Neas said, "or will be. And that's where the People who aren't going with us need to be."

"When we cut and run for the wild ocean and Shardan shores," Xandros said gravely. "We know not everybody will go. About half, really. But they need to be in Pharaoh's service, not the princess'. So they'll be safe when we go."

"Pharaoh won't cast them away," Neas said. "Not with the Libyans pressing. Especially since they're the men who kept faith."

"Not us oath breakers," Xandros said grimly.

I looked at him. What has brought this on? I tried to convey with my face alone. Of course these things are true, but until this moment Neas has heard none of it. What has changed?

I did not know what Xandros gathered from my expression. Possibly some inexplicable twitching.

He said, "Getting the People to Sais won't be hard. Basetamon doesn't like it that you spend so much time at the barracks of the Division of the Ram. You could tell her that the People would rather go to Sais and be close to their men since Pharaoh is going to use Sais to stage from rather than Memphis. If it's war with the Libyans, Memphis is too far south to be convenient."

Neas nodded. "I could. I doubt Basetamon will frankly remember that there might be some oarsman who stayed in Sais. It won't matter to her, not if I go."

"The problem," I said, "is getting you to Sais. Aren't you supposed to stay here?"

"I am," Neas said.

I mused, looking out over the waters at *Seven Sisters* riding high at the dock, empty of stores and crew. "The only person who can countermand Basetamon's orders is Pharaoh."

"And Pharaoh wants Neas in Sais, leading his ships.

After all, that's what he's paying him for," Xandros said reasonably.

"So we send a message to Pharaoh saying that Neas regrets that he will be unable to come to Sais in person because Basetamon requires he remain in Memphis," I said. "I can write out a message. I've learned enough scribing for that."

"And then Pharaoh orders him to Sais," Xandros said.

"I go to Sais, we settle in, and then those of us who are going just sail away." Neas turned and clapped Xandros on the shoulder. "Thank you for your counsel, my friend. And for yours, Sybil. That is what we shall do."

He turned and walked away into the night.

I watched him go. Xandros sighed and leaned on the rail, looking out across the river.

"What happened?" I asked. "Have you been out here talking to Neas all this time?"

He nodded. "He asked me not to speak of it to anyone." His face was troubled. I stood beside him, my shoulder almost touching his. "He asked me, on our friendship, to keep silent. We need to leave, Gull." His arm went around my waist, seeking warmth. "Soon, for his sake, not ours."

I leaned against him. "I'm glad he talked with you."

"I'm glad he's finally come to this," Xandros said. "Does your Lady bless this endeavor?"

I took a breath. The wind that blew across the river was just the wind, pulling at my hair and setting ripples to dancing on the water. There was no strangeness in it, no sense of Her at my sleeve. "She says nothing," I said. "I do not know."

"We have to leave, Gull," Xandros repeated.

I closed my eyes and said nothing. I still did not know

what I would do. The People would go with Neas, and those who remained would become something else. I could stay. No harm would come to me. I would be safe and welcomed at the temple. The choice was still mine.

And She was silent.

A FALCON
TO THE SUN

I wrote the letter from Neas to Pharaoh and saw it sent southward to Thebes in one of the courier boats in the service of Amon. A week passed, and the order came for our ships to sail for Sais. We were granted permission, by authority of Princess Basetamon, to take our families and goods with us to Sais, where we should live. Instead of barracks this time, we were free to take up abodes within the city in such places as we should wish. Prince Aeneas, however, would remain in Memphis and attend upon Princess Basetamon.

When I came to the Temple of Thoth the next morning it was with a heavy heart. I walked with Hry beside the pool and sat at last in the morning shade. "I do not wish to leave," I said.

He thought I meant only Memphis. "Daughter of Wilusa, it is not so far. Even for an old man like me. And you are not ordered to Sais. You could stay here."

"I cannot," I said. "She has given me this responsibil-

ity, don't you see? If it were only for myself, there is nowhere in the world I would rather stay, but I did not enter
Her service lightly. She has sent me to serve Her People,
and I must go." I bent my head and blinked back tears.

"Perhaps you will return from Sais at the end of the
summer," Hry said. "When the Libyans have been defeated."

I could not speak and lie to him, so I only shook my
head.

Hry put one hand on my shoulder. "Perhaps it is not to
Sais that you go," he said.

I looked up at him, startled.

He smiled at me. "Dear Daughter, do you think old age
has robbed me of my wits? I knew Wilusa of old, remember." He dropped his voice. "And I have spent my life in
the service of the gods. I know what they can ask of you.
What is it you see, Daughter of Isis?"

"I see a city in a distant land," I said. "I see young olive
trees growing on a hillside above a river, a stag breaking through the brambles and leading the hunt, a she-wolf
howling on a crag for her lost pups and laurel trees beside
a Shrine." There were shapes in the water of the pool, as
though I had been holding them back for months, keeping
the future at bay. "Fire leaping on a pyre, grain ripening
in the field. But the way there is not easy. The waters are
dark, and there is a mountain crowned in smoke, a path
that leads down into the darkness." I shivered.

Hry's hand was on my shoulder, and for a moment I
thought it was She Who Was Pythia who spoke to me.
"You do not fear the darkness, you who dwell in darkness.
You of all mortals need have no fear of Her sacred places.
When the time comes you will know what to do."

"He is a king," I said. "And I know how kings are made."

Hry nodded. "In every land it was thus. I too had my part when Ramses came to the throne eight years ago. I know the journey, and the price to come forth by day."

He kissed me on the brow. "Go in peace and with my blessing, Daughter of the Gods. When the time comes for you to return to the Black Land you will do so, and live here in peace all the days of your life."

I looked up at him. "Do you know this is true?"

"You will return," he said, "though a hundred years should pass, for your *ba* yearns after knowledge like a falcon for the sun. The doors of this temple will be open for you."

"I will come," I promised, "if it should take me a hundred years."

There was the sudden scattered sound of feet on stone, and one of the young door wardens hurried in. "Hry," he said, "a message has come from the palace. The Princess Basetamon requires your presence along with the Denden oracle. She wishes the oracle to tell her future and do magic for her."

Hry gave me one quick glance. "We shall come with all haste," he said.

I wrapped my black veil about me. "Do you have any paint?" I asked, and my voice was steady. Whether she knew what we intended or not, I should face her as what I truly was, as my Lady's voice.

WE WENT in a litter together, Hry and I. We did not speak. The bearers belonged to the princess.

The chamber where we were ushered in was nothing like the grand halls of the palace where I had been before. It was a small inner room. The walls were richly painted, every inch from floor to ceiling carved and covered in writing. There were no windows, and the room was lit only by a brazier in the middle of the floor and a pair of oil lamps hanging on chains. The floor was strewn with cushions. At one end an incense burner gave off a cloud of thick scented smoke. It was very close and very dark. Perhaps she thought this was a suitable place to greet an oracle, but it made the hairs on the back of my neck rise.

My face painted black and white, my black veil swooping behind me like a vulture's wings, I bowed in front of her.

Behind her I heard a faint shuffle, like padded feet. One of the cheetahs stood up from where she had lain among the pillows, her handler silent in a corner. The great cat's ears pricked forward.

"You may rise," the princess said, and I looked into her face. Close up, she seemed anxious, and her eyes were the color of honey.

"How may I serve Your Majesty?" I asked.

"Aeneas says you can tell the future," she said. "I want you to tell the future for me."

"Your Majesty, have you not foretellers in Khemet?" I asked. "Surely you do not need me."

Basetamon paced like a restless cat. "Of course I have foretellers. I have dozens. But none of them tell the truth. They cast lots and tell me platitudes. 'Caution is wise. The gods hold us in their hands.' They have no power. Aeneas says that you do."

"Your Majesty," I said carefully, "I am my Lady's

voice. But I do not bid Her to speak, any more than your handmaidens may bid you. It may be that the Lady of the Dead has words to impart to you and will use me thus, or it may not. She does not speak at my command."

The princess waved my words away. "Of course. I know one does not bid the gods to speak. But I want you to try for me."

"That I will do with a will, Your Majesty," I said. There was no other answer I could make, not to her, no matter how reluctant I might be.

"What do you need?" she asked keenly. "A snake? A dove for sacrifice?"

"I need nothing other than what you have here," I said. "Just the fire. There is no more to my magic than that. She will speak or She will not."

"There was a man in Great Ramses' reign who could prophesy and turn rods into snakes," she said. "He turned the river to blood."

"I will turn nothing into blood," I said, thinking that must have been quite a trick. I settled down on the pillows before the brazier, but my heart was beating fast. *Patience,* I thought. *If She does not speak I must do as Pythia taught me and use my eyes and my own mind, as I have again and again.*

Basetamon sat opposite me. I could see her pulse jumping in her throat. She was nervous too. Her hands twisted together.

"What knowledge does Your Majesty seek?" I asked, dropping my voice low.

"I want to know what will happen," she said. "I want to know if I will be happy."

"Are you not happy now?" I asked. Surely in all the

wide world if any woman had cause to be she did, who had beauty and birth and power, respect and good servants and Neas for a lover.

Basetamon shook her head, and her honey-colored eyes were distant. "I have never been happy. But lately it is worse and worse. My dreams are troubled and I cannot sleep. I have no desire for food, and it seems that my skin crawls. I dream of snakes." She looked into the brazier. "I was married to my uncle when I was nine. I was fifteen when he died, when he tried to kill my brother. Our son, my son, is thirteen and away learning war from my brother. My brother thinks this is best."

"It must be hard, to be parted from your son," I said.

She shook her head. "Not really. He never loved me enough. He grieves me." Basetamon looked into my face. "I want to know if Aeneas loves me. He says he does. I love him more than heaven and earth. He's my life. He's the only one who has ever belonged to me, body and soul."

She reached over and stroked the long ears of the big cat. "I will keep him at my side forever. He need not fear I will cast him off. He will be mine forever, and when I die he will be entombed with me."

A chill ran down my back that had nothing to do with Her presence. "Tell me about the dreams of snakes, My Lady," I said gently.

"I dream of snakes," she said. "Twining around my body. Pressing my limbs. I dream my bones crack. I cannot eat. You would not know to look at me that I was fat once." She spread her long thin arms in the firelight. "When I was a girl. When I was married. But now I cannot eat and I am beautiful. And I cannot sleep, and my eyes are bister. I am holy and wondrous."

"Did you tell Prince Aeneas that he should share your tomb?" I asked carefully, knowing that the Egyptians would consider such a very great honor, but that Neas should certainly feel otherwise.

Basetamon smiled. "I did. Not long before word came from my brother that your ships should go. I told my brother that Aeneas must stay with me because I am lost without him. I told Aeneas that he would be entombed with me, to lie beside me forever in the tomb, that our *kas* should dine together in the darkness. And then I bade him lie beside me and pleasure me with his tongue, and told him that when we are both corpses we will do the same."

I understood, then, why he had sought out Xandros. And what Xandros had not told me.

I struggled to keep my face bland, and keep the horror I felt from shading my voice. "Your Majesty," I said, "you do him too much honor. Your beauty must be as blinding to him as that of Isis! Remember he is only a mortal man!"

"I do remember," she said. "I wring him dry with my hands and he will not rise for hours. I wish he had Osiris' golden member, so that he might last forever in my power."

"But Osiris was dead," I said. "And His manhood was made of metal, not flesh, because Isis could not find all the parts of Him that Set cut apart and cast about the land."

"And one day Aeneas will be dead as well," Basetamon said. "And so will I. We are all going to be corpses, waiting for the natron. But he will be as fair on that day as ever. I told him that if he dies first I will keep him em-

balmed in my room until I die, so that we might lie together in one tomb."

"You do him too much honor," I said. "He cannot have
ever aspired to your companionship in the next world."
Indeed, I was not certain that he greatly desired it in this
one.

"Why not?" she demanded.

"You are as far above him as the sun is above the hills,"
I said. "You are the highest-born lady of Egypt. I am sure
Aeneas feels that he is unworthy."

Basetamon flipped her braids back from her long,
smooth neck, her beautiful hands restless. "He has the
body of a lion. And he is as fair as the desert falcon. He
is mine. And I make him worthy. Now prophesy for me,
Oracle! Tell me if I will be happy!"

I bent above the brazier, muttering nonsense words, my
mind working furiously. I did not think she could ever be
happy, because the snakes were within her, not without.
She walked in a darkness I could not penetrate.

"Great Lady," I said in my own mother tongue. "Healer
of hearts and minds, in Whose darkness we are all born,
walk with the Lady of Egypt and lead her to the fields of
peace."

Basetamon watched me, and the cheetah's eyes gleamed
in the dark.

I looked into the fire.

"What do you see?" she demanded.

If I had been at my own hearth I should have snapped
that I saw nothing because she would not be quiet for two
breaths. But I was not. And she was the ruler here. I simply took a long breath and exhaled it.

"I see fire," I said.

"And?" she asked breathlessly.

"I see flames rising," I said. "Smoke twisting in the air." *From a brazier,* I thought. *That's sitting right in front of me. Will she not be quiet if she wants me to see?*

"Like a sacrifice at our shared tomb?" she asked.

"Like a sacrifice," I temporized. "Smoke heavy with precious resins."

"What else do you see?"

"Wailing mourners," I said. "Throngs of wailing mourners. Priests and musicians. Even Pharaoh himself." I had never made up a prophecy out of whole cloth before. But as I spoke I could almost imagine it, Pharaoh standing by in his linen skirt, his face a mask of grief.

"Is he very sad?" Basetamon asked eagerly.

"Terribly," I said. "His face is stern and stricken. I can see that he suffers."

Basetamon put her hands together. "That's wonderful! A sacrifice at our shared tomb! Is it true that in your country you burn the dead?"

"It is," I said. "We build no such monuments as you do. Instead we build a funeral pyre."

Basetamon shivered. "How grotesque! Do you actually watch them burn?"

"We sing," I said, "and praise the dead. We offer libations and incense. And then we dance."

Basetamon shook her head. "How bizarre! But poor Aeneas will never endure that. He will lie beside me forever." Rising, she thrust a bag into my hand. "You have done me a great service, Oracle! You have my thanks!" The princess stood, her linen robes flaring around her. "Now go! And go to Sais with my blessing!"

"Your Majesty," I said, seeing suddenly a door open-

ing, "will you not come to Sais as well? Will you not bring
Prince Aeneas so that he may do deeds of valor for you?
To be worthy of you he must be great in war, the desert
falcon you have named him. Let him demonstrate to all
that he is worthy of the honors you have given him."

She turned. "Really?"

"Really, My Lady," I said. "I know he feels unworthy
of you, as I have said. Please grant his pride the chance to
do deeds of valor in your name that may be inscribed on
the walls of your tomb for all eternity!"

Basetamon smiled. "He would do this for me?"

"Only for you, Your Majesty," I said.

"Then we will go," she said. "We will go to Sais."
Reaching beneath the cushions she pulled yet another
bag out and pressed it into my hands. "Take these and use
them well."

I looked inside. One bag was filled with myrrh and the
other with frankincense, enough to burn a king. "Thank
you, Your Majesty," I said. Valuable as it was, I took it
with a shiver and could not help but feel it an ill omen.

WE SAILED for Sais. Neas did not go on *Seven Sisters,*
but on the great barge belonging to Basetamon. He did
indeed go to Sais at her side.

It was a pleasant journey. Our ships were crowded, for
our people had accumulated many goods in Memphis,
and it was more like moving households than ships of
war. But half, I reminded myself, would stay in Sais.

Xandros had spoken with Amynter. Amynter did want
to stay in Egypt in Pharaoh's service. When he heard that

Neas would release him from any oaths to him, he was happy indeed, though he loved Neas well.

"My luck is out," he said to Xandros as we stood on the bow of *Dolphin* in the evening as we all paused along the bank of the Nile. He shrugged. "A man's got only so much luck in his life. I've used mine on the sea and in war. And I've got my boys to think of. It's time for me to stay. I'll patrol this summer for Pharaoh, but then I'm leaving the ships. I'm going to get married and be a tradesman instead. It's not too late to learn a new trick. Let the boys go to war if they want. I'm done."

Xandros clasped his hand. "I understand. My time isn't yet, but I understand."

"Just get out in time," Amynter said. "I know too many good men who pushed their luck."

"I'll remember that," Xandros said, and smiled.

Maris would go. We thought all in all we should have three ships and a little more than a hundred men, with perhaps twenty women and twenty children in the lot. More of the married men would want to stay.

"So few," Xandros said, and put his arm around my shoulders. Together we watched the sun setting beyond the walls of the western desert, the river flowing remorselessly northward. We had no privacy, as there were five people in the bow cabin, but that meant that he had less chance of seeing me unclothed. I was wondering how much longer I could say nothing. Even in loose clothing it would become obvious soon. Neas hadn't noticed, but he was also considerably distracted.

"So few," I said. "But enough."

We didn't speak of it further. It wasn't time yet.

*　　*　　*

WE WERE FOUR DAYS in Sais. On the fifth night, a night with no moon, Xandros went round the sentries and the port watch. He told them that we were taking three ships on patrol downriver, as there were rumors of Libyans massing on the bank of the westernmost branch of the Nile as it flowed through the Delta and into the sea. This seemed reasonable enough. Three ships was a patrol. And we had patrolled before.

By night we loaded the ships—all of our people who were going and all of our goods. Rowers bumped into one another in unfamiliar places. Not all of any ship's company meant to go, and some of *Hunter's* and *Winged Night's* men wanted to come. So there was confusion in the darkness.

I stood beside *Dolphin* in the night, helping Tia aboard with sleeping Kianna pressed to her shoulder. Bai swung their bundles up and held the baby while Tia climbed. I smiled at him.

"Do you remember, Lady?" he said quietly. "When we left Byblos, when she was born?"

"I do," I said. "I remember how you brought Tia a warm cloak."

"And the boy," Bai said. "The one who was lost."

Both of us looked back up the dock to where Xandros was talking with Amynter, taking his leave.

Aren brushed past them and came up to me. "I'm not going," he said.

"What?"

"I'm not going," Aren said. His jaw was set. "I don't belong there, and I'm not going."

"Aren..."

"Pythia," he said, "you know I don't belong with you. I don't belong where you're going."

"Aren, what will you do? I can't just leave you here."

He put his hand on my shoulder. "I am the son of Triotes, and a man. I will stay in Pharaoh's service."

I looked at him, thinking of words. I had not thought of any when Xandros came down the dock. "Now," he said. "Neas is here. He sneaked off from the palace, but he may be missed at any time. We need to go now."

"Good-bye," Aren said.

"Are you certain?"

"Yes," he said, and embraced me. "Good fortune, sister."

I had always known he walked a path different from mine. "Good fortune, my brother," I said.

Xandros came aboard and went back to the tiller. It was Bai who reached down for my hand and helped me aboard.

"Good-bye," I whispered, and this time I knew it was forever.

Aren had already run back down the dock as we put off. *Pearl* went first, followed by *Seven Sisters*. *Dolphin* was last from the dock. We coasted by *Winged Night* and *Hunter*, tied up safe at their moorings. The river rocked us gently.

Past the silent docks of fishermen, past the wharves where the grain barges unloaded, we slid along in darkness, the sound of our oars quiet and beating like a heart. There were no shouts of challenge as we slipped past the Egyptian warships at their moorings. Behind me I heard Xandros call a greeting to a sentry, his Khemet smooth and fluid after a year.

"Good hunting!" the sentry called.

"Thanks!" Xandros replied. "We'll kill some Libyans for you!"

I went aft to stand at the tiller beside him. His hair was unbound and I watched his hands on the tiller, steady and firm. Ahead of us, *Seven Sisters* left a white wake in the water.

Xandros chuckled softly.

"What are you thinking?" I asked.

"I'm thinking that once in a while I'd like to leave a port in broad daylight with nobody after us," Xandros said.

I nearly laughed. "That would be nice, wouldn't it?"

Behind us on the broad terraces of the palace there was a sudden flare of fire. Almost at the same time I heard the drums start on *Seven Sisters*.

"Pick up the beat, Kos!" Xandros shouted. "Time to get moving!"

Our drums picked up, racing ahead.

"Right side skip the stroke!" Xandros yelled, and the right side oars hovered in the air while the left ones dug, turning us into the channel for the westernmost branch of the river, putting us midstream. We bumped a little as we crossed *Seven Sisters'* wake. The fire behind us was now obscured by date trees and palms that came down the riverbank. I could still see it faintly through the leaves, but Sais was well behind us.

"Pull!" Xandros yelled. "Keep it up!" He glanced at me. "We'll keep our best pace for a bit, just to put some distance behind us. I don't know what that was about. It may be nothing to do with us. But there's no point in taking a chance."

I nodded.

Night slid past like the walls of the Delta, tangled trees and undergrowth, reeds taller than my head. When dawn came pink and white over the river, the channel had narrowed to the width of two ships, with shallows on each side, and we slowed. Down the ship Tia and Polyra came out of the forward cabin and began taking skins of beer and loaves of flatbread to the rowers, who ate in turns. Ahead of us, *Pearl* and *Seven Sisters* slowed but didn't stop.

"How far is it to the sea?" I asked.

"A day," Xandros said. "We're going as much west as north right now. We'll come to the sea several days sailing west of Tamiat, the Delta is that broad."

"And then?"

"North across the sea," he said, gratefully taking a loaf of bread from Tia and biting into it without leaving the tiller. "That's where the Shardana live. There are several big islands, they say, and more mainland. They say it snows there, like on the highest mountains at home. And that there are forests so huge that you could walk for a moon without coming to the other side."

I tried to imagine it. But mostly what I saw was Egypt slipping away, the Black Land passing behind me, becoming the past.

"You didn't want to leave," he said.

I shook my head. "No."

"You didn't have to come," Xandros said.

"Yes, I did." I hardly knew how to begin to explain the reasons to him. But he would probably understand them anyway.

He gave me a sideways smile, his hands busy on the tiller. "I'm sorry."

"Oh, Xandros," I said. "Only you would think to say so." I perched on the rail beside him. Small as I am, my feet didn't quite touch the deck.

"All those scrolls. All that forever." For a moment he sounded almost wistful.

"They will be there," I said. "If there is one thing I learned in the Black Land, it is that it will not change soon."

"I thought it was another thing you learned," he said, cutting his eyes at me to see if I would laugh.

"That too," I said, and kissed him.

"Never distract the helmsman," Kos said, coming onto the rear deck. "Xandros, if you're going to pay no attention, let me take the tiller."

Xandros gave it over to Kos and sat beside me. Together we watched the sun rise out of the Nile in our wake.

THE PRISON
OF THE WINDS

To my astonishment, we had an easy passage. Even though it was early in the year, the sailing season just begun, the seas were calm and the weather was warm. The winds were light and variable, and while they did not hasten us northward, neither did they hinder us.

In twelve days we came in sight of land off to our left, a great mountain rising out of the sea, its heights ringed in smoke and cloud. I stood on deck with Xandros, and we watched the land come nearer while he held a steady course and Kos stood by the sail.

"I would guess it's the mountain they call the Prison of the Winds," Xandros said. "The Shardana told me it's the greatest peak on the island of Scylla."

"How big is the island?" I wondered. The shore before me seemed to spread and spread.

"Big. As large as the mouths of the Nile, they said. It's the biggest island."

"I wish they could have drawn it for you," I said. "In

Egypt they had drawings of the river and of the shores of the sea with names marked upon them and pictures of the inhabitants of all lands."

Xandros raised an eyebrow. "Did they have a drawing of the islands of the Shardan?"

"They didn't go that far," I said. I refrained from saying that they hadn't seen any reason for them to. Nothing important ever happened in the Shardan lands.

That night we pulled the ships in close to the beach, and sent men ashore. There was no village or settlement nearby, so we took the opportunity to fill our water casks where a stream came down to the sea. Most of the People were glad of the chance to sleep on land, and for the first time in many days Xandros and I had the cabin to ourselves.

I took a great deal of time moving things around and rearranging sacks of food and baggage, while Xandros lay down. It was dark, but I knew he was waiting for me, and when he stretched out a hand and laid it against my back I knew that it was time.

I knelt down beside him. "Xandros," I said. "There is something I must say."

His hand stilled on my back. "About Neas? Now that he's free?"

"No," I said. "No, not that."

"What, then?" His voice was even, waiting for a different blow.

I knelt in the dark, his hand on my back. "There will be a child," I said. "In the summer, when Sothis rises."

"Ah," he said very softly. Then he rose and went out of the cabin. I heard his feet going down the deck.

After a moment I got up and followed.

Xandros was standing at the stern, leaning against the tiller and looking out over the calm sea. He did not look at me. "You've known," he said. "You've known for a long time."

"Yes," I said.

"You should have stayed in Egypt," he said. I could not read his expression.

"I knew you'd say that."

The waxing moon was rising, making a path of light across the waves. I did not try to touch him.

"I can't keep you safe," he said, and his eyes were distant, as they had been after the storm, after Ashterah was lost. "I can't keep the child safe. I have nothing."

"I need nothing from you," I said.

Xandros turned, and his eyes were blazing. "Do you ever need anything from anyone? You sit wrapped in your preternatural calm, like you're watching us all from far away, like amusing little insects! Don't you actually need anything? Do you ever actually care?"

"Of course I care," I shot back. "You of all people should know that."

"You don't act like it," he snapped. "You don't act like any of us matter to you."

"You mean I don't act like I love you," I said. My hands were shaking now, not with Her presence but with anger.

"No, you don't!"

"Well, you don't love me either!" I yelled. "You love Neas, and that's fine. I understand that. You never pretended that it was me. But if it's not me, gods take me if I'm going to be the one who cries and chases after you! I don't need you, and we'll get along fine without you!"

"Stop yelling at me!"

"I am not yelling," I screamed. "You stop yelling!"

"I'm not yelling," he yelled back. "I'm screaming."

"No, you're not!"

"Yes, I am!"

From over on shore, Kos' voice rose in a sleepy shout. "I don't give a fuck if you're yelling or screaming, but cut it out so I can sleep!"

I looked at Xandros and he looked at me. And at the same moment we both started laughing. And then it was impossible to stop. I was laughing and crying and sat down on the deck at the stern.

Xandros sat down beside me and put his arm around me. "Pregnant women are strange," he said.

"Don't you dare patronize me," I said, sliding closer to him.

"I'm not patronizing. I'm just saying."

"Then just don't say."

"Fine." He put his head on my shoulder. His dark hair was damp and fine against my face.

After a moment I took his hand and folded it in mine. "Oh, Xandros."

"Do you love me?" he asked.

"Of course I do," I said. "I just love Neas too." His hand was warm around mine. We fit together. We always had.

"Well. If that's how it is." There was no resentment in his voice. Of all people, he understood.

"You love Neas," I said. I could hardly imagine him without that love, without Neas as his star to steer by, constant as any constellation.

He nodded. "Always. But you know where that goes. Exactly where it's always gone."

"So we console each other. Is that enough?" I wondered. I could belong to no man, be no man's wife, and never felt the lack of it before. But I should feel the lack of Xandros, feel his absence as keenly as a wound.

Xandros turned his hand in mine, the same shape, the same color of hands, like my own made male. "Enough for what?"

"For happiness," I said.

Xandros lifted his head. "I have no idea what that even means. I just get through each day. And you and Neas keep telling me that we're going to come out of all of this, but I can count. Our numbers keep getting smaller and smaller. I don't see the future. Right now I can't see any future. And now you tell me there's a child."

"Xandros," I said, and took his face in my hands. "Trust me on this one thing. If I had seen death before us, if I had seen this child's death, I would never have left Egypt."

"Truly?"

"Truly," I said. "I thought about it. But I came."

"And now what?" he asked.

"We wait for a sign," I said. "She will send one."

Xandros shook his head. "That's madness."

"That's faith," I said. "I'm in the business of believing in oracles."

He leaned down again, one hand touching my stomach very lightly. "When?"

"I told you. In the summer. When Sothis rises."

"Four moons?"

"Yes," I said, and smiled. "You've been a little preoccupied."

"I didn't want to know," he said.

"I know."

He did not look up at me, and I couldn't tell if the tears

were only in his voice or also in his eyes. "I can't keep you safe."

"I know you will try," I said. "And that's all anyone can do. But think of it like this—if my Lady can't keep me safe, how could you?"

Xandros laughed, and there was something looser in the sound, as though something in his chest had eased. "I keep doing this. Loving people who are god-touched."

"I know you do. Perhaps you should ask yourself why."

"Now you are counseling me again."

"It's a habit," I said, and pressed my face against his hair. "Xandros, keep me human. Call me by my name."

He raised his head. "Gull," he said. "You are Gull." And he laid his lips to mine.

WE WOKE to death. A wail went up from *Seven Sisters,* the formal funeral wail that accompanies death. Xandros and I sat straight up, and then he ran on deck.

Could Wilos have fallen overboard? I wondered. Yes, he was only six, but the boy swam like a fish and the seas were perfectly calm.

Xandros was already on the point of the prow when I came on deck. He called across the water, "Who is it? Who has died?"

Lide answered him. "Lord Anchises," she said.

"He died on the sea," I whispered. "In sight of the mountains of Scylla." I looked up at Xandros. "Let me get my veil and we'll go across."

They had laid him out amidships, his hair combed

about his shoulders. Lide stood by him, a veil over her hair.

"What happened?" I asked Lide, for there was no mark on him.

"His heart stopped in the night," she said. "That is all. He was an old man, forty-six years old."

Wilos came and stood beside the bier. He said nothing, his light hair catching the first rays of the sun rising out of the sea in an aurora of gold.

"Prince Wilos," I said. "Your grandfather was a great lord of the antique kind there will be no more of. Honor his memory."

He looked up at me. "Prince?"

"Yes," I said. "You are a prince. You are a Prince of Wilusa That Was, and of a kingdom yet to be. And that is what your grandfather strove for all his life."

Wilos nodded, his eyes on the still face. He did not cry.

In a moment Neas came up from belowdecks. He did not cry either, but his face was red.

"Sybil," he said. "And Xandros."

"I am truly sorry," Xandros said, and clasped him wrist to wrist. "If there is anything in my power to do I shall do it."

"We will burn him on the beach," Neas said. His voice was rough, as though he had already shed his tears alone. "And then we will celebrate with funeral games. We will celebrate nine days in his memory."

Xandros nodded. "It looked to me yesterday when we were filling the casks that there was good hunting in this country. We will hunt and there will be a proper funeral feast."

"If we are staying nine days I'll get over to the beach," Lide said briskly. "We can build an oven and a roasting pit if we're going to stay that long."

Neas nodded, his eyes on the near shore, the slopes of the great mountain. "Sybil, will you do what is proper?"

"I will," I said.

WE BURNED ANCHISES that night. The men had found wood, for there were plenty of deadfalls in the forest. Bai took Wilos and several of the boys hunting, and they managed to hit a couple of waterbirds. The men had more luck, and took a young doe. Meanwhile Lide had her oven and roasting pits, and we had made unleavened bread from the grain of Egypt.

It was a beautiful spring night, warm and clear, and the stars seemed close enough to touch. I stood beside the fire and sang the Descent in a clear voice, then the Greeting. My voice was not choked. I could not cry for Anchises. He had lived to do what he had wanted, and his son would be a king and his grandson after.

Neas tipped out wine for his shade, and Wilos solemnly cut a lock of his soft hair and laid it on the old man's breast.

Anchises had brought his precious grandson out of the fire, out of the ruin of the City. He had succeeded in all he aimed at, and now he rejoined Lysisippa in the land below. I could not cry for him.

The fire of dry wood caught quick and hard. Kos' drum came in deep and low. The wind from the beach picked up, and I stepped back lest the whirling sparks catch my veil. Across the fire I saw Kianna in Tia's arms, leaning back to see better, her eyes as dark as the night sky, following the sparks with her eyes, reaching up as though she might catch them, reaching toward Wilos.

Lady, I thought, *will she serve him as I serve Neas? One day when we are both dead and burned, will she sing the Descent while he pours the libation? May You will that it be so.*

WE WERE NINE DAYS on Scylla, nine days of rest. It was not that we needed the rest so much, but that we needed to remember who we were. It had been many months since the People lived according to our own customs without the clamor of the great city around us, with a cool wind off the sea and the rising thunderclouds in the afternoon. There were no clouds like this in the Black Land, no rain, no deer, no sounds of the sea. This land was new to us, but less strange than the one we had left.

On the fourth day I came upon Neas alone by the small stream that flowed into the sea. I was startled to see him, and he looked up as though he were equally surprised.

"I'm sorry," I said. "I didn't mean to disturb you."

"I was praying," he said, but he smiled and held out his hand. "But I don't need to be alone."

"For your father?" I asked.

"For Basetamon," he said.

I came and sat beside him on the edge of the stream, my twisted foot stretched out toward the cool water. "That was not the answer I expected," I said.

He shrugged. "Well, I suppose not."

"Are you glad to leave her?"

"Both yes and no," Neas said. "I can't even begin to explain."

I leaned back, looking up at the budding leaves above us, a small tree nodding over the stream. "She sent for me," I said quietly. "She wanted me to tell her the future."

Neas raised one eyebrow. "And did you?"

"No," I said. "I could see nothing for her."

He sighed. "They marry their kin in the Royal House of Egypt," he said. "They think nothing of giving a girl of nine to her uncle. And the marriage must be consummated as quickly as possible if there is to be an heir. Her son was born when she was eleven. She conceived before she even showed her first blood. Such things are not done in Wilusa. For an uncle to take his niece when she is still a child would be a blasphemy and a crime."

"The gods do not forbid things without cause," I said. "Often the child dies when the mother is so young, and sometimes she dies as well."

Neas climbed down onto the rocks in the stream, picking at the moss that grew there, his face turned away from me. "She was strange and beautiful, as clever as a man, as charming as the moon, and as changeable. One moment she would be playful and the next sad." He lifted up a piece of moss and examined it as though it were fascinating, his eyes on anything but my face. "One day she would embrace me with ardor and the next curse me and send me from her. She would call me barbarian and pet me as though I were one of her cats, showing my manhood to her servants and handmaidens and showing how it stood in her hand like a goat's, and the next moment she would tell me that I was her soul and that she loved me above all others." He shook his head and looked up at me. "I don't understand it."

"Neither do I," I said, and my voice was even though my heart was chilled within me. "Sometimes women are so. Often it is when there has been some great hurt, but I know no help for it except time and kindness."

"I tried to be kind," he said. "Not just because she held all our fates in her hand, though she did. But she was beautiful and stricken, and I thought that perhaps..." He stopped. "Did you know that she threatened you?"

"Why?" I asked.

"She threatened all the People at the end. She said that she would not allow me to love someone more than her. She asked me if I would love her still if she had Wilos killed, or my father, or you or Xandros or Amynter. I said that I would, but I would never look upon her again without tears, and, Sybil, you cannot imagine the fear that took my heart!" Neas looked away from me. "She cried and said that she would never do it. That it was lover's folly for her to be so jealous. But how could I be certain? She had the power to do it. And she liked hurting me to see if I would love her still."

Anger boiled in me. If I had seen Basetamon I should have broken all my oaths to shed no blood. But that was not what Neas needed to hear, so I said nothing.

"She said I had too much pride, and she would break it. And so she would have one of her servant girls torment me. And then she would slap the girl and send her away, hang upon me with tears and sorrow. Then she would be as calm and as clever and as quick as her brother, sitting in council as though she were Pharaoh. She would praise my wits to the generals and bid them obey me."

I reached toward his shoulder and saw him flinch, then deliberately allow me to touch his arm. I pulled my hand away. "Neas," I said, "Basetamon did much wrong."

"She did not mean to," Neas said. "She was haunted and spirit driven. And she was sad."

"Yes," I said, striving to order my thoughts. "But she still did much wrong. And you were wise not to trust her with the lives of the People."

He nodded. "I know. Each moon she went farther and farther. I don't know where it would have ended."

"It ended with you leaving," I said. "As was wise. What healing the gods may send her will come in their own time." I put my arm around his shoulder, feeling him tense like Tia, holding him as though he were Tia. "And they will send it to you as well. My dear prince, you have done everything that you could."

"I wish I were not a prince," he said.

"I know," I said. "But in that you have no choice. The gods have given the People into your hands, and you have held us all together and kept us safe. You are our king."

"I know," he said, and bent his head.

"You know that you must be, don't you?" I asked quietly.

Neas nodded. He looked at me and his eyes were dry. "Yes. There is no other way."

I sighed, thinking of what must come, and what I must do. "What do you know of how kings are made?"

"There has never been a king of the People in my lifetime, since Priam was killed when I was a child. I know there is something, some sacred mystery, but I do not know what."

"You told me on the Island of the Dead that you felt

like Theseus running the turns of the labyrinth, remember? That's an old story, and a true one. All kings must descend to the Underworld, into the realms of sorrow and grief, to Death's doorstep. If She judges them worthy, they return. Otherwise, they are swallowed up by the realms of Night." I looked at Neas, and took his hand. "Two companions may come with him to face the Shades, and Ariadne, Her Handmaiden, will guide him. But sometimes long before the hero ever walks into Night's Door he begins the long road that goes to the Underworld. He knows death and defeat and sorrow uncalculated."

"He runs the labyrinth," Neas said. "And I have run. And always you have guided me, and Xandros has been my true companion."

"Yes," I said. "And when you make that descent in truth, we will be there. You will not face the Shades alone. When you return, you will not be king alone." It took no oracle to say what Xandros' choice would be — he would go to the very depths of the Underworld for Neas, faithful as always, never counting the cost.

Neas nodded, and his face was taut but not fearful. "And Wilos? Will he someday have to face Night's Door?"

"If he is to be king," I said.

He shook his head. "I could not wish that on any man, much less my own son."

"Dear Neas," I said. "You cannot fight your son's battles for him. He will not be a little boy, but a grown man with his own sorrows and his own victories. And he will not be alone. Perhaps Kianna, or some child still unborn, will guide him or walk beside him as a true companion."

His eyes slid to my middle. "Ah, I thought so. Does Xandros know?"

"Yes," I said.

"He had better do what's right," Neas said.

I laughed. "You sound like I am your daughter!"

"You are my friend," he said, and clasped my hand wrist to wrist as though I were a captain and a man.

I squeezed back. "Yes," I said, "and shall be to the world's ending."

Together we walked back to the People.

W E SAILED from Scylla on a beautiful spring morning, leaving the ashes of our fires on the beach where the waves would wash them away.

The weather didn't hold. We followed the coast north, flanking the smoking mountain and coming toward the straits where the Shardana had told Xandros that the island of Scylla almost touched the mainland. We were in sight of the straits when the heavens opened and all the rains came down.

Xandros tied himself to the tiller, and I sat in the bow cabin with Tia, Polyra, and her son, Kianna on my heaving lap. Kianna kept up a low, steady whine to make sure we understood that she didn't like it at all, stopped only when her mouth was actually plugged by her mother's breast.

After a while I thought I would surely be sick. I went on deck and met Kos coming down the ship.

"Get back inside!" he yelled over the wind.

"In a moment!" I said. "What are you doing?"

Kos leaned close to me so that I could hear him. "I'm

going up on the bow to yell across to *Seven Sisters*! We can't row into this! Our oarsmen are exhausted and we're not making any way. We need to turn and get the wind behind us."

"We won't make the mainland then!" I yelled.

"Lady, at this rate we just need to make Scylla! We've got to get out of this! Sooner or later we're going to take one of these waves broadside!"

I nodded. "I'll go back in."

I heard him yelling across and related to the others what was happening. We felt the ship turn, the chant change as we turned downwind, the song stop as the sail rose half-way and the wind caught it. A moment later I heard Bai's oar coming into the rest position outside the door.

I stuck my head out again. Bai was leaning on his oar, his head hanging and the rain running down his bare back. The old arrow scar stood out pale on his chest. "We've turned?" I asked.

He nodded. "We can't keep it up," he panted. "We've got to turn back."

Night came while we let the winds push us. It wasn't the worst storm I had seen, but at dawn when I came on deck to rolling seas and scudding clouds I saw a familiar mountain off to my right, the familiar shape of a headland and beach.

I went up the ship and stood beside Xandros, taking him watered wine.

He gulped it down, his hands still on the tiller while I held it to his lips.

"We're back," I said.

He nodded. "There's where we burned Anchises. Right back where we were. A lot of effort for nothing."

Behind us I saw both *Seven Sisters* and *Pearl* loping along. "At least nobody seems to be damaged. I would guess that the Lady of the Sea wanted us to return. That there is some unfinished business here. But I do not know what it is."

"You don't?"

"No," I said, forestalling him. "And no, it's not a curse! I just think She wants us to do something. I need to find out what."

THE GOLDEN
BOUGH

When the rain ended Neas built an altar of tumbled stones on the beach and sacrificed to the Lady of the Sea. We had no lambs or goats, so it was flame and some of the myrrh Basetamon had given me. I assured Neas that myrrh was perfectly suitable for the goddess, and that in Egypt this was her accustomed food. Just to be safe, he poured out wine in libation as well.

"Great Lady," he prayed aloud. "Merciful mother of the seas and all the creatures therein, of all the birds that fly above it, You have brought us back to this place and we do not understand why. If You will show us, we will do our best to fulfill whatever it is that You ask of us. We will stay here nine days in Your honor, as we did for Anchises, and at the end of that time we will sail with Your blessing."

Nine days, I thought, would surely be enough for the

wind to change. And surely long enough for Her to manifest Her will.

And so we rested.

On the second day Wilos came to me while I was helping Tia clean fish for roasting. He stood shyly beside me and waited until I looked up.

"Yes, Wilos?" I asked.

"I found something," he said. "And I don't know, but it might be the thing."

"The thing?" I asked.

"The thing we're here for," he said. "I found it. I think it's a cave where a monster lives."

"A cave where a monster lives?" I frowned. There were some shallow caves up on the headland, and along the steep banks where the stream came down to the sea, but we had stayed here eleven days in all now without seeing anything more dangerous than a fox. Perhaps there were bears, but with all the hunting we had been doing, if there were bears surely our men would have seen signs of them by now.

Wilos shifted from foot to foot. "Will you come and bring my father?"

I brought not only Neas but Xandros, Kos, and Bai too, all of them with their swords and a couple of hefty spears. Bai also brought his bow. Neas didn't want Wilos to come, but I pointed out that he had to show us the way, and Xandros said that he wasn't too young for a bear hunt, provided he stayed well back, and he couldn't be any more trouble than me. Which was true. I was getting close to seven moons gone, and growing heavy and uncomfortable.

Quietly we went up the course of the stream. The day

was warm, and we walked for more than an hour. The sound of the sea faded into the distance. I began to wish I had reconsidered coming. Along the banks of the stream it was mostly rocks here, and the trees were small and stunted.

"There," Wilos said, and pointed.

The stream flowed through a small ravine, and up on the sides of the slope there was a grove of oak trees, their young leaves casting a dappled shade over the opening of a cave. I waited beside the stream with Wilos while Neas, Xandros, Kos, and Bai climbed up and investigated. They were gone a long time before Kos came out and called to us. "It's safe. You can come up!"

"What's there?" I called. If there was nothing, they would have all just come back down.

I climbed up. It was getting hot, and I was glad of the shade at the top. Wilos ran up ahead of me.

"What have you found?" I asked.

"It's all right," Neas said. "There's nothing alive here."

"The bones of a monster," Xandros said. He looked like he wished he were somewhere else.

"Come and see what you think," Neas said.

I stepped forward, letting my eyes adjust to the dim light. On the floor of the cave was a skeleton, the legs and feet still buried in the floor of the cave. It had ribs like a man, and I would have thought it was human if I had not seen the head. I knelt down beside it. Its skull was enormous and bulged in all the wrong places, with massive ridges of bone above its eyes and a jaw that jutted forward, a few worn square teeth still intact. I reached out and touched it very gently. The bone was as smooth and as cold as stone.

"See here?" Bai said. He lifted a stone that had lain beside it, sharpened on one side, whorls of white marking the striations in the flint. "It's some kind of ax or chopper."

I reached for it. "It is," I said. "I've seen people use stone choppers way up in the mountains above Pylos. Poor people who can't afford bronze."

"There isn't any metal here that I've seen," Neas said.

I turned back to the skeleton, pushing the dirt away from the ribs with my fingers. It looked like a man, almost.

"What is it?" Xandros said. "A Cyclops?"

"Maybe," I said. "But he had two eyes." My hands touched one rib, traced the reddish stains across it. "And he had friends. They sprinkled his body with ochre and laid him out."

"How do you know that?" Neas asked.

"The stains on his bones," I said. "It's how we bury priests. And the servants of the Lady of the Dead. We do not go to the fire, but sleep in the deep caves just like this."

They had laid him out. No corpse just fell into this position of repose, lying on his back with his ax beside his hand, his body sprinkled with ochre. Perhaps they had combed his hair on his shoulders, laid flowers around his body, cut locks of their hair to place on his breast. I could almost see it, and for a moment I thought I did. Strange, ugly people, but with drums and the wailing of women as they laid him here in the cave. Someone's lover, someone's father, someone's son. Had someone sung the Descent?

Xandros was edging toward the door. "I don't think we should be here," he said.

"If this is a sacred grave spot, we shouldn't be," Neas said. "The last thing we need is for the Lady of the Dead to be displeased with us."

"She will not be," I said. "If you want to go out you can. I will rebury what is left and sing the Descent for him."

"I'll help you," Wilos said.

"No," said Neas.

"I found him," Wilos said, looking up at his father. "And you can't expect the Lady to bury him by herself. She's pregnant!"

Neas' mouth twitched, but he couldn't refute his son's gallantry. "All right. Help Sybil, if you will. Is that fine with you?"

"Wilos will be a big help," I assured him. "And there is no danger."

Xandros looked clearly skeptical, but they all went out. The bright sun shone in through the cave door, lighting Wilos' fair hair in an aureole around his head.

"Thank you for staying, Prince Wilos," I said. "If you can help me move the dirt from that corner over here so we can cover him." I put his ax back beside him.

Wilos started digging with a will, carrying dirt in his tunic. I was certain that Lide would have something to say about laundry, but I said nothing.

The boy helped me pack the dirt down over his ribs and chest again. His little hands were brown and strong. "Do you think he was killed?" he asked.

I shook my head. "I don't see any broken bones or anything splintered. And he's missing most of his teeth, except a few that are very, very worn. See?" I showed him as we worked. "I think he was an old man."

"Like my grandfather," Wilos said.

"Yes," I said. I knew that he missed Anchises greatly. And that was no bad thing. Anchises was missed because he had been loved by his only grandchild.

"Do you think he was a king?"

"He might have been," I said. "Or a priest."

"I wish I could be a priest," Wilos said.

I looked up at his composed child's face, watching his own hands as he worked. "Do you?" I asked quietly. He was her grandson as well, Lysisippa the daughter of Priam who had been servant to the Lady of the Sea.

"Uh-huh. But I have to be a prince instead."

"You could be both, you know," I said. "Some of the gods have priests who do other things. And a king has to be a little bit of a priest."

"Will I be a king?" he asked.

"Yes," I said. "Someday when you are as old as your father is now, you will be our king and you will keep the People safe like your father does."

"That sounds really hard," he said, mounding the dirt softly over the skull's eyeholes.

"It is," I said. "Being a king is really hard. But you'll have people to help you."

"Like who?"

"Like Kianna," I said.

Wilos snorted. "Kianna's a baby. She's not much help."

"She won't be a baby then. She'll be Sybil, the Handmaiden of the Lady of the Dead. And she'll help you like I help your father."

He thought about that for a minute. "Will she be pretty?"

"I imagine so," I said. Kianna was a beautiful child, as

I had known she would be, with red-gold hair and great gray eyes, creamy skin freckled in the sun.

"Lide says she's a smart baby," Wilos said. "Maybe I should marry her. I mean, if she's smart and pretty and she's going to help me be king."

"Those are very important things to think of," I said, wondering how much talk Wilos had heard in Egypt, and how much Anchises had said. "It's important for a king to marry the right person. But I don't think you can marry Kianna, because she's going to be Sybil."

I patted the last of the dirt down. "Now I need to sing the Descent. Can you drum on the ground with your hands and help me?"

Wilos nodded, and I began the Descent, the long high part that comes at the beginning, and then the lower part of the lament. When I got to the change, Wilos came in singing above me, his little boy's voice as true and as clear as his father's, soaring over mine like a skylark. We finished together.

"I didn't know you knew that," I said.

He shrugged. "I've heard you sing it a lot."

"I suppose I have." I got ready to stand up. Too many times to have sung the Descent in so few months.

"Can I be a priest too? Besides a king?" he asked.

I looked down at him sitting in the stray sunbeams, shaking out his dirty shirt. His grandmother was Cythera, and his great-aunt was Kassandra, perhaps the greatest oracle the People have known. It was in his blood, in his very bones. And he was the firstborn, born to be a prince. Such things were not done in the City, but we were in the City no longer.

"Yes, Wilos," I said. "You will be a priest too. You

will be a priest of the king of the gods, and king of the People as well. There is no reason why you can't do both at once."

I reached for his hand and we walked out of the cave together.

In the grove of trees outside the men were practicing target shooting. Bai had his bow out, and they were taking turns trying to hit a particular tree trunk. Xandros was fairly horrible, and they had stopped and were standing around joking while Xandros hunted in the underbrush for his arrow.

He found it and brought it back to Kos. "You do better," he said, thrusting the arrow at him.

"Easily, my friend, easily," Kos said, fitting the arrow to the bow and aiming up at the tree.

Neas grabbed his arm. "Wait!" he said.

There was a flash of white in the trees. A pair of white doves flew circling through the air, alighting on the branch they had targeted.

Kos lowered the bow, and we all let out a breath.

"Doves," Neas said in a hushed voice. "We asked My Mother for a sign. There was a pair of white doves that nested in the eaves of the Great Temple of the Lady of the Sea where I was as a child. I remember them. I used to feed them pieces of bread and they would come to me. One of them would even land on my shoulder. It's the sign. She knew I would remember."

The doves sat on the branch, looking down at us. Then they took wing together, fluttering through the leaves and coming to rest a little ways away. Neas walked forward. They did not startle, only waited until he came near.

When he was beneath them he looked up. "What is it you are here to show me?" he asked.

They took off in a flurry of wings and he followed.

Six times they took flight and flew a little ways before alighting again, and six times we all followed through the sun-dappled wood, into the shade of a great oak as wide around as Neas and Xandros standing together. The doves alighted in its lower branches. I looked up. The doves cooed.

Twined around the branch were pale green leaves, a cluster of hanging golden berries, delicate and small.

"The golden bough," I whispered.

Neas looked at me.

"It is for kingship," I said. "To pass Night's Door into the Underworld and return unharmed we need those berries, for they are sacred to Death's Queen. They do not grow in Egypt, and only rarely in Akaiawa. You must get the bough without harming it. This is what the Lady of the Sea has brought you here to do."

"It's five times the height of a man up in the air!" Kos said. "There's no climbing that tree."

Neas' eyes went to Wilos' dirty tunic, then to the tree above.

"Son," he said, "take off your tunic and hold it between your hands the way you carried dirt, and stand beneath that branch." He reached for Bai's bow.

The doves took off, spiraling from the grove into the sky.

Carefully, Neas chose out the straightest arrow. None of us breathed while he fitted it to the string and pulled the bow taut.

The arrow flashed upward. It pierced the stem of the

bough where it held to the oak, and the bundle of leaves and berries dropped into Wilos' shirt.

Kos let out a cheer, joined by the others. Wilos whooped as Neas lifted the bough from the cloth and held it up.

I smiled. "Oh, well done, Prince Aeneas! Well done!"

With a triumphant smile he gave the bundle into my hands. "For you, Lady. Until the time comes to use it."

"That will not be long," I said.

WE SAILED AGAIN at the end of the nine days. This time the seas were calm and the winds were fresh but not strong, and two days later we came to the town that watches over the straits where they say the Charybdis lives. Messyna is a good-sized town with strong walls built on the headland, and the harbor is below with a village around it. I was worried at the reception we would find there, and for good reason, because by the time our ships came into the harbor they had assembled all the men of the town to repel us.

Neas had us put our bows below and Xandros called across to them in Shardan. The language is not the same, but it is similar enough for Xandros to make them understand the word "trade" rather than "give us your women and your food." After that they relaxed somewhat and let small numbers of us come ashore, though they did not unbar the citadel and the people who had fled there remained. Some of the men came down however, and were willing to trade.

Xandros, whose Shardan was best, did most of the talking. From them he learned that pirates were frequent on these coasts, and that there had been a group of Achaians here a few years ago who had made a great deal of trouble. Xandros told them what had happened with the great fleet in Egypt, and that it wasn't likely the Achaians would be back anytime soon.

We traded Egyptian beer for wine and olives, a fine bronze dagger for foodstuffs, and part of the bag of frankincense I carried for a considerable amount of grain, peas, and lentils, enough to keep us for several weeks. Their temple had had none for a year, with trade so poor. Indeed, we were the first foreign ship to come this sailing season, though we were getting into early summer.

We stayed a week, in the end. They had good port facilities, and Maris wanted to recaulk part of *Pearl*'s bottom where she had a small leak. It wasn't a big leak, but better to avoid trouble.

"A leak like that could open in a storm," Kos said. "Best to retar it before it gets worse."

So I sat, getting heavier and heavier, trying to stay away from the smell of the molten tar that threatened to make me sick. In truth, it was a lovely place to sit, with the air thick with summer and the warm sun playing on the ocean. I sat on the beach, Kianna grubbing in the sand, while Tia dug for clams to make a soup.

Neas came and found us there. He came and sat beside me, stretching his long legs out on the sand, burying his feet in the warmth.

"Another day," he said. "And then we're off again."

"Where?" I asked.

"Shouldn't it be me asking you?" he said.

I shook my head. "You are the king to be, and as you've pointed out, I know nothing about sailing."

He shrugged. "Northward along the coast, then. They say there've been no merchant ships at all this summer. I'm going to take some extra cargo aboard and take it north. We should make some good trades. And also, I want to find out where the swords come from."

"The Shardana swords?" I said. "They come from here?"

Neas nodded. "Northward up the coast are a people who have the knack of making them. If we're going to use them we need to know how to repair them and where to get more. They use them here, but they don't make them. What do you think?"

I spread my hands, my belly burgeoning beneath. "I see nothing. I haven't these several weeks, since we left the cave on Scylla. The child is taking everything now. I don't think I'll be able to see until she's born. I am too given over to life."

"A strange mystery," Neas said.

"Yes, but I have heard it is often so," I said. Bearing life, I was banished from Death's kingdom, dwelling above the ground as the Lady does when She casts off Her dark cloak and walks forth into the sunlight, flowers growing beneath Her feet. I had not imagined what it would be like to walk thus, to feel the bright summer air with no hint of the caves beneath it.

"North, then. And perhaps your daughter will put in her appearance soon, so that I am not bereft of my Sybil." He grinned.

"Not too soon," I said. "Not until Sothis rises and high summer comes."

*   *   *

AND SO WE SAILED northward up the coast, stopping at each little town and trading. Most of them were no more than fishing villages, poor places with a few dozen families who ran into the woods when they saw our sails. Sometimes there was no one left to trade with, and Xandros called through empty streets in vain, saying that we were not pirates but honest men, answered only by silence.

A moon later we were off the coast, and I stood by Xandros at the rail after we had left one of these towns.

"Does it seem to you," I said, "that there should be many more people here? These woods are rich with game, and the waters are full of fish."

"Good fish too," said Xandros. "And close inshore. They haven't been fished out. The seas around Wilusa were getting barren. We had to go much farther to find fish than my father said we had in his boyhood. After the first plunder of the city we fished more than we farmed. But these people don't seem to fish much. Or there are too few of them to make a difference."

"Pirates," I said.

He nodded. "A bunch of these towns sent men to the great fleet, men who decided to take a ship or two and sail with the Shardan. They're never coming back."

"They are in Egypt," I said, "with their foreskins cut, working in Pharaoh's fields."

"Or under the sea, where we put them," Xandros said grimly.

"Their wealth is gone," I said. "Who will fish the seas?"

"Nobody," Xandros said. "So they raid one another. All

of these tribes are at war with one another. They haven't got any choice. They just pass the loot back and forth."

"And it gets scarcer and scarcer," I said. "And each year there is less grain, fewer olives." Here too the world foundered, cities fell. Who could plant young olive trees, clear fields for grain, in such times?

"Which means they have to plunder or starve," Xandros said. "These are desperate men. If we stopped here we could catch enough fish to feed the People, even with only three ships. But how would we hold on to it? Someone desperate would come to plunder us."

"Could they, I wonder? With the new swords?"

Xandros nodded. "They might not be able to beat us in battle, but they could burn out the camp in short order. We have no walls, no safe place for you and the others to stay. So it won't do much good for us to fight off an attack if we know that the minute we go fishing they'll take you all as slaves and plunder everything."

I thought about that and saw no way around it. Building fortifications took a great deal of time, and as far as I knew there was no man among us who even knew how. Most of the men who had escaped Wilusa were seamen, not builders and townsmen.

MY PAINS CAME on the third night after Sothis rose. We were sailing just short of sunset, looking for a beach that was not too rocky to stop for the night. I had been feeling strange all day, elated and tired by turns, with a backache that would not go away. I was standing in the bow watching the waves and walking back and forth when my water broke standing there, drenching my skirts.

I cried out and Tia came running, passing off Kianna to Kos, who stood dumbfounded.

"Come on, now," Tia said. "Let's go below."

"I don't want to," I said. Somehow the idea of going into the cabin filled me with dread, maybe because I had seen Tia suffer there so long. "I want to stay here holding the rail." And then a wave of pain took me and I clutched the rail and held on.

When I opened my eyes again, Xandros was shouting across to *Seven Sisters*. The pains came again as I watched *Seven Sisters* coming toward us, and when they receded Xandros was stretching out his arms to help Lide aboard as they rode alongside.

Lide came bustling over. I was holding on to Tia's arms. "Here, let me see," Lide said.

"I won't go below," I said.

"Fine," she replied. "Kos, tell those men to mind their business. Tia, you're going to help me, and it will all go well. Sit down, Pythia. Let me see."

She got me down on the deck with my legs spread and made humming noises. Another wave of pain took me. When it cleared I looked at her.

"How long has this been happening?" she asked.

"Just a little while," I said. "Since my water broke. But I've been feeling strange all day and my back hurt."

She nodded. "Coming on hard, is it? Chances are it's been going all day, you just didn't notice. The babe is well down, and you're opening fast. Probably hurts quite a bit, but it should make it go faster. Tia, ask Xandros if we can make shore. If she won't go below I'd rather get on land."

Another pain took me.

Lide pressed my hand and I rode it out. Polyra had

come back and crouched on the other side of me. "Good, good," Lide said. "Opening nicely. Pains close together and fast. You're doing fine."

I didn't feel fine. But I didn't feel frightened either. It was like having Her inside me again, being possessed by something much larger. Life, I thought. By some strange goddess.

"Again," Lide said.

I heard Tia's voice somewhere far above. "Xandros says he's going to get in as close as he can to this beach. It's rocky, but it looks like small stones and we can get fairly close in."

Some part of me that was far away thought with amusement that it was unlike Tia to give a beach forecast, repeating Xandros word for word. Perhaps she was afraid.

"It's not like it was with you," Lide said to her over my head, and I knew I was right. "You were too young and the baby was early. She's ready. She's more than ready."

Waves cresting and receding. I could hear the waves on the beach. I clutched Tia's hand. Somewhere above the pain I could hear Xandros giving the order to ship oars, his voice breaking on the call. Water splashing around the bow.

"Come now," Lide said, taking my elbow and helping me up. "Between pains. Let's get you over on the beach. Tia, tell your husband to go build a fire. We'll need the warmth. Polyra, where's my knife?"

"Don't cut me," I said.

Lide pressed her hand against my cheek. "It's not for you, girl. It's for the cord. You're open all the way. I can see the top of the baby's head." Her voice changed. "Kos, get over here and help me lift her!"

Between the pains Kos took me up in his arms and got me over the side. Another wave, stronger than before, took me. I could hear him breathing hard, the splash of the seawater around his knees.

"Put me down," I said. "Kos, put me down!" I flailed.

"Kos, put her down!" That was Tia.

Waves, pushing me and pushing me.

"Not in the water, you idiot!" That was Lide.

My feet splashed ankle deep in seawater. "I have to. I have to," I said. I crouched down, grabbing Tia's arm.

Lide swore at Kos. "Another few paces wouldn't have killed you!"

The sounds of them running the ship in. Xandros' voice.

Tia ordering Kos: "Go take the ship. Go on. They're trying to run up."

I grabbed her arm tighter. Time stopped in a place beyond pain. Three drops of blood fell between my spread legs, dropping into the seawater. With an exhalation the child slid out, long, wide body dropping into Lide's hands, cord slithering after. One leg landed in cold seawater, and the child screamed.

It wasn't a tiny mewing sound like Kianna had made, but a full-throated yell, indignant and loud. The knife flashed. The cord parted, and Lide lifted the child from the dragging water.

"Ah there," she said with satisfaction. "What a big strong boy! You have a fine son, Sybil."

I felt Tia's arms around me, supporting me, and I reached out one hand to where Lide held him dangling free. Yes, he was a boy. His little phallus was erect and his scrotum swollen from the birth, olive skin and wide shoulders, a thick cap of dark hair on his head. His face was squinched up with screaming, his eyes clenched shut.

"Oh, oh, oh…" I said.

Another wave of pain, but I hardly noticed. "There's the afterbirth," Lide said. "All nice and in one piece. Hold still."

The sea took it. Salt water stung me on the incoming wave.

"Let me hold him," I said.

Tia helped me up. "Come this way. Bai is getting a fire going. Come out of the water."

I stood and Lide put him in my arms. His little fist opened and closed against my collarbone, and he cried like a bleating lamb.

"He's so big," I said.

They led me, half leaning on Tia, to the fire Bai was lighting, sat me down on someone's cloak with a blanket around me.

"He's a fine big boy," Lide said. "And a good healthy wail. Sit down now."

The fire flared. I held my son in my arms.

"He's twice Kianna's size," I said.

"Just about," Tia said. Her skirts steamed. We were all soaked with seawater.

I sat and watched the ships come in. *Seven Sisters* wasn't to shore yet. The sun was just below the waves and the stars were showing. It had seemed like an eternity, but it couldn't have been very long. I said so to Lide.

"Not long at all," she said. "Fast for a first birth. And a strong child at the end of it. Let's get you settled so he can nurse. Sometimes they don't want to at first, but it's good to try. Makes you stop bleeding better."

I waited in the firelight, my son at my breast. I lifted my nipple gently and rubbed his cheek with it. He turned his head and clamped on, his toothless gums surprisingly strong, a look of utter contentment on his face.

I sat there watching him, feeling receding cramps like waves going out to sea, strangely unreal, like I watched from above. In a few minutes Lide brought me some warmed wine, and I drank it drowsily. The boy closed his eyes and sighed, sliding off the nipple.

Xandros knelt down beside me. "Are you all right?"

I lifted a fold of the cloak around me so he could see. "He's a boy. He's a big, fine boy."

His hair was black, like mine and Xandros', with his father's wide shoulders and broad chest.

Xandros bent his head against my shoulder, his arm around me, tears streaming down his face.

There was a stir, a flare of torches. Neas, with Maris and Wilos, was standing at the edge of the firelight, as though at the door of a house. "May we greet you?" Neas asked.

Lide stepped back, opening an invisible door. "Prince Aeneas."

Xandros looked up.

Neas knelt before me. "Lady, may I offer my congratulations?"

"Thank you," I said, and opened the cloak again so he could see the baby.

"It's a baby," Wilos said.

Neas looked at him gravely. "What is to be his name?"

I looked at Xandros. In truth, we'd not discussed names for a boy. "Markai," I said.

Neas nodded and touched the boy's forehead gently.

"Markai son of Xandros son of Markai," he said. "You are welcome to our company, Son of the People."

Xandros met Neas' eyes. "Thank you," he said, and his eyes were full. "Markai son of Xandros son of Markai. My son and I will ever stand with you."

Wilos looked at me, and he smiled suddenly. "When I'm king," he said, "I promise Markai can be one of my captains."

"That's a good promise," Neas said, ruffling Wilos' hair. "May you be as true to it as I am to Xandros." And he reached out and clasped Xandros' hand, wrist to wrist.

The baby hiccuped and turned back to my breast.

ΠIGHT'S DOOR

I don't remember much about the first few weeks after
Markai was born besides him. He was a big boy, and
he wanted to eat constantly, nursing and sleeping and
sleeping and nursing again while morning turned into
noon turned into sunset turned into night. It all blurred
together for me after a few days, napping in the shadow
of the rail on *Dolphin* with him held close while we
skimmed over the blue waves, waking to find us at some
small village that would trade. I would fall asleep with
Markai held tight, and wake to find that I was lying beside
him in the bow cabin, the baby swaddled and warm, that
someone had laid a cloak over me to ward off the chill of
the night.

One night I woke in a panic, my breasts aching with
milk and reached for him. Markai sighed, and made a little grunting noise in his sleep, but did not wake. His brow
was cool and damp, his clout dry. It was nearly dawn. He
had nursed at midnight, but didn't seem inclined to wake
and nurse again.

I got up and went out into the predawn light. *Dolphin*

was run in on a beach of white sand. The waves rocked her a little as they washed against her stern. Xandros was on watch, sitting on *Dolphin*'s bow. He smiled when he saw me.

"Where's Markai?" he asked.

"Sleeping," I said, and came and sat beside him. "And that's a surprise. It seems to me he does nothing but eat."

"That will change soon," Xandros said. "Three weeks. And he's big. He's gone a full watch tonight. I was sleeping when you fed him. I went on watch when you were sleeping."

I looked around at the warm summer night, feeling the breeze off the water stirring my damp hair, my sweated body and heavy breasts. "I must look like a mess," I said.

Xandros put his head to the side, as though considering the matter carefully. "You look like a woman with a three-week-old baby," he said.

I laughed. "You should take up statecraft, with answers like that!"

"I thought I did," he said.

"I think you did too," I said. "It's not much like fishing, is it?" I looked out across the beach, the banked campfires, the People sleeping in the moonlight. Around the perimeter of our camp I could see several men moving, watchmen like Xandros, who had care of us while we slept.

"No," he said. "But there are good fish in these waters. This bay is magnificent."

South of us, the beach of white sand swept away in a perfect crescent, broad and wide, with hills rolling down covered in green. To the north, the mountain rose. When I looked at it, the hairs rose on the back of my neck, and I felt Her hand like a chill sea breeze. The mountain looked like some sleeping monster stretched out in repose, towering over the blue sea and dotted islands, its head wreathed in clouds or steam. "Xandros," I said.

"What?"

"The mountain."

"What about it?"

I couldn't take my eyes from it. "It's like the Prison of the Winds," I said. "Or Thera That Was. It's a forge. A gate."

He looked at it. "It's not doing anything. It hasn't. There's just that little puff of cloud over it that never seems to go away."

I shook my head. "I don't think it's doing anything now. But it will. Maybe a long time from now, maybe not. But it just is. Whatever it is. A gate."

"I wish you wouldn't prophesy before breakfast," Xandros said, but he looked nervous, like a pious man who is making a joke he shouldn't.

I put my head on his shoulder. "It's nothing to do with us. Not now. After all, it's not as though we're planning to live here. But I do wish I could get around to the other side, northward up the coast."

"That's where we'll go tomorrow. Today, rather," Xandros amended. "Why?"

"There's something there." I felt Her hand at my back, felt Her like a whisper in my mind. "One of Her holy places. I need to go there, and so does Neas."

"Why?"

"So he can be king," I said. "I knew when he found the golden bough that it would not be long. Just until Markai was born. She was waiting on him."

"The Lady of the Dead waited on Markai?" Xandros asked.

"Yes." I laid my head against his neck. It was nice to be with him alone for a minute while the stars paled above and the *Seven Sisters* sank into the sea. "She waited for life."

Xandros swallowed. "He's a fine boy."

"He is," I said. "And I love him more than I ever imagined possible." Which was true. But then, I had never imagined love very much.

Xandros nodded against my head. "Yes." He swallowed again, but his voice was steady. "That was why the Achaians killed my wife. She would not let them take the girls. She fought them so hard..." His voice broke, and he bent his face against my hair.

I put my arms around him and held him as he finally cried. I wrapped myself around him, as though it would make it better, though I knew that it wouldn't. I have seen enough grief.

When at last he looked up at me, the blue shades of night were going and the dawn was coming. Two years, I thought. It has taken him two years to cry. Two years, and another child to fill his arms. Below, I heard a hungry whimper.

"I need to get Markai and feed him," I said.

Xandros nodded. "Go on. No need for him to wait for his breakfast."

When I had fed him and brought him up on deck with me, the People were beginning to break camp. With Markai slung against my side, I went in search of Neas. I found him eating day-old bread beside the fire, having come off the dawn watch himself.

"Prince Aeneas," I said formally, though I did not look Death's priestess with grimy flyaway hair and a baby slung on my hip, "we need to sail around to the north side of the mountain, up the coast. There we need to make camp, and I need to go onto the slopes of the mountain."

Neas looked at me with surprise, but what he said was "If that is what your Lady requires, of course we shall do so, Sybil." He looked up at the mountain. One little puff of smoke rose, pink in the dawn. "I wondered," he said, his pale eyes distant. "I wondered when I saw it."

"It reminds you of Thera That Was," I said quietly.

He nodded. "It does. And I don't know why." Neas looked at me, led me a little way from the fire, where Lide was giving Wilos bread smeared with honey to break his fast. "Something strange happened in the night. I can't explain it. I'm not the kind of person..."

"You are not a priest," I said. "And yet you saw something."

Neas nodded tightly, and I saw that he was afraid, not merely unsettled.

"What did you see?" I asked. "It may be that it has bearing on your quest, on the journey you must take to be king."

Neas shook his head. "I have no idea. I hope not. And yet it was the strangest thing..."

"What did you see?" I asked.

Neas glanced back at the mountain, at the sea. "I was on watch last night, and everything was still. It was very dark, and I might have dozed off, I don't know. But I woke suddenly because I heard the sound of oars. I thought I saw ships. I could hear them in the darkness. They were moving under oar, and I was about to shout the alarm, thinking it was some remnant of the great fleet, until I took a better look. They weren't like any warships I've ever seen, though they were clearly warships. They had several banks of oars, nested one above the other, and they were huge, twice or three times the length of *Seven Sisters*. They were rounding the point, almost under the snout of the mountain, and the men were pulling like they were going into the Underworld themselves. I could hear the drums and the voices of their captains, the sound of the oars in the water, as real as anything." Neas' eyes were unfocused, as though he were still dreaming.

"What happened then?" I asked.

"The whole thing was lit by eerie light, as though the sky was on fire. And then I saw that it was." Neas shook his head. "The mountain was burning. The ships were coming toward us, toward a harbor town that was burning. People were rushing the docks, wading out into the sea holding their children over their heads while fire rained down from above. I could hear the commands being shouted on the decks, the ships getting as close in as they could. One of the ships caught fire and burned. They were picking up swimmers in the water. And for a moment I saw..." He stopped.

"What did you see?" I asked gently, as though he were an acolyte and I feared to break the spell.

"I saw myself," he said.

A chill ran through me.

"A young man on the aft deck of one of the big ships. He was wearing a bronze breastplate of some strange design over a scarlet tunic, but he was bareheaded, with brown hair cut short and a scar across his forehead. He was shouting out orders, trying to get alongside one of the big stone docks to pick up people. They were trying to back oars without breaking the lower bank against the dock. There were stones floating on the top of the waves like foam. A piece of burning stone landed right beside him and he just stepped over it. He was doing his duty, but all the while I thought he was looking for someone, someone he didn't see on the dock." Neas broke off and looked at me, blue eyes very bright. "Lady, can you tell me if this is something that will happen? And why I have dreamed this with my eyes wide open?"

"It may happen," I said. "But not for a very long time. As to why..." I spread my hands. "Perhaps it is that he was also reaching for you. After all, you have rescued people from a burning city aboard a warship under oar before. Perhaps the you that is to come was reaching back to you now, trying to remember across the River and draw from your wisdom. You are his memory, and he is your vision."

Neas shook his head. "That's very deep water for me."

"Yes," I said. "Even I can do no more than guess at the meaning of this. And perhaps we won't understand for many years to come."

Neas nodded. "Then we must go on with what lies ahead." He looked up. "It is time to be king."

"Yes, my prince," I said. "It is."

WE SAILED around the point, between the islands and the mountain. It reared above me, its sides green with summer, pastures and trees and dells all shades of green, lovely against the azure water. The day was cloudless and calm.

On the other side was a little village almost on the slopes, vineyards terraced into the mountain's side. The villagers ran in terror when they saw the ships, and it took until the sun was high to get them back and convince them that we wanted to trade.

"We need a place to camp," I said to Xandros, who was speaking to them in his ever-improving Shardan. "And ask them if there is a cave."

I knew exactly in the conversation when he did it. A hush came over the crowd. Xandros looked around. Finally an old woman, her white hair partially covered by a shawl, spoke. As she did, she looked at me.

Xandros translated. "She wants to know if you seek Sybil's cave," he said.

"I do," I said, looking her in the eye.

"Sybil is dead," she said through Xandros. "She died two years ago in the summer. She can give you no counsel."

"I am Sybil to these people," I said. "I am eleven years in Her service, and I have known the Mysteries. I am seeking Her cave."

The old woman looked at me. They all looked at me. I did not look the part, not with a young baby at my breast and my hair loose, my face unpainted. The townspeople did not speak.

I met the old woman's eyes. "Mother," I said, "will you not tell me?"

She nodded fractionally.

Xandros translated for her. "She says she will send her grandson to show you the way, but he will not go into the cave. She says you will not want to take the child. It is very steep."

I nodded. "Thank you, Mother."

The boy came forward, a clean-limbed boy about twelve or so.

I handed Markai to Tia. "If you wouldn't mind watching him a little while," I said.

She nodded. "It's fine. Don't be too long. I can feed him, but he'll want you."

THE CAVE was hard to find. The opening was in the shadow of a crag, just beneath a plateau in one of the cliffs overlooking a steep ravine. The mouth of the cave looked like a deeper shadow. I would not have seen it if I hadn't known what I was looking for.

I told the boy he could go, and across the language barrier must have made it plain enough, for he took off like a hare, back to normal places. I stood in the shadow of the rocks on the steep path.

"Great Lady," I said. "You have led Your handmaiden here, to this sacred place. If it is Your will that I should not disturb the silence of this Shrine, please let me know so. Otherwise I will know that I am doing as You intend. I will bring the son of Aphrodite Cythera here, that he may be king over the People in accordance with Your will. If I have misunderstood, please pardon my ignorance and teach me what Your wishes are." I stood in the silence. Around me the light tan rocks were riddled with lichen, pockmarked. The mountain slumbered.

I set my foot over the threshold and into the cave.

At first it seemed much like the one I had grown up in, except that the first chamber was smaller and a cleft in the roof meant that some light came in and that it was not truly entirely underground. There was a blackened fire pit, but the ashes were gone. No one had lived here for several years. There were no pots, no goods of any kind. I wondered if they had been buried with the old Sybil, and how long it would be before one came again, called to this place by blood or magic.

I walked through to the entrance in the back.

A long corridor not quite tall enough for me to walk upright was before me, cutting straight ahead into the earth.

I took off my shoes and laid them at the door. Yes, above were the hooks laboriously drilled into the stone to hang the veil. "A womb, a gate, a tomb," I whispered. I understood it better now than when Pythia had explained it. Birth and death, death and birth. It was a cave, a tomb, a birth canal. I walked into the darkness, trailing my hand along the wall and counting my steps.

Sixty steps without turns or side corridors. Behind me the light had shrunk to a lozenge of white. The cave opened into a great chamber, as tall as a temple, as wide as a hall. Five passages led from it. I sighed. I was going to have to learn this cave step by step. And that would take some time. A week or more, if I were going to make certain that nothing went amiss in the rites. I should have to artificially block off some of the passages so that no one went wandering during the rites since I did not know all of the turns underground. Given the honeycomb consistency of the stone, there might be hundreds of turns and crosspassages, some of them with dangerous drops. It would take time. I must do the work alone. No one except me and my acolyte could come in here. And my acolyte was a toddling child who still nursed.

"Great Lady," I said aloud to the echoing ceiling. "Great Lady, when the moon wanes I will bring Aeneas son of Anchises to Your halls. Thank You."

I turned and went out into the sun. This would require preparation, and my son would be hungry.

THE WORK took every bit of two weeks to complete. The People camped on the beach near the town of Cumai, the village nearest the Shrine. Each day I went and prepared, a few hours at a time, while Markai stayed with Tia. He could go half the morning without nursing, but still ate at least seven times in a day. He seemed as big as Kianna had been at twice his age.

On the day of the dark moon, Markai laughed for the first time. Then when it seemed to delight me, he did it again, his round dark eyes fixed on my face. I held him close and kissed his plump little belly, smelling the sweet baby scent of him, laughing in return.

Neas cleared his throat. He stood nearby, washed and bathed, his hair clean and shining, wearing a clean tunic. "Lady," he said, "I've chosen my two companions for the road. Xandros and Maris have pride of place, and neither will surrender it."

I nodded. "Very well, then. I will come and speak to them."

I stood in the sun and spoke to the captains, while the People assembled around them. "Aeneas son of Anchises," I said, "are you determined to take this road?"

Neas nodded. "I am," he said. "I will walk to the very Underworld itself, that I may seek counsel of the Shades and the blessings of the kings of Wilusa That Was. Does the door lie open?"

"It is easy to descend to the Underworld," I said, "to pass Night's Door. It's returning that's the hard part. Many heroes and sons of heroes have tried, and many have failed."

"I will try Night's Door," Neas said. He looked to Xandros on his right, Maris on his left. "My companions and I will try, for I would hold conversation with Anchises and the other fathers of my line."

I looked at the three of them. "You will eat no food this day, and will drink nothing besides water. When the sun has set, you will come to the Shrine following the path I have marked." I met Xandros' eyes, knowing as I did how he did not like the unknown. "Know that there is no shame if you choose not to come, for the Underworld is not a place for living men."

Neas nodded. "We will come, Lady."

THEY CAME. The sky was dark, for no moon shone tonight, and a bank of clouds was rolling in from over the sea. I waited within the first cave, a fire before me in the restored fire pit, my face painted and my hair pinned with ancient copper pins, brought from the islands who knew how many years ago. I heard their feet on the path before they were close, Maris stumbling and swearing in the dark, Neas rebuking him not to go near the edge.

I was waiting for them.

"Prince Aeneas," I said, and I saw them jump, though they had been expecting me. "Why have you sought Sybil, you and your companions?"

They came through the door and stood before me, armed and dressed as fighting men, each in their best.

"Because I would be king," Neas said. "If I am to lead the People, I must be king."

"If you are worthy," I said, turning my head away and cutting one outlined eye at him. "Sit."

They came and crouched around the fire together.

I reached back and brought forth incense for the fire, myrrh and frankincense from Egypt, bay and star of the sea from the cliffs above the Shrine. The leaves crackled in the flame. The myrrh gave off heady smoke.

From beside me I lifted a stone bowl, one of the things I had found in the dark corners of the Shrine, old beyond measure. "Drink," I said.

It looked like blood.

It was red wine steeped with the berries from the golden bough, steeped since we left Scylla and I knew that I would need this.

Neas drank first, then passed the bowl to Xandros, then to Maris. Last, I took one swallow. My head should be clearer than theirs, and I would have to nurse the child tomorrow.

I poured the dregs into the fire in libation and they steamed. And I began the songs. How Theseus went into the labyrinth and in the coils of the earth met the Minotaur, how he slew him there and returned, following Ariadne's thread. How beneath the earth he became king, and knew it in fact when journeying home he forgot to raise the white sail. Seeing black sails raised for mourning still, his father cast himself from the heights, and Theseus became king.

I saw their eyes fix, wide and dark. The floor seemed far away beneath my feet. I stood.

"Take off your swords," I said. "Take off your armor. They will avail you nothing against the beasts of the Underworld. Take off those symbols of pride, your bracelets and your linen worked with embroidery. You must go into Death as you came from it, naked as a child."

They disrobed awkwardly, and I knew it was working. Maris shivered in the cold.

"Come," I said, "if you are resolved on this." I lifted the veil and stepped into the dark. "Come."

Neas was behind me. "I am coming," he said.

Sixty steps in pitch blackness. I counted them. It was an eternity to them. I heard them breathing behind me. I walked faster, so that when I stepped out into the center of the great hollow they would not touch me when they stumbled out confused into the wide-open space.

"Son of Anchises," I whispered, and the whisper ran round and round the room. "Son of Anchises, what brings you to the River?"

And I saw it. I saw the barge poling toward us in the darkness, the ferryman with his skeletal hands.

Neas stepped forward. "I am come seeking my father, who passed this way before me."

"You are not dead," the ferryman said.

"I have come with the golden bough," Neas said, and it seemed to me that he held it in his hand again, as he had in the wood.

"Then you may cross," the ferryman said. "You and your companions."

We poled out onto the dark water and it lapped around the boat with many voices.

"Twice we cross the River," I said. "When we die, we cross this River, which is the Styx. And when we are born we cross the other River, which is Lethe."

"Memory," Neas said.

"For memory is sweet and full of delight, and if we do not leave it we cannot live," I said.

"Memory is bitter," Xandros said. "And if we carried it we would be mad."

"That too," I said.

"And still I would rather remember," Neas said. "I would take the bitter with the sweet."

"Ah," Xandros said, "But you are the son of a goddess."

"Here is the shore," I said, and it seemed we stepped off onto parched soil. The ferry melted into mist behind us. "We are in Death's land. We have passed Night's Door."

DEATH'S KINGDOM ☉

We walked through a dark wood. Overhead the stars were shining. The tall cypress trees muttered together in the wind.

"What is this place?" Neas said.

"This is the place that never was," I said. "The land where the sun has never shone, where the moon has never risen. Here we live in starlight."

"It's beautiful," Xandros said, and there was wonder in his voice. "It reminds me of the mountains behind Byblos, where the great cedars are." He stumbled a little against me.

Far off in the woods we heard a dove call, and then a voice. "Xandros?"

I turned.

Ashterah was standing at the edge of the wood, her long skirts made of silver, her face lit with longing and surprise, as radiant as I had seen her in the Great Temple of Byblos.

Xandros started.

Her eyes were dark and lined with kohl, and she smiled.

"Come," she said, and with a look back over her shoulder ran into the wood.

"Wait!" Xandros ran after her. "Ashterah, wait!"

Neas leaped forward after him, but I caught his arm. Xandros vanished into the shadows of the trees, into the wood as though he had never been.

"Why do you stop me?" Neas said. "We have to find him."

"No," I said, though there was a pain in my breast. "He has found what he seeks." I drew him by the arm and we walked on.

The sky lightened. The sun rose over the Egyptian desert, over the Red Lands of the west. Far overhead a desert falcon hunted in the still skies. The first rays of the sun turned the sands orange beneath our feet.

Maris sank to the ground, covering his eyes. "No," he whispered.

Neas knelt beside him. "Get up, my brother," he said. "Come now."

"No..." Maris moaned, and sank to the ground insensible.

"We must carry him," Neas said, getting his arm about Maris and trying to lift him.

I shook my head. "No," I said. "He has found what he seeks. I do not know what pain he met in Egypt, but it is here."

Neas stood and his face was pale. "Then I know what is to come," he said.

Before us were the banks of the Nile, the green fields and the walls of Memphis. We walked toward the city.

The walls were empty. The streets were empty. Trees swayed in the river breeze, awnings were spread against the heat of the day, but there were no people, no beasts. The markets were silent, wares displayed on tables. The wells were uncapped and filled with water, but there were no women drawing water, no animals drinking. Everything was still. The sun beat down on white streets, on palaces shining like burnished bronze.

Silently, Neas took my hand.

"This is a hazardous place," I said. "The sleeping city."

"For us both," he said.

I looked, and there was the temple. The doors stood open. I saw a movement out of the corner of my eye, and went to the doors.

Neas grabbed my hand and drew me back. "Take care!" he said.

There was an asp curled on the floor in the shadow of the door.

"Snakes are not death in dreams," I said.

"Are you sure of that?" Neas said.

I did not answer him, only went to the door. Inside, vast columns rose up into dim ceiling, dust making whirls of gold in the light that came in from somewhere far above. "Is this the future?" I asked. "Or the past?"

The snake spoke. "The gods do not see the future, for mortals write it. We can see only the past." It slithered nearer. "Come within," it said, and its voice seemed like my mother's. "And choose your own long destiny. This man is not your charge."

"He is my friend," I said.

"He is a flawed man," it said. "He does not love you. And he will bind you to his own destiny regardless of yours. Let go now. It is not easy, but you will be glad of it.

Otherwise you will be tied with blood and iron for many years."

Behind was the room of scrolls, shelves and shelves of them, stretching up into the light at the ceiling. Neas was silent. I looked at him and saw that he was frozen too, a look of sadness on his face.

"Look at him truly," the snake said, and it seemed that I saw an Achaian there, helmed and armed, a terrible wound disfiguring his face. "Patroclus of Achaia," it said. "And many more besides. He is born to arms, to kill and go down in blood." The snake's voice was sad. "He was your enemy, and now he is your prince, born to live in the ruins he created." I looked at him, and he was fair and strange to me at the same time, a man I had never seen and did not know.

"You tell me he is one of them, a man of blood. But you are telling me nothing I do not know." I had seen the love of battle in his face, the pleasure he took in the most daring plan, reckoning the cost and finding it worthwhile.

The snake's voice was filled with regret, and it seemed to me that it was the voice of She Who Had Been Pythia. "And you, daughter, might understand. You might be so much more. The world will grow old while you play men's games of blood and death, of wars and kingdoms and princes, and you sorrow for what might have been yours."

"Great Lady," I said carefully. "I know that You speak the truth. And perhaps I will regret; I do not know. But I am what I was born, and this is what I choose." My voice was stronger now, and my eyes were full of tears. "I am not wise or deep. I am not the river with its currents or the mountain with its secrets. I am not the worthiest or the best. I am not night, but fire. I love the dawn and the skies, the beat of drums around the fire and the passion of birth. I am not suited for the deep places, for Your Underworld. I am a lioness, and I must have the sun."

The snake changed. She stood before me lion headed, golden Sekhmet of Egypt, Her woman's body wrapped in scarlet linen. "There is nothing wrong with being a lioness," She said.

I bent my head. "No, Lady," I said.

She came closer and I felt Her breath, like a great cat pacing nearer. One hand lifted my chin, and I looked into Her eyes, as dark as the spaces between the stars. And I thought that She purred.

"All people see Me according to their nature," She said. "Do you understand?"

"I believe so," I said. "But, Lady..."

"If you are a lioness, then that is what you are. The bright fire of day is no less holy than the night." She looked up, Her eyes over my shoulder. "I commend you to My friend. May you have both Our blessings, Death's handmaiden."

I looked where She pointed. Behind Neas in the doorway stood a young man of surpassing beauty. His head was shaved in the Egyptian fashion, and His dark skin was shining with oil. He wore a linen skirt pleated and drawn, and a spear was in His hand. Behind Him rose the faint shadow of wings.

He looked at Sekhmet and shrugged. Then He smiled at me, a lopsided smile I had seen before. "Hello, Gull," He said.

"Mik-el?"

"I think we'd get along well," He said. "I've got some ideas."

"How can I serve You and Her too?" I asked. "Mik-el, I am already dedicated. And You belong to life, and to the world above."

"Have you not learned by now that they are the same?" She said. "Did Hry not teach you that as it is above, so it is below? Death without life is hollow and cruel, and life without death an empty mockery. All things must be in their time, in their course. For an old man to die when his time has come is not evil. You know that."

"I do," I said, and my voice throbbed. "But when a baby in arms is slaughtered, that is evil." I bent my head. "I have seen the world falling, Lady. Cities crumble one by one. More people than there are stars in the sky are starving. Men are desperate. And there is nothing I can do."

"You're already doing," Mik-el said. "What do you think you've been doing, trying to preserve Egypt, getting your people across the sea when they might otherwise be dead? You can't do everything at once all by yourself, you know."

"But I would," I said, desperate still with the longing. "Tell me how! How shall I raise dead men up to plow fields that are fallow? How shall I plant young olive trees?"

Mik-el smiled, and it was a beautiful smile. "One tree at a time," He said.

I bit my lip, and the tears overflowed my eyes.

"Come," He said gently. "If you are resolved, come. There is a city to found."

I nodded and took His hand.

*   *   *

AND THEN I stood beside Neas in a field of grain. He was crying. He knelt on the ground, hugging his knees.

I bent and put my arms around him. "What has happened, my prince?" I saw neither Mik-el nor Her, nor any sign of the temple.

"Did you not see her?" Neas said.

"Who?" I said.

"Basetamon. She is dead. She burned herself alive."

I felt a chill run through me, remembering the fire we had seen as we left Sais, my invented prophecy.

"When she knew I had gone with the ships, she built a pyre and burned herself. If we should not lie together in eternity she would lose it too, life and life after life." Neas shook in my arms. "She burned herself alive. Ah, gods! She burned herself alive!"

I took his face between my hands. "Neas! Neas! This is not your fault!"

"I knew that she might do something. I didn't think it, but I knew she might." He looked past me, to the edge of the fields where the woods met the river, as though looking after her. "I saw it. I saw her face blackening and her flesh sizzle, while her brother who had been called to the place stood there in horror and sadness. She killed herself because of me."

"Neas!" I grabbed both his hands. "What else should you have done? Stayed there as her concubine? You are not the one who changed her."

"I might have helped."

"And she might have killed you. Or killed Wilos or me or anyone else you loved. Madness is bad enough, but madness with power is terrible."

"She was not mad, only strange and sad. Only damaged. So terribly damaged."

"Neas." I had his attention now, and he was quieter. "Her healing is in the hands of the Lady of the Dead. You do not have that power. You never have. You cannot walk in the deep places with her, and you could not heal her. You are not a person who ever could. Should we blame the lion that it doesn't fly? Blame the ox that it doesn't swim?"

"I'm not an ox," he said.

"No, my prince. You are not," I said. "You are a man who tries to do what is best. And no more can be asked of you than that. No more can be asked of you than you ask of yourself, for already you expect more than any man."

"It isn't enough," he said. "I knew I could not be king. I have known since boyhood when men first began to sound me out about putting myself before the council in Wilusa that I could not do it."

"My prince," I said, "that is the Mystery." And as I said it I knew it to be true. "Any man who thinks he knows what is best, that he can mend all ends, should not be king. But to put yourself forward when there is no better man to the task and it must be done is not insubordinate. It is what must be done. You must do this. There is no one else."

"There's Maris and Xandros," Neas said.

"And do you believe either of them would make a better king?" I asked.

"No." He shook his head. "They are good men, and my friends. But no. They would not be better kings."

I took his hand and drew him to his feet. "Then stand, and walk with me there. I see Anchises coming for you."

In the rich meadowland along the river Anchises was walking, and it seemed to me he was different than I had seen before. His hair was gray, but he moved with the vigor of youth. Neas ran to him and they embraced.

"My son," Anchises said. "Know that I am proud you have come so far."

"I will not be the king you wished," Neas said abruptly. "Wilusa is no more, and I cannot bring her back. I cannot restore the past for you, or emulate my heroic uncles."

Anchises bowed his head. "I know. And I have burdened you too long with my hopes. I feared for you. And I was wrong to think that you would ever be less than honor requires."

"My honor or yours?" Neas asked.

"Mine," Anchises said, and his eyes were far away. "It is I who should have died for Wilusa, I who should have been there when they burned our temples and killed our kin, when Agamemnon ripped my Lysisippa's sister from her altar and raped her. But I was not there. I had gone to beg aid of the Hittite emperor. I did no deeds of arms on the field, and I did not even have the decency to die!"

Neas clasped his father in his arms, and at last I knew what had burned so, what had consumed Anchises with bitterness, this same guilt that burned too readily in Neas' breast. "My father," he said, "your service to the People has been hard indeed, but you have preserved us and come with us to a new home. If all the men were dead, who should preserve the memory of Wilusa That Was? Who should have saved Wilos? Who should have brought him from the fire, for he will be our next king?"

Anchises nodded. "He will be. That is assured." He

took Neas by the hand and led him along the river. I followed. "Come. There is something I want you to see."

Beside a willow that trailed in the water a young man was practicing with a bow. He was lithe and dark, with a heart-shaped face and brown eyes, long quick limbs.

"This is your son," Anchises said. "He waits here to be born. When the time comes he will cross the River and open his eyes in your world."

The boy did not look up, or even seem to see us.

"My son," Neas said, wonder in his voice. "Wilos' brother."

"Yes," Anchises said. "They will govern the People between them, the People of the sea and the People of the hills, and there will be no quarrel between them."

"And after?"

"Who can tell what the future holds?" I said. "So much depends on what we do. Whether we falter or not."

Anchises smiled. "And yet there are things that may be, a proud line and a proud city, son of Aphrodite. No, these things would not be if you flung yourself into the sea tomorrow, but you will not do that. I say to you the only thing one can say to a king. The things you desire may yet be."

Neas bent his head. "And that is the greatest burden of all. To desire."

"If you were free of desire you would not have tried Night's Door," Anchises said. "If you were not filled with longing."

"And then what should I have?" he asked, and his eyes were calm and blue.

"Peace," Anchises said. "Here, free of desire, is peace."

Neas looked about. "In these endless fields where nothing ever changes?"

"Yes," his father said gently.

Neas looked about, and I saw his face relax, his jaw unclench as though a fever slipped away, like a man terribly injured who has at last died, and with the final relaxation of muscles has passed beyond pain. I caught my breath.

Neas looked at me and smiled. "That's not for me," he said. "Better the pain and the joy too."

"That's what I thought you'd say," Anchises said.

I let out a breath I did not know I'd been holding.

"Come and walk by the River," Anchises said.

I did not know if the invitation included me too, but Neas held out his hand to me and I took it. It was warm and real, flesh, not fantasy.

All along the riverbank people were walking. Sometimes one would slip away, shouting farewells, exchanging embraces, joyfully promising remembrance. They stepped into the River, and its waters washed over them, pearl and silver streaming. And then a breeze took them, and they floated clear and light toward sunlight streaming down from above.

"What is happening?" Neas said.

"They are being born," I replied, and my voice was filled with wonder. "Twice we cross the River. When we die we cross the Styx, and come to the lands beneath and dwell here for a time. Then we cross this River, which is Memory, into the world above."

"They do not remember?" he asked.

"No," I said, and shook my head sadly. "Not even you. Not even me." I looked up at the light. "But that is not how we will leave this place. We will leave by the Gate of Horn, from which come true dreams."

I felt us rising up, saw the Gate of Horn before us, shimmering with a nacreous sheen. "We have dreamed in this place, my dear king. We have dreamed things that are true, and now we must return to the world above."

The light was blinding, and I clung to him. Brighter and brighter, until at last I closed my eyes.

I OPENED THEM.

I lay across Neas' naked body in the front chamber of the cave at Cumai, looking up at the bright sun pouring in through the cleft in the ceiling.

I pushed myself up on one elbow. My mouth was dry and my breasts were aching with the need to nurse Markai. I heard a moan.

Xandros was lying in the light coming in through the door, one hand almost in the ashes of the fire pit. He rolled over and threw up.

"Xandros?" I crawled over to him. "Are you all right?"

He nodded but did not speak. The color was coming back in his face, and his hands were steady.

I stood and went over to Neas. "Neas?"

He opened his eyes. For a moment they were blank, but then memory came flooding back. "Sybil?"

"Yes," I said. "Can you sit up?" I helped him sit.

Xandros called out to me. "I can't wake Maris!"

I stood again, more steady now, and went to him. I knelt down beside them.

"What is it?" Neas said from across the chamber.

"Maris is dead," I said.

*   *   *

WE MOURNED HIM and crowned Neas at the same time. For Maris there was a great pyre on the beach. Not only had he been *Pearl's* captain, but he was the sacrifice that sealed Neas' kingship, the man who had willingly gone into the darkness beside his prince and taken the death that waited. The rest of the incenses of Egypt went on his pyre, and we all wailed for him, his young wife, Idele, gray with grief, her belly swollen with the child he would never see.

I sang the Descent in a choked voice. Perhaps if I had not steeped the concoction so strong, or if there had been less…

He is mine, She whispered at my elbow. His heart was not so strong as his body. He gave himself for his king, a death he chose. He did not have to come.

I bent my head and let the smoke wash over me.

There was no crown, of course. The crown of Wilusa was plunder for the Achaians a generation ago. They crowned him with vine and summer flowers, toasted him with full cups of the local vintage.

Neas drank, and then they acclaimed him. "Aeneas! Aeneas! Son of Aphrodite!" They began the snake dance then, winding round and round the fire. I sat, and the wine was vinegar in my mouth.

Xandros came with our son in his arms, gave Markai to me and put his arms around me, his cheek against mine. "Don't," he said.

"Don't what?"

"Don't grieve for him."

"He was so young," I said. "It is my fault."

"I almost stayed too," he said. "I wanted to. I could

have stayed with Ashterah. I could have been healed of all this grief and pain. It was my choice."

"Why didn't you?" I asked.

Xandros rested his chin on my shoulder. "Well, there's Neas and you and Markai. I think I've got plenty of time in the future to be dead."

I smiled at that. "I suppose you do."

Xandros shrugged. "And so do you."

"The whole time I was singing the Descent I was thinking that I'm so glad it wasn't you. That's so wrong of me. To wish this grief on Idele and her child instead of on me..."

"That's the problem with love," Xandros said. "It makes you care more about one person than another."

"I can't not care anymore. I can't pretend that I don't feel more for Markai and Kianna than the other children. I can't pretend that I don't value your life more than other men's. And that's wrong in a priestess. Wrong, Xandros."

Xandros touched my face, the wet track of a single tear. "It's human. You can't help it. Only the gods can love everyone the same."

I buried my face against his neck. "I am so glad it wasn't you," I whispered. "That it wasn't you She chose to keep."

"Me too," said Xandros.

AB URBE CONDITA

We sailed on the fifth day, a gorgeous summer day with a following wind to urge us north-ward up the coast. The great bay disappeared behind us, the mountain sank into the distance. We fol-lowed the coast. Fields were ripening and poppies bloom-ing. The weather was perfect. There was a faint chill in the air at night that spoke of autumn, a lowering of the sun on the horizon. Summer was ending, and the harvest was coming in.

It seemed strange on *Dolphin* without Kos. Maris' second in command was much less experienced, and had only been at the helm since we left Egypt, so Neas pro-moted Kos as *Pearl*'s captain. It was true he was of low birth, but he had proved himself again and again. Xan-dros began teaching Bai how to steer. He already knew the chants, but when to use which orders was not some-thing he could see from the first oar, since the bow hid the sea ahead from him and he could not see any other rowers. Xandros let him take the tiller under his eyes, in-structing all the while.

We stopped and traded a little, but for the most part the villages were scarce. Perhaps there were settlements in-land, but we did not see them. At one tiny place, scarcely more than a collection of five or six houses and a couple of boats, we were ashore trading for fresh bread. I was walking Markai. He fretted sometimes, and we were walking along the edge of the field.

"See the flowers?" I picked one red poppy, golden centered, and held it up for his grasping hand. "Red is pretty."

Now, She whispered behind me. *Now. You must sail up the coast. Now.*

It was like the night in Pylos before the ships came, a dreadful certainty that something was about to happen. *Now.*

With the flower still in my hand I all but ran back to Neas.

"We must sail," I said.

He took one look at me and turned to his men. "Everyone back to the ships! We sail immediately!" Xandros looked up in the middle of the trade, one eyebrow rising. Then he concluded it as quickly as possible.

"Where are we going?" Neas asked.

It embarrassed me a little to see everyone running for the boats as though an enemy were at large. "North," I said. "North until She tells us to stop." I shifted Markai on my hip. "I don't know why. I'm sorry, Neas."

"Your word is enough for me," he said simply. "Xandros! Get *Dolphin* loaded! We sail!"

North, with a following wind. We sailed for two days without stopping, without beaching at night. And the shore passed beside us, golden and ripe.

The second night a fog rolled in, and we could not have seen *Seven Sisters* and *Pearl* if we had not all hung lamps at our sterns, something we had learned in Egypt.

Neas called over, and soon we all three came alongside.

Wordlessly, I handed Markai to Tia, and Xandros swung me across the gap between ships.

Kos climbed over *Seven Sisters'* rail on the other side. "We can't go on like this," he said without preliminary, and I thought how far he had come from the first council he had attended, when he had been too shy to speak. "I can hear surf off to my right. I have no idea how close it is, or how steeply the coast draws away. At this rate we're going to run up on rocks. We need to anchor and wait out the fog."

Xandros nodded. "I'm out on the seaward side, but I don't like this running without being able to see either. And there's a strange current here, closer inshore. I think we should wait."

Neas looked at me. "Lady? Prudence dictates that we wait, and seamanship demands it. What do you say?"

I felt nothing. She did not speak. The sense of urgency that had been pushing me was gone. I reached, and there was quiet. "We should wait," I said. "I do not see any danger in doing so."

Neas nodded, and Kos gave a visible sigh of relief. They had been willing to go on if Neas asked it, but they were glad not to. "Drop anchor!" Neas yelled. "We're going to wait out the fog!"

"It should go in the morning," Xandros said. "As warm as it's been, the sun will burn it off in no time."

Bai took the watch. Xandros came to stay beside me in

Dolphin's bow cabin, and while Markai slept, made love to me as quietly and gently as one can when trying not to disturb a sleeping baby a handbreadth away. Afterward, I curled onto his shoulder, and let the sea rock us both.

Perhaps it was the quiet, or the release of lovemaking after long waiting, but Xandros slept past dawn. I left him sleeping, Markai curled up in a little bundle near him, faces wearing identical expressions of repose. It was almost funny, I thought. They looked so much alike in sleep, damp black hair clinging to their foreheads. I went out on deck.

Dawn was coming and the sky was streaked with pink. The fog lifted off like a veil.

We stood out from a river mouth where a broad stream met the sea. It flowed between banks green with summer, and behind it rose slopes thick with trees, rolling hills and the shades of distant mountains on the far horizon. Seagulls cried on the winds. They dodged and dove as the sun rose above the hills, golden and brilliant. I watched, my heart leaping at the sheer beauty.

Neas stood on the deck of *Seven Sisters,* his arms upraised, the light gilding him.

Not wanting to wake people by calling, I climbed across to him. He saw what I was about and caught me under my arms, lifting me when the ships swayed apart. For a moment we stood like that, his arms around me, feeling the sun lift us both.

"Look!" he said. "That's not a water bird. What is it?"

Something large was winging toward us, scattering the seagulls in their diving. It flashed across us at mast height, its shadow dashing over Neas.

"It's a young eagle," I said.

The light caught its talons as it turned inland, flashing like gold.

Neas looked at me and I at him. "Yes," he said.

I nodded. "We should go upriver, my king."

As soon as the rowers were all awake we started upriver, *Seven Sisters* going first and very slowly, sounding the way ahead with a knotted rope weighted with stones. The river wasn't terribly wide, but it was deep enough and smooth enough for us to glide along. Away from the seashore there were trees and meadows, limbs bending down over the stream.

I stood with Xandros in the stern of *Dolphin,* for he would trust no hand but his on the tiller in the confines of the river. "Look there!" I said. "It looks like smoke from cooking fires."

Ahead, beyond a turn in the river, there were a few thin streaks of smoke.

Seven Sisters halted and drifted against the current, and Xandros yelled for our oars to still. We were within easy calling distance of *Seven Sisters* and *Pearl* behind us.

"Water's getting shallow," Neas called back. "We're going to try to find a channel on the left-hand side."

They crept forward again, only two oars beating.

"It's the dry season," Xandros said. "See along the bank there? The water is higher at other times. This river's perfectly navigable if it's still possible to get a warship up here in dry weather."

Neas found the channel, and we followed.

Along the bank the trees gave way to fields of barley and grain, ripe and waiting for the harvest. A vineyard was behind, grapes heavy on the vines, purple and dark.

Beyond were patches of other vegetables, all unharvested.

"There's something wrong," I said. "Where are the people? The grain is sitting ripe in the field and there are no reapers."

Xandros nodded. "There." He gestured with his chin.

One small corner of the field was mown, the stalks broken off haphazardly, as though by clumsy workers who took little care. Beyond it, an orchard of almond trees showed green in patches. Some of the trees had been burned.

They were shipping oars on *Seven Sisters,* gliding into the bank. As we came near we saw what they had seen. There was a fortified town just ahead. Before it docks came down to the shore, and gray stone walls rose up. It was a small place, no larger than Pylos, perhaps, with a plain wall and a pair of watchtowers no greater than four times a man's height. A few tendrils of cooking smoke rose, and I could smell bread baking. The gates were closed.

"Not again," Xandros said. He smiled at me. "I'm getting tired of coaxing people out to trade who think we're here to loot them and burn them out."

Neas and several others went over the side of *Seven Sisters* and walked back to us. "Think we should trade?" he asked.

Xandros nodded. "They seem to have plenty of food."

I leaned over the rail. "Neas, something is wrong. Why haven't they harvested? With that fog last night you'd think they would have wanted to get everything in before the damp comes."

The rest of the men were getting down from *Seven Sisters,* arms at the ready in case there was a misunderstanding. It had happened more than once, that we'd had to stand to arms before it was clear we wanted trade.

Neas looked across at the fields, and it occurred to me that he and Xandros had probably never actually harvested grain. They were seamen, not farmers. "You're right," he said. "It's strange."

There was a glint of metal on the walls, light glancing off helmets.

"Arm up," Neas said, and went back to *Seven Sisters* for his equipage.

I helped Xandros fasten his breastplate, his new sword at his side, his new shield on his arm.

Tia came and stood beside me. "What's going on?" she asked.

I showed her what we had been looking at, at the fields unharvested and the partially burned orchard.

Our men formed up. Xandros was calling something to the walls. I could see several armed men upon the wall, but they did not reply. Perhaps the language here was too different from Shardan.

"Why would the fields be unburned if they were attacked by an enemy? And if they haven't been raided, why aren't the fields harvested?" I wondered. "It doesn't make sense. Why haven't they done it?"

Tia gripped my arm. "It's the women. They haven't got enough men to harvest. So they've done only that one little corner. Someone attacked and they're planning to come back, like leaving a rabbit warren where it is and using it to trap a few when you want them. Why burn the fields and lose the food? They can leave them and come back for them when they're ripe. It's not like they can go anywhere!"

"Yes! I think you're right." I swung Markai against me and climbed over the rail, splashing into the mud and hurrying up to Neas.

He was not in bow shot of the walls, but he looked irritated with me. "Sybil, you're in too close. Back up. They're not answering our hails, and that fellow over there keeps shaking his spear at me."

"How many men do you count?" I asked him.

"Five on the walls," Neas said. "I'm guessing the rest are massed behind the gate and are going to come rushing out at any minute. You need to get back. And Tia too." He glanced behind me where Tia had followed, Kianna on her shoulder.

"I don't think there are any more men," I said. Quickly I explained what Tia had said.

Neas shook his head. "You may be right. Or you may not be. But they're not acting like they want to talk, and if they've got the number of men a settlement like this should have, we're outnumbered if they charge us. Get back on the ships."

"We have to talk," I said. "Let Xandros go forward and try again."

"They're not answering him," Neas said. "If he goes into bow shot he's going to get hit."

"Then let me go," I said, raising my chin. "They can see what I am. I'm a woman with a baby, and not an enemy who can attack them if they let me get close. Let me go with Xandros."

Neas opened and closed his mouth.

Xandros came up quietly. "Gull, are you sure?"

"Yes," I said with a quick glance at Tia. "I'm sure."

I arranged Markai on my shoulder so he was more visible, and took a step forward.

"Me too," said Tia. She stood beside me, Kianna on her hip, her long bare legs dangling. "If one is good, two are better."

"Those are your children," Neas said, and I could not tell if his voice was disbelieving or indignant.

"Yes," I said. And we started forward.

Xandros followed bare-handed, his shield against his back, ready to swing forward and cover me and Markai at his expense. "Oh love, you'd better know what you're doing," he whispered.

Lady, I thought, *I hope I do too.*

We approached the beetling walls. Xandros called out in Shardan, "People of this place, we mean you no harm! We are traders, honest men with families, as you can see! We want only to speak with you! Let there be no misunderstandings between us!"

There was a long silence. We saw them talking together on the wall, heads bent close. Then a voice called back in Shardan, though the accent was strange. "We see you and your children. But we do not want to trade. You have nothing we want. Get in your ships and leave."

Xandros looked at me.

I raised my voice. "We have men who can harvest your crops, and will trade their labor for a share of the grain."

They bent their heads to one another again. It seemed they conferred for a long time. "Is there one who speaks for you and will come within and treat with our king?"

"Yes," Xandros replied. "Our king, Aeneas, is here. He will speak with you."

Tia went back and changed places with Neas while

Xandros and I waited with Markai. Neas laid aside his sword and his helm and came forward.

He cocked an eye at Xandros. "Go back," he said. "I need you in command out here. You're my second and we can't both go in. And take Markai with you. Sybil goes with me. Her Shardan is better than mine."

Xandros gathered the baby from my arms. "You'll guard her."

"As if she were my own wife," Neas promised.

Xandros raised an eyebrow.

"It will be well," I said, and settled Markai in his arms.

And then Neas and I walked forward. The gates creaked open and we entered the city.

IT WAS a small city indeed, with dirt streets and low houses with tile roofs, one street wide enough for a chariot leading straight back, toward where presumably temples and the palace were. Two boys ran forward and shut the gates behind us, dropping a bar into place. They were only twelve or thirteen years old, not men under arms, and I knew that Tia was right.

A man in breastplate and antique greaves had come down from the wall, along the plank walk and staircase that ran along the inside. It was he who had called to us from the wall, and as he came near I saw that his left arm was missing at the elbow. I had not seen that at a distance. Three other men followed, and they seemed hearty enough.

"This way," he said. They surrounded us and we went quickly down the main street.

The palace was a long, low building with a roof of red tile and a portico held up by stone columns along the front. Smoke drifted up from a hearth hole in the middle of the building. The courtyard was dirt, not stone. Most of the houses were wood, on stone foundations. It was a very modest place.

And yet a weeping almond spread its boughs over the porch, and the temple across the way had a certain grace. The sky above was blue, and the ends of the roof were ornamented with fancy tiles.

We went inside. Autumn sunlight poured in through the hearth hole, illuminating a generously proportioned room with a floor of painted stone, a lion hunt picked out in colors. Blinking at the sudden darkness of the room around it, I saw motion along the walls, the movement of skirts. Before the hearth was a carved wooden chair. In it sat the king.

He was perhaps fifteen years Neas' senior, but his dark hair was already streaked with white. His robes covered his lap and limbs with folds of white linen and scarlet wool, but I thought there was something strange about the way he held his left leg, that the heel of his foot did not quite touch the floor. "You say you are traders," he said. "And yet I think you lie."

Neas raised his head sharply. "I am Aeneas, son of Anchises, King of Wilusa That Was. I do not lie."

"And yet you have come only to trade?" The king's gaze was sharp, and I knew him for a true ruler, a man worth reckoning upon.

"We have come to trade, yes," Neas said. "We have goods from many ports, and we are lately come from Egypt."

The king glanced at me. "And yet the woman there has said you will trade the labor of your hands for food."

"We do not disdain honest labor," Neas said. "And we are willing to trade that labor for food. We have our families with us, as you have seen, for Wilusa is no more."

There was a stirring behind me, but I could not turn to see.

"Well we know that Wilusa is no more," the king said. "We have heard so from men who fought with the Achaians in the great fleet that sought to loot the cities of Egypt. And we know that you fought for Pharaoh in that battle."

"Does that mean there is blood between us?" Neas asked. "For my part, I have no quarrel with you or your people. I do not even know the name of this city or its king."

"This city is called Latium," he said. "And I am its king. Latinus is my name, as it is the name of all who rule here. We did not send men to the great fleet. We have no need of mercenary enterprise here."

"Sir," Neas said politely, though there was steel in his voice, "politeness is an old virtue, and I had not heard that it was valued less in this land. We are mercenaries through hard cause. A king must do what is necessary for his people, no matter how few they are."

"Indeed he must," Latinus said, and he sighed. He seemed to come to some decision, for he leaned forward. "But sometimes answers may come in dreams, or the future be divined from the flight of birds by men who are skilled in reading such things. This morning I saw a young eagle flying up the river toward me, and he came and stood upon the roof poles of this house, and there he devoured a fox that he had caught. What do you make of this?"

Neas did not look at me. "I saw the same eagle as I stood upon my ship, and we followed it. But it is not I who am skilled in understanding such things. That is the role of Sybil, who stands here with me."

The king looked at me. "I had rather thought she was your wife."

"My wife is dead," Neas said. "My son and I are alone in the world." He glanced around at the hall. "And so are you, it seems. Where are the warriors who should guard your throne? The sons of your house who should wait at your side?"

"The sons of my house are dead," Latinus said, and his voice was steady and fierce. "They were killed by the Rutoli when we met them in battle, when I was sorely injured and the warriors of my people were slain."

Neas nodded. He could not have failed to mark the number of men, no more than ten all told, and perhaps as many youths. I had marked it well.

"The Rutoli are our neighbors to the north, and they are fierce men. They sent three ships to the great fleet, and only one of them returned. Since then they have made war with us, reckoning us an easier mark than Pharaoh." His dark eyes flashed as if to say that any who reckoned him an easier mark than the Great King of Egypt thought too little of him. They had their pride, these people.

"They came upon us by treachery, while we were working in the fields. Before we could arm, half our men were slain. More still fell in the battle that followed. We pushed them back and gained the gates, and they did not sit before us in siege. Why should they? They know that we cannot leave, and that they may return in force and finish what they have begun at any time. It is convenient to them to get their own harvest in before they come to claim us." Latinus looked at me, then back to Neas. "So you see, King Aeneas of Wilusa That Was, you have come at an ill-fated time to a cursed people. We wait for them to come, knowing that we at least will make the price of Latium dear indeed. What use are our forges and our towers when we do not have men to wield our swords or defend our walls?"

Neas nodded slowly. "And yet I am come to you unlooked for with more than a hundred fighting men. How many are your Rutoli?"

"Nearly three hundred," Latinus said. "And we can put no more than twenty men in the field, all told."

"Have they chariots?" Neas asked.

"No, they run as skirmishers," he said. "With spear or sword."

Neas looked down, and I saw what he was thinking. I saw the shape of it all in that moment, all the twists and turns of the labyrinth, all the paths over land and sea that led to this autumn morning. My heart leaped at the beauty of it.

Then Neas looked up and met the king's eyes, and a smile was on his lips. "King Latinus, your walls are stout and doubtless your men are stouthearted too. But you are right that they are too few to defend Latium alone. My people are weary, and we have wandered far over the sea seeking a land where we may live in peace and practice the customs of our forefathers, the sacred rites of our gods. A hundred and twenty-six men

I have with me, but only twenty-one women and twenty-two children. That is not enough, I think, to preserve the People. But it is more than enough to defend Latium and to harvest all the crops that wait in your fields, enough to fish these seas and mend your roofs. It is enough to plow fields that are fallow, and to plant young olive trees."

My breath caught and I bit down on my lip.

Latinus looked at him closely. "If you can do these things," he said. "If you can fend off the Rutoli and get our crops in so that we do not starve in the winter that comes, I will call you brother and give you whatever you may ask. I will call you my son and you will be king in Latium after me. I will give into your keeping the last treasure of my house."

I heard again the whisper of robes behind me, and she crossed to stand by his chair.

"The hand of my daughter, Lavinia," he said.

She was small and slender, no more than thirteen years old, with a heart-shaped face and big dark eyes, brown hair falling over her shoulder in a single braid. She put one hand on her father's shoulder and stood there looking at Neas, and her back was straight. If she was frightened it did not show in her face.

"She is my only living child," Latinus said. "And her inheritance is the kingdom."

Neas bent his head in respect. "Princess Lavinia," he said, "I shall undertake to defeat the Rutoli with goodwill, for your hand is an honor beyond price." He met her eyes as he straightened, and she did not flinch, child that she was in her white robe.

Neas stepped forward, and Latinus reached out his hand. "I pledge you my word."

Neas met his hand and joined it wrist to wrist. "And I pledge you mine. May all the gods stand witness to what we have resolved today, and grant us victory."

"May it be so," Latinus said.

LATIUM

We set to harvesting the crops of Latium with a will. The season was almost over, and the days left before the damp ruined the grain were numbered. Many of our men were sailors and had never done this work before, so it did not proceed as smoothly or as quickly as we might have wished, even with those women who were not tied down by small babies working too. I watched Markai and Kianna both while Tia worked, and tried to pick grapes as best I could with both of them with me. Markai was slung on my back while I picked. Kianna played around my feet, occasionally stopping to pop a fat ripe grape in her mouth. Then I would have to stop and pick the seeds out of her mouth, lest she choke on them. She was not yet old enough to spit them out properly. Markai dozed in the sun, his plump cheek against the back of my neck.

And always, always we kept watch for the Rutoli. It would not be long before they returned.

On the twelfth night there was a heavy rain, and when morning came the world was wreathed in fog. The river murmured quietly around the docks, swollen from the night's rain. The barley we had not gotten in was beaten down.

I stood with Neas on the wall just after dawn. Behind us, the smell of bread rose from the ovens of Latium, baking in round hard loaves with a sweet warm center.

"It will be tomorrow," Neas said with the certainty of an oracle.

I looked at him. "You know this?"

He nodded, still looking out toward the river. "I know war, Sybil. The harvest is ended. Soon the cold will come, and chill wet days little suited to campaigning. But tomorrow will dawn clear and bright, and tonight the moon is full. They will leave their town tonight, and fall upon us in the morning, thinking to catch the people of Latium in the fields, trying to get in whatever is left."

"This is what you would do?" I asked.

"Yes," he said. "Were I a raider in truth."

I voiced the thing I had been worrying over. "Can we win, Neas? They will outnumber us more than two to one. Latinus said there were nearly three hundred of them, and all told with us and the men of Latium we are less than a hundred and fifty."

Neas looked at me, and it was the same smile I had seen in Byblos. "We can win. They have not seen close order before. No man here has." He put his hands on the parapet and leaned out. "This is what we learned it for. This is the weapon, and this is the time. I feel it in every bone of my body."

"And the place?" I asked.

Neas nodded. "And the place. Here I will live, and the

sons of my house, for all the days of my life. Do you not feel it?"

"Yes," I said. He could have been a priest, were he not a prince.

"It is a beautiful place," he said.

Latium had no shining white walls, no great library, no temples with fine columns. There were no broad avenues, no high towers. It was a small town with dirt streets, wooden houses with tile roofs, docks, and a navigable river, arable fields.

"You will make it beautiful," I said.

Neas pointed off away from the river. "Those wooded slopes there face west. Can you not see them terraced for vines? And that overgrown field along there? An olive grove? And next spring we can put that fallow field along the river under the plow."

"Yes," I said. "I see that it will be so. You will rule well in this place, when Latinus has crossed the River and you have wed Lavinia."

He gave me a quick glance, then looked back out toward the river. For a moment he was silent and I thought he would not speak, but then he did. "Will she hate me, do you think?"

"For consummating the marriage?" I put my hands on the parapet as well. "You must consummate it. Otherwise it will not be valid in the eyes of our people or of hers."

"She is twelve years old," Neas said. "And I am twice her age. And not accustomed to a gentle young maiden."

"She is a princess," I said. "And she has been raised to her duty. She will do what must be done."

"But will she hate me for it?" he asked. "A queen who

hates me will bring us all nothing but sorrow. And I have no desire..."

To create another Basetamon, I thought. *To harm another that way.* I chose my words carefully. "You must consummate it," I said. "But you must be as gentle as you can. And this is difficult, I know."

"With two hundred people waiting to see the bloody linens?" Neas grimaced.

"My prince," I said, "they need to see blood. It is not important where the blood comes from." I held his eyes until I was sure he understood. "Better that the marriage be consummated privately and later, when there is time to take care and you understand each other better. And as for getting a son, well, there is no hurry between one moon and the next."

"Surely women will ask her," Neas said.

I nodded. "And you must see what she will say. But she seems a clever girl. As long as you do this in a way that does not seem that you spurn her, but rather value her so highly that you will risk no mistakes."

He nodded. "I do value her. Not for herself, but for the future. I must have a queen who is not my enemy."

"Perhaps in time you will value her for herself as well," I said.

Neas shrugged, but there was pain in his voice. "I do not look for love, Sybil. I am a king, and I was raised to my duty as well. But there are times when I wish I might be a simple ship's captain." He looked at me, and I felt the warmth in his eyes like the veiled sun. "Like Xandros."

"Neas," I said, and knew that I answered more than one question. "You are not."

He looked away, nodded. "I know." And we spoke of it no more.

THE RUTOLI CAME in the morning. An hour after sunrise they came over the most distant hill. We stood on the parapet and counted them. Latinus was right. Two hundred and sixty was my count.

In the courtyard below our men stood to arms. The men of Latium stood upon the wall. Those who had bows would use them, and the five or so without would handle the gates.

By the time the Rutoli crested the last ridge we were in arms.

I would not wait below. I could not. Markai was with Tia at the palace, but I could not stay there. Instead, I painted my face, put on my newest robes. Whatever happened, there would be many who needed me before the day's end. And after this long road, I would see the bloodshed that was shed for me and for my child, whether it was proper or not.

I felt no hint of Her displeasure, only Her presence. "Lady of the Underworld," I whispered. "Lady of Battles, Lion-headed Sekhmet, Lady of War."

Xandros looked up from the courtyard. *Dolphin*'s men were forming up around him.

I met his eyes.

He smiled and said nothing. There was nothing to be said. We knew everything there was to say, spoke with our eyes.

Now the Rutoli were before the gates, calling Latium to surrender.

Latinus had climbed the inner steps to the tower beside the gate, and he answered them himself in a strong voice. "We will not!" he cried. "If you want what is ours you must take it!"

I did not understand their answer, but I saw them shake their spears, heard their shouts.

The gate opened.

The Rutoli shouted again, beating their shields with their swords, challenges and curses.

Through the opening marched the first company of our men, *Seven Sisters*' crew in full array, a Shardan sword and shield for each man, four files of eight men, each covering the next. The stamping of their feet in perfect unison was like thunder.

Behind them *Dolphin*'s men followed. Past the gate they swung to the left, *Pearl*'s company following after. I could see Kos clearly in the front rank, the right front position that men turn on. They swung left of *Dolphin*'s men. Three companies stood in line, Neas on the right, Xandros in the center, and Kos on the left.

The Rutoli checked. Whatever they had expected of Latium, this was not it.

On the heels of *Pearl*'s men the gates swung shut. Our men waited before the gates. There was no sound. Our men did not shout or wave their swords, did not sing or cry out the names of their ancestors or gods. They just waited in good order, still and stern as the Nubian archers in Egypt.

The Rutoli shouted.

They were tall, strong men, it was true. Each wore arms of his choosing, and they stood in groups of family and friends, each with a leader of their house or line. Some

moved from one group to another. Some had swords, and
others short spears. They spread out, calling out threats
and boasts. I could hear their princes exhorting them, but
at a distance I could not make out the words.

Our men waited.

A breeze off the river lifted my veil. The sky was a
perfect autumn blue.

Their princes shouted, raising their spears. And then
they charged.

They broke off our lines like the sea off rocks.

In a rush and tumble of blood we met them, and they
crashed back. Ten or twelve men lay on the ground. Some
were moving and some were not. Our lines held firm. Not
one man of ours fell. In the ranks of *Pearl*'s men there
was a shift as two wounded men in the first line stepped
back to an inner rank, their shipmates stepping forward,
shields locking into place like a wall.

Again the princes cried, and again they surged forward
like the waves. Swords flashed, and the sound of men's
screams came on the morning air.

They broke again, and still our lines held firm. Three
men of ours were down now, but our ranks closed over
them. The shields of their shipmates protected them. I
heard Neas' voice, calm and carrying as though at sea.
"Stand fast! Stand fast, sons of Wilusa! Stand fast for our
gods and kin!"

A third time they charged.

Thirty or more of their men were down and would not
rise, and now they were filled with blood despair.

Not a man of ours moved. Not one broke the line.

This time when they broke I knew it was final. They
streamed away in ones and twos, some carrying kindred on

their backs, some limping with wounds or dropping their arms on the field. They fled for the tree line, and there was no one to call them to rally.

"Don't break the line!" Neas yelled. "Do not pursue! Hold the line!" We would not be lured out of formation by victory. A couple of men started forward, but their fellows caught them back. We stood. While the Rutoli fled in disorder from the gates of Latium, we stood. A dozen dead they left on the field, and forty more dead and wounded they bore away with them. As the sun rose up the sky, they left the fields before Latium clear.

When there were no more Rutoli in sight except for the dead, Neas stood down from arms. Men bent to tend the wounded. The gates of Latium opened.

I came down from the walls and went among the wounded.

There were not so many as I had feared. Ten men injured, and only two who seemed likely to die. The others had a variety of sword and spear wounds. One had a broken arm from a blow taken to the shield, and another a broken wrist. One man had a bad spear thrust to his leg, which I thought had injured the knee permanently.

The women of Latium came while I stayed with the worst wounded. I heard the splash of water as I bent over one and looked up to see Lavinia with a water jar in her hand. Her mouth was set against the stench. The water splashed but did not spill.

"Thank you, Princess," I said, and took the water jar.

She knelt down beside me and helped me lift the man to drink. "You have bled for our city," she said, speaking clearly that I might understand her.

"No, Princess," I said. "For what is mutually ours. For

a home at last, a free people. It is from our mingled blood that we will endure."

She looked down at the blood on her hand, where the wounded man had grasped at it. "From our mingled blood," she said. She knew as I did that our blood might flow together on the field, but where it should mingle was in the womb.

Neas came and stood behind us. He had a long cut on the inside of his right arm where the point of a spear had traced, but already it had ceased to bleed. "Sybil?" He stopped short when he saw Lavinia.

"The princess is helping me," I said.

"Ah." Neas was short of words. "Well. Xandros says he needs you over there. One of the men has died."

I got up. "I will go," I said. I crossed the tumbled earth. When I reached Xandros I looked back.

Neas was kneeling beside the wounded man, making some little joke with him, while Lavinia sponged the man's brow, a wary look on her face.

Xandros touched my shoulder, but did not embrace me. He would not, while I wore the paint. "What do you see?" he asked quietly.

"A boy with a heart-shaped face and skill with the bow," I said. And then I turned to him. "I see you." Well and whole, not a scratch on him, just dirt and other men's blood.

"Well," Xandros said with a rueful shrug. "I'm lucky."

"You are," I said.

"Only the gods know why." He glanced over his shoulder to where the dead man lay, one of *Pearl*'s rowers. His brother was kneeling beside him.

"Only the gods do," I said.

*   *   *

THAT NIGHT we burned the dead beneath the bright stars
of autumn. The next night, on a night of rain, we celebrated the marriage of a king.

Outside the rain drummed down, but inside the great
hall of Latium there was a warm fire, and our shadows
leaped on the walls, ours and the people of Latium alike.
I looked round at their faces. There were a few men and
youths, all the men of Latium, but it was mostly women,
I thought, women who had expected rape and pillage, to
be carried away from their lands and kin, their children
massacred or taken as slaves. Instead, they celebrated a
wedding.

I stood beside Xandros while Latinus put Lavinia's
hand in Neas'. Neas wore a tunic of scarlet wool bound
about with a golden belt, and his fair hair was combed and
glinted in the light. He towered above Lavinia. She wore
her white dress, and a saffron veil covered her face and
hair, golden as a cloud.

Her father held their hands together for a moment, then
let go. With one hand he gently lifted the veil from his
daughter's eyes. Her face was pale and still, carved from
marble. Neas bent and kissed her lips. She did not move,
though her eyes closed and then opened again.

Our men began to cheer.

I looked at her father. He was stern but not displeased.
This new son-in-law had done all that he might ask. His
people were safe. That is, after all, the first duty of a king,
and it must come before all else, even before one's own
child.

"I thank the gods..." Xandros said.

I looked up at him, leaned back against his warm arm. "What?"

"That I am not a prince."

I smiled and rested my head against his. "So do I."

At the feast I stopped to talk with Kos. It took a lot of wine to make the man drunk, and while half the celebrants were already beyond sense, Kos was still on his feet. I sat beside him at one of the long tables drawn up in the hall, and we watched some men from *Pearl* dancing on the table. Kos was looking somewhere beyond. I followed his gaze.

At the hearth the women were serving out the last of the food, platters of roasted fish that had been cooking in the ashes. I knew which one he watched. Now and again she glanced up at him, a cautious glance, but not without interest. She had curling brown hair and a broad forehead, a sharp nose and two little boys that followed her about, one three or so and one perhaps five. A widow, I thought. Twenty-five or so, with children at her skirts.

"Will you marry her?" I asked.

Kos looked into his cup. "Probably. If she'll have me." He met my gaze. "We've done a thing that could not be done. We've crossed land and sea to the ends of the earth to a place like we left. And they're glad to see us. I'd have carried off a woman if I had to, but I'd rather court one willing, and know what I'm getting."

"And you'll not kill those little boys of hers," I said. I knew what the women of Latium were gaining from the agreement.

"Gods, no!" Kos said. "They're likely boys. It seems that I'm the shipwright after all, and I must have some boys to train up."

"And some of your own to follow," I said.

Kos nodded. "If She wills. But I'd do no harm to my own children's brothers, new children or not. You know that."

"I do," I said. "But it's much more than anyone here could expect, taken in war." I had been born a captive; I knew.

Kos took a long pull at his wine cup. "I couldn't see how you meant to do it," he said. "You and Neas. Have some people welcome us, some place where we'd slide home like the sword to the sheath. But here everyone gains. We get a city ready built with people who want us, women who are ready for marrying, good walls, and good land. They get men who can defend what they have, and who won't loot them out or take them as slaves. You've traded us a life. And I have no idea how you've done that."

"She willed it," I said simply.

But it was never that simple, of course.

Across the room I watched Neas bend his head to speak with his bride. He was trying, I thought. And his Shardan was getting better.

Xandros and I did not follow the bawdy crowd that followed them to the bedchamber door. Instead, we slipped away into the rain, running across the streaming dirt streets to the portico of the temple. We stood there under the roof, gasping. The rain was cold. It glittered on his eyelashes.

"My dear, dear friend," he said. We were chilled, but his eyes were warm.

I laughed. My feet were covered in mud, and my hair was soaked. I was nothing beautiful or fine, but he kissed me anyway.

We clung together under the portico, the rain beating down, droplets bouncing where they hit the ground into a fine haze. After a few minutes we moved inside to the little room in the back where my things were. I drew him down beside me in the dark.

"Can it be real?" he whispered.

I touched his lips with my fingers, tracing the line of his lips, the curve of his chin. "We're home, Xandros. Home at last."

He kissed my fingers, warm lips on chilled white hands.

In the bright bedchamber of the palace Neas and Lavinia were in their marriage bed, a brazier to warm them and hanging lamps to light them, scarlet blanket folded at the bottom of the bed, white linens stretched clean and waiting. I hoped Neas did as I had advised. I hoped Lavinia was what I thought she was.

"You're thinking again," Xandros said. He kissed my throat. "You should stop."

"You're right," I said. I pulled him against me and we made love while the thunder cracked above us, while the rain thumped against the tiles overhead. At last we curled into blankets and lay silent. It was dark and warm and quiet, all sounds outside muffled by the rain.

"This is enough," Xandros said sleepily, his face against my shoulder, and I knew that he had finally answered the question he had asked so many months ago.

"Yes," I said. "It is." I kissed his brow and twined my hands in his long, soft hair.

THERE WAS ONE more thing to do.

It was winter before I found the cave. It was in the hills

a morning's walk from Latium, up the little river where it cut through a shallow gorge. Wolves had used it once, from the chewed and cracked bones littering the floor, but they were gone.

The entrance was low enough that I had to stoop, but the ceiling was high enough farther in. A passage led down and farther back. It grew too small to get through before long, but there were several side chambers, most of them too small for a man to stand. It was not ideal. Too small, and too distant from Latium to be convenient. And there was no water closer than the river.

But there was something about it, some thrum of power. I stood in the front chamber, a pile of gnawed bones before me, raised my arms and felt it. *This is the place,* She whispered. *This is where you have brought Me.* I stretched my arms high, feeling Her flex within me. *Here,* She whispered. *Here.*

And I let Her go, let Her flow out of me like water, into the stone, into the air.

I knelt on the cold floor, my hands against the stone. "Lady," I said, "I have done as You asked. Are You gone from me?" I should feel that loss like a parent, like a lover, all at once.

No. I am always with you, She whispered. *I am in you.*

"How shall I know?" I asked. "How shall I know what You want of me if everything is different?"

You will know, she said. *As you have always known. As I have always given you what you need. Everything is always different. The world ends, and then begins again.*

"I used to have nothing to pray for," I said. "And now I have too much. Markai and Xandros, Neas and Wilos, Tia and Bai and Kianna and Kos. Neas' child bride. Lide and Aren and Hry and the people of Wilusa, the people of Latium. All of them. I am not apart. I am not Death."

I felt Her presence wash over me and it was love. Death and life and memory. Babies breathing their first air and blood on the trampled grass. Anchises on his bier, and Markai shifting in the womb, the grain golden in the sun and the Nile alight with lamps for Isis.

"Dear Lady," I said, and bent my head, my tears falling like libation in the dust.

You are My handmaiden, She said. *I will call you when I need you. Go and love.*

SEVEN HİLLS

On his third birthday, Markai went to his father. Ceremoniously, we carried his bedding and clothes out the back door of the temple, down the street and around the corner, and to the second house. Markai carried his precious carved horse that Kos had made for him, and strutted along a little uncertainly while Xandros and I kept up a conversation about what a big boy he was now and how proud of him we were, and how a big boy like that needed to go out from the women and do big boy things all day, not baby things. From the threshold of the house Xandros had built we could see the roof of the temple.

There was a main room, with two sleeping cubicles behind. We arranged Markai's things in one of them, his bedding and his blankets, the soft deerskin swaddling that had been his when he was a baby. He had been here before, but not slept under his father's roof.

Xandros sat down cross-legged beside the bed. After a moment, Markai crawled into his lap. "Why does Kianna get to stay at the temple with the baby?"

"Because Kianna is a girl, and your mother's acolyte," Xandros said. "And the baby gets to stay because he's a baby. He's only four months old. When he's a big boy three years old he'll come here and you'll share this room with him."

There was a new baby by then, Karas, born in the springtime. He was Markai in miniature—the same round brown eyes, shaggy black hair, smooth olive skin, broad shoulders, and barrel chest. They both looked exactly like Xandros, I thought.

Markai looked around the room. "Where will he sleep?" he asked.

Xandros pointed to the other side. "We'll put a bed for him right there. And you and your brother will share this room, and you'll both come fishing with me."

"Can I come fish tomorrow?"

Xandros looked at me. I shook my head. He looked down at the top of Markai's head and grinned. "Of course."

"Xandros, are you…"

"I started at this age," Xandros said. "My father took me to sea. Besides, it's not a voyage or something, just a day's fishing. And he is a big boy now, out from the women."

I looked at Markai. He seemed so small, yet he was big for his age, strong and loud and a handful for the temple. In eight years he would have a rower's bench. Less, perhaps, given his broad shoulders. He would be learning his trade before long.

"You must be careful," I said to Markai. "And do everything your father tells you, if you're going to be a sailor."

He grinned. "I'll catch the biggest fish!"

The next morning I watched him standing in my old place on *Dolphin*'s stern, while Xandros maneuvered the ship away from the docks and down the river, his head held high and his legs planted wide with the ship's movement. I had not shown him that, nor Xandros. The blood of the Sea People, I thought.

I went back to the temple. Kianna came to me in the mornings only, and she would be there soon.

As I had expected, when the time came that she was weaned, Tia and Bai did not want her to go, so she came to me every other morning from sunrise until noon to begin learning what must be learned, and stayed at night with them. Tia had no other children yet. She had miscarried twice, and I knew she hated to be parted from her only child, so it was an arrangement that satisfied everyone.

KIANNA'S SEVENTH BIRTHDAY came almost on the Feast of the Descent. After the rites proper there was feasting, and Latinus sacrificed a cow, which, roasted, fed almost everyone. Afterward, the wine flowed and the snake dance began, round and round beneath the spring stars.

Kianna had had no part in the rite, but she had held my paints and brushes ready in the black linen bag tied around her waist, as I had done when I was Pythia's acolyte. I saw her sitting quietly watching the fire, not joining the other children in clamoring for the sweets Lavinia was distributing. Her long red hair lay across her shoulders and her snub nose was sprinkled with freckles, but her eyes were suddenly as dark as night, as dark as the spaces between the stars.

Quietly, I came and knelt beside her. "What do you see?"

For a long time she didn't answer. The sparks rose in the air where the wind took them. They did not reflect in her eyes.

"I see a funeral pyre," she said.

I felt Her at my back, Her cool hands.

"The king lies on his funeral pyre," she said. Her voice was very clear and calm, the voice of a dreaming child. "King Aeneas." My throat tightened, but she went on. "He's very old," Kianna said. "His hair is all white, and his arms are crossed on his chest, and his hands are twisted and old. I'm standing there and trying to keep my veil from blowing into the sparks. I'm singing the Descent. But why aren't you there? Where are you?" She jerked her head up, and her eyes were gray, a child's eyes filled with light. "I'm sorry! Was that bad?"

"No, sweetheart," I said, putting my arm around her. "That was exactly right. I'm not there because then you are Sybil in my stead, because you are there to sing the king to the River. Long years from now, when he is very old and you are a grown woman."

"A long time from now?"

"Yes," I said, pointing to Neas across the fire. "See? See how young he is now?"

Kianna nodded.

"It's good, Kianna. It means you are ready to be my acolyte in truth, that She has chosen you. And you have given me a great gift."

"By saying you'll die?" Kianna was confused.

"Of course I'll die," I said gently. "Everyone does. But to know that we will have long years of peace, and

that you will be Sybil after me is important. And good."
I stood up and drew her after me. "Come and get some
almond cakes, sweetheart. There won't be any left if we
wait much longer. Markai will eat them all."

LATINUS DIED the winter after Kianna was eight. He
lived to see his grandson, Silvius, Lavinia's firstborn. And
yet when he died it seemed that little had changed. He had
been ill for a year or more, and so when Neas at last became king of both peoples nothing was strange. Instead
of standing beside the carved chair in the hall he sat in
it. We had grown used to the red wool robe of a king that
they expected of him, and they had grown used to him, to
his ways and to his mind, to his hand always on the reins.
Wilos stood beside the chair on special occasions now,
with Lavinia sitting to the other side holding Silvius in her
lap, two sons, fair and dark, children of two peoples.

The People hailed them in two languages, and we
drank to the king that was, and to the king that from now
on should be.

Spring came.

The fields along the river were plowed and planted. The
almond orchard was in bloom, and new terraced fields on
the hill were thick with three-year-old grapevines spreading their leaves in the sun. The world was warm and
kind.

Neas came to me under the eaves of the temple. Karas
was three years old, and played in a puddle while I washed
out clothes for him and for Kianna.

"My prince?" I said. It was no longer usual for him to
come to me, rather than to summon me as a king should.

He leaned on the door frame. "Oh, don't get up. There's nothing official I need." Neas shifted in the doorway. "Everything's going well, don't you think?"

"Yes," I said carefully, waiting for the problem to be revealed. In truth, I couldn't think what it was. The spring planting was done, Lavinia and Silvius were both well, Wilos was turning into a young man, the weather was good and the People were at peace.

"I'm going hunting," he said abruptly.

"You go hunting often," I said, looking up. "And never have reason to speak to me of it."

"I want you and Xandros to come," he said. "Surely Karas is big enough to stay with Tia or someone for a day."

"He is," I said. "But why do you want me? Xandros hunts with you often enough."

"I want you to see something, of course. I want to know what you think." Neas shifted from foot to foot, less like a king than a boy with a secret.

"Then of course I will come," I said.

IT WAS A BRIGHT MORNING in late spring when we set out. It was more than the three of us. Whatever captains may do, kings do not go on hunting trips with only two people. There was Bai with his bow and five more men, four youths from Latium who were learning to hunt, the king, Xandros, and I. We made our way swiftly for half the morning, angling away from the river, inland and southward. It was very beautiful. Birds called in the flawless sky, and the sun was warm on my face and my skin. Xandros walked beside me, an expression of pleasure on his face. The men faded back and let the three of us walk together.

We were climbing a wooded hill when Neas finally spoke.

"The problem is," he said, "that I have two sons and one house."

"I have two sons and one boat," Xandros said.

Neas laughed. "Yes, but we can build more boats, if both of them are fit to be captains. But I have one kingdom, and what shall I do if I have two sons who are fit?"

"The Latins should rather have Silvius," I said, "because he is of their blood and their royal line. He is his mother's son. And yet Wilos is the elder by ten years, and your heir."

"Just so," Neas said.

"This isn't a new problem," Xandros pointed out. "You've known this was coming since the boy was born."

"I know. But you've given me the answer to it, you with your magic for statecraft."

Xandros raised one eyebrow. "I know nothing of statecraft, and I've given you no advice on this. There's nothing to give."

Neas laughed. "Yes, you have. Build another boat."

"Neas?" Xandros asked.

"Another city," I said. "I told you that you would found a city, and yet we found Latium waiting for us. Two princes, two cities."

We came to the top of the hill, where the trees gave way to an outcropping of stone and it was open to the sky.

"Here," Neas said.

I caught my breath. A broader river wound brown and swollen with rain through a lush forested valley. Seven hills rose around it, and here, on the highest hill, the sky stretched forever above. A faint cloud rose from the valley, from wet leaves drying in the spring sun, vapor lifting into the air.

"Here," Neas said again. "That river is perfect for trade, not far from the sea, and this valley is as fertile and as protected as I've ever seen."

"For Silvius?" I said.

He nodded. "It will take years to get anything going here, and it will take years for him to be ready to rule it. But knowing this is his..."

Will end any scheming against Wilos in Latium, I thought. I did not know that Lavinia schemed. I thought not. But her relatives would. And who was to say what Silvius himself might do, when he was past infancy and grew tired of his older brother's shadow?

"It's beautiful," Xandros said. He walked closer to the edge of the stone outcropping. It was not such a high place, but the stone made it seem such. His eyes were far away.

"I dreamed this place," Neas said. "A long time ago. And when I saw it I knew it."

I nodded. I did not feel what they felt. There was nothing of Her here. This place belonged to the gods of the heights, to the king of the gods, not to the Lady of the Underworld.

"Seven hills," I said. I thought again of the prow of his ship, as I had seen it in dreams when I was younger than Kianna was now. "Seven stars."

"Seven sisters," Xandros said. "It's fitting."

Neas nodded. "What do you think?" he asked me.

I spread my hands. "This is statecraft, not prophecy, my king. I think your plan is wise."

I walked to the edge and looked out across the green valley. There was too much to see. Too much potential, too many paths, and too many roads that might lead me back here to this place. There were too many shadows of the future here, shifting like seaweed in the currents. I could see nothing.

Neas nodded. "Then let it be so." He opened up his wineskin. "Let us drink, my friends. To a new world."

Xandros came and took it from his hand. "New worlds, Neas."

I stood between them, all of our shoulders nearly touching, a tight triangle. "And to friendship," I said.

THE LAST BATTLE

We had nine and a half more years of peace. Our families grew and our lands expanded. Our ships fished the sea.

Wilos was a young man with a wife of his own, a cousin of Queen Lavinia who had been a baby in arms when the Rutoli killed her father. Kianna was as old as I had been when black ships came to Pylos.

And it was she who knew, of course. The Lady of the Dead speaks most clearly to the young and to the old.

I woke before dawn one morning in high summer and wondered what was wrong. Perhaps I had dreamed, but if I had I did not remember. I looked about the room. Markai and Karas had long since left the temple, but their younger sister slumbered nearby, her light brown hair spread around her on the pillow. Ila was not quite six, the daughter to the Shrine at last. She was clever and pretty, but I could see even at her age that she was not chosen. Whatever it was that lay so heavily on Kianna did not touch her at all.

Kianna. Her bed was empty. It must have been her

movement that woke me. I got up and went out, into the main room of the temple.

The statues of the gods were white and silent in the predawn grayness, Aphrodite's carven face giving me a secret smile as I passed Her. Kianna stood in the doorway, her back to me, silhouetted against the growing light. So this was setting behind the far horizon. I came up beside her. "Kianna?"

She shivered a little, pulling her wrap tighter around her. "I thought I heard my mother calling, but that's impossible. She's over there in her own house. I dreamed that she told me to go to the top of the hill where Poblios' vineyards are and to be there when dawn came."

A chill ran down me. I kept my voice even. "Then we had best do as she says, hadn't we?"

Kianna looked at me sideways.

"Do you want your shoes?" I asked. I picked up my own sandals and tied them on.

She nodded. The strangeness had not left her face. "We should hurry," she said.

Together, we climbed the terraced hill in the dawn. Young grapevines stretched in ranks, each clinging to the other, the first grapes beginning on the vine. Kianna loped ahead of me on her longer legs and straight feet, pushed by an urgency that I understood but did not feel.

At the top we paused. We were barely in time.

Making for the mouth of the river were ten ships. The rising sun caught them in the light, picked out the devices on their sails, glimmering off the *Chariot of the Sun*.

One look was enough for me, and I thanked Her for Kianna's quick legs and quicker mind. "Run!" I said. "Run straight to the king, and tell him Neoptolemos is come with ten ships!" She hesitated. "Run!" I said. "I will come behind. Every moment counts."

She needed no more. Kianna took off like a young doe, threading through the vineyard far faster than I had ever thought to run.

The sun lifted red from the clouds. A death day, a red day, a day for blood.

Oh, Lady, I prayed as I ran, *please let Neoptolemos never have heard of close-order drill.*

By the time I reached the palace men were in arms. The king's pages were running throughout the town, fetching from their beds all the men who had not heard the alarm. Silvius and two other youths were swinging onto wiry little Alban horses to ride out to all the farms that owed allegiance to Latium. He kicked his horse forward, then drew up sharply as he saw me in the gate.

"I'm sorry, Lady," Silvius said.

I stepped back against the wall. "Don't mind me. Go!"

His horse needed little urging, young and eager as he. One touch and they sprang forward again, a three-year-old stallion and a boy of twelve.

I hastened inside.

Neas was being helped into his breastplate by another of the youths. He looked around at me. "There you are, Sybil. Kianna told me what you said. Is there anything else?"

"They were making toward the river mouth," I said. "But it looked as though some of the ships were heavy laden, and the summer has been dry. They don't know the channels, and I doubt they can get them this far up the river, with it as low as it is."

Neas nodded. "We'll go down to meet them. The farther we can engage them from the fields, the better."

All of our fields were laden with the harvest not to begin for several weeks yet.

Wilos came in, his wife stumbling after, her long hair down and tumbled across her back. He bent and kissed her, saying something I could not hear.

Neas saw my face. "Go," he said. "See to your sons, Lady. This is the business of war."

I went to Xandros' house, into the rooms where I had so often stayed. I could hear the sounds of them arming from the courtyard. I hurried inside. Karas was getting his things together.

"Karas," I said. I stopped. I could not think what to say next.

"I don't really want to go, Mother," Karas said. Fifteen and broad shouldered, there was no doubt that he would go. He had begun training in the drill when he joined *Dolphin*'s crew. "It's not for fun. But I must."

Markai came behind him to fasten his breastplate. He had the height Xandros and I both lacked, and at eighteen was as solid and as strong a young man as anyone could wish. The height, I thought, must be some legacy of his unknown Achaian grandfather, for none of us had it, but his common sense and level head was pure Xandros.

"I know," I said. There was no pretext to keep my son safe at home when boys three years younger were about the business of war, even Silvius, whose life Neas treasured. And where should we be, if every mother did the same? Who should defend our fields and gates then? Neas was right. It was best to meet them as far from the town as possible.

Xandros came and kissed me, to the embarrassment of the boys. I touched his cheek with one hand and smiled into his eyes.

"Don't worry," he said quietly. "I'll look after the boys."

"I know," I said. I brushed his hair back from his brow. There was gray in it now, but it was as soft as ever.

He nodded. There was nothing else that needed to be said between us. We had said everything in nineteen years, everything there was to say, many times over. And I should never tire of saying it.

I embraced Markai and Karas in turns, thinking how strange it was to reach up into my sons' arms. "Mind your father and be careful," I said.

Markai did not roll his eyes, but I saw him catch Karas' eye in a shared look.

Ila came shrieking in from the temple, her fair hair flying behind her. "I thought you were here!" She flung herself on Karas.

"I have to go, little sister," he said, lifting her up, her legs around his bronze breastplate. He was the kinder of the boys, if not the most responsible.

Xandros detached her and kissed her. Her long hair was in knots again. How it could get knotted while she was sleeping was beyond me. "We'll be back soon," he said.

He smiled at me over her head. "Come on, boys."

We followed them into the street, to the swift muster of men in the marketplace before the gate. Xandros began calling orders to *Dolphin*'s company, the boys falling in among the others. Though we now had five ships, and not all of the men were part of any crew, we still arranged drill in three companies, named for each of the three ships. They formed up on Bai, the right forward corner. There was silver in his beard now.

"All forward!" Neas called. "Open the gates!"

They marched out before the sun had risen an hour, *Seven Sisters,* then *Dolphin,* then *Pearl.* We watched until they were out of sight.

Kianna came and stood beside me and Ila. Together we watched the dust of their passage until we could see no more.

"Mother," she said, "I could take Ila and get her some breakfast."

"That sounds like a good idea," I said. My voice sounded perfectly steady and normal.

Kianna was good. Her hands did not even shake, and she picked up Ila and swung her on her hip. "Let's go have some bread and honey. It will be a long time before they come back." She looked down at me. "Where will you be?"

"The palace," I said. "That's where I should be."

I went into the great hall. Lavinia had the women making pallets around the walls and getting fresh bedding and cloths ready. Lide was with her, stooped and white haired. She looked at me and smiled.

"Two more good hands," Lide said. "Where's that acolyte of yours? We'll need her."

"She'll be along in a while," I said.

"Good." Lide bustled off to tend to something, leaving me and Lavinia alone.

At not quite thirty, her beauty was fading. She had the kind of face that youth gives charm to, but the tightening of her skin brought sharpness and defined her features too clearly for beauty here. In Egypt, I thought, they would tell her that she would be beautiful in death. I shivered at the memory.

"What will happen?" she said quietly.

"My queen, I wish I knew," I said. "I do not think it will all come to naught, but I cannot tell you anything more."

Her back straightened. A dowager queen, regent for a boy of twelve, his father and brother slain. It could happen. The dice were still rolling.

"I should like you at my side, come what will," she said. "As my lord and husband has ever held you." Her eyes met mine.

"My queen, I am at your service," I said. We had the measure of each other.

THE DAY WAS ENDLESS. The sun climbed the sky and began its descent from the height. I did not feel Her. Death was not here, but there.

Sometime after noon one of the children came shouting to the palace that dust had been seen, followed by one of the messengers with the same news.

"I should stay here and keep all things in readiness," Lavinia said, but I could see how she yearned for the walls.

"My queen," I began.

"Oh, go on," Lide said. "We've checked everything three times. I'll stay right here. But it's not as though the wounded are going to appear here unexpectedly."

We went to the walls together, barely keeping a decorous pace as befitted a queen and an oracle.

Dust indeed. But was it our men returning, or Neoptolemos? It was some time before we could see with the sun in our faces.

Neas was at the head of the line, companies behind him. Wilos was leading *Seven Sisters'* company, first as always.

I heard Lavinia catch a quick breath. "Oh gods," she whispered. "So few, oh gods so few."

The companies seemed half the size they had been when they marched out, and now we could see the farm carts following.

"Carts," I whispered.

The dust. I could not see any faces, begrimed and wreathed in dust as they were. I thought I recognized Kos' burly form in the first rank of the third company. I did not see them. I couldn't tell.

Kianna was beside me, and somehow her hand was gripping mine so tightly I heard the bones grind together.

A messenger had run ahead on weary feet, and below I heard the gates open. He came panting up the steps to the queen. "My Lady," he said, "the king bids me to tell you that it is a victory. He himself slew Neoptolemos of Achaia in mighty combat, and the *Chariot of the Sun* will trouble us no more."

I did not hear another word he said.

Markai was walking beside one of the carts, his head down. And I knew.

I don't know how I got down the stairs and out the gates. A number of women were running out. I suppose I was one of them.

I knew.

Xandros lay in one of the carts, a cloak thrown over the ruin of his body, his unmarred face still and quiet. Karas lay on his shoulder, as he had slept as a baby, the torn side of his face down against his father's shoulder. Someone had closed their eyes, though Karas' lashes were sticky with blood. Markai walked beside them.

Somehow Neas was beside me, catching at me with his bloodied arms. He had run from the front of the column, I suppose. He was saying things that were meaningless. "It was the third charge. We were almost done. Xandros went down. I didn't see what happened. I yelled at the boys to hold the line, not to break formation, to stay in the shield wall. Markai..."

Neas' voice broke. "Markai obeyed me. He stood firm. But Karas..." He ducked his head, tears streaming down his face. "He ran to his father and was cut down. I told him to hold the line! I told him, Gull, but he didn't listen. I yelled at him. He didn't listen..."

Something loosened inside me, a great wail. I began screaming and couldn't stop.

I DID NOT SING the Descent. My throat was closed from screaming, my voice raw. My hands shook and I could not paint my face.

I stood beside the biers while Kianna sang. The stars were coming in the night sky, and she had painted her face black and white, like the legends from the isles. Death stood veiled, black crowning her red hair held up with pins of copper, older than the bronze our fathers brought. Her voice was pure and true. Her hands were long and white. Twelve times she sang it at twelve pyres, so many were our dead.

Xandros and Karas lay together, the last pyre, father

and son, lapped under a fine scarlet wool cloak that I thought dimly must have belonged to Neas, the work of weeks upon the loom.

Ila clung to my skirts snuffling softly, but I knew no words to speak to her, just the mute coldness of my arms.

It was Tia who wrapped her arms around her, Tia who lifted her up and held her. I was struck with ice.

This is the last, I thought. *The last time I will look at his face. The last time I will see my baby. This is the last. The last time I will touch his hand. The last time I will see the way Xandros' hair rises from his brow. I will never see that streak of gray grow silver, will never see his hands grow old. I will never see Karas wed, never hear him laugh with his brother over some boyhood joke, never see him again.*

Neas was coming now, from the next pyre, Kianna with him, a great crowd of mourners following.

He stood at the head of the bier, and his eyes were red from the smoke of those already burning. He reached for a cup and poured out wine in libation, the best wine, the best work of our hands.

"Hear, oh People, the deeds of Xandros son of Markai, and Karas son of Xandros, most beloved of the People. In you, my friend, was all that is best of us."

He stopped, and looking I saw that it was hard for him to go on. Behind him, Kianna was as impassive as Death.

"A thousand times we would have been lost on the deep sea, a thousand times we would have been lost in Egypt or in strange lands, if it were not for Xandros son of Markai. No truer sailor, no truer soldier, no truer companion has there ever been, nor will be until world's ending.

My friend, the world did end, and you and I sailed beyond it, and safe into harbor at last." Neas poured out the wine.

"I cannot say all that I feel, or recount all your deeds, for they are too many and too mighty. There is not a man of the People who does not owe you his life, nor a woman or child of the People who has not relied upon you. And for you to give your son, your own blood, in this our greatest battle, is no more than I would have thought from you."

Neas raised his head, and now his voice rang out strong. "I say to you today that Markai the son of Xandros is a son of my house, companion of my own sons, my kin. Ila, the daughter of Xandros, shall be dowered as a princess of Latium, should she wish to leave the temple. No more and no less can I do for my brother."

His voice broke, and he could not go on. Neas bent his head and his voice choked.

Kianna came forward and gently took the myrrh from him and scattered it. Death walked in the firelight, and in Kianna's eyes I saw Her terrible compassion.

"It is over," I whispered. "It is really and truly over."

EPİLOGUE

The Achaians were broken and never came again. I knew this later, when I cared.

"They were nothing but rabble," Neas said. "Men of a dozen cities who hardly trusted one another, pirates and desperate men with nothing to lose. Neoptolemos styled himself High King of Achaia, but there is no such thing, and hasn't been since Orestes son of Agamemnon died. Mycenae is no more, nor Thebes or Pylos or most of the high palaces. They are sunk into dust. Now it is only Tiryns and a few smaller places."

We stood on the hill above Poblios' vineyard. Ten years had passed since the day Neas killed Neoptolemos. We had not spoken of it since that day. In the course of time we had spoken of many things, but not that. I was still his oracle.

The warm sun of early summer beat down upon us, and white threaded his beard. Above us on the hill, the bees were in the lavender. I lifted my water skin and drank.

"The world is not as it was when we were young,"

Neas said. "I hear from traders that Millawanda is fallen as you said it would long ago, and Byblos. Nothing endures but Egypt."

"They will endure forever," I said, thinking of their stories carved in stone, gods and heroes frozen forever in temples, in tombs on the edge of the desert. "The gods of the Black Land are strong."

"Men do not measure grain in tallies anymore, or write down the number of their measures. They do not build on the coast, but in strong places inland, and do not send their ships to trade far from home. The world has ended and the great days are past."

"We endure," I said. "And I cannot find what we have built so ill."

Below us, the pale leaves of the grapes entwined, and beyond them a grove of young olive trees stretched their boughs to the sun. Ila's husband was not a sailor, but a farmer with terraced slopes who planted trees that would bear for his children, and these were his.

"It is beyond price," Neas said and took the water skin from me. Sometimes we walked up here, when he had the desire to talk to his oracle privately. I had not given up that office to Kianna, though it would be hers one day to counsel the king, and the two young kings who would come after.

"I am fifty-three," he said. "And I have seen the world end and then begin. That is more than enough for one lifetime."

"It is, Neas," I said.

He took another drink and then handed the water back to me. I drank, pushing my hair back from my eyes, more silver than black now.

Down on the river one of our little coasters was coming up from the sea, a fishing boat back from a catch made at dawn.

"That's Markai with *Seagull*, isn't it?" he asked. Neas' eyes were not what they had been.

"Yes," I said. The coaster turned into the channel, her sail furled and her ten oars moving in perfect time.

"Do you think they remember us, those we have loved, beyond the River?" he said.

I turned and looked into his light eyes, as warm and as familiar as the sky above us. He had asked me this before, on the Island of the Dead, while the waves washed over the empty city, cool and bleak beneath the waters. I was less sure of my answer this time.

"My king," I said. "I do not know. When I was a child I was taught that when we pass the second River, that is Memory, we forget. But while we tarry in the Endless Fields we may remember. But now I do not know."

He smiled into my eyes. "My Lady, whatever we are taught, whatever the gods will, I will remember you until the end of the world."

I closed my eyes and then opened them, but he was still smiling at me. "My dear prince, I will remember you too," I said, and while I did not feel Her hand just then, I knew with every certainty I have ever felt that it was true.

Below us, the coaster was coming up to the dock. Markai was at the tiller, his chest bare and brown in the summer sun, his black hair held behind him with a piece of leather.

I leaned back on Neas' shoulder, and his hand went round my waist, holding my hand in his.

There was a squeal and my little granddaughter, four years old, ran shouting down the dock. Markai leaped lightly onto the stones and swept her up laughing, tossing her onto his shoulder, her long dark hair streaming.

And the world was mended.

AUTHOR'S NOTE

*B*lack Ships is based on *The Aeneid,* which is in itself a kind of historical novel. *The Aeneid* was written by a Roman, Publius Vergilius Maro, best known as Virgil, at the very end of the first century BCE. During this time, the early part of the reign of Augustus, there was a fad for all things Greek and for Greek culture, which of course included the two great epics, *The Iliad* and *The Odyssey.* Telling the story of the Trojan War and its aftermath as Odysseus tries to return home, *The Iliad* and *The Odyssey* remain classic stories of war and adventure today.

Virgil wanted to capture something of the thrilling beauty of these two great poems for Roman audiences in a way that made a new work that was uniquely Roman, and that could serve as a cultural touchstone in the same way. He wanted to tell a story that would both provide a context for Rome's history and that would be popular with general audiences as well as the most important patron, the emperor Augustus. The story he told is that of Aeneas, the last prince of Troy, who undergoes great trials on land and sea on his way to find a new home for the Trojan people, and ultimately to found the Roman people.

So Virgil's epic is my starting point, my first source. I have used the DC Heath and Company edition in Latin, published in Toronto in 1964, in which I first met Aeneas and his travels when I was in high school. There are any number of fine translations, and I encourage you to find them!

The historicity of the Trojan War has been debated at least since Virgil's time. The most accessible and inspiring recent book on the subject is one I have leaned on extensively, Michael Wood's *In Search of the Trojan War*, University of California Press, 1985. Carefully blending modern archaeological research with recently deciphered Linear B tablets, with sources from Egypt and Hatti, and with *The Iliad* itself, he presents the Trojan War as part of the crisis in the Mediterranean that precipitated a Dark Age that lasted for hundreds of years. This is the story I have chosen to tell — of the wanderings of the People not as an isolated event, but as part of the great displacement in this time of crisis.

But what of Troy itself? The city on Hisarlik that we know as Troy and that the Hittite archives knew as Wilusa was destroyed many times. Two particular sets of ruins, those of Troy VI and Troy VIIa, both date from this period. The two destructions may be as little as a generation apart. In short, they may bear the same relationship to each other as World War I and World War II. Does it not seem reasonable that over time people will conflate these two modern conflicts, and that Hitler and Wilson might be seen as antagonists, facing each other operatically in the same story? Perhaps that is what has happened here, that the events of both conflicts have been put together as the story of one war that lasted ten years.

I have set the First Trojan War, the one in which Gull's mother was made captive, around 1200 BCE, one of the later dates for the destruction of Troy VI. The Second Trojan War, the one that precipitates the wanderings of Neas and the People, is the destruction of Troy VIIa, around 1180 BCE. The cities were completely different. Troy VI was a great city with beautiful walls, broad streets, and lavish palaces. Troy VIIa was a "shanty-town" built on the ruins, with mended walls and palaces cut up into small apartments. This is Neas' and Xandros' Wilusa. It is also the city excavated by Carl W. Blegen, whose midcentury classic work, *Troy and the Trojans*, was recently reprinted by Barnes and Noble Books, New York, 2001.

Among the many books I have leaned on for the People's wanderings, I especially recommend two:

The End of the Bronze Age: Changes in Warfare and the Catastrophe ca. 1200 BC by Robert Drews, Princeton University Press, Princeton, 1995, is an incredibly insightful military history analysis of the change in warfare at the time, and especially of the impact of the new kind of sword on the chariot-based armies of the period. I have also leaned heavily on the Smithsonian Institution, whose collection of old- and new-style swords from the Aegean world was extremely helpful when I needed to go see Neas' Shardana sword!

The second book is *The Sea Peoples: Warriors of the Ancient Mediterranean* by N. K. Sandars, Thames and

Hudson, New York, 1985, which connects the dots beautifully between the people of Wilusa, Ugarit, Byblos, and Egypt. It brings the Sea People out of Homer and into history, detailing the great battle fought by Ramses III around 1175 BCE that denied the Sea People control of Egypt and at last provided an unbreachable bulwark against the chaos that had already engulfed most of the Mediterranean world.

One of the greatest dramatic problems I encountered in retelling some form of *The Aeneid* is the entire Carthaginian sequence, and Aeneas' doomed affair with Queen Dido. The storytelling problem is that Carthage was not founded until at least four hundred years after the probable Trojan War, and it would be completely impossible for Aeneas to visit it! However, in the actual late Bronze Age the great power was Egypt, where a princess could indeed wield the kind of power Virgil gives to Dido. We know Ramses III had sisters, but do not know their names. Basetamon is an invention of mine to combine historical Egypt with the famous story of Dido and Aeneas.

The sources on Egypt are myriad, but there is one that merits special mention because of the amount I used it in telling Gull's experiences, *Daughters of Isis: Women of Ancient Egypt* by Joyce Tyldesley, Penguin Books, London, 1994.

Another fascinating book that I used extensively in the Byblos section is Mark S. Smith's *The Early History of God: Yahweh and the Other Deities in Ancient Israel,* Erdmans, Cambridge, 2002. For the reimagined descriptions of the Thesmophoria and the mythological calendar of Greece, I was inspired by Jennifer Reif's *Mysteries of Demeter,* Samuel Weiser, Maine, 1999.

I hope that you will be as fascinated by this little-known period of history as I was, and that you will go explore some of the wonderful source material yourself! (A list of other useful materials appears on my Web site: www.jograham.net.)

PEOPLE, PLACES, AND THINGS

Achaian: archaic term for the Hellenes, the people we think of as ancient Greeks. Used in Homer, a better translation might be Mycenaeans

Agamemnon: the High King of Mycenae at the time of the Achaian expedition against Troy. In that war, he took the prophetess Kassandra as his prize, raping her and returning with her to Mycenae. He was murdered by his wife, Clytemnestra, who was in turn killed by his son Orestes, who was in turn pursued by the Furies

Ahhiyawa: Achaia, or mainland Greece, in the Arzawan language

Amynter: One of Neas' captains, of the warship *Hunter*. Father of two sons, the eldest of whom is Kassander

Anchises: Neas' father, a nobleman of Wilusa who was the lover of Lysisippa, the daughter of Priam who became Cythera

Aren: Gull's younger half brother

Arzawan: the language spoken by the people of Wilusa and the surrounding territories, including parts of the Hittite empire

Ashkelon: "the city of Ashteret," modern-day town of Al Majdal/Migdal Ashkelon in Israel, just north of Gaza. During the reign of Ramses III it was an Egyptian settlement

Ashterah: a eunuch priestess dedicated to Ashteret in Byblos

Ashteret: She Who Treads Upon the Sea, the Semitic goddess of sexuality, fertility, and the sea. She is the daughter of the god El, worshipped in Phoenicia and Judah. Byblos is one of the ancient centers of her worship

Bai: rower on *Dolphin* who is also a skilled archer

Basetamon (Princess): sister of Pharaoh Ramses III, and his viceroy in Memphis

Blessing of Ships: rite opening the spring sailing season, around the spring equinox and the end of March

Byblos: a city on the coast of modern-day Lebanon, known for its exports of wood and paper. The ruler of Byblos is Prince Hiram

Chariot of the Sun: Neoptolemos' flagship, painted with Helios' chariot on the sail

Cloud: one of Neas' warships

Creusa: Neas' wife, Wilos' mother, who was killed in the destruction of Wilusa

Cumai (Cumae): a town north and west of modern Naples, near Mount Vesuvius. In ancient times there was the

Shrine of the Sybil of Cumae and a reputed entrance to the Underworld

Cythera: one of the epithets for Aphrodite of the Sea. Also the title of the chief priestess of Aphrodite of the Sea

Demeter: goddess of grain and the harvest, mother of Kore Persephone

Denden: Egyptian name for the Wilusans

Dolcis: Pythia's servant in Pylos

Dolphin: Xandros' ship, with a leaping dolphin painted on her prow white on black, and red on white on her sail

Feast of the Descent (Skira): the festival marking Persephone's descent into the Underworld, and her transformation from Kore to Queen of the Dead. Takes place at the end of June

Feast of the Return (Thesmophoria and related rites): the festival marking Persephone's return from the Underworld and her reunion with her mother, Demeter. This is one of the main festivals of the year, taking place over a week in late October

Gull (also Linnea, Pythia, and Sybil): The daughter of a woman taken as a slave from Wilusa, Gull grows up in Pylos along the flax river until an accident causes her to become Pythia's acolyte

Hattuselak: Hittite gentleman of Millawanda, an old friend of Anchises

Hiram (Prince): ruler of Byblos, a city on the coast of modern-day Lebanon

Hry (He Who Walks in the Sunlight of Amon): a priest of Thoth in Memphis who had traveled in Wilusa before the first war. Hry is not a personal name, but a title held by the Lector Priests who had charge of sacred texts and learning. In context, it's something like "Father"

Hunter: one of Neas' warships, named for Orion, the hunter of the skies. Captained by Amynter

Idele: one of the captive women from Wilusa, wife of Maris

Idenes: the son of King Nestor of Pylos

Ila: daughter of Gull and Xandros

Iphigenia: the daughter of Agamemnon who was sacrificed by her father to raise the winds that the Achaian expedition might sail for Troy

Island of the Dead (Thera): the modern-day island of Santorini, Thera is a volcanic island in the Cyclades that had a thriving civilization during the Bronze Age. It was destroyed in a massive volcanic eruption around 1270 BCE

Jamarados: Captain of *Lady's Eyes,* the most experienced of Neas' captains

Kalligenia (the Ascent of the Maiden): the last rite of the Thesmophoria, in late October

Karas: son of Gull and Xandros

Kassander: Amynter's son, a messenger boy and substitute rower on *Dolphin*

Khemet (the Black Land): Egypt, more specifically the valley of the Nile, and the language spoken there

Kianna: Tia's daughter, promised to Gull before her birth as her acolyte

Kore (the Maiden): Persephone in her virgin aspect

Kos: Xandros' second in command on *Dolphin*. His younger sister is Tia

Krete: modern-day Crete, the seat of the Minoan civilization during the Bronze Age

Kyla: Illyrian girl who is Gull's friend in Pylos

Lady of the Dead: Persephone, the Queen of the Underworld who is the consort of Hades

Lady of the Sea: Aphrodite, specifically Aphrodite Cythera, who was born from the waves

Lady's Eyes: one of Neas' warships, captained by Jamarados

Latinus: King of Latium

Latium: an Etruscan town northwest of modern-day Rome

Lavinia (Princess): the daughter and only surviving child of King Latinus of Latium

Lide: a captive woman from Wilusa taken in the first war, she is also a skilled midwife and healer, as well as the mother of two young sons

Linnea: the name given to Gull by Pythia, meaning "girl from the flax river"

Lord of the Dead: Hades, ruler of the Underworld, husband of Persephone

Lower City (of Wilusa): The city had two parts, the Citadel, which was on the high mound of Hisarlik and enclosed by a great wall, and the Lower City which stood outside the walls presumably around the harbor. Few archaeological remains have been recovered from the Lower City

Lysisippa: Priam's eldest daughter, Kassandra's older sister, who was Cythera, the chief priestess of Aphrodite, at Mount Ida. Anchises was her lover, and Neas is her son

Markai: son of Gull and Xandros

Memphis: ancient capital of Egypt, later the second greatest city in Egypt. Near modern-day Cairo

Menace: one of Neas' warships

Mik-el: one of the warriors of the Phoenician god Baal, a young god who wants to champion the worthy

Millawanda: the Hittite name for Miletus, a walled city on the coast of Asia Minor

Mycenae: the greatest of the Achaian cities in the Bronze Age, it seems to have been the seat of a confederation of states throughout mainland Greece and possibly the islands. It may have been the home of the "Great King of Ahhiyawa" mentioned in the Hittite diplomatic archives. In mythology, that Great King was Agamemnon, son of Atreus, who led the Achaian assault on Troy. The citadel of Mycenae was discovered by Heinrich Schliemann late in the nineteenth century and has been the subject of many archaeological expeditions since then

Neas (Prince Aeneas): Son of Anchises and a priestess of Aphrodite (Lysisippa the daughter of Priam), the last prince of Wilusa. He was married to Creusa, who was killed in the sacking of the city. His son is Wilos

Neoptolemos: son of the hero Achilles, in mythology he is blamed for the murder of Hector's infant son Astyanax, several other members of the Trojan royal family, and with the rape and enslavement of Hector's widow Andromache. Perhaps this holds the memory of an expedition led against Troy VIIa in the generation after Agamemnon

Nestor (King): In *The Iliad* and *The Odyssey,* the king of Pylos, an ally of Agamemnon

Nubia: during the reign of Ramses III, a tributary kingdom of Egypt located southward along the Nile in modern-day Sudan

Patroclus: In *The Iliad,* the companion (or lover) of Achilles who is killed before the walls of Troy, thus stirring Achilles to vengeance

Pearl: one of Neas' warships, captained by Maris

Polyra: one of the Wilusan women captives in the second war, mother of a nine-year-old son who escaped the sinking of a fishing boat by swimming to *Dolphin* and being rescued by Xandros

Priam: former king of Wilusa, Neas' grandfather

Prison of the Winds: Mount Etna in Sicily, the most active volcano in Europe. In mythology, Aeolus, the god of the winds, was imprisoned beneath the mountain, and Hephaestus had his forge there

Pylos: city on the western shore of Greece, south of Ithaca. In the Bronze Age, there was a palace and settlement there that was deserted around 1200 BC. In *The Iliad* and *The Odyssey* this was the royal seat of King Nestor. The palace was excavated by Carl Blegen in the 1930s

Pythia: the oracle at any of the great Shrines, in a later period particularly that of Apollo at Delphi. In *Black Ships,* the old oracle to whom Gull is apprenticed

Ramses III: Pharaoh of Egypt from 1183–1152 BCE, he was the last powerful Pharaoh of the New Kingdom. He defeated sea raiders in a massive battle circa 1175 BCE, a battle commemorated in the carvings in the temple at Medinet Habu

Rutoli: Etruscan tribe living north of modern-day Rome

Sais: city on the westernmost branch of the Nile

Scylla: Sicily, especially the rocky coast near the Straits of Messina

Sekhmet: Egyptian lion-headed goddess of war

Seven Sisters: Aeneas' ship, named after the constellation of the Pleiades, known as the seven sisters. She has the stars painted on her prow

Shardan: people from an island in the Western Mediterranean, probably Sardinia or Corsica

Silvius (Prince): son of Neas and Lavinia, half brother of Wilos

Sothis: Sirius, the dog star. In Minoan mythology, it was known as Iakchos, the son of Persephone and Hades. The heliacal rising of Sirius is right after the summer solstice

Swift: one of Neas' warships, painted with the silhouette of a Pallid Swift, a small, quick bird native to the Mediterranean

Sybil: the title given to Pythia by the Wilusans, an oracle

Tamiat: Egyptian port, modern-day Damietta

Thoth: Egyptian god of writing, learning, speech, and knowledge, usually portrayed as an ibis or an ibis-headed man

Tia: Kos' sister, a young girl taken as a slave in the fall of the city. Mother of Kianna

Triotes: an Achaian, Gull's mother's lover

Ugarit: city on the coast of modern-day Syria destroyed by raiders around 1200 BCE

Wilos: Ilios or Iulus, the son of Neas, also known in mythology as Ascanius, who escaped the fall of Wilusa and his mother's death. Grandson of Anchises and Lysisippa

Wilusa: A city mentioned in the Hittite diplomatic archives that is probably the Arzawan name for Ilios (Troy). Also Uilusia in Hittite

Winged Night: one of Neas' warships, its sails painted with black wings

Xandros: Captain of *Dolphin,* and Neas' closest friend. His full name is Alexandros, a very common name in Wilusa, which means "guardsman." He was married and had two daughters before the fall of the city, when his entire family was killed

ACKNOWLEDGMENTS

There are many people without whom *Black Ships* would never have been written, beginning with two wonderful teachers, Janet Frederick Rhodes, who kindled in me a love of the ancient world and who always believed I would write novels, and Judy Arnette, who endured me through four books of Virgil's *Aeneid*, most of Caesar, and a smattering of Catullus in high school. The seeds of *Black Ships* come from them, and from my parents and their love of history. I also must thank my sister, Elizabeth Thompson, who remembers the first version of this story from our early teens as the *Tale of Aldith and the Sea People*.

I am deeply grateful to all the people who read *Black Ships* in progress and encouraged me at every step of the way. At the head of that list stands Tanja Kinkel, without whom I would never have finished the first draft.

I also must thank Lesley Arnold, Danielle D'Onofrio, Lynn Foster, Stephanie Grant, Mari Harju, Nathan Jensen, Gretchen Lang, Jessica Lee, Kris Lee, Kathryn McCulley, Anne-Elisabeth Moutet, Naomi Novik, Anna Sitniakowsky, Jeff Tan, and Robert Waters, for their friendship, their wonderful feedback, and occasional hard criticism.

I am most especially grateful to Amy Vincent, who not only thought it was good enough to publish, but who took the manuscript to an agent!

I have no gratitude deep enough for my wonderful agent, Diana Fox, who decided that she was going to sell *Black Ships,* no ifs, ands, or buts about it, and whose thoughtful comments improved the manuscript immensely; as well as Robin Rue of Writer's House. Likewise, I owe a debt of gratitude to Devi Pillai, who decided to take a gamble on an unknown author and to whom I will be forever thankful.

Last, in this, as in everything else I do, I would be lost without my wonderful partner, Amy, who makes every step in life an enchanted journey across a wide ocean.

extras

orbit

meet the author

JO GRAHAM lives in Maryland with her family, and has worked in politics for many years. *Black Ships* is her debut novel. Find out more about the author at http: jo-graham.livejournal.com.

interview

What kind of research did you do for Black Ships?

I've been interested in the period of the Trojan War since I was in high school, when I read *The Aeneid* in Latin and fell in love with Virgil and his storytelling. The thing about initially reading a book in a foreign language is that you have to go very slowly. The story really sinks in when you're doing thirty lines a day. I already knew at the time that it wasn't possible for Aeneas to actually visit Carthage, because Carthage didn't exist yet. So in my mind I mentally transported the action to Egypt.

Long before I started writing *Black Ships* I was reading about the period, and so the actual research was more brushing up on things and checking dates here and there.

If you could have dinner with one of your characters, who would it be?

Xandros, without a doubt. He can cook! And also I think it would be wonderful to spend time with him.

He's genuinely a nice person, and also interesting and intelligent.

What interests you about this period in history?

It's a period of change. It's a crisis. Up until this point, things have been improving for a lot of people — more food, more sanitation, more trade. But something's wrong, and the world is crashing down.

Historians and archaeologists are debating endlessly what caused the crisis around 1200 BCE, and nobody knows for certain. Was it a chain of events set off by earthquakes and the eruption of Santorini? Certainly that didn't help, but it seems unlikely to be the cause of economic disruption hundreds of miles away. Was it technology? Crop failures? Migrations of peoples in response to climate change? We don't know, any more than Gull does. But it happened, and it's fascinating to look at how people coped with that.

How long did it take you to write Black Ships?

A year. I started just before Christmas in 2004 and finished on New Year's Day, 2006.

What were other titles you considered for Black Ships?

Interestingly enough, I never had any others. My publisher debated a few, but it was *Black Ships* to me from the first chapter. It's from the haunting tablets from Ugarit, the last words of that doomed city. "The fleet is away. Black ships have been sighted . . ." That was an image that struck me and that came long before I started writing—looking toward the sea from a high place (the mountain road), looking toward the sea and seeing the black ships in the slanting dawn light and knowing what that meant.

What do you do to keep yourself inspired and motivated while working on a long project?

When I need to put it down, I do. I've found that pushing myself to work on it when I'm not ready just produces terrible work. So I go back and read original source material. Or I read or watch things that connect in some way in my head. Or listen to music that connects to the story for me. For *Black Ships*, the song that is absolutely Gull to me is Enya's "Book of Days." Go listen and see if you don't hear Gull there! And more than that, the entire tone of the book.

What was the first story you ever wrote?

A *Star Wars* fanfic about Han Solo as a child. I wrote it while waiting for my dance class when I was nine.

What do you hope readers will take away from your stories? What is it that you want them to think about?

That realism and enchantment are not mutually exclusive. That the world is a numinous place.

That said, that there are different kinds of heroics—Gull's quiet faith and courage, Neas' physical bravery and determination to do the right thing, Xandros' solid, generous doing what he has to without bitterness. And that all of them are within reach of real people. That we don't have to be the victims of big things happening around us in the world — we can overcome them and build something new out of even the most dreadful tragedy.

In what important ways is the era in which Black Ships *is set different than our own? In what ways is it like our own?*

It's different in many obvious ways, technology, etc., but it's similar in some very important ways.

Politically, the Mediterranean has had a number of very developed civilizations with a balance of power — the Hittites, the Minoans, the Mycenaeans, the Egyptians, etc. — who have had various conflicts over the past couple of centuries without a great deal of territory changing hands. And then, in the past hundred years, one after another major player has fallen into ruin. Egypt is left as the only superpower, an incredibly rich nation where there hasn't been a war on Egyptian soil for three hundred years. It's a volatile situation. And one that can't last.

What's on your bookshelf? What are the books you've read over and over?

Oh great question! There are so many! But I suppose these are the ones I reread just about every year.

Flying Colours by C. S. Forester

Kushiel's Dart by Jacqueline Carey
The Egyptian by Mika Waltari
Lord of the Two Lands by Judith Tarr
Tales of the South Pacific by James Michener
The Roads of Heaven by Melissa Scott
The Lord of the Rings by J. R. R. Tolkien
The Mask of Apollo by Mary Renault
The Eagle and the Nightingale by Juliette Benzoni
Imperial Woman by Pearl Buck
The Mists of Avalon by Marion Zimmer Bradley
Lammas Night by Katherine Kurtz

Which other writers do you think had an influence on your work and whose was the most important?

The obvious first answer is Mary Renault, whose books about the ancient world inspire me. I think also Judith Tarr, Mika Waltari, and Pearl Buck are obvious influences. In terms of my approach, I would have to say Marion Zimmer Bradley is a big influence, and also Katherine Kurtz.

Which of the main conflicts in the book is the one you are most interested in and why?

One of the things I find most interesting is Neas' conflict between being the person he feels he ought to be, the son of Anchises, and the person who can get everyone through this, someone with less rigid honor and more faith. Faith is not exactly a virtue of the Homeric hero. And neither are flexibility, kindness, or mercy. He really doesn't know what to do, for example, when he marries

Lavinia. Kindness to his young bride is not something anyone has ever taught him was important, and yet he wants her to not hate him and he wants to not scar someone as badly as Basetamon was scarred. He's a better person than his time teaches him to be.

What first interested you about ancient history?

I can't remember when I wasn't interested in ancient history! The first thing I remember being wildly interested in was when I was five. My mother watched the Elizabeth Taylor version of *Cleopatra* on broadcast television after my bedtime, and I snuck downstairs and sat on the steps and watched. Total love! My mother really encouraged my interest—it's an interest of hers, and we've always enjoyed talking about it.

What texts did you use for research/inspiration?

The one I recommend wholeheartedly for people who don't know a lot about the time but are interested is Michael Wood's *In Search of the Trojan War*. It really inspired me to see how to put the story together and how to place it in the context of the crisis around 1200 BCE. And that's where I first encountered the tablets from Pylos, listing the women who are flax slaves, including "the woman of Troy, the servant of the god."

Who or what influenced your characters?

I see the characters in the context of the entire story I'm telling, from the Trojan War to the modern day—the same major characters, weaving in and out of events, working together or against one another in different constellations. (Neas was telling the truth when he said he'd remember!)

So sometimes I look at something ahead and work backward. What are the things that would need to have happened for this person to have reacted this way?

reading group guide

1. Throughout *Black Ships,* Gull often has to make her decisions based on the situation at hand rather than the strictures that She Who Was Pythia taught her to abide by. What are a few examples of this, and how do you think they helped to shape Gull's complex character?

2. Does Jo Graham intend for us to believe that Gull has supernatural powers? Or could there be other explanations for her ability to see what others cannot?

3. In *Black Ships,* we constantly see the Wilusans trying to start over. How do we see their societal structure change over the course of their journey?

4. When the Wilusans arrive in Egypt, they are confronted with a society that does not adhere to the same social taboos to which they are accustomed. How do the two societies compare?

5. Basetamon, though quite beautiful and powerful, is a very troubled character. How much is she responsible for her actions regarding Neas? Is his response to her

behavior appropriate or should he have been more understanding?

6. When Xandros goes after Ashterah in the Underworld, what do you think is the impetus for his return? What does this say about his character's evolution in the novel?

7. Although Gull constantly worked in the realm of Death, she becomes utterly grief-stricken when Xandros and her son are taken from her. What do you think this says about her humanity versus her duty as Death's handmaiden?

8. In the final scene, do you think Neas' and Gull's relationship has developed beyond friendship (although his wife is still alive), or is it just a friendship that has naturally deepened with time?

9. *Black Ships* offers a number of parallels to our modern world. Gull comes from a world in which war has become a part of life. This is in sharp contrast to what the Wilusans see in Egypt: a society in which weapons are rarely needed and professional soldiers do the fighting. How is Gull's world like and unlike ours? Do we have societies today where war is part of life and societies where it's an extraordinary experience that most people never face?

introducing

If you enjoyed BLACK SHIPS,
look out for

HAND OF ISIS

by Jo Graham

Once, in a palace by the sea, there were three sisters born in the same year.

The eldest was born in the season of planting, when the waters of the Nile had receded once more and the land lay rich and fertile, warm and muddy and waiting for the sun to quicken everything to life. She was born in one of the small rooms behind the Court of Birds, and her mother was a serving woman who cooked and cleaned, but who one day had caught Ptolemy Auletes' eye. Her skin was honey, her eyes dark as the rich floodwaters. Her name was Iras.

The second sister was born under the clear stars of winter, while the land greened and grain ripened in the fields, when fig and peach trees nodded laden in the *starry night. She was born in a great bedchamber with wide windows open to the sea, and five Greek physicians in attendance, for she was the daughter of Ptolemy Auletes' queen, and her name was Cleopatra.*

The youngest sister was born as the earth died, as the stubble of the harvest withered in the fields beneath the scorching sun. She was born beside the fountain in the Court of Birds, because her mother was a blond slave girl from Thrace, and that was where her pains took her. Water fell from the sky and misted her tiny upturned face. Her hair was the color of tarnished bronze, and her eyes were blue as the endless Egyptian sky. Her name was Charmian.

Once, in a palace by the sea, there were three sisters. All the stories begin so.

My mother was a Thracian slave girl who died when I was born, so I do not remember her. Doubtless I would have died too, as unwanted children will, had Iras' mother not intervened. Asetnefer was from Elephantine, where the Nile comes out of Nubia at the great gorges, and enters Egypt. Her own daughter was five months old when I was born, and she took me to her breast beside Iras, a pale scrap of a newborn beside my foster sister. She had attended at the birth, and took it hard when my mother died.

I do not know if they were exactly friends. I heard it said later that Pharaoh had often called for them together, liking the contrast between them, the beauty of my mother's golden hair against Asetnefer's ebony skin. Perhaps it was true, and perhaps not. Not every story told at court is true.

Whatever her reasons, Asetnefer nursed me as though I were a second child of her own, and she is the mother I remember, and Iras my twin. She had borne a son some years before Iras, but he had drowned when he was three years old, before my sister and I were born. It is this tragedy that colored our young lives more than anything else, I believe, though we did not mourn for him, having never known him. Asetnefer was careful of us. We should not play out of sight of people; we should not stray from her while she worked. She carried us both, one on each hip in a sling of cloth, Iras to the left and me to the right, until we grew too heavy and had to go on our feet like big children. She was freeborn, and there was doubtless some story of how she had come to be a slave in Alexandria by the sea, but I in my innocence never asked what it was.

And so the first thing I remember is this, the courtyards of the great palace at Alexandria, the slave quarters and the kitchens, the harbor and the market, and the Court of Birds where I was born. In the palace, as in all civilized places, the language of choice was Koine Greek, which educated people speak from one end of the world to the other, but in the slave quarters they spoke Egyptian. My eyes were the color of lapis, and my hair might glow bronze in the sun, but the amulet I wore about my neck was not that of Artemis, but a blue faience cat of Bastet.

In truth, that was not odd. There were golden haired slaves from Epirus and the Black Sea, sharp Numidians and Sardinians, men from Greece fallen on hard times, mercenaries from Parthia and Italy. All the world met in

Alexandria, and every language that is spoken was heard in her streets and in her slave quarters. A quarter of the people of the city were Jews, and it was said that there were more Jews in Alexandria than in Jerusalem. They had their own quarter, with shops and theaters and their own temples, but one could not even count the Jews who studied at the Museum and Library, or who taught there. A man might have a Greek name and blond hair, and yet keep the Jewish Sabbath if it suited him. So it was of little importance that I looked Greek and acted Egyptian.

Iras, on the other hand, looked as Egyptian as possible and had the mind of a skeptic philosopher. From her earliest days she never ceased asking why. Why does the sea pile against the harbor mole? Why do the stars shine? What keeps us from flying off the ground? Her black hair lay smooth in the heavy braids that mine always escaped, and her skin was honey to my milk. We were as alike as night and day, parts of one thing, sides of the same coin.

The seas pile against the harbor mole because Isis set them to, and the stars are the distant fires of people camping in the sky. We could not fly because like young birds we had not learned yet, and when we did we should put off our bodies and our winged bas should cavort through the air, chasing and playing like swifts. The world was enchantment, and there should be no end to its magic, just as there was no end to the things that might hold Iras' curiosity. And that is who we were when we first met the Princess Cleopatra.

Knowing all that she became, it is often assumed that at that age she must have been willful and imperious. Nothing is farther from the truth. To begin with, she was the fifth child and third daughter, and not reckoned of much account. Her mother was dead as well, and the new queen had already produced a fourth princess. There was little reason for anyone to take note of her, another Cleopatra in a dynasty full of them. I only noticed her because she was my age.

In fact, she was exactly between me and Iras in age, born under the stars of winter in the same year, and when I met her I did not know who she was.

İRAS AND I were five years old, and enjoying a rare moment of freedom. Someone had called Asetnefer away with some question or another, and Iras and I were left to play under the eyes of half the women of the household in the Court of Birds. There was a fountain there, with worn mosaics of birds around the base, and we were playing some splashing game, in which one of us would leap in to throw water on the other, who would try to avoid being soaked, waiting her turn to splash the other. Running from a handful of cold water, I noticed a girl watching us with something of a wistful expression on her face. She had soft brown hair falling down her back and wide brown eyes that seemed almost round smudged in with sooty lashes. She was wearing a plain white tunic and girdle, and she was my height precisely. I smiled at her.

At that she came out from the shadow of the balcony above and asked if she could play.

"If you can run fast enough," Iras said.

"I can run," she said, her chin coming up. Faster than a snake, she dipped up a full handful of water and dashed it on Iras.

Iras squealed, and the game was off again, a three way game of soaking with no rules.

It lasted until Asetnefer returned. She called us to task immediately, upbraiding us for having our clothes wet, and then she saw the other girl and her face changed.

"Princess," she said gravely, "you should not be here rather than in the Royal Nursery. They will be searching for you and worrying if you have come to harm."

Cleopatra shrugged. "They never notice if I'm gone," she said. "There is Arsinoe and the new baby, and no one cares what becomes of me." She met Asetnefer's eyes squarely, like a grown-up, and there was no self pity in her voice. "Why can't I stay here and play? Nothing bad will happen to me here."

"Pharaoh your father will care if something happens to you," Asetnefer said. "Though it's true you are safe enough here." A frown came between her eyes, and she glanced from the princess to Iras, who stood taller by half a head, to me with my head to the side.

A princess, I thought with some surprise. She doesn't seem like a goddess on earth. At least not like what I think a goddess should be.

"Has he not arranged for tutors for you?" Asetnefer asked. "You are too old for the nursery."

She shrugged again. "I guess he forgot," she said.

"Perhaps he will remember," Asetnefer said. "I will take you back to the nursery now, before anyone worries. Girls! Iras! Charmian! Put dry clothes on and behave until I get back."

*   *   *

SHE DID NOT return until after the afternoon had changed into the cool shades of evening, and the birds sang in the lemon trees. Night came by the time Iras and I curled up in our cubicle in one bed, the sharp smell of meat roasted with coriander drifting in through the curtain door. Iras went straight to sleep, as she often did, but I was restless. I untangled myself from Iras' sleepy weight, and went outside to sit with the women in the cool night air. Asetnefer sat alone by the fountain, her lovely head bent to the water as though something troubled her.

I came and stood beside her, saying nothing.

"You were born here," she said quietly, "On a night like this. A spring night, with the harvest coming in and all the land green with the gifts of the Nile, the gifts of Isis."

"I know," I said, having heard this story before, but not impatient with it.

"He is your father too," she said, and for a moment I did not know who she meant. "Ptolemy Auletes. Pharaoh. Just as he is Iras' father. You are sisters in blood and bone as well as milk sisters."

"I knew that too," I said, though I hadn't given much thought to my father. I had always known Iras was my real sister. To be told it as a great truth was no surprise.

"That makes her your sister too. Cleopatra. Born under the same stars, the scholars would say."

I digested this a minute. I supposed I didn't mind another sister. She had seemed like she could be as much fun as Iras, and if she was a goddess on earth, she was really a very small goddess.

"You will start lessons with her tomorrow," Asetnefer said. "You and Iras both. You will go to the palace library after breakfast." She looked at me sideways now, and I wondered what she saw. "Cleopatra is to have a tutor, and it is better if she has companions in her studies. She is too much alone, and her half sister Arsinoe is barely two and much too young to begin reading and learning mathematics. You and Iras have been given to her to be her companions."

"Given by whom?" I asked.

"By your father," she said. "Pharaoh Ptolemy Auletes."